A FREE gift from Author **STEVE WINDSOR**

I0677209

The story of Eden's Garden as you've never heard it told. How man truly faced his first temptation.

The angel STEG has a dilemma, he can either fulfill his heavenly duty as the knowledge bearing serpent in the Garden—assist the daughter of Eden in bringing Life's light to mankind—or he can pursue a growing love inside of him that is beyond his control or comprehension.

STEG's love is more forbidden than any fruit growing in the Garden, and to pursue it he'll have to break just about every commandment he'll ever know, yet to be written or silently understood hardly matters.

But love is not one to wait and wane while it withers on the vine. Neither is STEG who, as the highest and most beautiful angel—the very first angel—is mere breaths away from being a god himself. Now, he'll either win the affection of the one he loves in the next 7 days, or he will incur the wrath of a God who purports to love him above all others.

Either way, the Garden will never be the same again. Because sooner or later . . . sin touches every god.

Get your copy of *STEG—The prologue Novella to THE FALLEN series Thrillers.*

Available in February 2015!

*Get My **FREE** Copy of STEG*

Available at http://vixenink.com/steg-free-offer/

Praise for the novels of author Steve Windsor

FURY

A FUTURISTIC RELIGIOUS FICTION THRILLER
(Testament 2)

STEVE WINDSOR

Vixen

VIXEN INK

FURY

A VIXEN ink book/Published by arrangement with the author

ISBN-13: 978-0692344521
ISBN-10: 0692344527

To the angry little angel in us all

FURY

Testament 2

RESURRECTION

— I —

YOU MAY *THINK* you know who I am, but like . . . you don't know shit.

My two best friends say I have quite a mouth on me. One of their boyfriends knows it's the truth. But I wasn't always like that. After I fell, I was worse. Still, none of it was as bad as my whole life.

Whoever I was before, Fury is my name now. This is my testament:

I'm cursing as I plummet, "Cocksuckerrrr!"

That's me, Mercedes King then—like I'm *even* telling you my full name—and I'm freshly flown off the roof, my rage-red hair all up in my mouth and shit. I'm falling to my death in my favorite underwear. The tight little pink ones I got in Cancun right before it happened.

I had to haggle the old jabbering Mexican woman for ten minutes so she would cut the credits on them. When she went to authorize my fake hex-card, I just jacked them and ran with my friends.

I know, I know. I'm a little shit. Get over it. There's a reason for everything. I'll get to it like . . . when I get to it.

I fell then, too. Right on my face and Tessa was just laughing at me and Brie—total bitch—didn't even help me when the old hag grabbed my hair.

Of course we got away—old ladies can't run. I wish we hadn't. If it wasn't for my dad. . . I don't like to think about the part that came after, but if it wasn't for him, I'd probably still be in a Mexican Protection cell with Donato and his raping buddy.

No, that doesn't mean I forgave my father for it. It just means he was a rich asshole with credits. Sometimes you need that.

But that was nothing compared to this, and I'm falling straight down from the penthouse of the Smith Tower in Seattle, my parents' little "love" nest.

It's hard to even think of them that way now, especially my dad. I'm glad I killed him. Rot in the dungeon!

Huh? . . . Yes, shut up, of course it's warmer than falling naked. Naked in Seattle is cold. What are you, ignorant? Nasty little purgatory. . . I'll tell you how all *that* works later. You won't believe me. I guess it's sorta funny, but kinda gross, too. And everyone gets to do it. Yes, even him. Jesus, especially him.

I'm working on getting that changed. Because. . . I mean like, come on, old people? I don't care if they are Man-monkeys or whatever other species Rain replaced them with. Those two. . .? That's just—eww! You know what I'm saying.

Christ almighty—now you got me blaspheming. But just listen to you wicked little bastards. I tell you I killed my dad and you're like, "You were in your underwear?" Shit never changes.

Whatever. Look, I'm trying to teach you something here, so shut up and listen. Hatchlings, always with the questions. Time to get cracked, dumbasses.

* * *

Thirty-eight stories is a long way to fall. Feels like it takes an eternity, maybe two of them.

You think I'm exaggerating? Trust me, some of you whining little purgies already know this, but it feels like a lifetime, at least. Because time doesn't go by like you think. A fall and a trial is one thing, but like, Judgment? That takes forever to burn through you.

"Time is relative," I think Jump told me once. Whatever that means. I do know this, different things seem to take longer, like waiting in line for meds at the State Med-mart, or for a guy to figure out how to give me an orgasm.

Seeing how ridiculous I look—flapping my arms and falling in my underwear—I guess I should have put on more clothes before I ran downstairs.

Can you believe that? Thrown out the window by the same asshole that saved me. That like, sucks *so* bad.

Really? Of course I'm pissed off about it . . . idiot! Stop talking over me. Anyways. . . What was I. . .? Oh yeah, it was probably the best thing that could have happened.

How *did* all this happen? It's not exactly how he told you. Let me tell you how life *really* worked. Wait, I don't think Salvation and Jump will be back from the arena for a while, why don't I just show you. Come on, follow me. What? . . . Of course we can, we're not dungeon demons. This is your Hell, not Purgatory. Stop asking so many questions. Are you coming or not?

And I flap my way up to the portal entrance with. . . I can't count all of you little purgatories anymore.

You wicked little shits are piling up like souls on judgment night—Hell's not hurting for humping hatchlings, is it?

Anyways, I'm only taking six of you—that's the rules. Rest a you gotta stay here.

Jesus! . . . Calm down, calm down! Trust me, trip like this, there's bound to be some bodies, so the rest of you will be like, on standby for your first flight. You can watch the fall, but you gotta hide, so they don't know where we've gone. Else it's deep shit when Jump and Salvation get back. Bet your flight-feathers on that.

I turn around and flap toward the portal, because I just can't look at those little pouty faces they make when they don't get what they want. I used to do that. It's pathetic.

Dammit! I always clip my wingtips on the edge of the portals—they should make these things bigger.

— II —

AS THE PROTECTOR of her two-thousand-year eternity, Life had been a god. No, she *was* God. And that *was* the right word . . . "was."

Now, her once brilliant and near-transparent white feathers were spotted and stained with patches of pink. Marks ground in from over half an eternity spent as a concubine in a cell, deep within the Dungeons of the Damned.

Life's shining black orbs glowed. She stared up blankly at her once beautiful archangel, turned vengeful master.

Lived had been her highest and most beautiful creation—an angel of light—until his ego surpassed hers and she was compelled to cast him into the bottomless pit below. Now he was the devil, Lived, the dark angel of light turned inside out and backward by God.

Life smiled when she spoke up at him. He was always more pleasant if she smiled, less rough, more like it used to be. In the beginning of the two-thousand-year eternity before this one—Life's own time as Protector—they were better together.

But that eternity was a distant, almost forgotten memory. No one spoke of the time of the Man-monkey now. And why would they? Rain almighty, the Protector of this new eternity—the god of her time —had decreed that none should speak of the Man-monkey's eternity. Those beings were considered far too dangerous to even tempt with thought and belief.

That life, and Life herself, were long-forgotten nightmares, locked behind iron bars of judgment and condemnation.

The once benevolent and all-powerful God, Life, endured the fate that Rain condemned her to suffer. She served the "devil" she "knew," on top and inside of her most mornings . . . and evenings, if it suited him. Though, in the dark depths of the dungeons, the change between day and night passed by unnoticed.

Life adjusted her wings and they scraped against the rusty red metal of her cellmate's feathers. And sparks dropped and bounced on the floor of their cell as they coupled. "Does she go back?" she asked Lived.

Lived—Dal, he used to be called, Life's dark angel of light—smiled down at his former master. His creator, actually, because she and she alone had made him and then twisted him into what he was now.

He had been dazzling once, the most and the highest angel in Heaven. But Life cast him from her side and into the pit—the lake of fire beneath the dungeons—for the simple act of disobedience. There, he ruled in Hell for a full eternity.

But then he and Life were vanquished—overthrown . . . by a child, no less. The Battle of the Books was a bloody one, pitting mother against son, and son against father. No angel in Heaven or Hell escaped judgment on that day. All faced justice. Not all found peace.

Afterward—once the Great Dragon of Judgment, Jump, defeated them—Jump's whelp daughter, Rain, stripped Life and Lived of their powers and cast them into the Dungeons of the Damned beneath the Arena of Reckoning. Before it all happened, they were the gods of their time. Now, the once God, Life and her evil devil, Lived, were less.

Lived's devilish breath no longer reeked of the vile bile of rotting souls, and Life's godly aroma no longer emitted the sweet, succulent scent of vanilla and molasses. Nor did her voice waft the wonderful sounds of women and children, wailing and crying. Sounds that Lived had so loved to hear.

Things were different. And not how Dal had imagined they would be. He had waited and plotted for two thousand years—an eternity spent planning to turn the tides of time against Life. But his plan had not borne fruit the way he intended. Failure was a disgusting taste that he had no palette for.

Lived's voice had less fire, his flames weren't as intimidating, and his fury was less formidable. Everything was "less" now . . . for both of them. The most egregious. . . When they woke from the last great nothingness—the dark sleep—this eternity was to be an everlasting impotence, imposed on them by the daughter of the very child that he and Life spawned to try and avoid it.

Thankfully, that part of their granddaughter Rain's new book was not literal. Literal or interpretation—the Word of Heaven and Hell, for Life and Lived, had changed for the worse.

Rain. . . Lived thought. The bright little star of light had condemned him and Life to live for this eternity, confined together behind iron-barred gates in a cell—alone with their failure.

Now, they were only allowed to hear the judgments above, never to witness them. Sweet sin and salvation a mere breath away—the smells of misery and mayhem everywhere, but not a drop to drink.

Their power stripped and their roles reversed, they would never be allowed to repent. Rain had made that clear. But Life was not one to be confined in a cage. Gods were funny that way. Cast out and imprisoned or not, she knew there were other ways. If she was not able to return to the throne as Protector through the front door, she would simply slip into the house of the Lord through the back.

Lived pushed his wings down harder against Life's and smiled as her brow furrowed. "You had a doubt that she would bend to my . . . *will?*" he grunted. Prisoner or not, submission was his right, and doubt played little part in that.

Jump may have defeated Lived in the Arena of Reckoning, his own lover may have smote him before the Battle of the Books, and Rain almighty herself may have stripped him of position and power, but he still had his wits . . . and his lies. Surely that was enough to defeat one small child, especially one without the wisdom of the world to keep her from ruin.

The seed of his and Life's plan was simple enough, but waiting for the fruits of revenge to grow was more difficult. "She will bite the apple," Lived said. And he pushed again. "These things take . . . *time.*"

Life winced a little as she tried to stay still. Then she looked back into her past and remembered.

How had she come to this fate? Life had ruled. She had made the garden and stocked it with fresh souls to worship her, but in the end of her eternity, every angel in the heavens revolted. And she was brought to judgment in the arena, condemned, and sentenced to be Lived's slave. But it wasn't the entire truth.

Ever since, Lived had tried, convicted and condemned her every day. The fate Life considered unacceptable had become her daily duty —her violating reality.

In the beginning of Life's eternity, Lived's danger and his passionate anger had been seductive, sensual . . . sensational. And every time they joined, she had experienced the white hot truth of the love she so longed to feel with her own creatures—to be loved and adored by the human beings she created. But each time, the fire she and her highest angel sparked, burned into her deeper. And sooner than she was prepared to, Life was forced to cast Lived's arrogance out of her Heaven and lock him in the bottomless pit. She would allow him to rule in his own kingdom, but never in hers.

It was a mistake, and Lived became the engineer of Life's destruction—the evil devil was now her master. He had used the son that Life bore him to inadvertently bring about both of their ends. As a result, in this eternity, Life was his to join with as often as he pleased. And it did please him often. Life knew who was responsible for that.

Rain. . . she thought again. The girl was becoming Life's obsession. But revenge would have to wait. She could tell by the evil grin on Lived's face and his disgustingly long tongue. . . He always slithered it around her breasts just before he finished. She was thankful he had cropped his huge, pointed tail. "No, my beautiful Day Star," she said. "I have no doubts." She moaned a little—she knew it hastened his ending. "None . . . what . . . so . . . *ever.*"

And then it was over and Life closed her big black orbs, and she forced a tear to run from one of her dark eyes—a drop of deception trickled down her cheek.

Lived slithered his tongue from his slave's chest and swirled it up the side of her face. Then he slowly savored the salty taste of his own revenge. And he pulled himself out and off of Life and stood up. He cawed above his head, and then he said, "You are still delicious, my love."

Life returned her feathers to their full brightness, stood up next to him, and shook her wings and her feathers dry. It felt like she would never get his burning-ash scent out of her plumage. *As you will be, when I feast on your failure*, she thought. The thought did not concern her—gone was the era when they would be able to smell the other's thoughts. Rain had stripped them of that power, too.

They both heard Rain's voice above, and they lifted their heads and spread their wings, listening to the roar of angels—the feathered followers, cheering in the arena above them. It was a constant reminder that the warmth of their eternity had ended. And both of them wished for nothing more than to return to its glory.

— III —

THE FIRST THING I notice is that like, my wing isn't the only thing that got fucked up going through the portal, because there's sirens all over the place, and I'm running from the PA's again. It's not where I wanted to resurrect and I tuck my wings into my back. Nothing to see here, just another Man-monkey chick running from Protection.

Life said the portal was more art than science, but this? Protection Agents? WTF on that?

It's not any fun this time around either, and I run. It's weird too—been a while since I used my legs like this. Why run when you have kick-ass wings, right? All I'm saying.

This memory isn't as scary as some I could think of—I ran from Protection agents before. *Screw it*, I think. I figure I'll just do the same thing I did then. One thing about a memory is that like, I already know what's going to happen.

I see it ahead—the exit's coming up. And I duck into the garbage alley between two tall scrapers. That's how I tricked them the last time. Nobody wants to look inside a Protection body-bin. You never know who you might recognize in there. Better not to know. Just pretend they never existed. *How did this happen?*

". . .King!" I barely hear the voice finishing up shouting my name. It catches me totally off guard, and then comes the part where he tries to arrest me. ". . .hereby remanded to Protection."

I look at him and I'm all wide-eyed and shit. He's got a black helmet, goggles, little submachine gun, black boots like they all wear. *Where did he come from? And how does he know my. . .?* "Remanded to Protection?" Who is he kidding? Liar. He doesn't even know he's lying, because he's been brain-scrubbed to believe anything they tell him. *Protection rookies. . .*

Probably the last thing my dear daddy gave me that didn't hurt. . . Before he—when I still believed in him. "Mercedes," he said to me, "if anyone ever tells you that you are 'remanded to Protection,' you run." I guess he would know.

However the sick bastard knew to tell me that, his advice saved me and my friends' more than once. But today, I run right into one of the very agents I'm running from—brain-scrubbed little boy with bullets —black-booted rapist PA. Kinda cute though, and I think about trying to fuck my way out of this alley.

I must be older now, because I didn't start thinking that way until . . . after. But I don't think it very long—smoking Salvation, I'm not a slut!

And before he can figure out that I'm not just some fifteen-year-old Bravo Mike jacker that he can snatch up and hand over to his Protection bosses, I fake like I slip, and then I slide backward on my back— between his legs—and just as my waist gets even with him, I kick him as hard as I can in the sack.

He goes down, clutching at himself. And none of them *ever* like *that.* By the time he crawls to his hands and knees and starts vomiting, I jump up, roll toward him, and bring the heel of my freshly jacked Betty-boot down on his lower back.

He screams in pain, and then he pushes off the ground and up to his knees.

Bravo Mike? Oh yeah, newbies. Sorry, I know you gotta play catch-up. Just don't take too long about it, because your granddaddy Jump is a miserable devil—no patience for anyone who can't keep up. Fall behind-left behind. Welcome to your new hell.

The Black Market—"Bravo Mike," so we could all pretend it didn't exist. And before you ask, "Betty-boots" are what Protection issues the chicks—what we all called them anyway. There's not many of them—chick rookies, I mean. There's plenty of Protection. Too many.

But no matter how many bastards or how few bitches Protection has, it's totally illegal for a citizen to have their boots. Normal citizen, anyways. For me, it hardly matters.

Don't fool yourself—you get kicked with a Betty, archangel or Man-monkey, that shit hurts. Huh? Of course I could *buy* them—I wasn't some bread-begging citizen—but what fun is that? We used to jack them—other stuff, too—at the Mike when we were bored.

Enough already, pay attention, no more questions for a while. Quit squawking at me! You might learn something.

I look down at the Protection agent's soon to be dead body and I frown a little. Before, this would have freaked me out, but that was a long, long time ago. I'm not even supposed to think about back then, anyways. *What's he doing alone?* I think.

And before this PA can decide whether he should hold onto his balls or grab his pistol, I spring at him, grab him by his goggles, whip his head back with them, and give him two open-hand knife chops to his Adam's apple.

And I feel it like, crunch on the second one, and he grabs his throat and spits blood and he's choking when he goes to the ground. And I jump on top of him and gouge him in the eyes—thumbs all the way in like Jump taught me.

He tries to scream, but nothing comes out, just a little bubble of blood. And then he rolls onto his side, dead. And I wipe my thumbs on my pants.

What? Well, what did you expect? Seven years of Martial Law classes. The last two of them getting the shit kicked out of me by my instructor. You know what it feels like to get kicked in the tits? Of course you don't, wicked little. . . Half of you *maybe*, but none of you other little purgatories.

Here's another little lesson I learned from Jump—mercy is for maggots. Maggot food anyways, because that's what you'll be if you don't learn this one. Old Jesus, I sound just like him. Dammit!

How did I get like this? I got like this because—I thought I said no more questions! Look, I was trying to take you back—start you at the beginning—but something's wrong with my resurrection. Oh . . . those *evil. . .!*

Mercedes, I think, *you stupid bitch. You should know better. Jump is gonna be pissed.*

— IV —

IF THERE WAS one thing Jump—the Great Dragon archangel of Judgment—knew after living in the shithole that Life and Lived used to call humanity, if he waited long enough, something was bound to get screwed up. And if it wasn't by him, then it would be at the hands of some other numb-nut . . . or "nookie" if he decided to go all sarcastic-technical on someone.

This particular nookie was becoming a pain in his ass. Really, Fury had always been that way, but some days were more uncomfortable than others.

Jump sat by the fiery lake with his head in his hands, running his fingers through the steel pinfeathers on his scalp, rubbing and massaging his mind to try and calm himself down. It worked better when Salvation did it. But his sweet savior liked to watch the games in the arena until the bitter end, and after a thousand. . . He had lost track of how many years they had ruled over Hell in this new eternity.

Jump spread his huge wings and shook his steel feathers. A fine mist of blood floated to the ground. He paid no attention to the remnants of the night's judgments. It was a habit by now, like a seahawk shaking water off its back after returning from scooping up a fish.

Most nights, before the last souls were judged, Jump flapped his way out through their personal portal to his own private hell—back to the warmth and solitude of his fiery lake beneath the dungeons. Once, when Fury brought him in to help prepare the new purgatories for their part in the judgments, he had smiled at them—Jump had a particular grin that spoke of wickedness beyond what he now ruled over in Hell—then he told the little hatchlings, "Once you've gutted a god, the judgments lose their . . . glory."

Now, he waited and listened until the noise from the crowd in the arena died down. And right on time—a few minutes later—though time was relative when he was waiting for his sweet Salvation to fly back from a party. . . So when Salvation finally appeared next to the lake, Jump stood up quickly, spread his wings as wide as they would go, and cawed angrily at her, "She's at it again!"

At the end of the last eternity—during the great cleansing of the garden—Salvation had been content to take a backseat to Jump's judgments. But after Rain took power, her new role had nothing to do with being a passenger on her husband's "rage train" outbursts. Sweet, nice, balanced and beautiful Salvation or not, there were times when she just wanted to reach out and choke him.

Salvation spread her own great gray wings, flapped them a couple of times, and then mirrored Jump's wings-wide stance. Then she frowned at him. "Rain almighty, what is it today?" she asked. "Seriously, you are mad every day. You need to give her a little breathing roo—"

"Not this time," Jump said. "And don't think I don't know what you're doing. They should've made you a mockingbird, or a parrot, or something. Squawk, squawk, squawk. Don't even—this is real shit, right here."

Salvation folded her wings behind her. Then she crisscrossed her ballistic fire-feathers to create the shield on her back. The shield was protection against attack from behind. And every angel in the new Heaven and the "new and improved" Hell learned how to use theirs first. Salvation's feathers fit together tightly, and the burned-in war-mark of the Great Dragon—Jump—shimmered black and gray on her back.

Salvation stared at Jump, crossed her arms, and puffed out all of her body feathers—another one of Rain's new "commandments."

Secretly, Salvation was glad that her daughter had the good sense to require that all the angels in Heaven and Hell leave their armored plumage out in public. Soul safety, golden guardian, not to mention avenging archangels, flying around throughout Rain's eternity, trying to deliver the justice and judgments of the new Words . . . naked, no less? That would not do.

For a thirteen-year-old turned protecting-god ruler, there would be no naked commune of angels flying through Heaven. Rain had made that crystal clear—the purgatories didn't need distractions like that.

Salvation wondered how the last two rulers ever got anything done. It was a miracle that it took two thousand years for their eternity to fall. She had no idea it had been much longer than that.

"Don't puff your plumage at me," Jump raised his voice at his wife. "I told her not to take those little shits out before they were fully fledged. Now she's. . . Who knows where she's got them off to. I swear to—"

"Careful," Salvation said, "you know how your daughter feels about cursing . . . and hypocrisy."

"Hypocrisy? Who you calling a hypocrite?"

"Listen to yourself," Salvation said. "Did *you* ever do what anyone told you to? You don't even listen to me, and that's supposed to be the law. Your daughter's law, by the way."

Jump stared blankly at his "better" half. He knew it was coming.

"Yeah," said Salvation, "let me help you out. The answer is no. That's why Fury makes you so nuts, and that's why you love her—she's just like you. Angry at the world for half your life, trying to burn it down for the other. You're lucky I don't tell—"

"Oh," Jump said, cocking his head and scrunching up his face, "so now you're a rat?" He smiled—he did love Fury for the angry, vengeful archangel that she was. He loved the banter with his wife even more.

"I'll *rat* you," Salvation said. "And don't even think about threatening me with that 'angels and demons' crap again either."

Jump knew his wife was no rat, and he also knew that there were some discussions that she would never have with their only daughter turned benevolent—if still a bit naive—Protector of the two Heavens. He had threatened Salvation that he would have the little "birds and the bees," angel procreation conversation with Rain. He knew "the talk" was way overdue, but he kept putting it off—it was a great chip to play if he wanted to end a spirited debate with his wife. Regardless, he looked forward to their "discussions." Salvation's anger kept things fiery hot, just the way he liked it.

Salvation could see another one of her man's pointless rants coming. She could also see that, though he was probably overreacting, Fury *was* missing . . . and so were the wicked little hatchlings that the girl was charged with training.

But Salvation had witnessed Fury in action during the cleansing of the garden at the end of the last eternity. Dubai . . . and Old Vegas . . . and then there was the Battle of the Books. Wherever she was, Fury would be fine. Besides. . . Salvation looked around the shores of the great lake of fire. "Where would she go?" she asked herself more than Jump.

"I'll tell you where she went," said Jump. He was starting to boil now, and for a dark soul turned angry leader of unruly angels in Hell, the boredom of this next eternity had him itching for somewhere to point his poison. "She's off flying them around the mountain again, showing off her wings."

"You blame her?" Salvation said. "Little girl is blazing fast. Faster than me, faster than—"

"Don't say it."

Salvation smiled back at him. Her man needed a little humility. "Way faster than you."

"Oh, to hell with this," Jump said. "Are you coming with me to find her, or not?"

Salvation looked around again. Most of the angels of the second Heaven. . . Hell had duties that kept the fully-faithed angels away from the lake at night, and without the new ones, things were quiet. It felt eerie to her, even for Hell. A pack of adolescent angels, flying around with a furious, fully-fledged, fallen archangel leading them? That was unpredictable and dangerous. "You don't want to wait a little," Salvation stated more than asked. "See if they show back up?"

Jump frowned. "You know better."

They both flexed their wings, pushed out all of their armored feathers, and threw their heads back a little, before cawing in their own special code. One thing they both knew—never ever leave the lake unless you were prepared for battle. Jump brought that with him from his time with Protection.

When they were both satisfied that their armor shields, ballistic fire-feathers and long, hooked talons were ready, they turned toward their private portal—the doorway to the darkness outside and the base of the Great Mountain of the Eternities.

When they turned around, they were greeted by the brightest light in Heaven or Hell, shining truth into every wicked crevice of their dark lake of fire and lies.

"Dammit. . ." but it wasn't Jump who muttered it and Salvation stared, searching for the words. "We . . . we were just coming to—"

— V —

"COMING TO VISIT me, Mother?" said Rain. And she shined the bright of her truth—the law of this eternity—brighter than she ever had. "How nice."

Jump squinted and reached for his sunshields. "God-goggles," all the hounds in Hell liked to call them. From the warm safety of the lake, of course, because using that word was the new blasphemy. "Shit. . ." he muttered.

Salvation flitted one of her wings a little and bumped it against Jump's side and he stumbled. Then she reached for her own sunshields —no one could withstand the blinding truth of the innocence of youth that Rain almighty brought to the Throne of Judgment.

Their daughter floated past the two of them as if they weren't even there, out to the edge of the burning lake. Then she stared out across the great burning waters, fluttering and hovering with her back to them. "I see that the great lake is having no luck in watering down my father's wicked tongue." She paused and turned her head just enough that they could both see her lips when she continued to speak. "It is a difficult task, even I must admit, but one that I am sure you agree is in desperate need of doing. A duty that I believe I asked you to assist me in accomplishing . . . Mother."

Neither of them could picture Rain as anything but the little girl they had lost to the State Med-mart during the last eternity, but for barely a teenager in their minds, she was remarkably condescending.

It was tough for any parent to watch their child grow up, but Rain had grown . . . beyond. Beyond the pettiness of the last eternity in the garden, beyond the violence and the thieving, and the viciousness of her predecessor, Life's, Man-monkey souls.

Rain surpassed all in power and restraint, and she had far outlived the "adorability" phase of her father's nasty disposition. She knew that Jump, however, had not outlived his surliness.

"The only thing I'm in desperate need of, little girl," Jump said, "is a good—"

"What he's trying to say," Salvation interrupted, "is that it's been a long time since you have visited us. And we are so pleased that you are here."

Rain continued to hover at the edge of the lake. Her snow white feathers, shined and glowed hot light, illuminating the lake like the Med-mart operating room that she had died in. "Yes, it's been quite a long time," she said. "Yet that is largely because I do not like it down here. Too hard to sort the truth out from the . . . untruths that were left here by your. . . I guess we all know that makes them my grandparents. How ironic is that apple, Mother? The evil Chosen One and her deceitful Devil, grandparents of truth and justice. The eternities do have their own sense of irony, don't they?"

Jump didn't even look at Salvation before he said it. "Ain't that a—" he caught himself. He knew that Rain had the power to end anyone, but he also knew what she did—he was the only thing between Heaven and Hell plunging into anarchy again. And no one wanted that to happen. Another war so soon after the last would be . . . "Unfortunate," he muttered.

Rain turned around, and for a brief instant she had a look of surprise on her face. Even Salvation looked at Jump in silence—she couldn't find the words.

Rain could. She said, "A"—she looked like she was searching for the correct word—"*wiser* choice was never spoken, especially by you, Jacob."

And Jump's face changed. There wasn't an angel in the two Heavens that would risk speaking his Man-monkey name, Jake, much less address him the way his mother used to. Dream mother or not, and daughter-turned-god or not, no one called him that. "Now listen, you little—you must be—"

Salvation grabbed Jump's arm. "You must be very tired," she said to Rain. She squeezed his arm just enough as she spoke again, "And we know that it is uncomfortable for you down here, so how can we be of —how can we help?"

Rain looked at Salvation's hand on her father's forearm, and then at Jump's face. She smiled at him and said, "The father was right. She really *is* your only salvation." Then she looked at her mother and shook her head. "How do you do it?" she asked. "He is simply beyond redemption."

Salvation smiled at who she now recognized as her innocent and benevolent, if not a bit mischievous, little girl. "Not beyond," she said. "A long, long way away, but not beyond. And . . . I like a good challenge."

"Challenge?" Rain almost laughed out loud. "He is just too much work. I should saint you." And she giggled and held up both of her hands above her head forming a big "V" with her arms. Then she said, "Saint Salvation—tamer of the great profanity of Purgatory."

And then they laughed—Rain and Salvation. And Salvation let go of Jump's arm.

They all closed their eyes because—sunshields or not—when Rain laughed nothing could protect you from her white light.

When the two of them quit clucking and chuckling, an awkward silence filled the stillness of the pit and the fiery lake. Jump stared at them.

Rain spoke first, "So, either of you care to tell me why I come down here and find this place abandoned . . . on a judgment night, no less? Now, I must warn you, it is no coincidence that this is the first time I have been to the lake in . . . years." And she looked at Salvation and winked. "I like what you have done with it. At least you are making *some* progress."

"I like it the way it is," Jump said. "No need to change what ain't broke."

Rain looked at Jump again. It was the second time he had surprised her since she had arrived. "Not a single profanity," she said. And then she looked at Salvation, straight-faced. "Maybe you can change—"

"Fury is missing," Jump blurted. He was tired of the game. "And she's got a whole pack a little purgatories with her. Now, unless you are down here to help us find her, you might wanna just let us get to it."

They all paused at that. It wasn't uncommon for archangels to take matters into their own hands—use their own interpretation, their own judgment when carrying out the Word. But there were no judgments, no orders to carry out in either of the two Hells—or down in the new garden, for that matter. Fury was training new archangels of the second Heaven and that duty didn't require leaving the lake.

"I see," Rain said.

"See what?" said Jump.

Rain had a touch of disgust in her voice when she spoke. "Well," she said, "it's no wonder you two aren't running around down here with your plumage pulled back. All alone, empty nest, with no one to care if you are—"

"Oh my God," Salvation said. Blasphemous, forbidden word or not. . . "I can't—I'm not going to be able to deal with that."

Rain frowned at Salvation. "Careful, Mother. I shouldn't have to remind you—language." And she looked at Jump. "One good thing I guess I learned from you, Father."

"Damn straight on that," Jump said. "Revolutions, little girl. Every last one of them started with words."

"A lesson many have paid dearly for us to learn," Rain said. She turned back to Salvation. "Wouldn't you agree?"

Salvation hung her head a little. "Yes," she said. She herself had paid the price—burned to ashes at the Battle of the Books at the end of the last eternity. "Forgive me, I—I. . ." This far into her daughter's eternity, she really had no excuse.

Jump rolled his eyes. "Relax," he said to them both, "she and her little buddy are locked in their little honeymoon suite, fu—"

"Jump!" Salvation shouted. She tried not to make eye contact with Rain when she raised her eyebrows at him.

Rain stared at both of them with a blank face.

Jump got the message. "I'll talk to her," he said. "Give it a rest."

"Please," Rain said. "I am not as naive as you may think." As the one responsible for the fate of billions, making her mother squirm was one of the truly enjoyable activities she had left. "And you two, armored up and angry war faces on both of you," she said. "I *hope* that's not what it's like."

"Oh, no-no-no," said Salvation. "I just—I can't."

And now Jump and Rain had a good laugh.

Once Rain and Jump stopped laughing at her, and Salvation quit picturing her little angel "growing up," she said, "No more . . . please. We have to find them and I don't have any idea where to start."

"Okay, okay," Jump clucked and chuckled himself back to serious. Then he faked like he was wiping a little tear out of the corner of his eye—the time for real tears was long past. Then he thought about it for a second. "Maybe she's got them in the arena . . . or destroying the dungeons, playing master and slave or some other messed up—"

"It seems to me," Rain interrupted her father. She knew their "talk" was coming soon enough, and she knew that he would give her the truth of how it all worked. The more important truth was, she had a truth of her own to tell, but right now there was a foul smell in the air. She could taste the seeds of revolt—it wasn't the first time—and she had spent enough hours with Fury to know that her friend would go looking for trouble when she was bored. As soon as Rain had felt it, she knew who needed to go investigate and clean it up.

Whatever flaws her father had, Jump had no match in his ability to extract the truth from an unwilling conspirator. Rain wondered how he did it, but she instinctively knew never to ask.

She continued, "I was just thinking, that whenever my rules are being broken. . . Any time the Word of this eternity is being challenged, it is usually by the author of the book from the last one who's behind it. And *that's* usually at her evil master's 'request.' "

"Ohhh . . . shit," Salvation said.

"Dammit," Jump said to Rain, "you should have smoked those two when you had the chance. Punished them once and for all the eternities."

"Sometimes. . ." Rain said.

Jump and Salvation watched as Rain turned and fluttered toward the entrance to the portal up to Heaven.

Rain continued to talk as she slowly flew toward the exit, ". . .it is much better to let someone live with their own failure . . . than to end their suffering for them. And sometimes"—Rain paused, stopped floating away and turned around toward Jump—"sometimes it is better to let people discover the truth on their own. To learn for themselves. And maybe, just maybe, they will come away more enlightened for the experience."

As Rain disappeared through the portal, the truth of why Fury was missing . . . went with her.

Jump looked at Salvation. "Was she talking about me?" He turned back toward the portal. "Or her?"

"She's so old," said Salvation. "I just can't believe—"

"You think she's already. . .?" Jump said.

"I try *not* to think about it."

— VI —

ONCE I'M DONE preaching to my little purgatories, I look down at the bag of blood PA that I just knocked to the bottom of this alley. *What the hell was a Protection agent doing in here?* I think. *Last time, I just ducked into this garbage alley and then Tessa and—*

"What did you do?" and I know that voice for sure. Brianna, pretty much my best friend, runs up next to me. "Holy shit, Em!" she yells at me. She barely stops running before she bumps into me. She's got her own Betty-boots on and she's panting like crazy, sweating down the front of her shirt. Brie sweats, totally sexy, but it makes her blonde hair look like shit. "Oh, bitch," she says. It's like her favorite word. "You have motherfucked us." One of her other favorites, mine too, I guess. And she nudges the guy a little with her toe, making sure he's dead. But I'm telling you, he's dead. I can smell it.

Let me tell you little rookies something, the first time you see a dead one. . . Let's just say there's no prepping you for that.

First time you see a messy sack of bones that used to be a living Man-monkey, the only thing you'll care about is ripping out its soul so you can get back to warm yourself by the fire with your friends. Because listening to grandpa Jump tell you some more of his warrior stories is way better than cleaning up Man-monkey guts.

Yeah, maybe you do know that, but when you—but like, after this, I don't know if I even wanna be back here. Anyways, Man-monkeys tend to freak out about death, so just be careful—they're unpredictable cocksuckers.

When Tessa runs into me, I almost trip over the Protection brute's body. "Tess?" I say to her. It's still a little weird to be back here. I don't know how long it's been since we've all been gone, but seeing Tessa makes the last eternity feel like yesterday.

"Glad you squeaked out, too," I say to her. "Now come on, we gotta ditch."

"Why'd you. . .?" Tessa says. "You condemned him?" She always asks like, totally obvious shit.

And I'm back in the garden with a bang. Two best friends and in deep shit faster than I was prepared for. My return isn't quite the way I planned it, so run we do. Out the other end of the alley and down a side street and then like, out into the crowded sidewalks. Then we start walking—just three little rich bitches, strolling and rolling with the citizens. Nothing to see here.

As we walk, I'm calmer than I would've been back as me—ten billion judged and executed souls since the last eternity—

What? . . . Okay, okay, three billion, but mine were harder. How many souls have you brought back from an eternity? . . . Uh-huh, that's what I thought.

My fuzzy math aside, it's hard for me to get worked up about one rookie Protection agent. Tessa, on the other hand—freaking. Part of the job, purgies. Better get used to that.

But for sure, if Tessa doesn't stop wigging, we are getting caught. I forgot how she was on the Cancun trip. And she's grabbing my arm and her eyes are flitting around, looking for more Protection agents. I know they aren't coming.

How? This close to my dad's office scraper. . . Even pumped up PAs don't want to mess around with his building. That's real security in there, not PA pussies.

I never noticed it—guess I should have—but it's raining. Seattle, go figure. It's totally weird though. I know I lived in it before, but I can hardly remember what rain on my skin feels like, and I shiver and goosebumps raise up all over me. And I don't remember exactly what that means, but it's not good.

All I can remember is that Hell is hot, and Rain. . . You know, she told me that she never liked the Seattle drizzle either. So now, Heaven is pretty much like the Phoenix Quarter in the summer, too—sunshine and saints and sinners, all blazing hot. I miss home already.

And the three of us are almost to the big automatic portals that twist open into my father's building—King and Tamanos Enterprises' Headquarters. K&T, the makers of pretty much everything . . . good and bad. I eavesdropped on daddy Frank and my mother enough to know that there's more credits to be made off the bad stuff.

Looking back. . . Hell, *being* back here is weird enough—the past or in my mind—but knowing what I know about my father and knowing what he did . . . I don't think the ass-kicking I gave him at the Battle of the Books was enough. In fact, I know it wasn't. And that's the main reason I'm—

I watch as Brie goes down without a sound, falling in slow motion in front of me, clutching at her neck. And blood spurts from between her fingers from the bullet hole in her throat.

I know she's been shot, because a split second later, Tessa and I hear it—*BOOM!*

And Tessa grabs my arm and she looks at me with wild eyes and yells, "Run!"

Then we both sprint as fast as we can toward the portal into the K&T scraper and I get there first, but Tessa slams into my back like a brick, and I hear another loud boom as we crash through the glass door and into the lobby, rolling over each other through flying shards of glass. Then I feel the hot blood on me. No clue if it's mine or hers or both.

And what the. . .? Like, I got no idea what the *hell's* happening, but I roll and jump up as fast as I can, because whatever it is. . . *This never happened!* I think. Then I yell down at Tessa, "Get up, bitch! We gotta get the—" But when I reach down to grab her by the hand, I pull her arm up and it's not attached to her anymore. And I look down and she's bleeding out faster than anyone is going to save her. I've seen that before. And I drop her arm.

Tessa screams and I look into her eyes, and then they roll back and she starts flopping on the floor. Blood is spraying everywhere—all over the light-blue industrial carpet. And I jump down on her and try to pin her down and put my hand over her shoulder, but like, a severed arm?

Blood sprays me in the face and she screams again and says, "My. . . Get my arm, Em. I want my arm. Don't let me. . ."

And then she slumps over and she's gone, and then the lobby goes nuts. There are screaming bitches everywhere—men, women, dudes in black.

"Motherfucker," I say to myself, because those are the building's security sentries, overtrained and contracted from Protection to guard . . . who knows what my father has in the basement of this scraper, but that's where they all come from—the door to the basement.

And now there's a half-dozen of them racing at me—guns up and plastic body armor clacking against itself as they run. I'm not getting away from them, so I spin, preparing to release. It's pure instinct, I know, and in another life—a different eternity—I would have loosed a few hundred fire-feathers at them and cut them all to pieces. Probably wasted a bunch of stupid, citizen gawkers in the process. But now's not then and like, nothing happens. Because my wings are camouflaged—tucked hard next to my spine—they're not going anywhere.

I guess I look pretty stupid, like a pirouetting ballerina, spinning around on top of her friend's blood in the middle of the lobby. But I'm no angel today, and now I'm—

A split second later, they are all on top of me, yelling and swinging billy clubs at me and shit. And there were actually only five of them—one of them's a chick. You believe that? But it feels like a dozen as they pummel the angel-shit right out of me.

And I can feel my bones breaking and I'm screaming and they are yelling and then everything just kinda mutes and slows down. And then none of it hurts anymore and I can feel my face scraping back and forth across the lobby's industrial carpet and I'm staring across the light-blue floor at Tessa's eyes and she blinks. *She's still alive?* And then I see her mouth my name with bloody lips. And then she closes her eyes and goes limp, and blood runs out of the corner of her mouth.

I hear my skull crunch and then the brightest star I've ever seen—brighter than beautiful Rain—flashes all around me. The last thought I have, *Rain help me!* Then I'm out, black, nothing. Nothing but the song—

With wings and stings we angels poke,
With fire and fury and black smoke.
We dream of things that most don't,
Because some can't and some won't.

FRANK KING STARED through the one-way glass in the observation room adjacent to Protection interrogation cell #2, deep beneath his company's research facility—the scraper he code-named *Genesis*.

His daughter's unconscious body—soon to be corpse if he didn't figure something out—sat slumped, facing across the room at the dark half of the cell, seated in one of the two stainless steel chairs that every interrogation cell had. The spotlight above little Mercedes' head cast a shadow around the legs of the chair . . . and her legs, strapped to them.

Frank glanced down at the freshly cleaned, stainless steel grate on the drain in the middle of the cell, under the table. The concrete floor sloped down from the edges of the room, forming a slightly sunken, cone-shaped bottom to an otherwise rounded room. The drain was still wet from the previous occupant and a tiny puddle of blood mixed with water hovered around the holes in the cover.

The stainless steel table in the middle of the room was oval-shaped and the legs were metal tubes. In fact, there wasn't a single edge in the room that a protectant could injure themselves on. Because inflicting bodily harm on a protectant was the sole responsibility of the two-man teams from Protection's interrogation squad.

Interrogators were hard men in their twenties. Men who had their consciences brain-scrubbed out of them so they wouldn't get in the way of extracting . . . anything they were told to. They would beat, bend over, and butcher anyone and everyone who ended up on the wrong side of the room's observation glass. The incentive, of course, was an "all orifices open" policy that Protection gave them as long as they produced results. They could extract or inject anything they needed, from or into a protectant to get answers. The consequences for failure were well known.

Frank still had a part of him that wanted to rush in and free his daughter from the tape that was the only thing stopping her body from falling out of the chair and onto the floor. *That's the drugs*, he thought. And he would know—his company invented them.

It wasn't that Frank harbored some sense of bond or duty toward his only daughter, it was more that he was indignant that someone would *dare* remand something that belonged to him.

The chivalrous parts of Frank died a long time ago. The parts left now knew there were far bigger, more lucrative things at stake. "What happened?" he asked the Protection Agent In Charge standing next to him.

The PAIC pointed his black, glove-covered finger at the glass. "She and two other females stole some Protection issue armor from a contraband shop we were tracking in the Black Market. When the market owner tried to stop them, one of them assaulted him and then they all fled.

"We tried to get her quietly, unfortunately a pedestrian compliance agent was in a garbage alley, relieving himself, and when she ran in there. . . We were planning to pick her up at the PA's precinct, but she —"

"No. . ." Frank said.

"She martial-lawed him up pretty badly," said the PAIC, "before she crushed his trachea and left him condemned in the alley." The agent paused, letting the consequences sink in. "Any idea where she would get that kind of training?"

Frank was silent. There was no need to talk about what they both already knew. Credits bought protection . . . from Protection, the cut-loose from accountability, brutal state agency that was responsible for securing "Peace and Prosperity" . . . at all costs, financial or freedom.

The rich knew that the "prosperity" part really meant commerce, and that was mandatory. Anyone in the way of that. . . The "Peace" part was an all-too-commonly forgotten option, secured with violent compliance. Goods needed to flow, one way or another. That's why the State allowed Protection to look the other way at the Black Markets. In truth, the "mike's" were some of the most efficient ways to "Pacify the Populace"—keep the citizens just below revolt.

The PAIC continued his explanation. "Regardless, our overwatch asset witnessed the entire incident from his position on top of the scraper above the Mike." He slowly pulled his gloves off and tucked them both under his right armpit. "As you are well aware, Mr. King, operational protocols specify that anyone interfering with a Protection operation in progress may be condemned at the discretion of the agent in charge of that operation. So I instructed my team to do that as soon as they had vectors on her and her accomplices. The team had no idea who she was or why she tried to run into this particular building."

Frank adjusted the collar of his shirt. The mesh armor "skins" that his Prime Officer Protection leader made him wear at work, constant-ly itched and irritated his skin. Not to mention that the scaled mesh made it hard to quill out a quickie with one of his secretary-body-guards at lunch. He reached down and adjusted the crotch of his pants. He would talk to his POP agent after he dealt with this latest uncomfortable "itch" he had to scratch.

Frank knew it was going to take a lot of credits, not to mention the free pharmaceuticals his company would have to "donate," to get his daughter out of this.

Before, it had simply been petty theft and mischievous vandalism. Nothing that a few credits to the right agent and some concessions in his company's lucrative Protection contracts couldn't fix. But this? Just defying a Protection agent could get the average citizen condemned down the *Genesis* elevator—ferried underground to the interrogation wing of the sanatorium across the street.

Then they would be tied up, tortured, and pitched into a body-bin in the alley outside—bound for burning. Fortunately for Mercedes, her father Frank was not the average citizen.

Frank frowned. Cracking credits in Cancun was one thing, but this would make his daughter's vacation bills look like spare metal for Protection traffic towers.

Still, he had a plan for his daughter, especially since his wife, Babette, had gone volatile on him. That was particularly annoying, but it was nothing compared to the change in her . . . usefulness.

It was the simplest solution and he was going to put his plan into motion on Mercedes' sixteenth birthday. He smiled a little. *Just as easy to move things up to today*, he thought. Once he paid off the PAIC, he'd head into the cell and get "reimbursed."

Frank reached into his shirt pocket and pulled out his hex-card. No need for cash, because every Protection agent he knew carried a six-point credit swiper tied to their personal accounts. And since he was wealthy—it didn't get any richer than the Prime Officer of State's sole drugs and detainment contractor—all he had to do now was determine the price. "She doesn't look too bad," Frank said. "I humbly thank you for sparing her life, agent. It won't happ—"

"Put that away," the PAIC said, "I'm afraid things have become a bit more complicated than that."

Frank knew that the entire process of bribing a Protection agent, especially a PAIC, was a negotiation—haggling was part of it. And this agent had two bodies on his hands—mountains of paperwork before he could burn them.

No matter how senior a Protection agent got, someone had to do the paperwork. And if a senior agent was too high up to be bothered with it, he would still have to listen to a whining rookie PA, squawking and hackling his feathers about the forms. No agent who had flown up through the ranks wanted to be associated with the Protection paper pushers—to a fully-fledged field agent, a P3 was worse than a citizen—always complaining and bitching for more.

"I understand," Frank said. "The bodies. . . Who are—who were they?" He had a pretty good idea who the other two girls were, and he had warned Mercedes enough times that running with them was going to end badly one day.

Frank routinely answered late night waves and then raced his Masari through the night drizzle to Seattle's downtown Protection precinct, where he had to credit-spring all three of them. It was better than listening to his wife bitch at him all night.

The first time Frank let Mercedes and her little "chick" friends spend the night in a minimum Protection cell—teach them a lesson—Babette kept him awake all night, screaming and screeching about what might happen to them. But in minimum, a protectant got fed better than most citizens ate in their habitats.

Dolphin, Dungeness, and donuts—the minimum D3 appetizers were like being at an overpriced Protection fundraiser. And the net-feed waves in the "cells"—if you could call the plush pillows and sheets in them cells. . . The waves in minimum pumped all the contraband channels. There was a reason for it, of course. The bribes it took to spring little rich chicks—take them back to their nests—were obscene.

The PAIC pulled out his wave-tablet. The two condemned protectants' parents had already been notified via mini-drone messenger—no need to waste a fully-fledged agent's wings on that duty. "Anthem, Tessa and Baines, Bri—"

"Brianna Baines. . ." Frank said. And then he hung his head. They were Mercedes' primary posse. She was going to need two new companions to fly around the world reaping trouble with. The only thing was, he knew that Tessa's father was deep into the state finance farm—his credits debt was racing faster than Frank's car. And with an unburned body in a cardboard box the only thing he would get for his bribe money, Mr. Anthem wasn't cracking credits anytime soon.

As for Brianna. . . Frank had footed the bill for her more times than he could count. Mercedes had even made him pay off the girl's boyfriend to keep him from telling some secret to her little frigid friend.

But Frank kept a rolling tab in his ledgers on them both—all of them, really—and he had planned to collect their debts in other ways soon enough. At least if they were alive he could have continued the trials on them. Now, it was just another bribe with no upside. "How much for them?" he asked. Better to just get it over with. It was clear that Mercedes' price was tied to theirs. Maybe if he sweetened the deal —sprinkled a little bonus for the agent. "I can work disposal off the books."

Disposal costs would be easy enough—K&T owned the Protection disposal contracts anyway. One extra corpse. . . It wasn't like anyone counted them.

The PAIC pulled his gloves out from his armpit, stretched them back onto his hands—they didn't leave them off very long. Then he put his hand into his pocket. He sighed and said, "I don't think you are understanding me, sir."

Sir. . . Frank thought. It was going to cost more than he planned, and that would have to come out of his wife, Babs', allowance . . . or her ass, he didn't care which. But her little brat was getting more expensive than his wife could bend over to pay for.

Frank looked at the agent. The man was still facing forward—they were single-minded and focused predators. Only this man didn't seem to be looking at Mercedes anymore. He was staring into the half of the room that was still bathed in darkness.

All of the Protection cells had lighting that was designed to keep a protectant blasted with bright light and the interrogators hidden, lurking in the black. That was part of the strategy of fear and intimidation. But there were no interrogation agents in the room.

Frank looked into the darkness. Once he saw his daughter, he hadn't even bothered to glance at the other half of the cell. He could barely make out the outline of another person, strapped to a chair—

bathed in shadows—directly in front of Mercedes, and only separated from her by the table in the center of the cell.

A third one? No wonder, Frank thought. He prepared himself for a bigger number. He leaned into the glass, trying to see into the shadows. "I thought you said they were"—he noticed a line of red, slowly making its way out of the dark half of the room and across the concrete floor, toward the drain—"dead."

— VIII —

BABETTE CABOT-KING—there had been no way her husband, Frank, was going to strip her of her maiden name. That was over twenty years ago, though, and ever since she seduced him when she overheard that he was the richest man in Seattle, Frank King had "stripped" her almost every day since.

Landing such a big catch was an easy thing to do—back then, Babette was bleach-blonde, brazen, and beautiful. But soon after she got Frank "in the boat"—reeled him through a huge wedding and a honeymoon to Cancun—he became an insatiable pig, sweating and grunting and making her swallow everything, including her pride.

He was sadistic, too. A little secret he hid until it was too late to get away from him. But after "Babs"—what the filthy dog liked to call her —woke up from a three-day experimental drug-induced dream, surrounded by state Protection doctors and rehabilitation agents, sporting a brand new set of silicone implants, aching in her chest . . . she knew she would never get away from him alive.

It was a fact she plainly understood, as one of the first things her husband said to her when she woke up was that the implants contained little wave catchers. And those receivers were connected to tiny titanium capsules of his pharmaceutical company's highly experimental interrogation serum. "Sleep syrup," they called it at the Black Market. A little bit would give you the most vivid and sensual dreams you could ever imagine.

But, depending on how you lived your life, the dreams could be the hottest and heaviest ecstasy you had experienced . . . or the most horrific nightmares, filled with God only knew what manner of raping demons and devils.

Anyone who woke up from a syrup sleep. . . A rich recreational user had a pretty good hope in Hell of recovery, but a citizen, getting it injected into their arm in a Protection cell. . . Best case once an interrogation team was done with them, was a 5150 hotel—the nuthouse. Even if they got lucky—somehow avoided the white-walled palace of pain—they would forever remember the drug by its street name, "Judgment," or simply "J."

Frank assured Babette that if she ever tried to run, he would send the wave to trigger release of the serum into her bloodstream. He showed her the little metal medallion with the symbol of a cross on it that he kept around his neck. Inside it, there was a little blue finger-print scanner about the size of a quarter-credit. After he showed her that, he let Babette see the satellite feed he had on his phone so he could track her every move.

The next day, Babette got a gun, a pistol from the Black Market. She knew it wouldn't save her from him, but one day she wouldn't care. Sure, guns were expensive—more than a citizen made in a year —but one of the few good things about her new life was that credits were not a problem.

She never worried about it being illegal—no rich person did— because being in minimum Protection for a few days on unauthorized possession was like taking a vacation from the Devil. She let herself get remanded to Protection every once in a while just to take a break. Frank always credit-sprung her anyway.

Yes, Babette lived a Protection prisoner's life, and that's where her husband kept her—high above the rest of the world—virtually locked in the penthouse atop the Smith Tower in Seattle's upper district.

Strictly speaking, she could go anywhere and do anything she wanted, so long as she did anything that Frank wanted first. But that wasn't freedom and when she finally realized it, she knew she was just like any other citizen—free to come and go as she pleased, but trapped in the chains of her life. A *rich* citizen sure, but a slave nonetheless.

So she used her "new-won" wealth to torture her tormentor in the only way she could—she cracked-credits on his hex-card, buying anything and everything she could get her freshly primed nails on. Travel, trinkets and tobacco were her favorites, but if that got too boring she simply stopped by the Church and donated . . . right after she "confessed" her sins. And there was no way to get those credits back.

The church had figured out how to hide money long before her husband made a single credit. Even powerful people had no idea how to recapture revenue from the religions of the world. That drove Frank particularly nuts. To an evil business baron, credits to charity was the worst way to waste wealth.

Babette sarcastically told him the donations were to make sure that he didn't go to Hell for all the sins he had to commit to get them. But to Frank, it was wasteful. "Gifting green to God," he had said to her, "you might as well burn it."

And she thought about it too, but that wouldn't have allowed her to pay for her other favorite pastime—banging the benevolent.

* * *

Babette bent over and gripped the sheets at the head of her super-king bed in the lower loft of their penthouse suite at the top of the Smith Tower. She normally used her daughter's loft in the tower's tip —made the maids clean Mercedes' sheets instead of her own—but Mercedes had the building maintenance change the security code on the portal to her loft. The little bitch's room was locked up tight.

Babette frowned—thinking about it was getting her out of "the mood." It was getting harder to keep her little teen twat in line.

When Mercedes was young, it had been easier. Print up some fake fan tickets to her daughter's favorite wave-star concerts, post them on the ice-keeper, and whenever the little miscreant didn't do what she wanted, Babette ripped the tickets up in front of her and said, "And that's no concert for you!" It didn't take long for her daughter to catch on to that trick.

But the locked portal to Mercedes' room hardly mattered anymore —if her husband didn't know by now, he was too stupid to ever figure it out.

Babette moaned and said, "Fuck me!" Her head heaved forward. "Grab my tits."

And she felt the familiar pain of fingers squeezing too hard. "Aaaaah!" she winced and yelled. Just because she had to endure it when her husband did it. "Son of a bitch! Don't rip them off! What the. . .? Get off me!"

Incoming wave . . . Incoming wave . . . Incoming wave. . .

The annoying voice from the loft's integrated communications net ground on Babette's ears like fresh-primed nails on a wave-tablet.

Frank had found a young secretary at his company for the voice synthesizer module to mimic. The girl's annoyingly "helpful" voice drove Babette crazy. More after she bumped into the little slut on one of her few visits to the *Genesis* scraper downtown. Visits which really had only one purpose—Frank liked to show off Babette's breasts to his business buddies.

Incoming wave . . . Incoming wave . . . Incoming wave. . .

And Babette's "lover" jumped up and scrambled to the corner of the room—out of view of the communication feed camera.

Babette didn't even bother pulling the covers over her—she already knew who it was. So she stood up, naked on the bed with her hands on her hips. There was only one reason that the feed hadn't automatically answered—her husband was giving her time to shove anyone she had out the door and get covered up. "Accept," she said.

And the 3D holographic feed projected in front of the wall opposite the foot of the bed, and her husband's face and torso appeared in full color. "Babs," the projection said before her husband realized. "Jesus Christ, what are you. . .? Put some clothes on!"

"Why?" Babette said. "I'm hot."

For the last few years, Babette had faked hot flashes and migraines to see if that would get her husband to leave her alone. It worked for a while, but in the damp cold of the Pacific Northwest Quarter, it was hard to claim "hot flashes" to delay her husband's advances.

Frank's image on the holograph frowned. "Jesus Christ," he said, "we both know that's bullshit."

Babette got down on all fours on the bed and crawled toward the feed camera. "What do you mean?" In his office, all the way down-town and in the middle of the day, she could tease and torture Frank without worry of "retribution." Immediate revenge, anyway.

"Knock it off," Frank said, "this is serious. Get dressed and send the father back to church. Where is he?" And Frank's projection turned and looked behind him. Then Babette was shocked when he almost whispered, "Never mind, I'll deal with him later. You need to get your tits down here . . . *right* now."

And the holographic projection disappeared and then the grinding voice hit Babette's ears again—

Wave terminated. Have a nice day, Babette King.

Babette stood back up. "Bitch," she muttered. Then she looked over at the father. He was wide-eyed and a little less "faithful," standing in the corner with a sheet around his waist. "Hah, you wanna put that in your little book? If I was you, I'd get a gun." She glanced at his waist, and then back at his face. "Probably a little bigger than that one." Then she smiled—she wasn't finished.

When the father didn't move quickly enough, Babette frowned a little and motioned for him to come back into the bed. The father hesitated.

"Aw, sweetie," Babette said, "I'm just kidding, he's not going to do anything. He has an image. Besides, you're the largest church in the city—everyone comes to you to confess their conscience. He knows that. All it's going to cost you is a few secrets." And she rolled onto her back and spread her legs. "Now . . . get back in here."

— IX —

THE ARCHANGEL FAITH flapped his tired wings and slowly fluttered toward the portal to the dungeons. He was exhausted, but it wasn't because he was an old, boozing and blaspheming believer. His days as a Man-monkey priest were long gone. Jump had confiscated his flask and Rain had pardoned him for the rest. But neither of them could remove the weight of his conscience, hanging like an anvil of guilt around his soul. A Rosary of remembrance, reminding him of who he really was . . . who he had been.

But Faith's body was strong—angels were stout creatures with few, if any, physical weaknesses. So whatever ailments and addictions he had as a Man-monkey were left behind when Fury lopped off his head in his own church. An act he forgave as it was only so Rain could carry his soul and forge her way back into Purgatory in order to save eternity from Lived and Life.

It seemed like more than an eternity since Rain had ferried his essence into the arena. There, Father Benito Benedetti was judged, turned into the dark archangel, Faith, and then burned to ashes by the devil, Lived.

But Rain almighty resurrected him . . . just as she did every last soul in the old Heaven and Hell. It was her first act as the Protector-god of this new eternity—the kingdom of Rain's reign.

The aftermath of the night's judgments passed beneath Faith as he flew. The smell of burned souls on the floor of the arena assaulted his nostrils, and smoke mixed with ash slowly wafted up toward the transparent domed ceiling of the Hallowed Hall. And that smell, mixed with the sweet fragrance of vanilla and molasses, alternated a feeling of despair and hope in his own soul.

Rain's new eternity was all about nurturing the natural balance of power. Good and "not so good," she would say, "two sides to the same soul." Good relied on evil and evil could not exist unless it were defined by good. So she forced them both to depend on one another for survival. It was how wars were avoided.

Faith smiled and flapped his wings a little faster. How such a young ruler had come to understand the nuance of that concept gave him renewed faith in all their futures.

"Faith." That was the name they gave him after he was judged in Heaven. Before that it was "the father," and before that, "Father Benito." That was his favorite. It was the name he received when he started his journey toward understanding the true nature of God—graduated the seminary. Now, the very name of the previous protector was synonymous with evil and treachery and it was forbidden to speak it. "God" was blasphemy.

Faith understood why Rain had commanded it to be so—the woman. . . Finding out God was a woman was still the hardest thing for him to reconcile when he finally saw Heaven. Now, when he allowed himself to stop and remember it all, he realized he had come to grips with quite a lot.

Losing his own faith, defiling his church with all manner of sin and sinner, and then authoring the blasphemous book that would end eternity—the *Book of Blood* that wiped out humanity itself. . . Yet all of that paled in comparison to that other thing.

He could barely think of it, but falling into the grasp of that temptress woman. . .? Faith knew that it wasn't a small miracle he had ended up above the lake of fire, tucked into the first Heaven as if he wasn't who he knew himself to be.

The "first" Heaven. . . "For one Man-monkey's Heaven," Rain had said in one of her speeches before a particularly long night of judgments, "is simply another's second Heaven." What she really meant was another one's Hell. But Rain led by example—she had never spoken a profanity or blasphemy, as a girl or a god. Before or after the end, if Faith remembered correctly.

That was the way he wrote her in his book and he was responsible for all of it—the Battle of the Books, for certain. For Faith was the author of the end of humanity. He wrote his *Book of Blood* as a protest against the *Bible*, because God never spoke to him the way he imagined. It was the word of a revolution in Hell—the coup that overthrew God and the Devil and ended their plans to enslave all the souls in the two Heavens for another eternity and then . . . forever.

The Battle of the Books had put so many in agony. . . The fallen angel, Faith, was not worthy of the Heaven where he now lived. He felt that understanding growing in both of his hearts.

The Rosary-covered prison bars in the dungeons beneath the Arena of Reckoning were still where all of the worst souls were kept. Souls so vile and hateful that even Rain believed them to be beyond redemption.

No angel in the two Heavens understood why Rain left the dungeons intact after the great darkness of oblivion ended the last eternity and ushered in hers. But for an innocent young soul who allowed even the most repugnant of the Man-monkeys from the last eternity to repent. . . If Rain couldn't save an angel from their worst selves, they probably weren't worth saving at all.

Located just above the great fiery lake, the Dungeons of the Damned were constantly hot and muggy. The walls dripped black blood from the wrong hearts of the wretched and crimson-red blood from the right hearts of the righteous. All of it spilled, since time began in the Garden, in the arena above. The life liquid of evil and good, slowly oozed to the floor—Chinasian water torture to the souls imprisoned there—a constant, dripping reminder of their failures and follies. And no eternity could change that fact.

Faith folded his wings behind him and interlocked their feathers to form his shield. They formed the sunburned, shimmering image of a bright, shining-white star—the symbol of the brightest soul that ever graced the Pearly Gates of Heaven—the warmark of Rain the almighty.

Then Faith pushed out all of his armored feathers and scraped their steel together, checking to make sure they would work if he needed them. As he did, the sounds of metal echoed down the tunnel.

He gazed down the dungeon's dark passageway. Despair and anger loomed in the air and the scent of pent-up violence fought its way into his nostrils. The dungeons weren't hot from the flames of the lake below alone—dark souls sweltered sin and suffering from every cell. The heat stuck on Faith like lava from the shores of the lake.

The dungeons glowed and flickered a deep orange and black. Cells lined both sides of the long, dark tunnel. Faith knew it ran in a huge circle around and underneath the entire edge of the arena above. And other tunnels crisscrossed underneath the arena, cutting the big circular passageway around the edge like the spokes of a great wheel. And each of those tunnels were lined with cells, as well. All of it led to one place, the center of the arena—the destiny of souls.

As Faith walked, black shadows flitted and fluttered in the corners and crevices of each cell. He glanced at the bars on their gates—great, rusted-iron pillars that were covered with the remnants of Rosary beads. The cult charms were how Life had imprisoned bright and dark souls. Now, each cell was locked and branded with the molten-iron seal of Rain's star. To break a seal was blasphemy and punishable by annihilation—the only way for an angel to truly die.

Any angel in the two Heavens and any being in the new garden could be resurrected from death—the ten billion souls lasted through each eternity—but annihilation was permanent. It was a fate that all feared, and no seal had ever been broken.

A raspy, vile voice whispered from the shadows of its cell, "Faith. . ."

And Faith jerked his head toward the voice. A figure flitted into the blackness.

Across the tunnel, another voice whispered and lisped like a snake, "Faith. . ."

He moved away from it.

And then another crowed at him, "Faith!" And he spun around to face it.

And this time, a caw echoed from down the tunnel, "Faith!" He backed away, toward the edge of the tunnel. And then he bumped into the bars on the cell behind him.

Then a voice was right in his ear. "Ah, Father Benito," the voice said.

Faith tried to flap away from it, but a burning hand grabbed his wing and he could feel the red hot coals on the back of his neck. And the heat singed into his feathers . . . and he knew who it was.

Lived was just another clever way that the evil creature disguised himself. But whatever name he had come to be known by—Dark Angel of Light, Day Star, Lucifer, Liar, or "Long-licker," as Jump liked to call him—to Faith, the vile, red-winged angel who had tortured him and then burned him to ashes in front of a million faithful and fallen angels, was the worst of all of them—the devil, Lived.

"It seems you are well known here," said Lived, breathing heat into Faith's ear. "Almost as famous as I am. However, thinking about it, maybe it is infamous." Lived paused and they both listened to the cawing and crowing echo through the dungeon. "Listen to them. Why, it almost sounds as if they believe you are one of them, doesn't it. What do you think, father, do you belong down here? . . . Or perhaps you are simply here for a . . . conjugal visit."

Faith's neck burned and he winced and cried out, "Aaah!" Then he clenched his jaw and leaned into the pain. He knew he deserved it. "I am not. . . I will never—"

"Lover?" a raspy, seductive voice growled from down and across the tunnel. Then a slightly maniacal laugh and then a small giggle followed it. "You are so long in . . . coming."

"Ahh. . ." Lived whispered, burning flame into Faith's ear, "there she is." And he let go of Faith's neck. Faith stumbled forward a half step. "Go ahead, then," Lived said. "Who am I to stand in the way of . . . old lovers?" But then he grabbed Faith again and breathed hot fire into his ear when he shouted, "Give her tits a squeeze for me, father!" And he slowed down a little and ran his long tongue around Faith's ear. "And oh, by the way . . . peace be with you." And then he looked across and down the tunnel, at the darkness of the woman's cell. "And also with you . . . nasty little whore." Then he let go of Faith again, and he threw his head back and cackled loudly, "A match made in Hell!" He looked behind him. "Just like ours, my little lamb."

— X —

WHEN I WAKE up this time. . . *Thank God*, I think, not even catching myself in my blasphemy. But whatever, because the sun is warm, I can feel the sand between my toes, and I'm lying on my stomach with my top untied, tanning my back on my big orange beach towel. I recognize where I am immediately—the hot-ass beach in Cancun, Mehico baby! Been coming here since I was thirteen. Booyah!

But damn, Tessa's arm blown off? And that interrogation room? That resurrection sucked. That detention—I've gotta be more careful —these thoughts and flashes are like playing Russian roulette with a machine gun. Lying *cocksuckers*—I should have known. *You're in it now, Mercedes*, I think. Then I turn my head, looking to see if they're with me. I make sure not to lift up and have my boobs pop out when I do it. Not that they're huge, but—oh, whatever.

No, of course I don't care *now*, you little humping hatchlings, but I'm probably about like, thirteen or fourteen on this resurrection, and in Man-monkey years that's like. . . Shit, I don't know. All of you are so good at math, you figure it out.

Anyways, I'm too little for you shits to go gawking at my gods, I know that much. . . . Huh? . . . Well, we aren't *in* Hell, now are we, so I can say anything I want. Trust me, the Man-monkey. . . I guess you would call us Woman-monkeys. Hah! Totally funny . . . whatever. But women were always screaming and moaning for God during sex. My mother—*all* the time.

When I first caught them. . . Oh shit, never mind, I've said too much already. I told you I'm saving that for later. Maybe I'll just take you down there. It's sorta hard to explain—better for you to see it for real. But now is not—I don't want to right now.

What? . . . "Gods?" Seriously, that's what you want to. . .? It's what Jump calls them, because like, when he first saw Life, he couldn't stop staring at hers—total old-man perv. He told you that story, didn't he? . . . No? Well, I told you about old cocksuckers and sex. Can you imagine him and grandma Salvation. Yeah, try and scrape that off your feathers. Sick!

Now listen, just calm down a little, try to enjoy the sun. You were all just bitching about the cold like, five minutes ago. So shut up, I'm gonna cop some Z's. Don't let me burn, okay?

And when I look, there they are—Brie and Tessa—tanning their boobs, lying face up on either side of me. Exhibitionist little. . . And Brie—not much to tan on her, but Tessa. . . Not now—I can see that —but when she was like, fifteen, when she laid on her back we would call her "pit-tits." She was huge. Lucky bitch.

There, are you happy now? Sick little purgatory pervs.

Anyways, I'm glad to see both of them, because dream or whatever —sure they're bitches, but they're *my* bitches. And dead? I don't *think* so.

And I'm pretty excited to go out with them tonight. That's what I remember—party night in Cancun and there's no minimum age. I put my head back down, smiling—it's been a while since I felt that way about either one of them.

We never really did much, back then—now. Mostly we just yacked and jacked and smacked a little yayo. Maybe not now—we look a little young to be snorting coke *or* shooting J. I don't remember when we actually started that. About the same time we started sucking dicks, I gue—

Hey, hey! Whoa. . . Chill. . . You don't know me yet. Judgmental little shits. Do you know how all this works? . . . Do ya? . . . No, you don't. None of you were Man-monkeys. None of you were at the Battle of the Books, either, were you?

Shut your heaven-holes—it's called rhetorically . . . or something. Yeah, don't answer.

Well, I *was* there, and I was—and I'm in charge of all a you. God-dammit this job sucks. Now you're making me commit blasphemy again. I can't wait until you deliver your first souls to the arena. You have no idea. Hell and Heaven, none of you are even full-fledged archangels yet—featherless little. . . A little dick sucking will be the least of your worries.

You're asking too many questions. I'll tell you everything when we get back. You little—in fact, you don't stop squawking at me, you aren't going to want to go back, because I'm making Salvation hammer you. You can bet that. Out . . . of . . . *control!*

Hah, well you *should* be afraid. You ever heard of Vegas? . . . Of course you haven't. That's because me and Salvation burned it to the ground, idiots. Aw shit! And now you got me talking about Vegas.

* * *

A couple of hours of suntanning with infant oil, and Tessa and Brie's baked brown breasts later, and the three of us are headed to the Bravo Mike to do a little jacking. Because every place has one, oh yeah.

And then I think about it and I remember. *Oh no. . .*

"Why don't we ditch on the shopping?" I say to them as we walk.

Brie stops. "And a bitch says what?" she says. "The party's not 'til like, nine. I can't tan anymore. So what are we gonna do until then?"

But I keep walking, eyeing the market ahead, and Tessa keeps walking with me.

Brie catches back up. "Bitches. . ." she mumbles. Then she says, "What *should* we do, then?"

"We could boot some liqs," Tessa says. She likes the sweet booze. Brie and me, the hard stuff. Tessa looks at me. "Got any credits?" she asks.

"Jesus," I say, because like, I know she's not *that* hurting for credits. "Doesn't your dad give you *any* credits? How did you even get on the flight?" I close my fingers and thumb, snapping my hand at her face. "Mute—I don't wanna know." Because, private jet or not, everyone pays for the flight.

Brie bumps into me on purpose and I stumble, kick a rock that goes shooting off the trail. "We can't all be Kings, bitch," she says. "Stop ragging her. I got credits. And she's right—it's hot. I could use a Blonde Bimbo or three."

Blonde Bimbos—nothing but trouble: shot of coconut rum, shot of peach schnapps, shot of Tuaca—if you can even find "T." If you can't, sub in some State swill like, mixed with OJ and vanilla and shit. Throw some pineapple juice on top of the whole thing to make it go down without a frown. . . I like mine blended, but Tess and Brie—on the rocks, all the way.

Over Brie's bitching, I barely hear my wave tablet singing and going off in the bottom of my big beach bag. By the time I open it—

. . .King, you have an International wave . . . Incoming wave . . . Incoming wave. . .

We all stop and Brie looks at me with her big, blue, jealous eyes. "Oh *my-God*, how did you get that? He's like, my favorite singer *ever!*"

And I already know that. I made one of my daddy's techno-junkies reprogram the voice-synth module on my tablet with the little wave-star's voice. I did it just to fuck with Brie. I smile and dig in my bag for my wave tablet. "Identify," I say, pushing past my extra pair of panties to get to it.

Franklin James King, Prime Officer, King and Tamonos Enterprises. . . Incoming wave . . . Incoming wave. . .

Brie has her hands on her hips by now, because she knows that I couldn't care less about her favorite singer. She laughs a little. "Such a bitch," she says, "I love it, totally illegal. How the—you must live in minimum."

I smile down at my bag. "Got my own room."

Tessa is just shaking her head—she knows me. "You mean *cell.*"

And I finally find my little, transparent glass tablet at the very bottom of my bag. "Shit. . ." I say. It's got infant oil all over it. "Dammit." I wipe it off on my swim mini, put it up to my ear, and then I hold it there with my shoulder while I dig in my bag for my swipes. "Accept"—the phone chimes, letting me know it's connected —"Hi, Daddy, how's Seattle?"

I'm wiping my hands when he starts in. He doesn't even bother with the weather chit-chit. All he wants to know about are the credit comms he's getting. I already know he has alarms on every tab of my hex-chip. Six little auto-waves, ratting me out to him when I'm cracking too many credits.

So I tell him, "I had to get a new swim—"

And he launches off into some shit about credits and my mom and other stuff. Not like he's going to go broke off one swim mini, Jesus.

"Because that one didn't fit anymore," I tell him. It's the truth, because they *are* starting to grow.

I can tell he doesn't get it, because he's asking me why I need the expensive one. As if I should be buying the surplus synthetics that the citizens wear.

"Yes," I say to him, "the bottoms *did* still fit. But my boobs *don't.*" *That should shut him up.*

I'm pretty sure it works, because there's a long silence on the other end of the wave. But then he goes right back at me.

So I grab my wave tablet and hold it away from my face. I look at Brie and Tessa, busy trying not to giggle. And I open and close my free hand at them and rock my head from side to side, mocking my dad's voice, because we can all still hear him ragging me.

When I put the tablet back to my ear, I barely catch the last of his "sermon" about credits. "No, I'm not kidding," I say. And I put my finger to my lips and motion for them to be quiet. Then I hold the tablet out in front of me, flat in my palm. "Holo."

And the 3D holographic image of my dad's head projects above the wave-tablet.

Then I point the vid-port at my cups and I say, "See, look."

And I wasn't shitting him—they are even bursting out of this year's mini-top. Anyways, I know it will probably shock him enough to shut him up, because whenever I bring up that subject, he gets all freaky and sends me to my mother.

"Uh. . ." he says.

Then I point the 3D port at Brie and Tessa and say, "Say hi to Brie and Tess, Daddy."

And they both wave at him all cutesy like we talked about. "Hi, Mr. King." Both at the same time—they are so good.

Then Tessa leans in and fakes a little kiss at him, but it's really so he can get a little look down her mini-top.

And we all figured that out quick, because the best thing about boobs—totally distracting. And it works pretty good, because Daddy is like, "Uh . . . hi girls."

And for a guy that has like, hot supermodels for personal assistants, he is pretty easy to distract. It's totally funny . . . and gross. And I scrunch up my face from behind the 3D hologram—at Brie and Tessa —and they both giggle.

"Mercedes?" the projection asks.

I move right next to Brie and Tessa and point the 3D port at all of us. "Yes, Daddy?"

"Well," he says, "it sounds like you girls are having a good time.

Just—"

"Totally awesome, Mr. King," Tessa says.

"Uh," he says, "that's . . . good, really good, Tessa," he says to her. "Just try to stay out of—I don't want to have to spring all you girls again, okay?"

"No problem whatsoever," Tessa says. "We're just playing around at the beach, Mr. King."

And I can feel Brie looking at her, because what the. . .?

"Sounds good," my dad says to Tessa. "I'll trust you to keep Mercedes' hex-card under control, then?"

And I have to cut this shit off right now, because I'm starting to get. . . It's just—eww! So I point the 3D port at me and move away from them. "Okay, Daddy," I say.

And I glance over at Tessa and she's giving me that, "What the fuck?" look.

So I raise my eyebrows at her and give her my own look back. Then I turn back to my wave tablet. "We just have one party to go to, and then a little shopping. Nothing major, I promise."

And his head turns and tries to look toward Brie and Tessa, but I have the vid-port turned too far and he can't see them, Tessa for sure. His head turns back and he says, "Just take it easy on the tag-popping, okay? Your mother's driving me nuts with it. She's totally out of. . ."

I don't listen to the end of it, but when he stops talking I say, "Absolutely." And I'm trying not to look annoyed, but—"TTY, Daddy."

"I'm trusting you, Em," he says. "We talked about this."

I try not to raise my eyebrows. No clue if I do or not. "I got it," I say to him, "easy on the credits. I gotta go. Terminate."

The 3D projection retracts and cuts off whatever *Daddy* was going to say after that.

And I look at Brie and she's staring at Tessa and then I look at Tessa.

Tessa shrugs her shoulders and scrunches up her face. Then she looks at Brie and leans back away from her a little, because Brie is moving into her face. "What?" Then Tessa turns back to me. "You said flirty. That was flirty." And she looks at Brie again. "*What?*"

Brie's got her arms crossed now and I can tell she's trying not to smile. "Holy bitch. . ."

"*Serious*," I say.

And Tessa jerks her head and looks at me. "Oh, come on. Screw both of you! If—if Brie did that, you would be all"—she rocks her head side to side at me—" 'Oh, that was sooo funny! Brie, you are so wonderful and I just want to kiss you right now. And you are so cool.' "

Brie can't hold it back anymore. She starts giggling. A little at first, but then more than I like.

I put my hand on my hip, throw my wave tablet into my beach bag, and then I look into the bag and say, "Block previous wave." Because I don't wanna hear that ever again. Then I look at her. "That shit is *not* okay. *Not!*"

And now Tessa is laughing with Brie and they high-five.

Brie is so excited to get one over on me that she starts running in place, and then she stops and points her finger at me. "Smackdown, bitch."

"Oh *my-God*," I say. "No *way!*"

And Brie bends over and just laughs. "Bitch," she says, "your dad is a perv."

"Totally," Tessa says, putting her hand on Brie's back. It makes Brie stop and stand back up. And I think they have enough sense to stop, because I'm over it. But then Tessa says, "Totally cute, though."

Then Brie starts laughing again. And Tessa is laughing again, too.

Now I'm just grossed-out. "Gross," I say to them. Now I *really* want to go jacking, because that is just. . . And I stomp off toward the mike and flip them the "angel-ass" with the first two fingers and the pinky of my right hand. "Sluts," I say behind me.

When Brie and Tessa catch up to me, I refuse to look at them. And the Bravo Mike is getting closer, and I can see the brown-suited Mexican Protection agents at the entrance—shit's a little different in Cancun—PA's are right out in the open. And I'm so pissed, I forget why I even care.

"What about the Blonde Bimbos?" Brie giggles. And I can tell she's only half-trying to be serious.

Even though I think it's a pretty good joke, I'm still annoyed. But I'm starting to remember something. "I'm not talking to you."

Tessa leans next to me, puts both her arms around mine as she walks beside me. "You just did," she whispers.

I try not to smile. "Or you," I say to her. Then I slow down a little, because now I *do* remember. And before we have to sit in a cockroach-infested Mexican Protection cell again, while my dad waves credits to Raul the rapist—"Duh," I say to them both, "you know I'm not drinking that without any T. Why don't we just go—"

"Which is why. . ." Tessa says, and then she lets go of my arm and reaches into her big beach purse—she jacked it at the same place I did

—and she pulls a pint-sized bottle of the brown sugary booze halfway out of her purse.

It's a pretty stupid move—and I'm back to annoyed—because we are almost at the entrance to a "Mike" and—

Brie tries to grab Tessa's hand and push it back into her bag. "Bitch," she says to her, "put that away. Are you crazy?" And now all of us are looking around and Brie and I are serious, because we know. Waving a 3D holo around is one thing—everyone knows a wave tablet is worthless to anyone but the person it's voice-matched to— but contraband liquor? Gold's cheaper.

I don't think Tessa was even thinking about it. "Ow," she says. And she twists away from Brie as she walks and shakes her hand off of her. "Get off me, bitch. It's just T."

"And this is a Black Market in Mexico," I say to her, "and that shit's —how did you get that, anyways?"

Tessa laughs. "Mute," she says. "And stop being a bitch to me. I was just jacking with him. It's not like I—"

I stop, and both of them stop with me. And now I'm scared. "That's not what I—I don't care about that!" I look at the bottle of contraband booze in Tessa's hand. "What are you think—"

"Aaaah!" Tessa yells, and then she falls down, face first, flat on the ground. And a kid runs past us faster than I think the little brat should be able to. And he's got, like, tan burlap for clothes, or some shit. *Mexi-jacker!* I think.

And he is fast as hell and I look at his feet, pounding the dust as he runs. *He's got no shoes.* But what he does have, is Tessa's bottle of Tuaca in his hand, and he's booking it straight at the Bravo Mike gate.

"You little bitch!" I yell at him. And I frown, but then I smile. Corrupt Protection gate guards or not, jacking right out in the open. . .? The gate agents are gonna mess him up. But the little jacker jets right past them and they don't do anything.

"Mother—*bitches!*" Brie yells at the Protection agents. And she's down on her knees, trying to help Tessa get back up.

And Tessa isn't saying anything. She's just kinda moaning a little. *Little shit*, I think. But the little jacker just saved us the trouble of trying to get rid of that bottle. Then I look back at the gate and the Protection agents are walking toward us.

Brie holds up her hand at me. "Em?"

I look at her hand and at first I don't get it, because it's just got clumped-up sand and dirt on it, but when I look closer . . . it's covered in blood.

"Great," I say, "now we gotta go to the hospital. This is just—" But when I look at Tessa's back, there's a little slit just above her swim-mini and it's pumping dark blood.

Liver, I think. Because, like I said, I've seen that before, too. "Tess!" I yell down at her. And I drop down on my knees next to Brie. And she's pulling on Tessa, trying to roll her over. And I grab on too and I look into Brie's eyes as we roll Tessa over. And I can tell Brie is shitting —there's no faking fear. "We gotta get her up and to a med—"

But when we get Tessa on her side, she's not screaming or crying or yelling in pain, or anything. Her eyes are rolled back and they should be white, but they're like, totally black. And then her whole body shakes like crazy.

I hold Tessa's body down, but Brie lets go and kicks herself away a little. "Judgment," she says. And then she stops scooting. "Oh bitch. . ."

I know what she means—little jacker stuck Tessa with Sleep Syrup, too much of it. And if the liver wound doesn't kill her. . . I look back at the Protection agents, running at us now, and I scream, "She's stabbed! . . . Judgment! Juicio-juicio!"

I know, you little shits are right—I am—I was stupid. But there was nothing we could've done anyways.

— XI —

JUMP FLEW, BEATING his huge gray wings in long, powerful strokes, pushing his great steel feathers against the snowflakes that fell from the clouds above the Great Mountain of the Eternities.

The air around the mountain was ice cold. When he did catch up with Fury, there was going to be some hell. No angel in the second heaven liked being out in the cold. And the ruler of Hell having to fly through it?

Not that it would stick to Jump's feathers. His blood boiled so hot that Salvation worried he would melt the snow right off the peak of the mountain. But he was the Great Dragon, and archangel "search and salvation" was not in his job description.

Jump looked over at Salvation, flying beside him. "She's not out here in this," he said. "This is total—when we find her. . ."

Jump's wingtip scraped against Salvation's and she banked a little to avoid colliding with him. He tended to drift in the direction he was looking when he flew. "Careful," she said. "Don't make me pull your license."

Jump banked hard into her path and Salvation pulled up and spun around him to avoid crashing. Then she drifted back behind him a little.

"I'll give you something to pull," Jump crowed back at her.

Salvation shook her head and smiled. Her man was testy. They needed to find Fury or she would spend the rest of the day listening to him rant. "Careful," she cawed at him. "I'll have to get you glasses, too."

Jump must not have heard her, because he didn't even look back.

Salvation scanned the mountain. She zoomed her vision into every crack and crevice of the valleys below it. There were flowerites, treetippies, and snow leopard fairyflies—their big white and gray wings camouflaging them against the rocks and white on the slopes of the mountain—all of Rain's favorites as a child. Well, not the fairyflies. Rain created those after Salvation explained to her that she would have to create something for real snow leopards to eat. That would mean lambs for them to slaughter. And judging dead souls in the arena was one thing, but creating animals just so something could rip their guts out for breakfast? A child didn't understand that.

So Rain made them into fairyflies and gave them slopes of snowgrass to munch. There were lots of living beings on the mountain that Rain had created during the genesis of this new eternity . . . but there was no angel Fury.

It began to snow harder. Once that started, Salvation knew it would be days before Rain made the sun come back out. It was as ironic as Hell being the second Heaven, but Rain loved Christday snow, too.

"I don't think she's out here," Salvation screeched in front of her. She flapped her wings hard to catch up to Jump. It was difficult. His wings were so big that no angel in Heaven or Hell could catch him if he was at full speed. Except for the one they were looking for, that is. Luckily they weren't attacking anything today, so her husband's pace was manageable. "We should check the arena," she shouted through the snowflakes.

"You know she's not in there," Jump cawed back. The touch of annoyance in his voice had turned to a slap. "When I get my hands on —"

Salvation dove and then used her speed to pull up—right in front of Jump—and she flew as fast as she could toward the top of the mountain.

And Jump frowned, spun upside down, did a couple of loops, and then powered in front of her.

Then she followed him in silence all the way through the rotating, transparent domed roof of the great Hallowed Hall.

They tried to avoid it as long as they could, but they both knew where they had to check next. It wasn't the arena.

Jump rubbed his foot across the chipped diamonds and rubies on the floor of the Arena of Reckoning, remembering the spot where he had torn Life apart and then had his heart ripped from his chest by his own daughter. Then he looked up and toward the edge of the field.

The stars above the transparent roof made the gemstones of the arena sparkle, and they cast tiny reflections into the grandstands. The long, railed perches in the grandstands were usually filled to bursting with the steel armor and feathers of the fallen and the faithful of the two Heavens, all of them cawing for judgment, justice, and in some extreme cases . . . jail.

He and Salvation stood side by side, as they once had, in the middle of the arena, silently eyeing the portal entrance to the dungeons below.

The arena was a wild and barely controllable place on judgment nights. Long screeching and cawing matches, where dark and light souls were judged. Condemnation or salvation was delivered with equal fury. None who passed through the great Pearl Gate—the bright, pearl-covered portal entrance from and to the garden—were ever the same after, and all were required to endure.

Rain had wanted to change the process—it seemed far too violent to her—but in the end, harder souls prevailed. Jump had asked Salvation to speak to their daughter about the ways of the world of the old Man-monkeys . . . and those of Rain's new creations. For every species he could think of, from the old eternity to the new, only grew stronger through struggle.

That wasn't quite the way he put it when he fumed at Salvation by the lake of fire. She smiled at him, remembering his words.

"They gotta be tough," he had told her. "Go tell your daughter I'm not letting any pee-pissing purgatories stink this place up."

Translating understanding and meaning between Rain the innocent and the Great Dragon of cynicism. . . Salvation had her hands full most days. She looked at the spot on the arena floor.

During the Battle of the Books, Salvation was smote there and her feathers had been burned to a powdered ash around her. Remembering the pain still made her feathers prickle, and she reached next to her and held Jump's hand. She squeezed into his metal pinfeathers . . . just hard enough.

Jump looked down at Salvation's hand on his. She had a firm grip, tighter than when she held it on judgment nights. And he followed her gaze to the spot on the arena floor. "Still a bitch, huh?" he said.

Salvation nodded her head and continued to stare. "Like it was yesterday. She is such a. . ."

Once Rain resurrected Salvation from the ashes of Life's lightning bolt, Jump had raged for the one responsible to be ended by annihilation. A judgment that only Rain could render. But his daughter had other plans for the "Chosen One" and her dark angel, Lived. So, locked in the dungeon they were, condemned to a fate Rain believed worse than annihilation.

Jump did not agree. "If she won't do it, I'm going to rip her apart again," he said. Then he walked toward the portal to the dungeon.

Salvation pulled back on his hand. "That won't change a thing," she said. "You've done that—she always . . . she will never. . . Nothing good comes from fighting with her. She just resurrects worse."

Jump stopped at the end of Salvation's outstretched arm. He stared at the portal. "I'm not after good," he said. Then he looked back at his wife. He was wild-eyed and thirsting for the blood of the benevolent. "I'm after *gone*."

Salvation knew how to handle her man. She smiled, stepped toward him and pulled his hand behind her back, and then she hugged him and ran her fingers through the pinfeathers on his head with her free hand. As she stared behind him, silently assuring him that she was okay, she caught a shimmer of light at the edge of the arena. "Remember. . ."

Then the portal to the dungeons twisted open and out fluttered a familiar figure. The portal twisted shut behind the dark shape.

Salvation watched as the angel fluttered, meandering playfully like a little purgatory with a new fresh frock of feathers. But bathed in shadow, illuminated only occasionally by sparkles from the gemstone floor, it was hard for her to be certain. And then there was the way he was flying. The archangel that Salvation knew hadn't shown a spark of light since . . . she couldn't remember when.

Jump had calmed down a little. "Remember what?" he whispered into her ear.

Salvation continued to watch the figure flit and flap. "Father Ben?" she muttered. She had never gotten used to calling him by his new angelic name, Faith. "What's he doing down. . .?"

Jump let go of Salvation's hand and pulled her other one out of his head feathers. Then he turned around to see. At first he didn't say anything, because from the way that the angel was flying, there was no way it was him. He zoomed his gaze in on the figure. Then he smiled, remembering the little priest that had poured molasses over his wounds on the floor of his church.

The father, Faith, had been a little "tin-tit sucking boozehound," Jump had called him back then. A faithless clergyman who had resorted to carrying a flask of State swill with him wherever he went. Jump had only seen him a handful of times since the old geezer's *Book of Blood* had overthrown Life and that long-licker, Lived.

The man had been judged, executed, torn apart and burned to ash, and if Rain hadn't shown up, they would have annihilated him for all the eternities, too.

But the last Jump had heard of him, Rain had pardoned him and the "old cocksucker," as Fury liked to call him, was safely tucked in Heaven with the rest of the self-righteous hypocrites on the mountain. He could barely remember the last time he saw the man.

Jump took a half step forward. "What's he doing fluttering around down here?"

Jump had moved in front of her, so Salvation had to take a step to the side in order to see the fluttering father again. Something wasn't right. She whispered to Jump, "He came out of the—"

"Hey, father!" Jump yelled across the arena at him. His voice boomed a little too loudly and the sound echoed off the grandstands on the other side.

They both watched as the figure jerked to a stop and hovered in place, looking all around the arena for the voice that probably just scared the shit out of him.

Salvation eased up next to Jump and, she didn't know why, but she continued to whisper, "A bit jumpy, don't you think."

Jump closed his eyes and lowered his head a little. Salvation had always had a bit of a "featherbrained" sense of humor, even in life. "Oh, that's just pathetic," he said, clucking a little. "You are no good at that. You know that, right?"

"What?" she said. Then she frowned at him. "No-no, I mean he is —he's *acting* funny."

"He's a priest," Jump said, "and a nutbag. You know what they do to them in there." Of course it was blasphemy to belittle the author of the book that started the revolution in Hell, but he knew Salvation wasn't ratting him. He might take an ass-chewing later. At worst, he'd get the cold wing for a night or two. But benevolent god for a daughter or sweet salvation for a wife aside, he'd say what he wanted, deal with the consequences later—it was kind of a motto.

Jump turned his head toward Salvation so he could enjoy the look of disgust on her face. "Of course he's acting funny. They probably let him out of his straitjacket so he could go find a little purgie to pump."

Jump was reckless, and a brute of a warrior as archangels went. Salvation knew that. She had witnessed it too many times.

Most hounds in the new Hell learned their lessons well—pain was a wonderful teacher. But Jump. . . Over and over again, he was so much like a big anvil that she could beat her head against until her feathers bled and he still wouldn't listen. So it was no surprise to her that he did nothing when she yelled, "Shields!"

Jump watched Salvation spin around, slam both of her wings together behind her back, and crouch down so fast. . . The first thought that flashed through his mind was that she was having some kind of PTSD reaction to being back in the arena where she was killed. "Battle-beak," he'd heard more seasoned archangels call it, because instead of slowly bobbing your head like a pigeon before a big fight, a scared-shitless angel would slam on his shield and nod his head like they were having a seizure.

Jump looked down at Salvation's shining shield. He could just make out little golden specks of light in its reflection. "What are you. . .?" And it looked like the little specks were getting bigger. He turned back to look toward the father again. "Shit!"

It wasn't hard for him to recognize the gold streaks, rocketing across the arena at them. Kill ten billion souls in the garden—he had seen a lot of tracer rounds in his "career" as a Man-monkey, not to mention fire-feathers in his new job—flaming, ballistic quills, rocketing across battlefields like shooting stars of death, cutting assholes and angels to pieces.

He spun just as the first feathers clanged against Salvation's armor. Jump slammed his huge wings together a split second too late and a bright gold fire-feather pierced into his back and started melting into his steel plumage. And the searing pain shot up his spine and he yelled, "Motherfucker!" It was his favorite pain "killer."

"Get down!" Salvation yelled at him. "You're going to get shot!"

"I *am* shot!" Jump yelled. "Get that thing outta—aaaah! It's burning."

Salvation jumped up and straddled her man's back, shielding him from the rest of the volley of feathers.

With a searing spike sticking out of him, Jump's wings couldn't fit together to make his protective shield. But the firefight—ambush was more like it—was over faster than it started. Whoever it was stopped as fast as they started firing.

That couldn't have been the father, Salvation thought. There weren't many fire-feathers—a dozen, maybe, twenty at most. Considering an archangel could fire hundreds of flight feathers with a single combat spin, Salvation knew they were lucky.

She looked across the arena in front of her. The feathers that missed them were busy burning bright gold holes into the grandstands. When she was sure there weren't more on the way—couple of seconds maybe, because she still had to get the burning one out of Jump's back —she stood up and spread her wings hard. The burning quills stuck in her shield, splintered and sparked and fell to the ground.

Then she spun fast and loosed a couple hundred of her own feathers back toward where the golden streaks started. She watched her own grey-streaking feathers fly across the arena and embed in the grandstands. Then they burned down to sparks. There was no sound. She zoomed in and looked around. Whoever fired at them was already gone.

Salvation reached down and, without a word from her or a whimper from Jump, ripped the burning gold spike out of his lower back.

"Goddammit!" Jump yelled. Then he felt the hot liquid oozing down his back. "Fucking molasses."

Salvation threw the spike to the ground and then plucked out one of her own flight feathers and began to heat it up to a bright red glow. Another feather from behind it—like shark's teeth—filled the gap in her wing back in.

Jump screeched in pain. "You gotta burn—aaah!"

Salvation pressed her red hot feather onto the wound in Jump's lower back. It burned and seared and smoked like the branding iron they used on the whores and whoremongers during judgment. Then she pulled it off. "Stay still," she said, because squirming around caused scars.

Jump had plenty of battle-brands. He screeched and grimaced and stood up and said, "*That*"—his face contorted in pain. He reached behind him, trying to rub it—"is gonna leave a *fucking* mark."

As long as he was cussing and bitching, Salvation never feared for her husband's life. It was when he stopped that things were serious. She looked across the arena at the portal entrance to the dungeons. "What was he doing in. . .?"

"Blind bastard was shooting at us," Jump said. He tried to bend over, but it pulled at the feathers and freshly-melted flesh on his lower back, and he screeched. "I'm gonna kill him!"

— XII —

FRANK KING LEANED back in the big leather chair in his executive office, and then he crossed his feet on top of his huge glass desk. He looked out the window.

The forty-eighth floor of K&T's downtown scraper, *Genesis*, overlooked most of the city. On any day that the fog didn't drown it in gray mist, that is. Today was one of those days where he couldn't even see the old granite sanatorium right across the street.

He looked at his wave tablet, flat on the glass desktop by his feet. And he waited for the call that would tell him the deal was solid.

One thing Frank learned early on in his career, synthesizing highly lucrative drugs in the K&T research and development department, was that if he wanted to speed up the time to market—avoid all the red tape and rigmarole of State compliance bribes and bellyaching, not to mention the humanitarian assholes gumming him up with picketing and paperwork—he needed to move all of the human trials . . . to Mexico.

That had worked like a charm for a long time. Mexico had so many impoverished "citizens" that there was no shortage of uneducated, starving farmhands who would volunteer to get injected to keep their overblown Catholic families in beans and babies for another month.

But when one of his "investigational" drugs resulted in a few hundred permanently "drunk" Mexicans, wandering the streets blathering, and pissing blood on anything and everything in their path, until they finally ran out and just keeled over and shriveled up on the side of the street. . . Well, even starvation seemed better than becoming the equivalent of a mindless zombie with no bladder control—it got real hard to find local volunteers south of the border.

So K&T had contracted with the Mexican Protection agency's interrogation division to help them "Procure Investigational Trial Subjects," the secret internal memoranda stated. The cost was minimal and pretty standard for a waste-world "handshake" contract—a couple of villas in Spain, three Masari sports-guzzlers, and one G12 private aircraft. Tiny drops in the multi-billion-credit bucket of blood money that K&T would make after a successful human trial.

The hardest things about the negotiations were the personal "tokens" that the Mexican agents wanted in exchange for their corrupt cooperation. Most of them had a taste for supermodels and wave-stars, which weren't a problem, because those people were used to the game.

Throw enough credits at a person whose depth was that of the average Seattle rain puddle, and they *would* do just about anything. Hell, Frank knew they would do anything. He paid and "tested" all of them before he put them on his corporate jet and flew them to their new "gig" in Cancun.

Sure, some of them got roughed up—a couple of them pretty badly —but credits trumped crying . . . in any world he knew. Unfortunate-ly, a few of the "corrupt cocksuckers," as Frank liked to refer to his new business partners when he came home to bang Babette, had more "juvenile" tastes.

International wave . . . International wave . . . International wave. . .

Frank pulled his feet off of his desk and leaned forward in his chair. He looked at his wave-tablet and said, "Identify."

Identity unknown . . . International wave . . . International wave. . .

Frank frowned. His geek IT pukes could figure out whether a call was domestic or not, but the State still controlled most of the technology that made identifying International wave ID's possible. And he knew State had too many international "friends" to give up that techno. The list of dictators that they didn't want anyone to know they were friendly with was huge.

Regardless, checking was just a habit—deciding whether he wanted to take a call or not—but he already knew who was on the other end of this wave. "Accept," Frank said. Then he picked up his little transparent wave tablet, held it up to his ear, and put his feet back on his desk. He held the tablet with his shoulder while he reached his hand down the front of his slacks and adjusted himself.

The voice on the other end sounded angry. English, Spanish, or incoherent gibberish, angry was angry.

Frank pulled his feet down and sat up in his chair. He spoke into his tablet, "Whoa-whoa, slow down. What do you mean, unusable?"

He listened while a low-level Mexican Protection agent with a piss-poor understanding of English tried to explain how one of the two girls Frank sent to Cancun for his boss, had become "unusable" in his translation.

"How in the. . .?" Frank spoke into his phone. Then he thought about it. "Wait, which one?" he asked. If it was. . . There would be no end to his wife's wailing.

Frank understood only one word of the response—"chichis." He knew which one that was. He breathed a little easier—Babette's bitching avoided—though it hardly solved the business problem.

Then the agent was speaking some bullshit, back and forth between English and Spanish, and Frank started to get pissed. Normally, he would have had one of his supermodels in training—one of the ones who had made the trip to Cancun before and picked up a little Spanish along with her case of crabs—interpret for him. But he wouldn't risk that on this "transaction."

"What the Christ is 'juicio'?" Frank asked. "No-no, I don't care what it is. No, listen—stop talking, dammit! Two? What the—I already sent you two! I just saw them on the tablet not more than thirty minutes ago. They were both fine. So if one of them got "unusable," that on you."

There was a long pause, and then some more broken English mixed with Spanish, but the request was clear.

"Oh no," Frank spoke at his tablet. Bleating wave-stars and babbling bimbos was one thing, but ferrying more minors south of the border? The paperwork was insane, and the credits to get a minor without a passport or an immunization history. . .? This one had been expensive enough.

Two extra off-the-books private flights, a full battery of immunizations, not to mention the syringes, a Mexican villa complete with catered party, *and* the expensive bottle of Tuaca he gave the one with the tits, *after* he made her "thank" him for paying for her flight. *What was her name?* he thought. *Tess-something?*

She was one of the new members of his daughter's pussy posse. It would've been cheaper to contract a Protection team to go down there and kill the son of a bitch he had to deal with. "Tell that—tell your jeffy or hefe, or whatever, I'm not sending any '*uno mas*' nothing. Nada, you hear me. Nunca—*no mas chicas*. Use what you got." Then Frank pulled his wave tablet away from his ear and spoke at it angrily, "Terminate." Then he threw it at his desk, and it spun across the top of the slick glass surface and then it arced in slow motion, off the other side before it disappeared over the edge. "God *dammit!*" he shouted.

— XIII —

WHEN I WAKE up this—like, I don't even remember going out. And I'm groggy and everything is pitch black and it's hard to breathe. Feels like I'm suffocating or choking or something. I need air.

And there's something on my head and face and I try to move, but my arms and legs are tied down . . . to something. A chair, maybe? Because I can feel that I'm sitting down. Then I remember. "Tess?" I whisper. Nothing. . . "Tessa," I say it a little louder.

There's a little crying behind me and then a voice whispers back, "Em, you have to be quiet." And then Brie is whimpering behind me, and it sounds like she's trying not to, and she's just—I can feel the fear. "Please, please, please!"

And that is not Brie's normal voice. I'm a little freaked out myself, because this whole resurrection thing is going totally shitty. I can't control a bit of it. "I'm trying," I whisper at her. "What's happening? Where's Tess?"

And then Brie just starts crying. "I don't know, I don't—they took her body . . . somewhere."

I struggle against whatever I'm strapped to this chair with, but I'm going nowhere.

"Don't do that," Brie whispers. "I—I tried to—"

"Where are we?" I whisper again, trying to turn my head behind me. "I can't see."

"Please," she's trying to whisper, but now it's more like hissing, "I don't want them to come ba—"

We both hear the laugh at the same time. And we both go dead silent, because it's like, whoever it is, is right in front of me. Then someone yanks my head and pulls at my hair. And whatever was on my head comes off and some of my hair rips out with it. "Ow!" I yell, and then I squint my eyes at the light. "You bast—"

SMACK! Then the voice says, "Surprise, señorita!"

The sting across my cheek is nothing compared to how bad my ears hurt when Brie starts screaming behind me. And it's a hideous, terrifying screech and she barely pauses to catch her breath before the next high-pitched wail starts.

And one of the men—there's another one behind the one in front of me—*Protection agents from the Mike?* He starts laughing at Brie. And he walks across the room and past me and I shut my eyes, because I just don't want to see it. *SMACK!*

And Brie's still screaming, but mixed with crying now, and—*SMACK!* And he's still laughing at her.

"Stop it!" I yell at him. "You're hurting—you bastard!"

And I can tell that Brie is trying to stop crying, but she's getting close to hysterical, alternating screaming and whimpering. And he just won't stop. *SMACK! . . . SMACK! . . . SMACK!* Every time Brie makes a sound, the guy hits her.

And the other one moves closer to me and he laughs, too.

I look at him. His unshaven, sweaty face smiles on its way down toward my head. "Get away from me, motherfucker!"

He leans down and his mouth is right in front of my face. I can see the spittle in the corners of his lips, and the gold fillings on his two front teeth, and the leftover lunch between them and it's just *sick* smelling. His breath is nasty when he speaks, "Your little friend. . ." he says. His English is shitty—he's never left Mexico. ". . .she like to doing the screaming."

Then I start whimpering and shaking and I bounce up and down in my chair, because I just wish Brie would pass out so she didn't have to get hit anymore. And I look and the room is big and—but it just feels like the ceiling is caving in and the walls are going to crush me. And stomach acid rises up in my throat and it stings and I cough.

And—*SMACK!* The sound comes from behind me again. And I just don't know how Brie is not passed out, but at least she's quit crying, and now she's down to a little whimper. And I hear her spit, and then she struggles to say, "God please . . . please don't. . ."

I can almost taste the sweat on the motherfucker's face when he speaks again, "*Es bueno*, you know," he says. His breath feels hot on my face. "Because, Donato . . . he like to doing the hitting. Sometime, I think. . ." And he stands up in front of me and looks over my head and he laughs and then I hear the one behind me—Donato? He laughs too.

And then I try to be quiet and not move or say anything, because at least he's not hitting Brie anymore.

Then the one standing up in front of me pushes himself at my face and I think I see something moving underneath his pants, pushing on the outside of his zipper, like it's trying to get out. *Don't let it get out*, I think. Then he says, "I think he like to do the hitting . . . better than the fucking. Eh, amigo?" And he laughs and spit sprays down on my forehead. I close my eyes and think about praying, but for what? To who? I don't know.

And Brie starts crying again and I wince, waiting for "Donato" to slap her some more.

But the filthy dogs laugh at each other and the one in front of me has his crotch right in my face and—

What did you say? . . . Oh, that's just *nasty*. "Bite him in the dick?" . . . Like, that's what you got? . . . Uh, huh. . . Stupid . . . little . . . *bitches*.

So let me ask you something, geniuses. What are you going to do about the fact that you are strapped to a chair, huh? And there's another guy with him? And who knows what other assholes are outside, so—eh, you aren't learning *anything* down here. I can't believe I brought you.

What? Well, if I *was* an angel, sure that would work. A lot of things would work, wouldn't they? I would probably already be talons deep in this stinky bitch's guts, watching *him* scream while I caw and cackle at his buddy and beat *him* senseless. Yes, *Bravo!*

However. . . Now, do you remember what grandpa Jump told all of you about what comes after that word? . . . You're right. So you should know that today, I'm not an all-powerful archangel at all, and here comes the truth.

International wave . . . Incoming wave . . . Incoming wave. . .

"Accept!" I shout it without even thinking. *SMACK!* I take a slap to my face. I taste the coppery metal of blood in my mouth, and I work my jaw and I spit, but trust me, my mother's hit me a few times and the bitch can swing, so my ear's ringing, sure, but my wits aren't beat out of me yet. "Help-help-help!" I yell behind me.

And I think Brie gets it, because she starts screaming, too, "Help us! Help us! Please help us!"

I don't think Donato and his breath-stinking, gold-toothed buddy know what to do, because they don't hit either one of us.

And I can hear the voice on the other end of the phone, yelling and crackling, but I can't understand it and I don't recognize it either. But I don't care who it is, and I yell again, "Holo!"

And the room lights up with a little blue glow from the 3D projection of my wave tablet. But it's behind me on Brie's side of the cell, so I can't see who it is.

Brie screams, "Bab—Mrs. King, help us!"

SMACK! And after that, Brie doesn't say another word.

"Oh my God, Oh my God!" and that's my mom's voice on the holograph, "Brie? Brie!"

Blue light flashes around the room—one of them has my wave tablet. And they struggle with it—probably never even seen one before. And I can hear them yelling at each other in Spanish. And then they are yelling at my tablet.

"Mom!" I yell. And I know where we are. I've been in plenty of the minimum ones, but never like this. "We're in a Protection cell in Cancun and Tessa's dead."

I barely notice the gold-toothed one coming back, before a bright star shoots through my head and I scream at the top of my lungs and then another blinding light. And then everything goes dark.

Yes . . . of course she's dead. There was a stainless gurney in that room with us, and the only look I got at her—she wasn't moving, I'll tell you that. What? . . . No! . . . She's better off. Because why? . . . I don't—really, you're gonna ask me *that?* . . . Because she got raped, too, that's why. I already know that. Tessa couldn't have lived after that.

Calm down, calm down. Listen, it's going to be okay. If Salvation can handle—I'll be okay. Look, I'm not going to lie to you, Manmonkeys are some twisted bitches. Maybe some of you squeamish—you might not want to watch this next part. I already know what happens, it's pretty bad. Nothing compared to what comes after, though.

RAPE

— XIV —

THE DRIVE TO her husband's office scraper downtown was horrible. Babette listened to the thunder from drone strikes and then the sirens went off. And all kinds of crazy citizens were jamming up the roads.

She had to hold her little pistol on her driver at one point and tell her, "Drive on the sidewalk if you have to, but you better get us around it."

"What about them?" the girl had asked. "There's citizens everywhere."

Babette knew that the tall, blonde twentysomething was just another one of her husband's concubine spies. She would just as soon have shot the girl in the head and driven herself, but Babette was in a hurry. Anyway, she knew the girl had skills. She was a trained "VIP tactical security pilot," Frank had told her when Babette complained about her husband's slutty new driver. Soon after the girl showed up, Babette decided that if her husband was going to screw anyone he wanted, then she would, too.

"What citizens," Babette had said to her. It hadn't been a question, and she knew the girl clipped at least one unlucky pedestrian as they sped down the sidewalks.

Citizens were always causing traffic delays. What did they need to keep guns for? They didn't have anything worth stealing anyway. If a citizen wanted a gun, they should just join Protection. Though,

Babette knew that you didn't "join" Protection. That's who was behind all the drone strikes and the guns were what they were after. She knew that . . . *all* about that.

She knew Frank's company made the scent-tracking drones that Protection used to find anything combustible down to the size of an ant's ass.

They tested the scent-seeker modules at the security ports first. If an incoming citizen, or any other lowlife entering the country, tried to bring something even remotely resembling explosives on a plane or a ship, the sniffer drone would scent it. Then, depending on the color of the security threat at the time, it would automatically call a Protection team to come snatch that person up . . . or simply terminate the domestic terrorist right then and there.

In fact, one unlucky idiot had brought a relic smoke lighter with him and the butane fluid in it had got him a one-way trip to the 5150. The nuthouse cracked his skull open like a . . . well, like a nut. Babette knew all about that, too.

Once Protection proved out the scent-seekers at the ports, they equipped every Vengeance drone in the sky with the modules. Now, a citizen would have to bury a gun so far underground in order to keep it hidden that it would be virtually useless to have it. And if he did get stupid and dig it up—get a little gunpowder residue on his hands—a Vengeance's scent-seeker module could find him in a couple of hours.

Kaboom! Babette thought. She grinned a little, but then she looked down at her breasts and closed her eyes. She shook her head a little and frowned. "Asshole," she muttered.

Her driver had looked in the mirror when Babette said it. "*Excuse me,*" the girl frowned in her mirror at her as she careened the car down the sidewalk. *Probably when she ran over the citizen*, Babette thought.

"Not you, sweetie," Babette had said to her. Then she smiled and waved her gun at the girl to get her to turn around. "You just keep your eyes straight ahead and don't talk. Pretend you're sucking my husband's cock."

That shut her up.

Babette stood in Frank's office and pointed her little pistol. She alternated yelling and waving the gun at him. "You have to get her out of there! I'm not letting you—that's not happening to her."

Frank held his hands up and gingerly pressed the security alarm under his desk with the tip of his shoe. He only had to keep his wife busy for three minutes—the elevator ride up from the detention cells beneath the street—five minutes at most. He could do that. "Easy. . . Taaaake it easy," he said. "She's going to be fine. Nothing's going to happen. Just fine."

Babette waved her pistol. She didn't even care if he blew up her breasts. It wasn't happening to their daughter, too. "Don't 'Babs' me, you bastard—you know. . . I—I know that's bullshit." She shook the barrel of her gun at the wave tablet on Frank's desk. "So pick that thing up and get her out of that shithole."

"I reeeally want to," Frank said. He paused longer than he normally would—ticking off seconds in his head—before he spoke again, "It's just . . . not . . . that . . . simple."

"She's your daughter!" Babette yelled past the tears streaming into her mouth. "You're just gonna. . .? How can you do that? She's coming back here all messed—what, you think you can just buy her a new set of tits and say happy birthday, sweetie? You telling *her* to buck up, Frank? You bastard!" She pointed her pistol at his head and grabbed over her other hand, holding the pistol grip with both now. "I should —I should—"

Babette's mascara streaked down her face. Back before they got married, she had thought it would be a good idea to work side by side with Frank at his company. It was a short-lived delusion, because part of being her new husband's secretary meant she was also a negotiating tool for him to use . . . any way he saw fit. Just another corporate asset.

On their honeymoon in Cancun, Babette had experienced that fact firsthand. Though she hadn't remembered anything until it was dragged out of her during one of her therapy sessions, over a year later. Once she finally remembered being drugged and raped in a Mexican Protection cell for the sport of one of her husband's business buddies, she threatened to divide from him and take half of everything he had. Three days later, she had new implants in her breasts. A couple of days after that . . . she got her gun.

Frank moved his hand to his necklace and pulled out the little medallion that held the beginning of Babette's end. "Careful," he said to her, "There's nothing to be gained here by—"

"You think that thing—I don't give a"—Babette was well on her way to hysterical—"go ahead, push it, see what happens." She laughed a little "mental patient off her meds for a day" hysteria. "I bet I— which one you think is faster, the Judgment or one of these bullets? You wanna find out?" She raised her eyebrows up so high that it stretched at her cheeks. She shook her head and she squeezed the trigger. "Let's find ou—"

Bang!

One of the greatest things about his company's sleep serum drug was that depending on the subject's mood—agitation, in Frank's wife's current case—the dosage could be dialed up or down to match it. A dose of Judgment could take a person either way.

If a Protection interrogator wanted a detailed testament, he would keep the amount low. That would produce a nice, euphoric, waking sleep that mimicked the old heroin high . . . without the vomiting and addiction, of course. Then that protectant would spill the details of damn near anything.

If a Protection interrogator wanted some pain thrown in—if he needed a quick and dirty testament from a protectant—he would just dial up the dosage a little. Of course the side effect was that the information would be sprinkled with all manner of cursing and profanity and hallucinating delusions.

Then again, if an agent wanted to skip the long-winded testament and go straight to the execution phase of a Judgment overdose. . . If he wanted to kill someone and avoid all the blood and bullets and booming sounds, then . . . the sky was the limit.

When Frank tripped the executive protection alarm in his office, the Prime Officer Protection agent on duty in the basement of the K&T scraper hadn't known what to expect.

Most of the offices at *Genesis* had hidden wave feeds that he could have watched on his wave tablet—assessed the threat, and then responded with better information, matching the dose in his dart-pistol to the disaster in a room. However, the Prime Officer of K&T had his office suite swept for wave snatchers and hidden feed cameras on a daily basis.

So when the agent poked his little pistol through the centurion slit in the security hall adjacent to Frank's office, he would recount later in his post-incident briefing and subsequent blizzard of paperwork, that he shot the PO's wife with an injection of "medium" load and "average" potency.

And that it was a "split second" before the woman's "unauthorized firearm discharged" and she "fell to the floor." Which, as Protection protocol clearly stated, was why he brought in a clean crew and immediately ushered her to the sanatorium facility.

According to the woman's CID badge, she would be spending *another* three days in one of the State's premier complimentary accommodations. This time, however, it would be the 5150 sanatorium scraper across the street—the *Fifty*.

— XV —

FAITH, HE THOUGHT. Father Benito Octavio Benedetti. That's what they used to call him. It was half an eternity ago if you counted the time like a Man-monkey did. But every being's eternity was different and Father Ben—he could hardly think of himself as a man of faith anymore. His wings sagged as he realized the depth of his own self-deception. Which was nothing compared to the secret he had kept from everyone else.

His *Book of Blood* was a tale of revolution and he wrote it in his own blood to overthrow the Devil. And for that, Rain pardoned Faith for everything he had done. He was brought into her flock—the faithful followers of Rain almighty, the brightest soul in all of the eternities.

An angel's death was excruciating, and Dal—that liar, Lived—had killed Faith in a most violent and painful way. But it wasn't before the reborn father was able to deliver his final words of wisdom to all the angels in the arena.

It was a sermon that he had waited a lifetime to deliver. A speech to motivate angels to move mountains—cast dictators out of power at the hands of the very ones they oppressed. And in the end . . . it had worked.

He had never intended. . . Faith smiled, remembering Jump's words as they sat together in the father's church on the night before the great cleansing of the garden. "Intentions are like assholes," Faith's fallen friend had told him. "Everyone's got 'em . . . and they're usually full of shit. You gotta decide who you are, then be that. No *intending* to it."

So who was he? . . . What kind of angel was Faith?

Yes, he had been forgiven, but not for his greatest sin. Absolution for that could only come from one place, and she was locked down in the dungeons.

Faith had flown to the entrance of the dungeons below the great arena . . . so many times. After every night of judgment, he would wait until the stadium cleared. Some nights it took forever for the grandstands to empty. The cawing and screeching and crowing and cackling seemed to last for hours.

Every angel in the two Heavens enjoyed a good trial and the judgments were intoxicating to watch. Even if they weren't, no one was allowed to miss the condemnations and salvations. Keeping faithful and faithless followers pacified and obedient was an art more than a science. Every ruler in all the eternities had their hands full with that.

But when the judgments were over and all the golden guardian angels had flown back to their posts and barracks, Faith would tentatively fly to the entrance to the dungeons and just . . . hover.

He knew Babette was down there—condemned as one of the worst souls imaginable. For she had let her own daughter be raped at the hands of. . . And when he thought of it, Faith would fall to his knees on the floor of the arena. Tears blurring his eyes, he would look up through the roof at the stars in the black and wonder if there was any truth up there. And if there was, could it ever find its way to his love in such a dark and desperate prison?

Faith had come to this point many times before, but today was different. Today . . . he stood up, fluttered to the portal and watched it twist open. He landed in front of it, closed his wings tightly against his back, and then he stepped inside.

Faith stared at Rain's seal on the iron-barred gate to his once-lover's dark and desperate cell. "How. . .?" The words just weren't there. "I never intended to—"

Bathed in the blackness at the back of its cage, all that could be seen of the woman he knew when he was a priest were glowing red eyes, piercing into him like red-hot pokers burning through the black of his past. But this creature in the cage was no woman now. It spoke in a raspy and raw voice, "To wha—" The creature coughed, hacking to clear its throat. It spit and then it spoke, "Intended to what, bury your faith in my pussy?"

The sound of its voice repulsed him, yet the memory of who it once was aroused him at the same time. And he closed his eyes, trying to control his swelling weakness—his own feelings of faltering faith.

"Half a—" the voice crowed and coughed. "Really, half an eternity you waited?" The creature growled and Faith watched its eyes move in the darkness as it paced back and forth. When it stopped, the eyes turned toward him. "You make me wait for over half an eternity? I'm glad my master burned you, you whining old cock!"

And a great cawing and screeching sound roared from down and across the passageway.

The creature snapped its jaws a few times at the sound—Faith could hear its teeth chomping. Then it stopped. "I'm sorry. Yes, well . . . mmm, it's been . . . it's been a long time, Benito. How did you stay away from my little baby that long? Do you think you can find her friends? So dark down here." The voice was barely female now. She laughed and then growled. "Maybe you should just lick your way to them," she whispered. "That always worked for you."

A putrid smell of rotting blood wafted to the edge of the cell and then through the bars on the gate and into Faith's nostrils. He sniffed hard and then coughed and choked and spit at the taste in his mouth.

Mere seconds later, all manner of creature and being—foul and feathered, ferocious and fecal-smelling—began wildly cawing and crowing and howling. There were even some soft yelps behind him that sounded like barks, which made Faith pause. Because though demons, devils and dark souls were all spared annihilation in the great arena . . . there were no dogs in the dungeons.

An unfortunate bite when Rain was a child—back in Life's eternity —sealed the fate of canines beyond reasoning with her. Canines would have no souls. The law was second only to her "don't touch me" covenant. And Faith glanced over his shoulder, into the darkness of the cell on the other side of the tunnel. Nothing stirred there.

A dog? Faith thought.

The uproar down the passageway continued for a few seconds and then it died down to occasional caws.

The creature in the cage in front of him growled and Faith turned back toward its cell.

"Ah," it said, "they already know."

Faith leaned in and grasped the bars on the gate with both hands. He put his face between the bars and squinted. His eyes were much better than they had been back in life—he was nearly blind then and wore thick bifocals—yet even an angel's razor-sharp eyes could not see into the black. "They know what?" he asked.

"Look at you," the creature growled and laughed, "always poking your face into tight places you shouldn't." And then it choked and coughed—the sound of hacking up phlegm. Then it sounded like it spit on the floor again. When it was finished, the voice said, "Sorry"—it cleared its throat—"occupational"—and it coughed and spit again —"occupational . . . ha—*ha*—hazard. . . . I'm sure you understand. You remember, don't you, sweetie?"

"How could I have. . .?"

"Yes," it growled at him, "how could you have abandoned us? Left me to rot for so long! How could you have?"

"I had no choice," Faith said. "He made me—he said he would kill —"

The creature let out a loud roar like a lion. Then it shouted, "Shut your filthy mouth!" Then it faked crying and sobbing, mocking him. "Oh, Babs, the devil made me do it, the devil made me do it! You priests with your lies and your—I should have cut your cock off, so you—"

"Please!" Faith cried. "I am trying to—"

"Half an eternity!" it roared at him. "You call that trying? I guess I didn't need to cut your cock off, because you're impotent. Why did she even give you dicks?"

A loud screech and moan from down and across the tunnel, interrupted the creature's accusations.

There was barely a pause though, before it yelled back, "Fuck you, bitch, they could have *pissed* out their asses." Then the red eyes turned back to burning from the darkness at him. "Piss out your ass,

Benito . . . like a lazy cow! . . . Why didn't they just cut your dicks off when you joined the church? That way, you would have never been able to—now that's faith, that's commitment to God."

The scream from down the tunnel was louder this time, and it felt to Faith like there was a warning in it. He knew who it was, but the— Life hardly had power to follow through with a threat. *Does she?* he wondered.

The creature in the cell yelled back down the tunnel, "Next time, *cut* them off!" Then it turned its attention back toward Faith. "Dumb bitch," it muttered. Then it whispered to him, "Don't worry, lover— too late to cut *yours* off, isn't it."

"Babette, please!"

"Fool!" it yelled. Then it raced to the front of its cage, at the gate. And the creature stopped just short of Faith's face and snapped its jaws and bared its fangs at him.

The hideous animal looked nothing like the woman he had visited in the Smith Tower back in life. She had snakes for hair that hissed and struck at him. And there were oozing pustules on her face and her mouth breathed smoke.

Faith shoved himself away from the bars and flapped his wings at the cell gate, hurling himself across the dungeon tunnel. His back slammed into the bars on the other side, and then he closed a wing around his face. She—it was just too hideous to look at. His wing was over his eyes, but Faith closed them anyway and he wept. "I am. . ." and he couldn't contain himself. "I—you are right. I am so . . . so sorry. I can't. . ."

"What's the matter, Benito?" she said, cackling like a crow, "Don't you want to lick my tits anymore?" Then she growled louder. "Look at me! Look at what you did to me!"

Faith couldn't—his beautiful lover in Life's eternity had turned to a twisted nightmare in this one. And he knew he was to blame.

"What, you want to suck on your little flask first, you boozing bastard? I've got something better for you to suck! Look, I said! You owe me that!"

And Faith opened his eyes and slowly raised up his wing.

A blood-soaked paw reached out from the iron bars behind Faith's head and grabbed him around the throat. He tried to jerk himself away, but the paw squeezed and choked him and he gurgled. He kicked his legs and flapped his wings, beating them back as far as they would bend behind him.

Faith's wings slammed the bars on the cell behind him and then another paw was under one wing and it wrapped around his feathers and the steel bone along his wing, and then pinned it against the outside of the cell. Now he couldn't struggle and he couldn't breathe and the dark dungeon got fuzzy.

The paw on his neck loosened its grip. "No, no," the voice behind Faith growled lowly, "relax, everything's going to be fine . . . just fine. We don't want you to pass out, do we?"

Faith coughed and choked and grabbed at the paw on his neck.

The creature behind him smelled like a wet dog that had just rolled in fresh shit. It repositioned itself, maintaining its grip on Faith's neck and wing. Then it spoke again, "We wouldn't want him to choke to death, would we, Babs?"

Faith heard his—the creature's voice growled back from across the tunnel.

"I just want to talk to you," the dog's voice behind him said, "that's all."

Faith barely recognized the voice—so long ago. But he would never forget the evil bastard's calm and collected demeanor. The cold and calculating manner he used when he threatened him, lying to Faith's face. Well, not Faith then. Back then he was a—

"Father Ben," the growling dog said, "you are looking good. Come to visit your little dove?" the voice asked. "Seems like you're always visiting her when she's locked up in a cage. Why is that, do you think? Okay, okay, maybe not always. Sometimes your little visits are in my bed, aren't they? Or were—can't tell what's past or present down here. So *dark* all the time. Hard to tell if it's night or day, much less what eternity it is. I guess that's what being in a cage feels like."

The dog repositioned itself again, moving its head and stinking breath back and forth, from one side of the back of Faith's head to the other.

Dirty dog, Faith thought. *Frank King. . .*

"What do you think, Babs," Frank growled over at her, "is this as good as the *Fifty?*"

Her voice growled back, "It's better than the Smith."

"Yes," Frank spoke into Faith's ear, "you remember my loft, don't you? Wait, don't answer, don't answer. We all know. I watched you up there . . . with my wife in my bed. That was some nasty—she would never do that for me. I even threatened her tits—nada."

"You are such an—"

Frank barked back across the tunnel at the creature. Then he turned and spoke to Faith again, "I had to drug her to get in there. Then she started with that menopause-headache crap. The first time I caught you two. . . I thought she was just handling it with her little lady's companion. Imagine my surprise when I saw you show up on the building security wave.

"I mean, are you *kidding* me? A priest was—nobody at the club believed it! So you know what I did? I brought them to my office and let them see for themselves. Hell, we were just gonna wave the backup file over some secretaries and beers, but I'll be damned"—Frank chuckled to himself—"Now that's funny! Huh. . . Oh, yeah. I'll be *God* damned if my remote sentries didn't net in another live wave, and you two were at it again. And that got me thinking . . . maybe that wasn't the first time."

"Let him go," The creature across the passageway pleaded. "Please . . . let him go."

Frank ignored her.

Faith struggled on the floor. And as the dog told his story—with the parts that he obviously didn't like—he squeezed tighter on Faith's throat, alternating between choking him near to death and letting him gasp for air to stay alive. Back and forth between Heaven and Hell— Faith was friends with that misery.

"You know how many times you. . .?" Frank the dog said, "They must have kept you in the basement of that church forever. Thirty-three times, Ben. I don't think I . . . I can't even *remember* that far back. I watched you two for years after that. I didn't think she knew, but when I waved in that day. . . You remember, don't you? Standing in the corner like a little kid, covering your prick. Maybe you don't remember—eternities are funny like that. Eh, doesn't matter. What am I saying? It all turned out, right? I mean, here we are—the three of us—old friends."

Faith choked a little and his eyes rolled back in their sockets. His body started to shake and his wings flapped wildly.

"You're killing hi—"

"Shut up!" Frank yelled at her. Then he let go of Faith's neck. "He can't die, you dumb bitch!"

Faith choked and coughed and sucked for air. Technically he *could* die, but his death wouldn't have been permanent. Though all of them knew that angel resurrection was as traumatic as getting killed.

Frank the dog wrapped his long claws around the back of Faith's head. He pointed Faith's face across the tunnel at Babette's cell. Then he whispered in Faith's ear, "So you've come to see your beautiful lover. Well, let's get a good look at her, shall we?"

— XVI —

NO, YOU IGNORANT little purgatories! Aren't you paying attention? My father is *not* coming to get me, so stop asking me that. If you haven't been watching, he was the one who put me *in* this cell. What? Oh, Jesus, stop cawing—it's me that has to go through it, not you.

You're bigger babies than Rain. Shit, blasphemy! She's going to kick my—now I gotta pray. See what you little shits are. . .

Mighty Salvation, full of hate. Jump be with thee. Blessed art thou amongst the fallen, and blessed is the seed of thy womb, Rain. Oh, holy Salvation, mother of Rain, pray for me, make my armor strong at the hour of my judgment. Amen.

Yeah, you *better* say it with me.

Any of you little purgatory bitches tell her I said that, I'll fire and fury every last one of you. Better yet, how about like, I just put you in the arena with no training . . . and no hope in hell of surviving, either!

Annihilation? You'll think annihilated. I don't know what's worse, getting beat to shit and raped in this cell, or listening to all of you whining. "Oh, Fury, who's coming to rescue you? Oh, Fury, why didn't your mommy save you?" Listen to yourselves . . . grow some talons, already!

And when I wake back up, they are all over Brie, because I can hear her screaming and yelling and crying, and then I hear her clothes rip, but I can't see anything because they've still got her behind me.

I rock my head back and forth so hard I think my neck is gonna break off, but the chair won't move. And I can't move.

And in between the crying and the slapping and the laughing behind me, Brie is grunting and crying and then she says something that scares the living shit out of me, "Mommy." That's it—the last words she ever spoke.

"Get off her!" I yell, but no words come out and it's kinda like I lose energy or something, because my voice sounds far away. "Dirty cocksuckers. . ." And I have no idea where that came from, because I'm. . . Then it's like, I leave my body and it's not really me.

I float above the whole room—above my body taped to the chair. *Duct tape, no wonder*, I think.

I hover for a while, while they work on us. And from up here, we look like work to them. Not like I imagined it when the bag was over my head.

One thing that scares me is this huge—I don't wanna think about it, I just want it to go away. It's kinda like a big snake or like, two snakes wrapped around a long shaft or something. And when they stick it in Brie, her head tilts back and her eyes roll back and turn black, and then she just falls over and she's out . . . or dead . . . or I don't know what. But when they poke it into my body—in me—a blinding white light shoots through my head and I squint, and I think I yell, but there's no sound and then my body goes limp, and I start convulsing or something. It looks like a seizure, only I don't have those.

And then another white light and then—but I'm not dark and I'm starting to wonder if resurrecting was the best idea I've ever had, because I just wanna go back to Hell.

I watch them roll another gurney into the cell and then they put Brie in a big black bag and zip her up and then she's on the gurney. They wheel her out of the room and the last thing I hear is a great screeching sound from the gurney's wheels and then the white searing light in my head again and I'm dark—out.

— XVII —

FAITH SAT ON the floor of the dungeon kicking his legs and wings, struggling against the filthy dog, Frank's, claws on the back of his head, forcing him to look at the creature. He peered across the dark dungeon tunnel at his once beautiful lover, Babette, in her cell.

Babette. . . Faith had failed her at the *Fifty*—abandoned her in a sanatorium in life. He hadn't been able to—they both paid the price for it with their lives. And when their souls hung in the balance, he had failed her again.

Babette had become a hideous hound of Lived's hell . . . and it was Faith's fault. Now, he could barely look at her body, but when he was finally able to force himself to look at all of her, he realized the creature—his Babette was pregnant.

"Ya see there . . . *father* Ben," Frank the dirty dog said. He held Faith's head and forced him to look closely at Babette, now lying on her side with her belly heaving and something pushing against it from the inside. "How do you suppose *that* happened?"

Lived smiled at the smell, then he looked down at Life, busy trying to tame his snakes. After a few moments, he spread his wings wide and cawed out above his head.

Life got to her feet and walked to the edge of their cage. She peered through the bars, down the tunnel and across to the cell. She had the time for her plan to bear fruit. She would endure until that fruit was ripe. So she played her part. "Your little bitch is bursting at her seam," she said. "Your seed finds a path to the darkest of dungeons." She felt to her own stomach, busy churning from the performance of her duties. Then she laughed and cawed down the hall at the three of them, "She is a wretched wench, father. And you have condemned her to a fate more disgraceful than damnation." Then she turned back to Lived. "How are you able. . .?" She looked at his snakes and frowned. "How do you persuade them to bathe in her breaches? She is appalling!"

Lived was just coaxing his two-headed snake back to its nest. When he finally pushed it beneath his feathers, he looked up and then he shook all of his plumage. And the remnants of Life's scent misted their way to the floor. "Why, Your Majesty," he said, "the same way I am able to bask in yours. Yours are a . . . small matter, however." He moved beside his current concubine-slave. "One hole is as satisfying as another." Then he cawed down the tunnel at Babette King's cage. "Isn't that true, Hole?" he shouted. "She screamed for you, Faith. Not even the decency to call out my name. Benitoooo!" Lived howled down the tunnel.

Life's lip quivered. She bit at it, attempting to silence her inner-God. It was an ever-increasingly difficult task. "How can you tolerate yourself? . . . Filthy beast."

Lived cawed a little and laughed, "We hounds are not known for our . . . discerning tastes."

Down the hall, Life's Dogg, barked and whined back to his master.

"You see," Lived said. "Dog in a cage—we merely search for somewhere to bury our bones." He turned and howled back at the dirty dog. "Dogg!" he yelled. "Set him free, Frank. He's gotta go save her . . . again."

The hound down the hall barked a few times and then howled back.

Lived turned to Life. "Why doesn't he obey?" he asked.

"He does," Life said. Then she called down the hall to Dogg, whistling and moaning a little. "Let the father loose, my pet. He has to re-find his faith."

Then she recited the prayer.

And with no more than that the filthy animal, Dogg, let Faith loose. "Have fun, Benito," he said. "I hear the *Fifty* is . . . unforgettable. Owooooah!"

And Faith stood and adjusted his wings, stretching them to make sure they weren't injured. He winced at the pain in the one Dogg had held. Then he rubbed his throat. He looked down the great tunnel to the light shining from their cell. "Very well," he said softly, "I am ready."

Faith stood in the darkness of the arena, just outside the portal to the dungeon. Seeing Babette like that was more than he could take. He bent over, fell to his knees, spread his wings and dropped the tips of them onto the floor of the arena, trying to steady himself. Then he vomited everything in his stomach. When he was finished, he spit and stood up.

As hideous as Babette looked when Frank forced him to look at her in the dungeons, he still loved her. But now he pitied her even more. Because now he knew the truth about his lover.

The first time he visited her in a place like that, he could never bring himself to believe it. At the *Fifty*—the 5150 sanatorium for the insane—he had denied the truth of her words. He flapped his wings and lazily fluttered off the arena floor, slowly flying to nowhere. And he closed his eyes and remembered.

— XVIII —

THE *FIFTY* WAS an old granite and iron sanatorium with tiny slits for windows that no living body would fit through. A fact that was proven over and over by insane addicts who tried to squeeze their skulls through the barely six-inch-wide slits. Most failed, but the few who succeeded were killed by the orderlies, jerking the unfortunate souls' cracked skulls back in.

Powerful people used the *Fifty* as a convenient place to dispose of the weak. And torment them, Faith knew, because anyone who could afford to put someone in there could afford to have them killed and disappeared much easier . . . and cheaper.

But that wasn't how the mind of a Man-monkey worked. Treachery and revenge and retribution needed to watch misery. That infection needed to see suffering, ooze over its enemies, and then burn and choke them with a dark black oil of desperation and hopelessness.

Father Benito hadn't known that when he became a priest, but he learned it soon enough. Even the clergy would condemn a "heretic" to the *Fifty* if that person was in danger of overthrowing their authority.

Power was like that—a big, fat, lazy bully that continually gorged itself on the misery of its faithful followers. It would grow and grow until it was such an obese behemoth of worthlessness that no one could remember the reason it existed in the first place. The trouble was, once they did figure it out, it was too late. Because a bully was only happy when it was beating the shit out of some ninety-pound weakling. And those weaklings were usually the very citizens it was supposed to protect.

The *Fifty* was the pinnacle of the rich and powerful's domination over the weak and pitiful. A place where no one you knew would enter—if anyone even knew you were in there. For most, it was a lonely place where, if you weren't crazy when you went in, you would wish you were by the time you got out. Few left on their feet.

The outside of the downtown sanatorium was a lonely-looking pillar—a big behemoth, completely out of place, crowded on every side by the high-tech, hyper-connected, mirror-skinned scrapers of the world's new masters. But if someone were on the inside of the *Fifty*, there was only isolation.

Once inside, most prayed that they just lived through it—got back to their life. Or they begged for salvation or redemption or forgiveness —anything that gave them comfort to endure their daily misery. But no prayers were answered inside the *Fifty's* damp, bloodstained walls.

In the *Fifty*, the Protection sentries that guarded the halls and cells would laugh at the praying "guests" and say, "You won't find God in here, but He'll find you."

If someone was lucky, that was the truth. They would leave the *Fifty* in a big, black, rubberized body bag, zipped up on one of the facility's many gurneys—rolling stainless steel tables that they were strapped to and then tortured. Tormented for three days for information, or because someone paid a sentry enough, or to train Protection agents in the art of interrogation, or just for the fun of a businessman with enough credits, taking his lunch break from a scraper across the street.

Credits. . . There was only one other class of people that had an all access pass to a *Fifty*—the clergy. More specifically, one of their representatives. And that's just what Father Benito Octavio Benedetti was, a representative of his faith.

But on this day, he wasn't there to save souls, and it wasn't so that he could administer last rites and redemptions, though that was a job that was in desperate need of doing. No, the head priest of the largest church in the city was in charge of tending to the clergy's "affairs" inside the sanatorium. His job was to make sure that anyone who the church paid to have sent inside . . . never came back out. And the clergy paid hefty sums of credits so that he could come and go as he pleased, unmolested by paperwork, procedures, or Protection agents, for that matter.

So no one even blinked when Father Ben swiped his Citizen ID badge—the magnetic card containing every last detail of his life—and no one said a thing when the security portal twisted open and he walked inside.

The nice middle-aged—though a little weathered for his time—priest with the soda-bottle thick glasses and the not-so-subtly hidden flask in his robe, walked right past the indifferent Protection sentry agents, and right by the scream-filled interrogation cells with the staring and stoic orderlies outside, then ambled nonchalantly past the sentry in front of the doctors' private lounge, and finally sauntered between the two Protection sentries, standing at attention on either side of the two big wooden doors of the entrance to the pharmaceutical company's private wing . . . just like he owned the whole place.

It was nothing out of the ordinary for Benito—he was ignored so often on his visits that some days he wondered if the "organization" he tended affairs for *did* own the building. The only difference from a hundred, maybe a thousand other trips he took to the *Fifty* was that on this day, it was Benito's own "affair" he was tending to.

— XIX —

AS SOON AS Salvation told Jump that she had seen Faith flutter out the portal to the great dungeons. . . "You mean, before that little shit shot a fire-feather into my back," Jump had reminded her. He had a way of personalizing trouble.

Jump had actually flown to the other side of the arena, trying to pick up Faith's scent so he could go "beat the living shit out of that backstabbing boozer." But the putrid piss smell of fear was mixed with a smell so disgusting that even Salvation's highly developed sense of smell couldn't tolerate it long enough to follow. And that was a concern.

It took a little convincing on Salvation's part—Jump wasn't one to let go of a knife stuck in his back, figurative or literal—but she finally got him calmed down by explaining to him that if they were going to figure out why Faith had been down in the dungeons in the first place, they would probably need Rain's help to do it.

That launched Jump off into a tirade about finding Faith, ripping out some of his flight feathers, and forcing him to tell them what was going on.

Salvation knew that there were dark things—darker than even the darkest archangel in Hell could conjure up in his head—left over in her husband from Life's life, but ripping out flight feathers? "That's just . . . wrong," she had said. "You might as well geld him."

Jump had been so pissed about the fire-feather in his back that he thought about doing that very thing.

Salvation had wondered so many times about her husband's "occupation" when they were Man-monkeys in life, but she had somehow intuitively understood that she really didn't want to know.

Well, she wanted to . . . but she didn't. Because even in life, her husband had subtly warned her, "A pinch of curiosity . . . can get a whole lotta trouble pounded into you. The kind of trouble you wish killed you." It was about as much as she ever got out of him.

In the arena, as was the case in most situations, calmer beaks prevailed, and Salvation led her wild demon of a husband to Rain's throne room and then they waited while the golden guardians fetched her.

Jump stood outside on the huge stone steps, impatiently waiting for his daughter to grace them with her presence. He rubbed the wound on his lower back. Angels healed quickly, Jump quicker than most, but there was nothing quite like the sting from one of the faithful's searing, steel feathers. Once a little purgatory got shot in the arena, they never made the shield mistake again.

But Jump had made that mistake. "Shot me in the back," he mumbled. "Crazy old man shot me. *Me*."

Salvation waited on the steps with him, more patient on the outside, but a torrent of anger on the inside. Someone would pay for shooting at them, judgment night would take care of that. But her man *had* gotten shot. "Yes, yes, someone shot at you," she said. "Like that's the first time."

"Why do you always have to go disagreeing with me all the time? It's just—"

"That's not the right question," Salvation said.

"Then what is?"

"The question is . . . why?" said Salvation. "And the father—Faith . . . of all angels? He has no—why would he do that?"

Jump frowned and shook his head slowly. "What was he doing down there, anyway?"

A familiar, bright-spiking light shined out of the throne room, and Salvation and Jump covered their eyes and then they both reached for their sunshields. A split second later, Rain fluttered out in front of them, her wings and entire body emanating brilliant white light. "I'm afraid that would be my fault," she said.

Flanked on each side by two of her golden guardians, busy shading their own eyes with their wings and reaching for their own "God-goggles," it was like visiting the queen . . . *just* like it.

"*Your* fault?" Jump said. "*You* told him to shoot at me?" He had no idea what to do about it, but it pissed him off anyway. So he looked at Salvation and did what he always did. "You believe—what are you going to do about that? She had him *shoot* me. She is just—that is some disrespectful shit."

"He shot at both of us," Salvation reminded him. Then she ignored Jump's rant and looked at Rain. "Who's down there?" she asked. "Other than those two?"

"I don't give a *fuck* who's down there," Jump said. "I got shot."

Rain giggled at her father. "Your feathers look fine to me." Then she looked at her mother. "Seriously, he is like a child." She looked back at Jump. "Stop angel-aching like a little purgatory," she said to him. Then she looked up at the roof of the Hallowed Hall. "You are upright, the stars are shining, you have a wonderful wife—everything is right in your eternity."

Jump knew it wasn't. "Okay, okay," he said, "you two wanna play dump on Jump with yourselves, go right ahead. But this has turned into more than a little game of hide and seek the sinner. And me getting shot right after, by that little tit-sucker—and before you even start"—he held up his hand at Rain—"I'm talking about the booze, so don't get your pinfeathers in a wad. I've had enough annoying little quills for one day."

Salvation and Rain stared at Jump. And Rain tried not to grin when she said, "What are you referring—"

"Oh, hell no," Jump said, frowning, "I'm not finished, not by a long—you sit back and you listen to *me* crow for a while." Then he looked back at Salvation, now standing with her arms crossed and her hips cocked to the side. "I don't know who you two think you're dealing with, but we're deep into my realm of expertise now. You know better—missing children and backstabbing priests. I know that kinda shit . . . all too well. It never changes and I told that little—I told Fury not to go messing around with things more evil than her."

"Who—what evil things?" Rain asked. "What was she asking?"

Jump jerked his head toward Rain. He was pigeon-bobbing now—it always happened right before and right after a good fight. "You missed a few things back in life, sweetie," he said. "Probably time to catch you up."

"Now?" Salvation asked. She didn't know if she was ready for Jump to have the "talk," much less stand there while he did it.

"That's just—" Rain frowned and scrunched up her face at her father. Then she looked at Salvation, standing as uncomfortably as a mother could, listening to her husband explain the "angels and demons" to her only daughter. "Mother, you did that with—ich!"

Jump laughed a little. It was his turn to lean on Rain's comfort zone. His wife's too, when he thought about it. Doing it was one thing. Talking about it after. . .? He shook his head and smiled at Salvation. "More than once."

"Jacob!" Salvation said. It was all too much. "That's enough—it's just—it's TMI." Fury taught her that little saying.

Jump frowned at her—he knew. "There's no such thing. You see, that's the trouble with . . . every—every damn thing, if you ask me."

It was another rant. Salvation saw it coming. Rain did, too. Somehow both of them knew that in between the screaming and cussing—the crowing and cawing about justice and tyranny—there were little tidbits of truth, sprinkled through the anger. And if they listened closely, there were also hints about who Salvation's husband and Rain's father had been. Way back, before this half eternity, before the end of the last eternity, before he was just an angry citizen sick of the system. Because if they listened carefully they knew that a long, long time ago, Jump—Jacob Blake—was the system.

So they both listened, stood silent while Jump explained the facts of Life's life . . . the real ones.

"Everyone always trying to cover shit up," Jump muttered. "Hiding and scurrying like little rat-monkeys, stealing some other rat's meal. Buncha pigeon-toed pussies, pretending to be tough guys, passing laws and pounding on people every damn way they can."

And that might have been a little too far into Rain's comfort zone.

"Careful, Father."

Jump barely broke stride in his sermon. "Careful," he said, "gets you killed, little girl. You go getting too careful—beg for too much protection from . . . from every scary thing you *think* might happen. Pretty soon, only way to "protect" you is to lock you up—remand you—protect you from yourself. Because if you're that big a pussy, then what good are you to the rest of us?" It wasn't a question. "And once I do that. . . After I'm totally responsible for delivering for your whole existence . . . well, then I just *own* you. And that, ladies, makes you a goddamn slave."

CRACK!

Rain's bolt of lightning sent Jump flying backward. It wasn't meant to kill him, just remind him. "I've warned you about blasphemy!" Rain shouted. "There is no purpose—"

"There's a purpose, Rain," Salvation said. Then she walked over to her daughter—Jump would be fine. *Arrow in his back was worse*, she thought. And she put her hands up to hold Rain's shoulders. When her daughter recoiled backward and gave her mother a "Rainly" look, Salvation put her arms down. "Forgive me, however . . . you might want to listen to your father, once in a while. He is right about more things than you could possibly know."

Jump was just getting to his feet, dusting himself off. Only half paying attention to what Salvation was saying, because whether it could kill him or not—and battle after battle had proven that it couldn't—lightning stung like a bitch. But he caught that last part, and it caught him off guard. "Thank you," he said. And that surprised even him, and he stood straight up, wide-eyed, and looked at them both, like a little kid who had just said the "F" word for the first time. "Yeah, well . . . anyway. . . And stop hitting me with the damn lightning. It hurts."

Rain looked at him with more empathy than Salvation had ever seen. "Father," she said, "I am. . . I should not have—"

"*Yeah*, you should—"

"Jacob!" Salvation shouted. Then she raised her wings and her feathers fluttered a little toward Rain. And she motioned with her head, too.

Jump looked at his daughter. God or not, the little girl inside her was feeling guilty. "Yeah. . ." Rant all day about idiots—easy to find the words for that. Comfort his—reassure the protector of Heaven and Hell that everything would be okay? . . . Not so easy to wail words for that. "I'm fine—I can take a punch. Just don't do that a—"

"You just can't help yourself, can you?" Salvation said to him. "That's not what she needs right now. What she needs now, is a plan. So unless you have one buried inside one of your little speeches, you need to stop talking and we'll figure it out ourselves."

"Damn. . ." Jump said. He looked at them both. Salvation was serious, but he knew that she didn't understand the depths of the evil he smelled when they went to try and find Faith. There was only one angel in Heaven or Hell who smelled like that, and Salvation didn't know why she was right, but they were damn sure wasting time getting to him.

"Do you have a plan, Father?"

Jump walked back to the steps. Then he spread his wings as wide as they would go. And neither Rain nor Salvation had seen him do it anywhere but in the arena. . . Though that wasn't entirely true, because Salvation *had* seen it at the Battle of the Books, but that was so long ago.

Jump's wings caught fire and he pushed the flames up high above all of their heads and let them burn and smoke for a few second before he let the inferno die down to a campfire-sized flicker of flame. "Yeah, I got a plan," he said, nodding. Then he smiled the wicked grin that made Salvation both excited and scared screechless at the same time. "Time to fight fire . . . with fury, ladies." And he turned around —wide wings trailing flames and smoke as he did. "Time to go dick with the devils in the dungeon."

"Shit. . ." someone said behind him. Who said it? . . . Any angel's guess.

Salvation flapped her wings and swooped around the edges of the Arena of Reckoning, just in front of the normally pigeon-packed grandstands, slicing her razor sharp flight feathers through the bathed-in-black air above the arena floor, warming up to play her part.

It was a decent plan, from what she knew of them anyway. She was only worried about one thing, and she flew faster and faster thinking about it.

Teaching Rain about the facts of the afterlife was one thing, but one of Fury's classes, instructing new hatchlings in the theoretical operation of ballistic fire-feathers and their proper application during battle, never prepared a single one of the little purgatories for the first time they were penetrated by a burning hot quill. And gray, orange, or cherry-red hardly mattered—an innocent little purgatory, not to mention Salvation's darling daughter—practically speaking, still a little naive young deity. . . The first time always hurt the worst.

If Rain's part of the plan went poorly. . . Salvation swooped up in the air and screeched in anger. That was just not going to happen.

Jump stood on the floor of the arena and watched Salvation fly around the edges of the grandstands. She flew to the center, just below the roof, and then she swooped and swirled, and twisted and turned and dived at the arena floor like she was in a real battle.

It reminded Jump of the first time he saw her as an angel, screaming her way down out of the fog above Seattle to pick up that molester's black soul. Jump still felt guilty about the whole thing. Of course he hadn't known then, but it hardly mattered to his wife when he sunk his talons in her as she tried to collect Frank's soul. She went bleeding and limping to who the hell knew where, while Jump used the evil bastard's wriggling worm of a soul to get into Purgatory.

He yelled up at Salvation, "Hey, don't overdo it." Then he muttered to himself, "Can't fly around in the dungeons anyway."

And if they couldn't, then he knew that he would have to rely on his talons if his plan went to pigeon-shit on them. He flipped them out—the ones on his feet, too—and he sharpened the ones on the tips of his fingers with one of his flight feathers. When he was satisfied that it could cut through steel like a feather through Faith's head—he still had to get to that little prick—he cawed up at Salvation, "Get down here, will ya? It's just about time."

Salvation screeched back at him. She knew the time. The smell of lust was already starting to waft its way out of the dungeon and into her nostrils. After she swooped down and landed a few yards behind Jump, she walked up to him and said, "I swear to Christ—"

"Careful on the blasphemy, babe," Jump said. Then he smiled and looked at the portal to the dungeon. He rubbed his chest. The scars from the lightning, not to mention his ripped-out hearts, had healed. The shadows and echoes of the pain had not. "She's in a real fucking mood tonight."

Salvation slapped him on the back of his head and his pinfeathers stung. "Don't even *talk* like—that's it, I'm going in!"

Jump was confused. It had been a while since he had taken a crack on his crown. He prickled his head feathers. "Like what?" he asked. Then he thought about it. "Oh, shit, that's not what I meant. Jesus, don't say it like that."

"I didn't say anything, *you* did," Salvation said. She started for the portal. "I'll rip his guts out!"

Salvation had a thing for guts. Truth be told, every angel in the two Heavens went for the guts first in a fight. It was the softest and most easily picked apart place on . . . any angel or other creation you were fighting.

It was also, Rain informed them after she was ordained as Protector and gained the historical knowledge of every eternity since the first, a buried instinct left over from one of the very first eternities.

It seemed that one of Rain's Protector predecessors decided it would be a good idea to populate the entire garden with intellectually ignorant, prehistoric-looking birds.

That didn't turn out too well, however, and the end of that garden ushered in like every eternity before it. The inhabitants fornicated with such reckless abandon and proficiency that eventually, they ate everything in sight—mowed the garden down to a dusty wasteland—then . . . they ate each other.

* * *

Jump grabbed onto Salvation's shoulder. "Not just yet there, wild-wing," he said. "Couple more seconds." He really only did it to bring her back from wherever she was in her head. Putting on a warface was one thing—Man-monkey in a black Protection van or angry archangel before a judgment trial—puff up your feathers too much, and it was just as likely that the other guy, or angel, would pluck 'em.

Salvation jerked her shoulder away from him. Her chick was in the dungeon . . . with that disgusting, lecherous liar and his self-absorbed, wannabe benevolent bitch. There was no telling how much trouble Rain was in. She spread her wings and flexed every steel feather she had until sparks showered the ground.

Jump stepped back. Better for her to just get it out before she went in. He shook his head—as much in awe as anything else.

And Salvation screeched above her head and all of her talons scraped out and she stretched her arms above her, and then closed her hand to a fist. She gripped her fingers and talons so hard that they sparked against the steel feathers on her wrists. Then she crowed out a loud war cry.

Now that he saw how worked up she really was, Jump figured it was just as well to let her go in sooner. Leave her lashed to the leash much longer and she might not be able to stop herself before they got the information they needed. Corpses didn't talk. Jump had seen that plenty of times. "Go get 'em, tiger," he said to her.

And Salvation raced at the portal to the dungeon and it twisted open and a light like neither of them had ever seen blasted out of the entrance, and both of them had to shade their eyes with their wings.

They went for their sunshields as all manner of hideous howls and whimpering wails screamed out of the dungeons. They fell to their knees and held their ears. It took a couple of seconds for them to shake their heads and push the pinfeathers around their ears to muffle the sound enough so they could stand up.

Jump was behind Salvation, so he had no idea what she saw inside, but whatever it was, she didn't like it. She screamed the loudest he had ever heard her screech before. "You sick son of a bitch!" she yelled. Then she ran at the portal. Her wings slammed into the sides of the entrance to the dungeons and sparks flew as she forced her way through. And then the portal twisted shut behind her.

Jump was left standing in the dark of the arena, eyes still trying to adjust to the "dark-light-dark" blasting they just took. His ears still rang from the sinful sounds that singed them.

The thing about plans was, even the best ones could go to shit when the feathers started flying. And Salvation cussing and flying into the portal . . . was *not* part of the plan.

— XX —

LIVED SMILED AT his concubine, Life. She was busy watching the fall from the corner of their cell. It was an activity that no ruler would deny even the worst of the condemned. For watching beings fall to or from the garden was as effective at controlling followers as television had been at stupefying ancient Man-monkeys so their rulers could enslave them. "Ah, darling," he snarled and said to Life, "how they frolic in the misery of their loved ones. Your beautiful creatures are so"—he put his hand to his mouth—"*lively*, dare I say."

It had been a long time since Life had felt anything but contempt for her Man-monkeys. She observed the fall with the indifference of a dictator watching elections. She had long ago realized that she set loose the very vermin in her garden that caused . . . and then required its destruction.

Life had believed them to be faithful and manageable followers. In the end, that was not the case. So she and Lived created an abomination—an offense against her own laws. And in their hypocrisy. . . If their son, Jump, the Great Dragon of Judgment, and his bitch, Salvation, hadn't done it, Life would have burned the entire garden to smoking ash herself just to be rid of it.

Life smiled wide. Jump and Salvation had help . . . hadn't they? She stared at the image of the two girls in the prison cell. Not much different from her own cage, she mused. Life watched Fury fall from her own delusions. It was one of the few joys she had, confined in her own dungeon, watching while she waited to be vengefully violated by yet another of her creations turned against her. "They are already dead," she said to Lived.

"Aw," Lived replied, "do not fret, my love. They were doomed to fail. For you were their mother."

Life frowned at him. She had desperately needed her children to love, obey, and honor her covenants . . . and they had failed her in every way she could imagine. And many ways that she simply could not. Watching them fall—reveling in their misery—was pleasing to her, but it was far more joyful to rule over them and mete out judgment and punishments—salvation and damnation—with a randomness that only a god could take pleasure in.

Now, Life lived a god's sentence. It was why Rain left her alone with her failure and lack of power.

To a slave—a citizen—a prison was no different from most of their lives, but to a ruler, being powerless was as miserable a punishment as they could imagine. "Is this how it is to be . . . forever?" she asked Lived. "You are to rule over a kingdom of one, stripped of every fallen soldier you once had, save for a barren and abandoned deity to torment." She stood up and her black orbs glowed. "You strut in your cage like a lion in one of their zoos, pretending you are fierce and ferocious while you are fed a steady diet of delusion and defeat." She knew she was boiling Lived's blood. That was what he needed. It was what she wanted. "Yes, you are a great and powerful devil, my Day Star. A master of *nothing*."

Lived's blood *was* boiling, but taking her by force had become boring and there were truths mingled with her words. That was the best place to disguise them, he knew that. Sprinkle the proper amount of truth in with the lies he wanted to tell. . . Soon enough, there wasn't a Man-monkey or archangel birthed or created that could tell the difference.

Lived paused and thought about the best course forward. "And yet . . . I *am* your master," he said. Then he slithered up behind her, grabbed her by the shoulders, and hissed into her ear. He ran his long tongue down to the middle of her back, to just above her. . .

Life closed her eyes—it was pleasurable—her tactic had failed. She might as well enjoy what little she could. An eternity was a long, long time. She knew that all too well. Yet, the time to turn the tables would come soon enough.

Lived slithered his tongue back into his mouth. He licked his lips with it on the way. "A master whom you openly defy every instance you find occasion to speak."

Life smiled in front of her, away from him. Her plan might succeed after all. "Forgive me . . . my master," she said. Then she stepped forward, pulling herself from his grip. She lay down on the blood-sweating floor of their cell. She spread herself open—wings and will. Then she retracted all of her once-beautiful white feathers and she spoke softly up at him, "Shall I lie here and pretend for you again?" Then she spoke more harshly, "No, no . . . *not* that." And she quickly stood up, walked angrily away from him—across the floor to the edge of their cell—and then she leaned against the bars on the iron gates. She spread her wings wide and her legs this time, too. Then she hung her head. "Take me, my great and powerful master . . . please," she mocked.

Lived growled at her.

And then Life raised her head and squeezed on the bars as hard as she could. And she gritted her teeth as she shined her feathers and wings to brighter than she had since being cast into their cell. "From behind, so I may be *spared* the *torment* of looking into your eyes . . . at my greatest failure's *impotent soul!*"

Lived was livid. He bared himself —retracted all of his body feathers—and raced across the cell at Life, snarling and spitting flames, his snakes hissing as he ran. No one—god, girl, or grandmother in hell— could be allowed to speak . . .

The brightest and warmest light in Heaven *or* Hell shined and blasted white-hot truth into the dark lies of the dungeons. It far outshined Life's glowing brightness. And all manner of vile creature howled and cawed and crowed, and then ran for the safety of the corners of their cages, trying to escape the burning bright. But there was no escaping truth. Truth was simply there for all to see . . . and so was Rain.

Rain floated down the center of the outer ring of the dungeon tunnels. She rarely justified a visit to the insidious place. It felt like some of it. . . The taste in her mouth and the smell in her nostrils would last for days after she left.

The creatures down here were condemned and abandoned with good reason, and they cowered and covered their glowing red eyes as she passed their cells.

But one particularly vile soul—Jump had warned her against keeping the putrid pup around—raced at the gate to his cage, snarling and biting at the bars as he spoke, "I'll eat your soul," he spat, "and then I'll fuck your mother in the ass, like I—"

And Rain lifted her hand with as much effort as a steed swatting a fly with its tail and—*CRACK!*

A huge bolt of lightning blasted the disgusting creature and it lit up to a white-hot, star-shining glow, and then it exploded into sparks and glowing chunks of smoking flesh and blood. The chunks wriggled and crawled, trying to reach the other parts and when they did, each part caught fire and melted back into the other.

Rain turned up her nose and scrunched her face. "Disgusting," she said. She kept floating down the tunnel. One of the "perks" of power was that she didn't need to fully flap her wings to hover above the ground. She could simply flutter them. And faster than most angels could even see, her wings vibrated like a hovering hummingbird and she hummed slowly down the passageway.

Behind her, the creature struggled to recreate its miserable shell.

"She was entirely justified in killing you," Rain said. She looked ahead of her again—at the cells upon putrid, piss-smelling cells of forgotten and filthy souls she condemned. "Anyone else care to tell me who they are going to. . .? My mother? It is no wonder that my father —he is right, I should annihilate *all* of you."

While the dog-creature was busy picking up the pieces of its putrid existence, probably preparing to assault Rain's heritage again, the rest of the "occupants" in the dungeon crowed and cawed and screeched at the light. To dark souls beyond redemption, the light of the truth burned like acid. The wailing continued.

"All of you," Rain said. She stopped and hovered, humming in front of the cage that housed the worst of them. "You two blasphem-ing schemers in particular." She stared in at Lived.

Lived stood with his plumage fully retracted—naked—seemingly dumbstruck, and for the moment at least, screechless in mid-stride.

"Ich!" Rain said to him. "Put on your plumage, liar. That thing is disgusting!" She looked Life in the eyes. Her once-ruthless master, vanquished by Rain's own father, still gripped the bars on the gate to their cell. "And you, the Chosen One of your children, look at you. Have some dignity—cover yourself. How far you have both fallen!" Rain turned away from their cell and spoke to the rest of them, "Now you see," she said. She turned down her bright light—just enough so the creatures would stop screaming, but not enough to allow the dank dungeon to return to its shadowy self. "All of you, this is how those that you defiled were treated. Burning in agony at your deceptions, poisoned by the fruits of your lies, wanting for justice while you delivered only *misery*. You are beasts . . . best sent to slaughter, I am told. And yet I wonder . . . is there none among you worthy of re-demption?"

None spoke or made noise. The silence was deafening. Rain could smell the fear—putrid piss-smell of Purgatory—of fallen angels in limbo, too afraid of the Devil to speak. She wrinkled her face and debated breathing through her mouth, but then thought better of it—she knew the taste would be worse. "As I suspected," she said, looking up and down the huge tunnel. "You yourselves realize the futility of your forgiveness." Yet she knew Lived would not. His long tongue could not be expected to remain tied for long. So before he untied it, she swung her arm behind her and without looking back, she pointed right at his wrong heart and said, "Look what they have all sacrificed in the name of your black heart." She pulled her hand back. "See what he has offered you—evil and iniquity and the loss of your innocence. How violated you must all feel, sacrificing your beautiful souls to this liar. Defiled and desecrated for him and for Life. And to what purpose? A few moments of his pleasure? Of hers?"

Indeed, Rain was correct about one thing: Lived never remained quiet for long. The flames of his voice hissed and spit behind her, "Sacrifices? What do you know of this? You do not understand their sacrifices. Were it so, I would gladly offer them. Yet, you are not pleased with burnt offerings, either . . . as we all can see. And still you ask each of us to make sacrifice with a humble spirit, Rain the almighty. Yet you reject our humble and repentant hearts . . . as you always have."

Rain's voice screamed as an eagle, "Silence, you blaspheming liar!" She turned to face his cell again. "None shall recite from her book. And you—you twist her words around your tongue as you speak."

"As I happily twist it around her tits, you impudent whelp!"

"Do not tempt—" Rain started to say, but then she cut her statement short and tried to calm herself. It would do no good, threatening a devil who had himself threatened billions upon billions of souls. Trading taunts with an expert was not part of the plan. That was a task better left to someone with the . . . proper skills. And that someone would arrive soon enough. "Your temptation is wasted on me, liar," she continued. "You will find no quarrel with me. Your warring ways are no longer welcome in the house of the Lord."

"Lord?" Lived said. "Hah, you are a little girl, playing with matches." He waved his hand back and forth, motioning up and down the tunnel at the remnants of his followers. "But all of these little sticks *burn*, sweet and innocent child. You would do well to remember that."

Life had covered herself in her white plumage. The small patches of dingy gray and pink on them now had grown larger since Rain's last visit. No doubt from half an eternity spent on her back on the floor of their cell.

And the great mother of the last eternity knelt down and cowered at the rear of the room she and her lover now called their dominion. From behind her lying lover, Lived, Life stared back at Rain.

In order to look at her, Rain had to gaze right past Lived's snakes. "Oh great Garden of Eden, how do you tolerate. . .?" She closed her eyes and tilted her head up a little. Then she opened them and looked Lived in the eyes. "I have warned you, put it away before I crop it like your tail, you miserable—" Then she noticed something and she stared at Life's black orbs, glowing slightly, covered from Rain's light by Lived's shadow. Life's orbs rarely did that, and Rain thought for a few seconds. It was clear that Lived was not going to put on his plumage, and she considered fulfilling her promise of cutting his snake. It could wait until Jump finished with him. "He really tempted Eve with that . . . *thing?*" Rain asked Life.

Life blinked her orbs a few times, obviously trying to turn down their glow. "It was a different eternity," she replied. Then she stood up.

Rain pointed at her—right at her eyes—carefully positioning her arm to block her view of Lived's snakes. "Different. . . Yes, I remember this, great mother." She swirled her finger a little at Life's eyes. "In that time, those only did that when you were excited about . . . something. I remember how you watched me fight for your judgments." She looked up at the ceiling, oozing and dripping above the cell. "And since there are no trials tonight, I wonder . . . if it is not your beautiful Day Star—which clearly, at this point, how could it be —then what, may I ask, has you so . . . aroused?"

Lived's hands were on his hips now, and he stood as an evil Adonis —legs spread and chest puffed like a peacock. Then he spread his great bloodstained wings as wide as their cell would allow and the tips scraped and sparked against the granite walls. He made sure to place one of them directly in front of Life, obscuring most of the top half of his concubine's body. All that peeked over was the top of her head . . . and her shining orbs.

Wings were one of the ways that angels "spoke." Often times communicating more than speech. Right now, Lived was threatening Rain, while at the same time controlling his concubine—exercising what little power he had left, as well as defying Rain's orders. Because truly, her words were, in effect, the law of this eternity.

Laws were for followers, however. And the three of them under-stood that constant all too well. Kings . . . *and* Queens made them to control subjects, *not* the other way around.

So none of the three should have been surprised when Rain spread her own wings wide, mirroring Lived's, then put her hands on her hips and pulled back her blistering-white plumage . . . all the way. She smiled at Lived, right through his eyes, then she turned her gaze to Life. "We shall play games then. How . . . quaint."

— XXI —

"WHOA-WHOA!" SALVATION yelled. "No-no-no!" she screeched ahead of her, shouting far down the dungeon's dark tunnel, toward the source of the white light in front of her. "Rain almighty! What are you *doing?*" she yelled, and then she sprinted and jumped and flew. And the portal twisted shut behind her.

Jump stood outside the portal for a couple of seconds, staring at the closed entrance. His eyes were wide under his sunshields. He took them off. Salvation never cussed, much less at her only daughter.

Whatever she saw in there, they were off the plan already. Luring the ornery demon away from his concubine so Jump could interrogate her in private was not going to be very easy if they went in there all beaks blazing and feathers firing. You couldn't get a voluntary testament from someone like that. They'd just clam up, grit their teeth, and make you torture it out of them.

Nothing after that was reliable. Torturing someone got them to talk, but they said anything to make the pain stop.

Jump ran to the portal entrance, waited for it to twist open, and then folded his wings tight behind his back and stepped through it. "Take it easy," he shouted after Salvation. She was already well ahead of him. "You know you can't do that shit."

If Salvation was in a mood, she could fly almost as fast as Fury. And it didn't get any moodier than her using profanity. Jump ran behind her, flapped hard, and tried to fly after her.

The passageways down the middle of the usually dark and damp tunnels in the dungeon glowed brightly for some reason. But they weren't big enough for an angel to fly along. In fact, they were built that way on purpose.

It was written in the first book—the *Book of Eden*—the testament of the very first Protector of the very first eternity—that the dungeons should prevent dark souls from escaping. As such, they needed to be built so an angry soul could not fly through or out of them.

Salvation's wings scraped and sparked along the stone ceiling and floor of the passageway—the tunnel between the cells. And she screeched and screamed in front of her as she flew, ignored the scraping and kept flying. She ignored Jump cawing whatever he was cawing behind her, too.

Jump's wings were far too big to fly inside the dungeon, and it only took a few scraping, sparking flaps for him to crash to the ground. Then he stood up and ran, leaving his wings slightly open so he could glide every few steps. He tried to look ahead and find out what had his wife so angry, but he couldn't see beyond her flapping wings.

One thing was certain, whatever was ahead of them was as bright as Rain and he wondered if the great mother, Life, was blasting her brightness again, showing off for the few spectators she had left.

Whoever it was, clearly the light was pissing Salvation off, because he hadn't seen her this angry since they faithfully waited outside the operating room at the State hospital, only to find out that their daughter was . . . in a better place.

Jump was almost to the source of the light, when Salvation veered to the side of the passageway and slammed into the gate of one of the cells. Then she violently flapped and clawed, flailing her wings wildly through the bars, screeching and cawing at whoever the unlucky bastard was inside. Because if any of those blows connected with whoever was in that cell, they would be in a world of shit.

But the light was still bright and Jump adjusted his sunshields. After their first fiasco, he and Salvation brought them whenever they went to the dungeons.

The first trip underneath the arena, it was kinda like leaving on a foggy morning and not even thinking twice about bringing sunglasses, then squinting all day while the afternoon sun burned pink slits into the whites of their eyes. Bringing sunshields to a dungeon was about as intuitive as . . . *Sunglasses on angels*, Jump thought. It worked, but it still felt weird to him. But the Chosen One, Life, still had her bright —one thing Rain let her keep—so he was glad to have the shields.

And then Jump saw her—Rain, pushed behind Salvation—on the floor and totally naked. "Put on your damn plumage!" he yelled. And he grabbed her by the arms—"don't touch me" covenant be damned —and he spread his great wings wide, shielding his daughter from whatever was behind him. "Right now!"

"Do not touch—"

"Save it, little girl," Jump said. And he looked at Salvation. "You better hope she guts someone. You're in deep shit."

And Salvation's steel wings were busy beating the shit out of the bars on the cage behind him and when she flapped them behind her to deliver another blow, they scraped steel with Jump's and huge sparks flew. But she kept thrusting them into the cage.

Once Rain pushed her feathers out, Jump hurried her down the tunnel a safe distance away, then he told her, "Stay *right* here!" And he ran back to where Salvation was still battering and sparking the iron cell.

"I'll tear out your guts!" Salvation screamed at the figures inside the cell. She continued reaching and clawing at them. "How dare you!"

When Jump got to her, he understood why.

Lived was standing with all of his feathers retracted and his serpents hissing—no mistaking what they wanted. And Lived cackled and laughed as Salvation's wings barely missed clipping him. "You should get better control of your bitch," he said to Jump. Then he leaned in a little—just out of reach—looking toward Rain. "Probably both of them." And he tilted his head back and let out a loud caw.

And the fallen demons and devils in the entire dungeon cawed and cackled and screeched at their master's call.

Life leaned into Lived's back and pushed him gently into the pathway of Salvation's wings.

One of Salvation's wingtips sliced across Lived's chest and he screamed out. And black blood—molasses from the garden—spurted out and then red blood shot from his arm, and he screamed like a hawk and swung his wing back at Life.

Lived's wing slammed into Life's chest and she went rolling toward the back of their cell, ramming into the wall. And she whale-moaned out a long sorrowful sound. When she was finished, she sat up and coughed. Then she laughed.

And Lived raced at her and he was on top of her, and he dug the talons on his hands into her chest and Life screeched loudly.

Lived hoisted her up off the ground with no more effort than a great fork-horned owling snatching up a field mush. Then he looked into her black orbs and he growled.

By now, Salvation had stopped her futile assault on the cell. Jump stood beside her. She breathed heavily, like a cheetah after running down a gazelle . . . if they existed anymore. Jump tried to hold her shoulders to calm her, but she shook him off violently. "Get the—get off me!" And she looked at Rain's seal on the gate to the cell.

Jump caught her glance. "Don't even think about it." And he grabbed her hand.

Salvation tried to pull against Jump's hand, but he held her tight. Then he looked in at Lived, squeezing his talons into Life's breasts. He laughed a little. "Looks like you could use a little help yourself . . . *Daddy*. What's the matter, trouble in Purgatory?"

That stopped them both, and they looked at their creation—Lived forgetting to squeeze and Life trying not to wince.

Jump crossed his arms and frowned at them. "Are you two finished?" He raised his eyebrows. "Put her down or so help me, I'll pull this seal off and rip the guts out of both of you . . . *again.*"

Lived dropped Life. He didn't even know why. And she fell to the floor in a pile and crouched on her hands and knees. Blood flowed from her breasts—crimson red from her right heart and black molasses from the wrong one on her left. And she hung her head down and watched it drip.

"Don't even," Jump said to her. "Jesus Christ . . . stand up, Your Majesty, you're fine." He couldn't manage an ounce of pity. Then again, that was how the father had made him.

Salvation was still fuming. "You're. . .? Mercy?" she said. "For them? They were going to—he had his plumage down!" And she rushed at the great iron bars and swung a wing in at Lived again.

But Lived was too far back for anyone to be concerned, and Jump pulled Salvation away from the cell. She protested a little—her wings jerked, and she cawed at her husband. Then she stood next to him and crossed her arms, too.

Lived had calmed himself enough. This was more excitement than he had enjoyed in a long . . . *long* time. "Look, darling," he said to Life. Then he reached down and held his hand out for her.

Life grabbed hold and allowed him to help her to her feet.

Lived squeezed her hand hard on the way up. Once Life was standing, he let go and put his hands back on his hips. "How delightful, it's the house of hypocrites, come for an evening visit." He leaned forward, trying to look around Jump and Salvation, at the light from Rain down the hall. Then he turned back to Life, her own light back to bright. "Is it evening?" he asked her. Then he looked back at Salvation. "One never knows, down here. I did say *evening* appetizers, did I not?" Then he turned back, looked down the hall again, and then back at Salvation and then directly at Jump. "Though, you—you have *come* a bit early. Then again. . ." And he looked back at Salvation, still fuming. "Could it be? Maybe that is why you are so furious. What has you so angry? Great Dragon letting loose his fire too quickly in his old age?"

Once Rain was satisfied that her plan was well in motion, she walked back to where her parents stood, and then she played her part in their plan. "I must apologize for my unkingly—"

Salvation was hardly finished with her naive little ruler. "Apologize?

You are in so much trouble. Do you have any idea what this bastard is capable of? I'm so—I'm gonna—I. . ."

Rain stared at Lived on purpose, ignoring her mother. In half an eternity, she had learned . . . things. And yet the seductiveness of a male's snake was still intriguing.

When Salvation saw where her daughter was looking, she flung her wing over Rain's face. Then she looked at Jump and motioned with her head a couple of times at Lived. "Can you *please?*" she said.

Jump looked at Lived, still standing and smiling—now with *his* arms crossed—his feathers still back and his snakes stretching straight up, flitting their forked tongues toward Rain. "Jesus," he said, "put that thing away or I'll blind you with it."

Lived looked down at his snake. "Ah . . . yes," he said, "how rude of me." Then he twisted his hips and pointed them at Life, reminding her of what was to come later. And he pushed out all of his great blood-red plumage and folded his wings tightly behind his back, forming the long staff with the twisting snakes and angel wings on his shield—the warmark of his legions, the Hell he once ruled over. "The innocence and gullibility of youth—wonderful, isn't it, darling?" He smiled at Salvation.

Salvation gave him a frown and merely tilted her head as a warning.

"Must be positively infuriating for you," Lived said to her. "Her curiosity—how will you ever keep her from resurrecting her lust? Ah, how I wish we could go back to simpler times. Back when we weren't all so . . . tied up about our bodies. Before we were beaten senseless with our own desires."

Rain had pulled her mother's wing from her face. Now she was glowing and smiling at Lived. "And what desires might those be, great liar?" she asked.

"Rain!" Salvation said to her. She tried to put her wing back up over Rain's face, but her daughter gave her a condemning look and held up her hand. Salvation frowned, still slowly raising her wing. She pleaded, "Please, he is the most—he will inject you with lies!"

Rain pushed her mother's wing down all the way. Then she stepped in front of her, directly in front of the cell. She looked at Lived. "He will not lie to me," she said. "Will you, Day Star?"

Life could see Lived's snakes, writhing and wiggling beneath his feathers. She may have grown disgusted by her cellmate's assaults on her, but Lived was *her* beautiful creation and no child would toy with something that rightfully belonged to her. Not the other one and certainly not this one.

She would not lose any more, anyway, for Lived was one of the few things she had left from her reign of pain and terror. Life stepped in front of her devil and said, "You are no *god*, girl. Do not toy with animals you cannot hope to control."

Salvation and Jump both gasped a little. Open blasphemy would usually send Rain into a tirade about manners and land someone a pile of shitty angel duties, at the very least. Jump knew Salvation was still going to have to answer for using that forbidden word when they came into the dungeon. But Rain held her hand behind her back at them, motioning them both to be silent.

Life glanced behind the little insolent bitch and then she looked Rain in the eyes. "You think you can rule over the desires of devils?" she said to her. "Over your father? Hah! He is my—our son has no *ruler*. He placates your innocence. I can smell it on him."

Jump raised his eyebrows at that little tidbit. He had kicked this bitch's lying ass. Just as easy to do it again . . . now that he knew the secret. But Salvation eased her hand over his and held it.

Life stared at Rain and continued, "Great *Dragon*. . . You have little hope of controlling a desirous demon, much less this angel of light or his bastard son." She turned behind her and looked at Lived. When she turned back, her black orbs had turned wild. "I have managed this liar for nearly *two* eternities. And only through my own failings were any of you able to challenge him. He is foul and ferocious, little girl, and he will fuck you until you are a faithless, featherless purgatory!"

And Jump just about stepped in on that one, because—

But Salvation leaned on him and squeezed his hand harder. She looked at Life's light. It was glowing now and Rain was letting it. And it seemed, at least for the time being, that Lived's ego was letting his concubine sing his praises. It was perfect.

Life's black orbs glowed dark blue around the edges when she started speaking again, "How many are your works, O Rain almighty? None! . . . In wisdom I made . . . them . . . *all*. The Earth was full of my creatures . . . long before I sent your soul to it. Everything was already created, and you presume to renew the face of the garden? After I commanded it destroyed?"

More blasphemy, Jump thought. There would be a helluva reckoning at the end of this day. And yet he was confused when Rain let Life continue again.

"The Earth was mine and everything in the world and the universe," Life said. "And all who lived in it! For I founded it upon the seas and established it upon the waters. And the universe was formed at *my* command, not yours, so that what was seen was not made out of what was visible, but what I saw . . . *me!* . . . And *you*"—she pointed at Rain—"*you* took it from me."

"I say this to you for I am your redeemer, who formed all of you in my womb! . . . I am *God*, who *alone* stretched out my bosom and spread out the earth . . . by myself!"

And now Jump thought she was starting to sound like less of a deity and more like a spoiled little rich bitch.

"And I will send you back to the dream you called life," Life growled at them. "Back to your trial and your judgment and your resurrection. . ."

Now they could all see that the god, turned jealous lover, had finally snapped, because she was glowing white hot and even Lived was moving away from her, toward the back of their cell, cowering like a lion from the whipping words of his master.

And lightning bolts started to form in Life's eyes and Salvation knew they were almost there, and she gripped onto her husband's arm again with her other hand, because she could feel him wanting to do something—he had no idea.

Then Lived's face went slack . . . and his mouth slowly fell open. Then he said, "No, you ignorant—"

But his arrogance was surpassed only by that of his creator's, and Life almost yelled when she finally said, ". . .just like I sent that furious little bitch!"

— XXII —

WHATEVER THE GOLDEN Guardians told you little pissing-purgatories about rape back in that angry dream you think is reality, I can tell you right now, it's complete bullshit. Rape is not that rare. And the murderous mayhem you just saw back in that Mexican Protection cell, that wasn't like it went down.

Because like, Man-monkeys *love* rape! They love rape almost as much as they love war. Because if they didn't, there wouldn't be so much of it.

Listen, the best way I ever heard it. . . Even if he is a wicked bastard, he knows some shit. Don't get that old without—here's how it is: If you are born or you get created or whatever—okay, so let's say you're a lion, back in Life's eternity, if you want.

So you're a lion and that's the way she created you, and you're all, I'm a lion, right. So you go around doing what lions do. And in this case, what you do is, you eat. Simple enough—some things are simple. Bitchy as she was—is—she made some simple shit.

Okay, so you eat. And you don't care what you eat, because like, you're a lion. Zebras, deer or whatever, hyenakins I think she called them, hippos or hunthounds—doesn't matter, not the point.

Now, you're out doing all that eating, and you're tearing out guts and chomping on throats, and pretty much ripping and raping and pillaging your way through anything you want.

What? . . . Never thought of it like that, but yeah, just like an archangel . . . *which* none of you will ever get to be if you don't shut up and listen to this story!

You done? . . . Okay. So, because she made you that way—lion—you eat everything alive, while it's like, still living. And I do mean living—feeling the last part of anything that it will ever call life again, because whatever unlucky, furry little bitch you happened to claw down that day, it can feel every last thing.

Every bite you take of it with your big fangs, every last claw you scrape across its back, tearing into its flesh, and every organ you rip open with your blood-soaked face. And then that thing is just dead, nothing on the outside but rotting meat and nothing on the inside but maggot food. Even its soul is gonna stink when you fly down to collect it.

Oh my G—I know animals don't have souls. Aren't you paying *attention?* I don't know how much more hate I can waste on hammering this into you little—focus!

The lion? Well, you—you just walk away. You go back to whatever rock you live on and you lie down and just like, sleep and shit. You lick the blood off your balls or whatever. And then you know what you do? . . . Not even close. First thing you do is you try to find—you just do it again. Because you're a lion, that's why! Jesus!

You were hungry, you ate, you took a shit, and then you're hungry again. Because you're a filthy lion.

Oh, but don't worry, because pretty soon, because you don't know any better, or you just don't give a shit. No one will ever know how a lion thinks.

What? Yes, yes, except another lion, that's true. But you don't even care about other lions . . . unless you wanna fuck one.

Let me tell you a little something they never showed much on the PIN nature waves—too like, offensive or something, I think they said. Anyways, a lion will kill its own babies so the bitch lion wants to do it again. You believe that? That is some benevolent being, creationist shit, right there, don't you think? Eat its own *babies!*

Where was I? . . . Yeah, you get caught. Right out in the open, killing like you were created to, and you get snatched up by a Man-monkey and thrown in a cage. Zoo, I think they used to call them. "For your own protection." I loved that one.

A zoo. Now, they just call it Animal Protection. Why? Who knows why Man-monkeys do anything, idiot! They just do it—they're crazy hypocrites. But here's what happens next.

Now, you are just like, lazing around in your cage all day, waiting for the guy who brings the food. And you're shitting and yawning and all the curious Man-monkeys come to gawk at you in your nice, safe little cell—cage. And to them, it looks like you couldn't give a shit, because you're all fed and happy and farting or whatever.

And maybe if you're lucky, they put you in with a girl lion so you can pass the boring day away, fucking. And if the Man-monkeys are lucky, the two of you make a vicious little baby lion. But even that's boring, because it's not like the little baby lion is ever getting out anyways.

What? . . . You're not gonna eat that little—you don't *have* to. Bitch lion isn't going anywhere, so what's the point to that?

And now, like, you're locked up for years and years, and to you it seems like eternity goes by, one of them at least, because to a roaming and raping lion, a day in a zoo is like an eternity—relative time, remember that shit? Still confuses me, too.

Now, the Man-monkey that feeds you gets lazy one day, and he's all chucking the food in and there's blood all over and *whoops!* Yep, he slips into the cage with you, and you know what you do?

No! Are you even paying attention? You eat him, that's what you do! . . . Why? I just told you, because that's . . . what . . . you . . . do. It's what all lions do. And I don't care how long they lock you up in Heaven or back in Life's garden, lions eat things. No amount of resurrection or redemption rehab is fixing that. Nothing to fix. You're not broken, you're just dangerous . . . to everything else. That's not broke, that's just Life. She's a bitch.

Listen, a lesson grandpa Jump hasn't taught you yet—you don't like something dangerous and it's like, not even broken? Only thing you can do with it, get rid of it—kill it before it kills you. Understanding it is a silly little dream, just like life.

What? . . . Rape? Rain almighty! Save me, Salvation, what do you think I've been talking about?

Shut up! You're so—now, I'm not even answering questions anymore. I talk, you listen. That's how it's gonna be from here on. You *will* learn this shit, Rain help me, or I'll give you to someone who will teach it to you the hard way. That's how I had to learn it, and let me tell you something, you wide-eyed, whining wingnuts, it's no lamican roast by the fiery lake, either.

When the people you thought were your protectors get done with you. . . After they twist up your mind—turn you upside down and inside out, they will put *you* on trial in front of everyone, not the bastard who did it. And then they'll infect your soul with their vicious judgment, and they'll sentence you—condemn you to a lifetime of guilt, locked in a cell with yourself. And then they'll annihilate any chance you have at redemption. And God or Rain or Eden or whatever eternity's Protector you think is coming to save you, won't be able to resurrect one ounce of pity for you.

There's no eternity in Heaven or Hell that can wipe that out. There's only two times you will know after that—everything before . . . and every miserable thing after. That's just the way it is.

Last thing, you will never *ever* see it coming.

— XXIII —

LONG BEFORE RAIN almighty and long before the Lord almighty, Life's, eternity. . . All the way back to the very first eternity—the eternity of Eden—the Protector Eden had commanded that the dungeons be built in a very specific way.

She decreed that since the dungeons would house some of the most vile and dangerous souls, sinners, and sodomites that would ever be brought to creation, there could be no risk of letting them escape.

The only entrance to the tunnels and passageways of the dark dungeons underneath the Arena of Reckoning would lead right out into the arena—into the open for all to see. Any escape attempts would have to be carried out in full view and truth of the stars above the Hallowed Hall. And this safeguard, it was thought, would prevent any dark soul, plotting escape, from harboring any hope in their hearts of avoiding detection.

Even the always-skeptical golden guardians liked the design. With only one entrance to secure and nowhere for a prisoner to flee but out into the center of the arena, the drudgery of guard duty was easier to abide. And since it would only take two guards to secure the portal entrance, the rest of the guardians could take their turn patrolling the tunnels and then take a break from the tedious duty of keeping evil angels caged up.

It also meant that they could enjoy some of the more stately duties entrusted to the guardian angels in Heaven. Duties such as escorting evil souls in and out of the dungeons during the judgments, or brand-ing the condemned with molten fire once they were judged, or the best task of all—Protector protection. "Guarding gods," the golden angels referred to it. Before Rain's reign outlawed the word, that is.

The food was more succulent, the scent sweeter, and the class of angel more stately, as well.

However, security safeguards—locked down and impenetrable front gates—were only as effective as the people or angels patrolling them. And even if the front entrance to the dungeons was Purgatory-proof, all Protectors required their own private entrance, so they could sneak in through the back.

But just as it had since the dawn of despots, the "rules-are-not-for-the-rulers" rule would eventually lead them straight to damnation. Though, they never considered themselves vulnerable until it was too late.

Had Rain known any of this, she might have taken a little more care when she cast the current occupants into the dungeons and left them down there to rot. With fewer and fewer golden guardians dedicated to patrolling the dark tunnels and passageways, the evil souls were left largely alone with their bitterness, to plot and plan and bemoan their captivity.

And had she known any of it, Rain might have realized that one of the occupants in the great dungeons harbored a secret—one which Rain believed only she knew. A special prayer that would allow them to resurrect any soul in the dungeons, freeing them from their tor-ment and misery and allowing them to unleash that anger and rage back in their own life.

And if that person—a Protector with the power of penance—decided to try and free themselves, then it was just a short flight away from resurrection—escape.

There had only been one imprisoned soul in all the eternities who had successfully escaped the dungeons. Life had sent him back to try to regain control of her garden. But it wasn't to be, and the entire trial and judgment had ended with disastrous results.

That unfortunate angel had ended up spiked to a cross, speared, and bled out next to thieves.

Lived sat with his wings against the granite wall of his cell, brooding. His cellmate had divulged vital information to their enemies. The whelp and her parents *were* his enemies, but no one could wrong him as much as Life had.

Yet more immediately damning was the fact that she had been bested by the child, Rain. He looked across the cell at Life and growled. Eventually she would pay. As would they all.

Life stared back.

"Well," Lived said. He bounced back several times against the wall, before he clasped his fingers together and stopped, "that was—that was simply. . ." He sighed, and furrowed his brow. "I have no taste for you now. You cast me from Heaven for less offense. What fate shall I. . .?"

Life sat on the opposite side of their cell, trying to understand how Rain had deceived her. She knew *how*, but she didn't understand how she had let the child manipulate her so completely. *That insolent little bitch*, she thought.

Understanding arrogance and jealousy in oneself was difficult, even for a god.

But for a devil? Why would he even consider it?

Lived cawed, crowing a little at her silence. "Yes," he said, "for you, it is much better to remain silent, it seems. Because we have witnessed enough of the fruits of that folly for one day. We—I commanded you to send her back for a *reason!*" he shouted. "I bade you one—you have managed to fail me on the simplest of tasks."

Life was used to Lived's crowing, and she knew they would have to attend to their son and his daughter by the end of it all. Yet by the time any of them realized the depth of her plan, it would be too late for them all. "It is hardly—it is of little concern," she said. She measured her words carefully. "They will waste themselves *and* time in understanding. There is precious little of that remaining."

"Little concern?" Lived crowed. "You divulged everything! Ignorant. . . So this is how they taste Hell—why they fear it so. Trapped in a cage with failure . . . for eternity. Misery . . . torment. The taste is so vile in my mouth."

You are vile, Life thought. "This is no hell," she said. "Hell is trapped beneath an angry little fledgling, penetrating you while he continues to attempt to play at God. And I would have never believed it had I not witnessed it myself, but you have become quick to relent. How did you become so. . .? You fold your wings at the first gust of wind. That is a weakling's way, and I did not create you to be a weakling!

"What fate shall I save for you, my failed creation? Because clearly, you are of no use to me if this is how you respond to deception and threat. I wondered how he bested you in the arena, and how I killed you so easily. You are a *featherless* fledgling!"

Lived cawed wildly and then he laughed thunder down the tunnels of the dungeon. And all the creatures in it knew what usually came next. They crowed and cawed and screeched and howled and their sounds echoed down the passageways. Lived stood up and pulled back his feathers. He spread his wings at her and stretched them, scraping his blood-stained steel feathers against each other, sending sparks to the floor.

Life sat against her wall and eyed her creation's display. As easy as she had been to fool, there was no deceiver like one of her creation's snakes. She watched the two heads slither out and then point toward her and stiffen.

Wisdom. . . Life thought. That's what she had bestowed upon the snake. She created all the other beings in her garden with such beauty, that it seemed the most intuitive of decisions to make.

Temper unrivaled beauty with godly intelligence. Life never understood how mistaken she could be. With Man as his vessel, the snake quickly turned vile and manipulative, and it perverted her beautiful Man's soul. And it used him to slither and slink through the garden, telling lies and tempting everything it could to get anything it wanted. And what it wanted was fruit.

In Life's eternity, the sweet blossom, Eve, was the snake's first devilish meal. And from there, the succulent seed that Eden entrusted to all the Protectors of the eternities after hers. . . Eden's garden plunged into chaos.

Life's creations fornicated with such reckless abandon that they quickly grew out of control like rats. She sent plagues and famine and pestilence to try and control their proliferation. None of it slowed the swelling tide of Man's thirst for more fruit.

The single-minded, insidious focus of the snake. Life knew it was the source of her ruin. She looked from Lived's snakes to his face. "Ah," she said, "it seems you are not the sole ruler in our small kingdom. Perhaps his heads are more useful than your own." She looked back at Lived's snakes, now rigid and angrily staring at her. "When I married the two of you together, I had hoped for a better result. Yet, his wisdom has only given you the power to deceive, and your beauty and arrogance have given him a singular taste for fruit. You cloud each other's minds such that neither of you can think to save the other from destruction. You wish to fornicate while our great mountain falls into ruin? Imbeciles. . . You fornicate, my beautiful Devil, when you should fight."

Lived's snakes hissed up at him, bidding him to ignore her and plunge them into Life's fruit. But he hesitated, sifting through her words for the truth.

Life smiled. She had learned to manipulate her vengeful captor once again. She pushed herself off of the floor and got on her hands and knees, facing away from him. She hung her head and smiled through her hair—her slave turned master was returning to her power. "Your master's wishes shall be fulfilled, my devil," she said. "Do as he commands—give him my fruits."

Lived roared and growled down at his snakes and they cowered and softened and slinked back toward his waist. And he pushed all his feathers back out and over them, and then fire sprang from his wings. "I am your master," he said, "and I shall decide whether we bath ourselves in fruit . . . or blood!"

Life knelt in the middle of their cage. She spread her wings wide and her feathers glowed bright white. The beings in the dungeon howled at the sting of their light.

Even Lived shrunk away from her bright. Then he growled down the passageways. "Silence, putrid pigs," he said, "or she will resurrect every one of you!" Because that's what he was about to do.

Resurrecting a condemned—as their ruler, Lived believed it was his right. But only a Protector of the great eternities had that power—only a god could send someone back to their life.

Lived would have done it without her—spoken the words to open the portal back to life, recited the Prayer of the Protectors. But for anyone *but* a Protector, speaking the words was pointless.

He hadn't believed it, at first—he had warned Life not to lie to him. But trust was a scarcity in the deceit-filled dungeon, so he violently fed her fruit to his snakes to be certain she was telling the truth. When Life finally relented and told him the prayer, he released her. But when Lived spoke the words, nothing happened—she had told him the truth.

Life, it seemed, had her own personal pet—a lap dog, in every sense of the word. And they would send him back first, to quicken the pace.

She spoke the words of Eden—the Prayer of the Protectors: "Sweet mother of mayhem and mercy, Eden, I am Life, your banished child. Bring us redemption now, and the sweetness and the power of resurrection!

"I send up my sighs, mourning and weeping in my dungeon of tears. Turn, most gracious Protector, thine eye of mercy and thine hand of mayhem toward him, deliver him from his exile, return him unto my eternity, the bastard fruit of thy womb, the fallen archangel . . . Dogg."

— XXIV —

THE LAUGH WAKES me back up. *Thank God,* I think, *my daddy—*

"Look at you," he says to me, "God's glorious little children. All twisted and tied up, wondering what in the—trying to figure out what in the two hells is going on, I bet."

"Daddy?"

He smiles and his teeth are crystal white, and now I have no idea what he's talking about or who this guy is, because like, I know he looks like him—I don't even know where I am. Well, I'm still in this Mexican Protection cell, I can see that, but I'm starting to wonder if it's real.

"Mr. King," Brie says from behind me. And she's—she's still alive? "I—I wanna go home."

Brie's alive? I think, *What's going. . .? Oh, shit.* "Tessa?" I say.

"She's fine," his voice is like smooth peanut butter on pancakes.

I can smell the syrup. *Mmm!* And I smile and giggle at him. That's what he used to make me when he stayed home from work. It wasn't very often, but every once in a while it was pretty cool, ya know.

"I'm just letting her sleep," he says. "She's probably pretty tired after all of that."

And, I mean, he's standing right in front of me, and I know it's him, but that is *not* my father. And I just stare at him. I don't even struggle against the tape holding me to this chair. Because it's like, I don't even care.

"Everything's going to be just fine," he says again. And I believe him, ya know . . . because. . .

But something's—he's just not right, but I don't feel scared anymore, I'm just . . . curious or something. I wanna figure it out—put the pieces together like a little puzzle.

His clothes are pressed and creased, his hair is combed tight, and his shirt—he's not even sweating. And in Cancun, that's like, just impossible. In this room, for sure, because I'm soaking wet and I can taste the damp in the air. But he's like . . . too perfect-looking. Like, I don't know how else to put it.

I know he's my father, and I know in my head—and I should say "gross" or "eww" or something like that. I mean, that's what I would —what I should say, right? That's what I would've said . . . then.

But that's not what I say, and I don't even know why, but the words float out of my mouth so easily, "Cut this tape off for me, Daddy." And that is not a voice I've ever used before. For sure not with him. "I'm hot and sweaty."

I'm staring at his face. It's about all I can fu—all I can do. And now I—I don't want to curse, but *goddamn* I feel good! And I don't know why, but I don't even think that's a curse word, is it? *Hell, I don't care! Or maybe it's just f*—I can't even think it.

Then I hear Brie. "Mr. King," she says, "can you untie me? I gotta pee first. And I think Em can. . ." And she giggles.

Before what? I think. And Brie's voice sounds kinda wrong—not how I think she should talk to my dad. It's kinda like . . . when she's talking about jacking the Mike, or when she's drunk or something.

"She can wait," Brie says. And she giggles some more. "Because like, she all ready screwed my *boyfriend.* She's fine. She doesn't need—did you know that? . . . He told me that."

I laugh at her and then I giggle, too—I did screw her boyfriend. Didn't cum, though. It was over too fast, was more like it. But that wasn't now. It was later than this, and it was his fault . . . and I don't even care. When I talk again, I slur, "He tol' you? I can belief. . . What a big *baby!*" I think I feel—yep, I'm drunk. "Yes . . . I . . . did, and he sucked. . ." And I laugh and shut my eyes. "He sucked, I sucked, we all *sucked*. Gooood *stuff!*"

Then I think I hear something rip. More rips, and then Brie's laughing behind me and giggling. "Whoa," she says. "Wheeeee, we're flying!"

And I open my eyes and it's blurry and I blink a couple of times, but that doesn't—it's all foggy and stuff. And I squint real hard, and there goes Brie. *Whee!* I think. And she's flying, and it looks like Daddy's carrying her. That's so nice. Oh, that's sooo *pretty!* "Flutter, flutter, little fairy," I say.

And Daddy flaps his wings and they *flyyy* away.

"He's a dirty little dog," I giggle. I close my eyes and my head bobs, and I jerk it back up. "Bimbo. . ." I say as the door shuts. She's so—I don't *even* care—it's fun. I just feel . . . good. And that's a *good* thing, right. This is silly—my *voice* is silly. "Blonde Bimbos." They're jus' . . . *nasty.*

— XXV —

SAFELY BACK IN their cell after resurrecting Life's favorite guard dog, she and Lived casually watched the fall. The thick, dank air of the dungeon was cut by knives of cawing and crowing, and screeching and howling from—it was getting harder and harder for either of them to tell whose followers were whose. But they were both accustomed to the constant sounds of despair and torment from the fallen. It would have concerned them more if the dungeon cells were silent.

Once Life finished the Prayer of the Protectors, Rain's seal had been suspended and a portal in the cage of their filthiest fornicator, Frank the dog, had opened. Then Lived commanded the dirty animal to step through it. When the beast resisted, Life whale-moaned and cawed down the hall at him.

Then the humping hound of Lived's hell, Dogg, leapt through the portal and disappeared.

Every angel's fall was different. For an archangel, to fall from grace was to question their very existence. "How could God create me this way?", "Why am I here?", "What made me this way?" And one of the biggest ones, "If God made me, then why was I cast down?"

But the most important question any angel would ask once they relived the horrors of the life they only thought they knew, "How do I get back to Heaven? Or Hell, as the case may be?" Falling was a scary thing . . . but it wasn't the scariest of things. Resurrection was worse.

If an angel chose to go back to Life's garden—they had to choose—the life they thought they remembered was never the same. Because pigeoning around in the past was a tricky business. And if a Man-monkey caught an angel—figured out what it was. . . Well, the one time the Man-monkeys caught a fallen angel from heaven—the first time they caught one of God's children returning to the garden—they nailed him to a cross, stabbed him with a spear, and then let him bleed to death like a criminal.

No angel in either of the two Heavens had volunteered for that fate since. Now, resurrection was no better than punishment. Yet it was unclear who the punishment was intended for, because an angel back in life could either be a Man-monkey's worst nightmare or wind up as his next midnight snack.

Life turned her gaze from the fall. "*This* was her life?" she asked.

"How she wanted to remember it," Lived said. "Intoxicating, is it not?"

Trapped for half an eternity with her devil turned raping beast, Life had finally begun to understand the magnitude of the miseries that she had wrought upon women. "By the time she returns, she will be less than Hole," she said.

"You blame Hole for this?" Lived said. "This is *your* doing, not hers."

"Spare me," Life said. "You would have tormented her far worse."

Poison her own words and use them against her—it was always Lived's best response. " 'I have two daughters which have not known man; let me, I pray you, bring them out unto you, and do ye to them as is good in your eyes.' " He let that verse sink in for a moment. "Tell me, my love, is it better that he give her to strangers for them to violate, or simply follow your words and tend to the matter himself?"

"You are a . . . a twisting liar!" Life said. "These are not my words, they are—"

"Oh," said Lived, "they are in your *Bible*, so naturally I just assumed. . ."

"Yes, yes—they have misinterpreted and bastardized its entirety"

"They *did*," Lived said.

"What?"

"Did."

"What are you. . .? Oh, yes," Life said. "So they did."

It was easy to forget that a fall was simply an angel's way of interpreting and making sense of their past life. It was closer to a hallucination than any reality from the past. Questions and regrets and sorrows an angel remembered on the way down were just part of their judgment, the real precursor to resurrection itself. Nothing was true . . . but to a falling angel, everything was real.

And that was the key—belief. If enough fallen angels believed in something . . . or *someone*, then who was to say what was real and what was not? Because laws were only obeyed when people believed they were real—that the judgments of the ones who made them were just. And it did not get any more "real" than Fury's fall.

"Why did you choose. . .?" Life turned back to watch the fall. "What makes her so special?"

Lived would not tell her why he had chosen Fury to start the revolution—return things to the way they had been before they were both cast into the dungeons. If they could twist her up enough—and they had plenty of dark souls to send down to do that—then by the time she hit bottom, she would think that down was up. Which was perfect if one wanted to overturn a young whelp and her reign.

Lived smiled at his cellmate. He knew she was becoming distracted by the fall, watching one of her precious children of the garden resurrect her nightmares and beliefs. But he might have to remind her again who her master was. His snakes stirred beneath his feathers. It could wait. So could they. "It is really quite simple," he said. "She is the only angel Rain takes counsel with, for all of her . . . 'advice.' "

"Ah," Life said. She had already known the answer, but deception was in her nature. She might be able to send her children back for their belief, but for Life there was no going back for hers. She smiled and grinned into the image of the fall. "Ironic," she said softly.

Lived furrowed his brow at the back of her head.

Life could feel her *temporary* master's gaze behind her. His breath was hot on her neck. She smiled to herself, then turned her face to a straight-lined blank slate. Then she turned around. She looked into his eyes and then down at his snakes, busy wriggling, trying to squirm themselves free from their "master's" restraints. "It seems that Rain—our little bright light . . . has a blind spot."

They both looked back at the fall. Their hound, Dogg, was just finishing up with the second one in the cell.

Life hadn't felt anything but disgust for her "lover" for a long, long time, but watching her guard dog take pleasure in his work had her stirring. She would pretend as long as she had to, but even a deity had desires—many, many desires. "He is a despicable and filthy animal," she said, "yet he does take pleasure in serving his master. Tell me, how do you control—when he is finished, how will you keep him at bay? Presumably, you are not going to let him roam the streets. I don't think that will end well, if I remember correctly."

Lived laughed out loud and the rest of the dungeon cawed to join suit. When he was finished, he said, "Strutting around with a crown on your head, claiming to be a king, was sure to draw attention to *him*. The wrong type of attention. I warned you of this." He chuckled as he remembered yet another one of Life's swelling legions of debacles. "It was a miracle that they didn't burn him at the stake." He paused to see if Life would respond, but she remained uncommonly silent. No doubt feeling the truth of his words, he surmised. "But no one pays heed to a stray dog, digging and scratching in a dark and dank alleyway, sniffing and smelling for a place to bury his bone. And we know just which alley to point him at."

For Lived, the insatiable devil, had a personal pet of his own. Far down and across the tunnel, a small roar echoed down the halls. Then it turned to low growling and screaming like a cat in heat.

And Lived smiled and gazed down the passageway at the cage that housed Hole—the whoring demon-angel that he knew in every way imaginable. "Isn't that right, lover?" he cawed.

— XXVI —

THE ARCHANGEL DEMON, Dogg, was a "dog." The disgusting canine concubine that Life kept in his cage as her own "boy-toy" pet. Before, she had fed him with her own dark desires whenever it suited her. And compared to her current cellmate, it was debatable which one was worse.

Dogg was full of hell and fury, sinister and seductive as a Man-monkey—such an incestuous and conniving bastard—that his soul had trouble converting to even a dark demon's form. Locked in the dungeons for his crimes against one of Rain almighty's most cherished friends, Dogg simply got worse.

His eyes caved in and his belly got fat, and he grew fangs that were misshapen, like his crooked crotch-snake's crawl. His claws were constantly filled with the remnants of rock, broken free from scratching the floor in his cell after he'd just taken a shit.

And like any dirty dog, left untrained and to himself, he rolled in his own excrement whenever he thought about . . . whatever a dog thinks before he frolics in his own filth.

But the worst thing about him wasn't the smell. The most vile thing about him was that he was the worst leg-humping nightmare of a bitch-in-heat-sniffing hound that had ever been married with one of Life's monster snakes. Dogg was simply the worst demon in Lived's hell.

* * *

But as hideous as the humping hound had turned after the end of his life—as bad as Frank King looked after Jump threw him out a window and watched his sack of bones splatter on the street below—when Life resurrected the vicious and vile Man-monkey back to the land of the living. . . In Dogg's egotistical version of his recollection of being alive, he looked as smooth and as seductively sinister as any "heartbreaker and cherry-taker"—he liked to joke with himself in the mirror—could look.

His hair was jet black with the wave of a parade float princess. And no matter how many bloody bodies he remembered chewing through at the *Battle of the Books*, his teeth were shinier than Life's pearly white feathers.

In Frank the dog's resurrected version of the land of the living, he was a god, as beautiful as any one of them had been. A projected delusion that helped him in more ways than his favorite—violating the faith out of innocent souls.

Dogg licked the blood from the corner of his mouth. Then he smiled and stared down at the woman, still strapped face-down to the gurney inside her "suite" at the sanatorium.

Her back was clawed bloody and some of her hair was pulled out. And there were bite marks on her buttocks that oozed deep red blood.

Dogg adjusted inside the front of his pants—his snake too limp to protest—and he tucked his white shirt in tight under his belt. Then he rolled his shoulders around until he was satisfied that his shirt was as near to perfect as he could get it. "And that's that," he said. Then he turned around, getting ready to leave.

"God. . ." the woman's voice barely made sound, "please . . . help me."

Dogg stopped in his tracks. He didn't turn back. He looked at the door to her interrogation cell and squinted just a bit, debating. "You're fine," he said, frowning. "Everything's gonna be just fine." And then he growled. "And you got it backward—the name's Dogg, bitch," he said. "You remember, don't you, Babs?" Then he opened the door and left.

As Dogg walked down the long, dark hallway—barely lit by the flickering red bulbs inside their iron-cage housings above the doors to the cells—he glanced at the priest walking toward him from the far end. And then a little song popped into his thoughts and he bobbed his head back and forth and shuffled his feet a little lighter as he silently hummed the tune:

Two little love birds lying in bed,
One rolled over this is what he said.
Little bird, little bird why so red?
Don't you know you're already dead?

By the time Dogg finished amusing himself with his little bedtime ditty, he was almost to the priest. And he sniffed first and then smiled and looked the shaking little man up and down as they passed.

The old man's knuckles showed signs of scraped blood, hastily washed raw. He rubbed his Rosary with one hand, and cradled and gripped into his disgusting book with the dirt-filled fingernails of the other.

The first thing Dogg smelled was the liquor on the man's breath, and then the putrid-piss smell of fear and the acidy taste of anger behind it. Then a faint scent of the dried blood on the pages of the book, rammed into Dogg's nostrils and he almost salivated. He barely smelled the gunpowder and grease on the gun.

As he passed the wrinkled old God-giver, Dogg let out an involuntary growl. He smelled the man's thoughts and smiled. Then he raised up his hand and leisurely pointed his finger and thumb like a pistol. He winked at the priest and curled the corner of his mouth. "Khik," he clucked.

The priest stumbled and almost fell.

"Careful with the booze, Benito," Dogg said to the priest. "Makes it hard to wake that little snake up." Then he turned back toward the exit and kept walking, faking a few barks as he sauntered. "You'll meet your God soon enough, girls," he shouted behind him. And then Dogg pushed the doors at the end of the long hall, and he howled as they swung slowly closed behind him, "Owoooooah. . ."

— XXVII —

FATHER BENITO WALKED carefully down the long hallway inside the interrogation wing of the sanatorium—K&T's private torture facility underground and across the street from the Genesis building at the *Fifty*. He knew that's where Frank would send her.

Babette had waved him in hysterics, screaming at him through her wave tablet, yelling something about Frank kidnapping their child.

She had threatened to kill her husband more than once during Benito's and her "talks." She had ranted and raved about what an animal he was, but when Benito turned the wave to a hologram, Babette was shaking a gun. And when she looked over her shoulder and yelled for her driver to bring the car around to the front of the tower, he knew that she was finally serious.

Benito begged her not to go. He was clear across town, and there was no way he could get there in time to stop her, but she terminated the wave before he could reason with her. He was left standing in his office, alone with a decision.

Going after Babette was a difficult choice to make, but he had done far more dangerous things, infinitely more life-threatening. So he dug up his gun—it was buried in the basement, right next to his book. He worked so fast to resurrect his little personal protection pistol that he nearly ripped out a fingernail and scraped all of his knuckles bloody.

The drive through the rain to the big brick sanatorium building downtown was nerve-racking, and Benito's guzzler was almost sideswiped by several Protection vehicles speeding past him. Then some Traffic Compliance agents had detoured him around a road-block down the street from the sanatorium, and he thought he would never make it in time.

Sirens and gunfire were nothing new on the streets of any major urban zone. The drizzle-drenched streets of Seattle were no different, but diverting a well-marked vehicle of the clergy meant bigger trouble than Benito had ever seen.

Church vehicles were behind only Protection "snatch and bag" teams when it came to traffic right-of-way. Even emergency vehicles had to yield to a clergy-marked guzzler. That could only mean one thing—something worthy of a MARR, Protection's Mobile Assault and Resistance Response vehicle, filled with Citizen Compliance twentysomethings, black-clad and ready to black-bag someone for interrogation.

When Benito swiped his ID badge and scurried into the building, gunfire and explosions echoed from a few blocks down the street. He thought he had heard huge crashes of breaking glass, too.

After he walked through the evaporators, just inside the front door, his mouth dried out and it felt like there was sand in his throat.

K&T Enterprises had invented the technology to create the zero humidity zones—"Z-zones" or just "Z's," in citizen slang.

The Z's were one of the few technologies that actually made some citizens' lives easier, especially if they were the ones who had to mop miles of smooth floors inside an office scraper. But for anyone who worked inside or visited one of the huge buildings, it was better than walking around all day like a slowly drowned rat. Every scraper in the city had Z's to keep Seattle's liquid "sunshine" outside where it belonged.

It was well known—the human body being composed of roughly sixty percent water—that anyone passing through a Z needed to drink water immediately after. The side effect was that if they didn't, they would be out cold in five minutes from dehydration. Sooner if they were prone to sipping State swill like Benito.

"Catching Z's" at the *Fifty* was not a good idea, but Benito was so preoccupied and nervous that he forgot to stop at the hydration station and get a drink.

Once Benito was dried off and all the way inside, he tried to act as casually as he could. Raising the suspicions of the *Fifty's* staff was not a good idea, either. In addition to the schizoid paranoia of the sanatorium's numerous resident Protectants, there wasn't a person who worked inside the eerily-lit, granite dungeon who wasn't at least a little bit "mental."

Something got on anyone who stayed too long in a sanatorium. A deep haze drifted over their soul that at first felt lethargic, like being really tired and on the edge of sleep. If they lingered too long—let it infect them to the point that they came down with a case of "Fifty-fever"—fell asleep at the switch in their job, or on a visit in Benito's case. . . The *Fifty* had a habit of swallowing people up, and then shitting them into a body-bin in the garbage alley.

At the very best, the people who worked there could only imagine what it would be like to wake up inside your head, strapped down to a gurney as an unwilling "guest." And no one on the outside but the powerful people who would never end up there had any clue about the torturous hell inside.

But Benito knew all about the lost souls trapped inside the *Fifty*, images of rape, torture and murder burning into their minds, creating for themselves their own private hells. The only thing he didn't know was anyone who had burned their way out.

When the door at the other end of the long hall creaked its rusty metal hinges open, and out strolled Frank King—the very man Benito had hoped to avoid—he figured that was just what was about to happen to him. He knew he was going to burn for his sins.

The man sauntered toward Benito, smiling and almost dancing to some silent, whistling tune in his head.

Benito gripped his book and rubbed his fingers so hard into his Rosary beads that he thought he might crush them. He only let up when he felt the searing pain from his ripped fingernail.

He would have to drop something if he wanted to dig his pistol out from under his robe. But that would be something that wouldn't go unnoticed. And even if he did somehow get his gun pulled before Frank's Prime Officer Protection detail raced down the hall, where would he go?

The POP's were too highly trained for one lonely priest and his little 9mm pistol to stand a chance. And Benito wasn't a cardinal. If he were, he would have his own POP's and he wouldn't need the gun in the first place. It was all ludicrous and he began to question his sanity. What could he hope to accomplish?

With his long-buried handgun, Benito was a marginal shot at best. And once the alarms rang, six highly trained Protection agents would spring from nowhere and kill him. He'd seen it before, during a failed escape attempt that ended in a bloody, bullet-ridden body, oozing out its life right in front of him.

No, the only thing that would happen if Benito shot Frank now, was the man's POP's would riddle him with bullets . . . if he was lucky. Then there would be no one left to pay for Babette's "therapy" at the *Fifty*. Absent that, she would become a lab rat or a sex slave . . . or both.

The gun was a last-ditch defense, a security blanket meant to deny a tyrant his tyranny. Benito knew that if he had to pull it out, it wouldn't be to save his life or hers. It would be to save her soul, end her misery if he could. And then he would use it on himself to prevent the Protectors from condemning him to the same miserable fate.

It was a horrible dilemma—none of it was part of his primary mission—and given the eternal consequences of such a blasphemous act, *two* of them, really. . . But Benito had found love, and not where he'd meant to. He would have a reckoning with his destiny sooner or later, and he would answer to God or the Devil soon after that. But today, the love they had *all* denied him was locked up in this hell, not theirs.

Benito kept walking toward Frank, squeezing the symbols of his faith as he prepared himself for judgment. He prayed in his head to be saved from the damnation that the man walking toward him would bring, *Hail Mary, full of grace. The Lord is with thee. Blessed art thou amongst women, and blessed is the fruit of thy womb, Jesus. Holy Mary, Mother of God, pray for us sinners, now and at the hour of our death. Amen.*

And then Frank was just a few feet away, smiling as he surely prepared to imprison Benito's soul. *He's smiling*, Benito thought. *He never smiles at me.*

And then Frank. . .? Only it wasn't Frank . . . but it was. Benito looked more closely.

The man resembled Babette's husband—a dead ringer, for sure. But he was more like a copy, or a clone or some cinewave actor who was too close to tell the difference unless he was standing right next to the original man. Benito frowned a little. The man was just too . . . "perfect" was a word he would never use to describe the bastard, but that's what he looked like, perfection.

And then Babette's beast husband was right in front of Benito, and the man raised up his hand and pointed his fingers like a gun at him, and—*BOOM!*

That was the sound Benito heard inside his head, and it actually felt like a bullet ripped into his chest and exploded his heart, and then exited through his back, ripping flesh and bone and bile out the back of his black robe. And he stumbled and almost fell.

"Careful with the booze, Benito," the copy of Frank said to him. At least that's what he thought the man said, because the sound was muffled and it seemed slower than real speech. And then he felt like his head was slipping into a gooey bucket of molasses. "Makes . . . it . . . hard . . . to . . . wake . . . that . . . little . . . snake . . . up," the copy said in slow motion. And then Benito felt dizzy, and he stumbled a little . . . right before he closed his eyes and went black.

When Benito woke up, he had a splitting headache . . . and he was surrounded! At least that's what it felt like, staring up at two nurses, an orderly, and the two black-clad Protection sentries from the entrance to the interrogation wing.

His vision was fuzzy and it felt like there were ants, scratching their way up his throat. Benito touched his forehead, carefully feeling the lump throbbing and growing there. Then he slowly sat up and reached for his shirt pocket, feeling for the gun under his waistband as he did. Then he pulled out his thick, black-rimmed glasses—he was one of the few citizens that didn't want a State Protection doctor "correcting" his vision with a laser. One of the lenses fell to the floor.

"I'll get that, father," the first nurse said. Then she let go of his arm and knelt down to pick it up.

Benito noticed that the girl—most of them were barely in their twenties—took particular care not to bend at the waist. *She's a veteran*, he thought. The experienced nurses knew better. But at least there was still *someone* at the *Fifty* who wanted to help people in need. It certainly wasn't the raping orderly behind her.

Benito recognized the big man from the description that one of the poor souls he'd given last rites and redemptions provided. She had whispered in his ear . . . just before she died of infection from a perforation to her cervix.

The second nurse knelt down next to Benito the same way the first had. She held a glass of water to his trembling lips. He put both of his hands on hers and sipped. Benito drank all of it in one long guzzle. Then he wiped his mouth with his sleeve. "Thank"—he coughed a little and cleared his throat—"thank you."

The orderly towered over him. "You all right, there, bub?" the big man asked. "Copping some Z's, are ya?" He smiled down like a huge cat, picking its teeth with its claw while it eyed a tiny canary.

Benito knew he had to get that image out of his mind, because that would show on his face. *Don't be weak, don't be weak*, it was all he could think to change what he was sure was nothing *but* weakness, written all over his face. Showing frailty at the *Fifty* was a sure step to staying there. "I'm fine," Benito said, barely making eye contact with the orderly, before looking at the first nurse. "Yes, fine, fine. Thank—thank you. I think I forgot to drink. . ." Another step was attracting the attention of any other body part on one of the sanatorium's orderlies. "Thank you, thank you," he said again, just for good measure. Then he wobbled his way to his feet.

As the nurse handed Benito his broken lens, she smiled a hesitant grin and then wiped it away. She glanced quickly at the orderly, before grabbing up her colleague by the arm and whisking her away down the hall, and then out through the double doors.

Benito knew that if the orderly was going to snatch him up, it would be better if the nurses weren't around to show their disapproval. More than one staff nurse had become a permanent guest by catching the "eye" of the wrong orderly. And there wasn't a "right" one in the entire building.

Benito had no idea where they found them. The huge and hateful men that Protection used to maintain order inside the prison. Whether it was a sanatorium or prison—there was precious little difference—the orderlies were only out-menaced by the Protection sentries themselves. In fact, orderly duty at the sanatorium was one of the shorter career paths to being asked to join Protection—go to the academy. And then, if a person could stomach the training, he might get to be an interrogator one day. Then, who knew, maybe Protection

Agent In Charge—the most coveted job that a black-clad thug could aspire to.

Benito shuddered—physically shook his upper body and head—at the thought of this orderly running anything.

But that caught the eye of one of the Protection agents. And the man stared through his goggles at him. He gazed at Benito like they all stared at citizens—the indifference of an old guzzler mechanic, figuring out if he wanted to take the time to wipe up a single drop of spilled crude. "I don't know, father," the agent said. He reached for the comm-button on his shoulder, activating the mini-wave-unit on his helmet. "I'm waving medical—get you checked out."

Benito grabbed the agent's forearm on impulse, and quickly jerked his hand back as fast as he could. It wasn't fast enough, and the second one rammed the metal action of his submachine gun into Benito's outstretched arm.

Benito yelped a little and grabbed his arm with his other hand. Spiking pins and needles of pain shot into his elbow and then up his whole arm, and he winced hard and tried not to cry out. "I'm sorry, I'm—" he tried to get the apology out, but the barrel end of the second agent's submachine gun was right in his face.

And then the agent punched his rifle at his forehead and sent a spike of pain into Benito's already swelling forehead, and he stumbled backward and grabbed at his head.

"Thirteen-thirteen!" the first agent shouted into his shoulder. "Agent engaged! Agent engaged!" Then he let go of his shoulder and pointed his gun at Benito.

"I'm sorry, I'm sorry, I didn't mean—"

"Benito Octavio Benedetti," the first agent said. Then they both moved right at him and held their guns inches from his face. "You are hereby remanded to Protection! State your compliance!"

And things were happening too fast, and once they found his pistol he'd be killed or worse, and Babette was—

"Threat severity, over?" the first agent's helmet-mini squawked the wave back.

Benito's mind raced. A "thirteen-thirteen"—"assault with intent to defy"—Protection agents only ran to one code faster. He would be beaten and tortured and then given to the orderlies for good measure. The last thing his soul would ever see would be a body-bin in the alley. *Never see her again*, his mind cried. "I didn't mean to—"

"I *said*," the second agent's voice was angrier now, and Benito could see the fire in his eyes, glowing and growing, "state your intention to *comply!*" And the agent bent his elbow and leaned in fast and he smashed his forearm into Benito's face.

Pain spiked into Benito's eyes, and a bright light flashed and he fell to the ground. He grabbed at his head and the pain—he couldn't see, and then his ribs caught fire and he screamed. The agents kicked him in the legs and the ribs, and he put his arms over his face and tried to roll away. He caught a flash of white and then the orderly was down on his knees, punching him in the chest.

"Submit-submit," the orderly yelled as he swung over and over. "I can do this all day, ya old idiot. Submit!"

"I submi—" but Benito took another punch to the gut before he could get the full statement out. He gasped and coughed blood, and then he curled into the fetal position and urinated down his leg, soaking his pants and the floor.

* * *

When there were still courts and not just mountains of paperwork to bury someone under, agents were often asked why citizens had been beaten so badly during the process of remanding. The standard agent response—they taught it at all the academies—was, "The potential protectant resisted submission to judgment, and subsequently the Protection agents responding were compelled to force compliance." It never went any further than that.

It was a small matter that saying one word was difficult enough while someone was being beaten to death, much less trying to spit four of them out in the correct order. The courts checked the box on the judgment form and then the protectant was remanded. Dead or alive hardly mattered.

Benito knew he had to get the words out to make it stop. "I submit to—" Another punch felt like it nearly caved in his chest. He gasped and then sucked for air.

Laughing while he worked—Benito could feel that the orderly was enjoying the chance to prove himself in front of two potential future comrades. "Goddammit," the man laughed as he swung, "you pissed on my floor, ya little shit!"

But Benito gritted and yelled this time, "I submit to judgment! I submit to judgment!" Then he coughed and groaned.

The orderly swung again, but an arm caught his just before he hit Benito in the head. The second Protection agent wrapped his arm around the orderly's and held back hard. "He's submitted—no further force is necessary, citizen."

The orderly got a disappointed look on his face. "No further force" was bad enough, but that wasn't the worst thing the agent said to him.

"Citizen," about the worst thing any Protection agent—wannabe-agent orderly or full-fledged agent—could be called. But there wasn't one single thing the big man could do about it. Well, there was one thing. . .

Drunk on the adrenaline of beating an old man senseless, the orderly resisted. It was the one thing he could do about being called a lowly citizen—the wrong thing.

As strong as the huge orderly was, when he pulled his arm away from the agent as hard as he could, the agent flipped and then he slammed down hard on his back on the concrete floor. And the agent let out a huge groan, but then rolled away from the orderly as fast as he could.

The move wasn't necessarily so the agent could escape; it was more that the man knew, in the ensuing response that followed a "thirty-one, thirty-one," more than one Protection agent had been killed by "friendly" force. Because a "thirteen-thirteen" by a weak old priest was one thing, but "deadly defiance" against an agent of Protection. . .?

The first Protection agent didn't even bother reading the orderly his rights to recourse. There wasn't a rule, much less any law, that said he had to. *Brrrrt-brrrrt-brrrrt!* The agent's squatty little submachine gun spit 9mm lead rounds so fast that the whole thing was over before the last of the ejected casings hit the concrete floor and echoed little tinks down the hallway.

Benito clutched at his ears and laid in his piss on the floor. His ears were ringing a little from the sounds of the rounds. If it weren't for the suppressors on the Protection agent's gun, he would have probably been deaf. Every Protection agent on duty and off were required to wear the squishy, sonic-barrier balls in their ears. Priests . . . were not. Benito was, however, required to administer last rites and redemptions to the dying or dead.

He looked across the hallway at the bleeding, bullet-riddled body of the orderly who had just beaten him. And he searched for the faith and forgiveness to give the man his last R's. Benito was silent. Whatever rights the sadistic bastard had left, he would have to exercise them in Hell.

"Donato Ortega Gonzales. . ." the first Protection agent recited the requirement at the man's lifeless body. Even after a citizen was dead, it made the paperwork easier. The barrel on the agent's MP7 hadn't even stopped smoking when he finished it, ". . .you are hereby released from Protection." Which was just an overly complicated legal way of saying "condemned," the citizen's slang term for dead.

— XXVIII —

"WHAT THE HELL do you mean, you can resurrect people?" Jump asked Rain. A thousand years into this eternity and he had never even heard of such a thing, much less believed that his own daughter was capable of it . . . with a prayer, no less. "Why would you—who would want to go back to that shithole?"

"Calm down, calm down," Salvation said to him. "I can handle this." She tightened the feathers on her wings and tensed up the shield on her back. Then she looked back across the Throne Chamber of the Protectors—the residence of every Protector—at her daughter.

Rain was perched on top of the Throne of Judgment, like a white dove on a wire. And her back was to the Sword of Power—the huge stone shield and sword that formed the back of the throne. Rain was flanked on each side by a single golden guardian angel, each wearing sunshields to protect themselves from her bright.

Between the two beautiful guardians, Rain appeared older and more menacing than a thirteen-year-old girl should. But no angel really knew another's "true" age—the relativity of time. Some ancient archangels acted like fledglings, and there were hatchlings in her and Jump's hell, with the viciousness and cunning of a fully-fledged fallen. But this new deception—"What do you mean you can resurrect people?" Salvation raised her voice and said. "Why in—why would you do that? . . . And why the *hell* didn't you tell us?"

Rain hopped and flapped down from her perch. And when she did, everyone in the room could see the words on the throne, reminding them that she was no longer Salvation and Jump's innocent child.

Rain walked down a couple of steps, tightening her own wings behind her back.

The guardians both stepped forward with her.

Then Rain stopped—one step above Salvation—and she cawed in a tone that was unmistakably defiant. "I was unaware that I was required to inform you of all of my duties and decisions," she said. "Regardless, it is not people."

Salvation didn't hear the last part. She leaned forward and shook her head a little, pointing her finger at Rain. "Oh, don't even—don't take that tone with me," she said. "I'm still your mother."

Jump took half a step forward. "Don't talk like that to—"

But a quick look and an angry squint from Salvation cut off Jump's warning. Then she said nothing. Two eternities in, if her husband didn't know by now, he'd be reminded when this was all over.

Jump raised his eyes in surprise at her and held up his hands in front of him. "What?" he said. "She can't talk to you—I'm trying to help!"

"Don't," was all that Salvation had to say. And that was that. She turned back toward Rain, now floating in the chamber, just like they had all seen Life do at the *Battle of the Books*. "Stop that," Salvation said to her. "This is serious, Rain. It's not some—those two are the most conniving creatures you can imagine, and if that bitch can resurrect—this is so bad. You have no"—she shook her head—"we could have helped! Maybe prevented any of this from ever happening in the first place. Now we've got—Faith is shooting at us, Fury is missing with a bunch of our hatchlings, and now this? You're playing with fire and that bastard is made out of it. Resurrection? . . . Jesus Christ!"

One of the benefits of being chosen as Protector was gaining access to the historical *Library of Lambs*. A huge hidden hallway surrounding the throne chamber of the Protectors like a moat. The outside edge of the circular stone tunnel was packed with rows and rows of scrolls and books, and parchments of all shapes and sizes.

The fruits of authors and scribes—stories of long-past eternities, and those not that far gone—stood at attention like soldiers of wisdom past, floor to ceiling on the stone-chiseled shelves, silently waiting for those with the will to command their wisdom.

In preparation for the first time that Rain was to sit on her new throne, she had cleared her chamber of all but her most trusted advisor—her friend. She was a little nervous at first. The weight of the responsibility of being Protector had her apprehensive that she would not be able to shoulder the task, much less wield the power of the position to the benefit of all.

"To the Benefit of All." That was the edict of the Protectors, chiseled deeply into the granite on the stone shield that formed the back of the throne's perch. And that was the double edge of the Sword of Power. It was the task that came for those who sat in judgment on the throne—the power and the responsibility of gods.

After the sun set on the end of Life's eternity and at the very dawn of her reign, Rain had walked up the steps, tentatively at first, silently excited and afraid at the same time. It was a scary thing for a young Protector, so she was also quietly happy that she was not alone.

Rain—Amy Blake—had felt so powerless in her life, constantly under the watchful wing of her father, while assaulted on all fronts with situations and people she had no idea how to handle on her own. She had only had a glimpse of her powers at the end of the Battle of the Books, but to go from that to all-powerful god? "How will I do it?" she had held the hand of her confidant and asked.

"To the Benefit of All." . . . It was the "all" part that confused Rain the most. What did that mean? For certain, it was difficult to miscon-strue a word like "all." However, "benefit" was a term open to wild interpretation. One man's benefit—or woman's or angel's, for that matter—was sure to affect another's. So what prosperity could she bring to one that would not bring poverty to another? The "win-win" result that her father sarcastically joked about was lost in her under-standing of how to bring it to reality.

"All. . ." It was like a hammer that swung wildly, over and over with the intention to hit a spike on the head. And yet Rain missed each attempt to understand the point. She had stared at the words on the shield of the throne with her friend . . . for minutes it seemed before either of them spoke. "What . . . what does it mean?" she had asked herself as much as her companion.

"I'm sure I don't fucking—uh . . . I have no idea," her friend had said, failing at practicing her new ruler's cursing covenant. "Why don't you just like, sit on it?" she had suggested. "See how it feels."

Rain hesitantly let go of her companion's hand, slowly climbed the remaining steps, and then tentatively flapped her wings and landed on the throne's shining silver perch. Her head had immediately jerked up toward the ceiling and great clouds and lightning formed above her, and her eyes rolled back and turned a darker shade, and her eyelashes fluttered and then the feelings all blasted her mind at once.

Empathy and contempt, sadness and joy, and confusion and . . . understanding came down in little jolts of electro from the clouds over her head, like the bolts from the former Protector, Life. And blinding light blasted Rain's thoughts, and self-awareness and knowledge melded with her soul.

Rain's friend had rushed up the steps to the throne to come to her aid. But there was no help that her new ruler needed in swinging the sword of power. What was happening to her *was* the point.

So when her friend grabbed onto Rain's arm, a small bolt of lightning knocked her back down the steps. Rain lowered her head and looked at the angel, doubled over in pain on the floor of her chamber. Rain shouted, "You mustn't touch!" Then her head jerked toward the ceiling again and she shook for what seemed like minutes, at least.

When it was over, Rain's eyes returned to normal and she lowered her chin all the way to her chest, staring down at her hearts, and she *did* understand . . . more than she ever wanted to.

When she raised her head slowly and looked at her friend, Rain had changed . . . forever. Gone was the frightened and frail girl of her eternity as a Man-monkey in the garden, left behind was her youthful naiveté as a newly-crowned Protector, and lost was her innocence and folly of youth. And she understood her own nature and that of the garden and the natures of all of the creatures in Life's eternity. And Rain knew what she must do to ensure that the failures in that god's realm . . . did not repeat in her own.

There was no way she could explain it to the only confidant she had ever trusted. Regardless, Rain knew it was not something to be explained to an archangel, much less a fallen one from Hell. Rain's responsibility was a godly duty . . . and only gods could understand it.

So when she looked down from the throne at her friend and smiled, Rain's face was different . . . but the same. "I am prepared." It was all that she had said to her confused and frowning friend.

But before either of them could say another word, the Throne of Judgment began to slide. And its great granite legs ground rock against rock, sliding back the full depth of its legs, slowly revealing the treasure beneath it.

Rain stared down from her perch at the front feet of the throne, into the black hole and the steps down to the dark. And then she looked up at her friend and smiled a knowing and playful grin.

Her friend stared back, uncharacteristically silent for a few seconds. But seeing the comforting smile on her newly-empowered Protector's face did nothing to quell her quivering feathers. And the angel shook her wide wings and pushed out her plumage. "What," Fury squawked a little and asked, "in the motherfuck . . . is that?"

Fury had been a little hesitant to follow. She tiptoed her way down the stairs under the throne like she had snuck out of her loft back in life. But safely beneath Rain's chamber, the two of them stared at the seemingly endless supply of books and, more to Rain's purpose, knowledge.

"Humph!" Fury said. Then she crossed her arms and peered as far down the tunnel as she could—to the point that the passageway bent in an arc and she could see no farther. "I guess now you're gonna like, say we have to read all this shit. I'm not—"

"Not all," Rain had cut her off and said. "For now, only the most important . . . of this *shit*," she giggled at Fury. Then Rain closed her eyes and pushed her thoughts toward the book.

And Fury got a guilty look on her face, one she usually reserved for her mother back in life. Then she scrunched up her face, turning it into the look that she reserved for her treacherous father, "Look, I'm sorry I—"

"Shhh," Rain put her finger to her mouth. She didn't open her eyes, but she smiled. "I'm being all-powerful," she giggled. She never opened her eyes, but she knew. "And stop frowning, it makes you look mean."

"*He*," Rain replied to Salvation's Jesus slip, "though I've warned you of this blasphemy countless times in the past." She frowned at both of her parents. "What shall I do with the two of you? It is not just that you so openly defy my words, while others choose to follow them willingly. . ."

"Stop talking like that," Jump said, "it's driving me nuts. Thee-thou all-powerful, omniscient bullshit."

Rain giggled at her father.

And Salvation frowned back at her. "This isn't a game, Rain," she said. "Those two are evil and they don't play games."

"Oh, I would beg to differ, Mother," Rain said.

Jump rolled his eyes, but remained silent. It was obvious that his daughter—once Rain started speaking like that, she usually couldn't be persuaded to stop. But it smelled like she had some devious plan up her benevolent sleeve, so he listened. He would stop her if it got too annoying.

"Beg to differ?" Salvation said. "Beg to differ, what?"

"It is all a game," Rain replied. "Only the consequences and the stakes vary."

Salvation thought about that for a moment. Rain understood many things, but salvaging her out from under Lived's snakes—it was just too disgusting a thought. "He almost—you were naked!" she shouted.

Rain understood more than her parents knew, even if she had not endured the "talk" with her father. "And yet here I am—blossom intact, with the information I needed."

"Oh, my—" Salvation said, wide eyed, but still trying to control her blasphemy. Then she looked over at Jump. "This is Fury's doing," she said to him. "That girl—"

"What did I tell you," Jump said.

"She is not a girl!" Rain said a little too loudly.

It startled Salvation and she turned back, readying another reprimand.

But Rain gave her a wild look and Salvation held back whatever she was going to say. "She is an archangel of the fallen," Rain said. Then she looked at her father. "A faithful hound of your Hell, in case you have forgotten your place in all of this. And it was your duty to protect her, and now . . . now she is lost!

"She is fallen again at the hands of that evil creature, and I had no idea—none—that Life had this power. Fury will have to fight for the very essence of her soul in order to get back. And neither of you even knows what that means. So . . . we can sit here while you reprimand me for my actions," Rain's voice became more urgent and commanding, "*or* we can help Fury find her redemption!"

Once the aftershocks from Rain's reprimand died down, she and Salvation and Jump came to the understanding that Rain was more worldly than her parents knew.

"It is the only reason to send someone back," Rain said to them. "Put their faith on trial to bring them to a better judgment—save their immortal soul from Hell, bring them to redemption and faith and—"

Jump frowned at Rain. It was his now and the place wasn't that bad. "What the hell's wrong with Hell?" he interrupted. "I've cleaned the place up. All the damn hypocrites and liars are in Heaven anyway. Why would she want to—?"

Salvation gave him another look. "Enough," she said, "that's not helping anyone. Maybe Fury doesn't *want* to be in Hell anymore. Did you ever think of that?" There was something in Rain's voice before. And it had popped up again as she explained the consequences for an archangel who had lost faith in both Heavens. Without redemption when she was judged and condemned, Fury *had* ended up in Hell. But there had to be a reason that she wanted—"You're saying she went down there and *asked* them . . . to send her back?"

"Free will," Rain said. "It is the only way. She has put herself back on trial for her sins."

"Oh shit. . ." Jump muttered. He'd heard enough. If everything they were saying was true. . .? "This shit again. What the hell did she —she didn't do anything wrong. So she's in Hell, so what? It's not like that anymore. It's a perfectly fine place to spend eternity. What could she have possibly done to ruin her soul anyway? And don't go talking about that cleansing the garden shit, either." He pointed to Salvation. "We all did that. And it was a good thing, too. Place was a shithole headed for worse than what we gave it. You know they were going to eat each other, right?" He pointed at Rain, then Salvation. "Either of you want to go through that? We did that place a favor!" Then he pointed back at Rain, shaking his finger several times. More angrily than he should shake it at the almighty. "And all her new creatures are better off for it. Jesus, guilt-guilt-guilt, it's like walking around with a cross on your back. What's the point? How does anyone get any shit done up here?"

"Wait," Salvation interrupted her husband's rant. It was getting them no closer to a solution. His part would come soon enough, she knew that. She also knew that she wanted no part in another "clean crew" mission. It would take more than one eternity to get all of the garden's blood off of her feathers. "What is she—what does Life get out of this?" she asked. "Or her bastard boyfriend? They aren't going anywhere." She looked at Rain with the question in her eyes. She asked it anyway, "Are they?"

Rain's explanation was more of the same. Rules and regulations in some book, beyond the average angel's comprehension.

"So," Jump interrupted Rain, "if you're the only one who can resurrect yourself, then it doesn't matter. So why are you so fired up about it? I'll go down there, teach them both a lesson, then we get Fury's little ass back here—badabing—sick little game over."

Rain scrunched up her face when her father mentioned Fury's body. "Disgusting," she muttered. She looked at Salvation. She could see that her mother understood what she had meant. Rain looked back at Jump. "That is *not* what I said."

"That's exactly what you said."

"No," said Rain, "what I said was, that only a *Protector* can resurrect herself. If she feels that she has been unjustly—"

"Yeah," said Jump, "and what I said was, since that's you, then—"

And then he finally figured it out. And he looked at his wife. The answer was written all over Salvation's face. "You're kidding me! How in hell's she gonna do that?" He shook his head. "She just won't die."

Jump's continual blasphemy and cursing didn't seem to be riling her daughter up like it normally did. Salvation could see that Rain was letting her father's uncontrollable irreverence slide for the moment . . . and that was curious. She tucked the thought away for another time, because if what Rain was saying was true, the situation was worse than just one lost archangel, towing a pack of most likely panic-stricken purgatory hatchlings.

It sounded like Fury was in real trouble. Salvation knew the girl's life had been pretty miserable, and if she was going back to face all of that. . . But that was nothing compared to the havoc that Life would wreak on everyone if she somehow got back into power. "I just don't understand how she's going to do that," Salvation said.

Jump did . . . understand. There was nothing real back in life, or the land of the unloving, for that matter, that existed outside of someone's belief in it.

"I do." It was all he had to say.

To Salvation, short and not-so-sweet answers from her husband meant things were about to get serious. Jump would rant and rage all day about nothing, or really dangerous things. It didn't matter, precious little actually happened while he was blustering. But when he was about to put on his uniform . . . before, or dress up like an ordinary citizen to go out into the night . . . after—when neither of them were sure if he was coming back or not—the answers got quick and choppy, and there was no more hint of his ornery self.

Salvation knew Jump was steeling himself for whatever he had to do next. "Spill it, then," she said to him. She motioned her finger in a circle, pointing to her husband's face, which was slowly turning to a granite slab. "Because I know what all *that* means."

Jump held out his hand toward Rain and waved his fingers quickly a few times, motioning for her to hand it over. "The book," he said. It wasn't a request.

Rain protested briefly before Jump gave her his look—the one he rarely used with her, in life or after. "You're in charge," he said. "There are no rules . . . so give it to me."

Rain handed her book to him. "It is—"

Jump grabbed it a little rougher than he wanted to. Then he thumbed through the parchment on the pages. After a few moments of silence while he read, he said, "Seems to me. . ." The writing was more of the same unrecognizable gobbledygook in a long-forgotten language, but he ran his finger across the text like they all knew to do now, and the sounds of the ten billion former inhabitants' souls of the garden wailed out the translation for him. ". . .there's a few holes in your little story." He paused and turned to Salvation. "Can't anybody write a goddamn book that makes sense anymore?" Then he turned back to reading without waiting for an answer or a reprimand for his blasphemy—he hadn't wanted either one. He moved his fingers across the text again, continuing to translate as he read, "Thee, thou, shall," he muttered. "Same shit, different damn deity." When he was finished, he looked up at Rain and said, "So that's it, she says this prayer, and she can send anyone back she wants?"

"I believe so," Rain said.

"You believe so," Jump said. "Uh-huh."

Now they're both doing it, Salvation thought. Then she looked at Jump.

Jump caught her gaze, but he ignored it. "Wanna know what else?" he asked them both.

Salvation grumbled a little. When Jump got his self-satisfied grin— right before the catastrophe that he'd been warning her about was just about to happen. . . He actually enjoyed being right more than he was ever concerned about the disaster.

"Yeah," Jump said to her, "you *know* that's not good, don't you?" Then he turned back to Rain. "Whoever she sends . . . only one way back."

And then there was more grumbling and fidgeting from Salvation.

"Uh-huh," Jump said to her. He raised his eyebrows and got a fake smile on his face, "But wait," he continued, "there's more."

Rifling through the *Bible* during church as a kid, then rereading it so he could understand all of the clergy he had to deal with on the job each day. . . Then there was the father's unholy *Book of Blood* that he had to interpret to save . . . well, every damn thing. . . Jump had gotten pretty good at "interpreting the Word." He figured if the God-dogs could do it, how tough could it be?

So he read and read and reread for hours, sifting through hidden meanings, finding the truth between the . . . "misinterpretations" Father Benito had made him start calling them. Because that's how language worked—nuance and nonsense. Say one thing and mean another, it was just like Protection. Because what "protection" really meant was punishment and pain, and he knew that's what would happen to Fury if they got a hold of her.

"Let me just read you this part here," Jump said to them both, "see if you can figure it out."

Rain looked at Salvation. "Do we have time for—?"

Salvation shook her head at Rain, raised her eyebrows a little.

Jump read the passage, " 'And the Chosen One's children did mourn at her passing, and she was thrown into the pit with her lie. And thus it came to be that she was resurrected in their hearts and minds.' "

Salvation looked at him. She knew better than to take the bait. Her husband figured he knew exactly what it meant, and whatever he had figured out, it wasn't going to be good.

"And so that is where I placed them," Rain said to him, "just as the text instructed me to. They are both in the pit, no more than a memory to those they once oppressed."

Jump smiled and looked at his wife. "Now ya see," he said to her, "that's exactly what I'm talking about. Plain English—just like guns. You don't put it in plain English, and everything is open to—you see what I'm talking about, right?" He looked at Rain and then back at Salvation. "She's smart as hell. But you go writing all holier-than-thou shit, and everyone reads it a different way. So then that means none of it's the truth . . . and all of it is. And that's just another way of saying something is a lie."

"What?" Rain asked. She knew her father had to come to it on his own. Otherwise, she would never have given him the book. And it wasn't as if the Protector could order him to do it, especially under the "benefit of all" covenant that gilded and guided Rain's hand in every decision she had to make. But a task like this one her father had to figure out for himself.

"Right here," Jump read them the passage again. When he was done, he said, "Same pit as her lie? . . . You don't get that? Let me ask you a question. What if life is not *for* eternity? What if this little section right here means that life—she is eternity? What then?"

Rain and Salvation's eyes got bigger and they looked over Jump's shoulder at the text.

Then Jump said, "The big lie—L.I.E. You tell one long enough, pretty soon that's the God's honest truth."

Jump's blasphemy fluttered out of Rain's throne chamber, along with any hope they had of "ferreting out the truth the easy way," as he put it. Everything from there on would be the "other" way.

Rain wanted Fury found—she *needed* her found. Because Fury was the only one who understood both sides of her. The weight and the responsibility of eternity and the need to be young and free—the yin and yang of power that Rain felt after she perched on her throne. But now she knew her friend understood it, too. Fury was trying to find truth, while she was trapped in her own lie.

— XXIX —

I'M STILL OUT, or in the dream or some other shit, because everything is still black and there's another song in my head. But like, I don't recognize a word of it.

Rain's reign go away,
Boil my blood another day.
If the night turns into day,
Burned to ashes you shall stay!

And I'm freaking out, because the last thing I remember. . . *Where are all those wicked little shits anyways?* I think. And I have no idea, but I—I think that singing sounded like. . . But there's just no way she's down here.

RAGE

— XXX —

JUMP KNEW HE was missing something, but he couldn't quite rage his way to it. Some little hidden "gem" in between the lines and the lies in the resurrection prayer book that Rain had somehow dug up.

Book of Birth? Another goddamn book of the "benevolent." He was getting fed up with reading them. Self-serving pages full of piss.

Rain had said she found the book in an "unknown" library. She would only describe it to him and Salvation. Jump had never even heard of a library in the two Heavens, and he had been everywhere in them—up, down, sideways.

But it made sense that the lies had to be written down somewhere, and Rain assured him the library was real. She also assured him that he would never see it. That little statement of defiance annoyed Jump even more.

Transparency. . . Sooner or later, every ruler in the free and forgotten universe decided it was a bad idea. No use having a bunch of pesky archangels, or citizens for that matter, questioning the validity and stupidity of your decisions. They just wouldn't understand, anyway. How could they?

Jump wrinkled his face and held up the book to look at it again. *Book of Birth*, he thought. Brains, babies, or buttholes—he didn't care what they were called—he was about to give a couple of "lost" archangel wannabe-Protectors a lesson in the "book" of brutality. A book that he helped write, coincidentally.

He gripped his whip and slowly flapped his wings across the arena toward the portal entrance to the dungeons. Jump needed time to steel himself—turn away from anything left, human or angel, and go to the dark place in his past. The place where only pain existed . . . and punishment.

Jump was alone—the only Protection interrogator ever who preferred, or had been allowed, to do the job by himself. That was a long, long time—it seemed like another life. Some other person that he no longer remembered. But what he did remember was how to get information out of someone. Someone who had every incentive in the world not to give that information to him. After all, what greater incentive was there to stay silent than the loss of your life after you spilled your guts?

There had been no question of whether or not Rain and Salvation could help in some way. Jump wasn't going to let his wife see him in that "light," and a bright, white "queen" couldn't allow herself to be bathed in the blackness that it took to get the job done.

"Plausible deniability," they used to call it before Protection's time: pretend it never happened. Or if you got caught at it, you had absolutely no clue it was happening on your watch. Didn't matter if it was a Protector or president, or priest for that matter—deny, deny, deny. Outlast any inquiry you allowed to take place. And over and over again, citizens proved it was the best strategy for getting them refocused on their own misery and off of questioning the authorities.

Jump knew Rain had manipulated him into the suggestion. He let her. And whether it was "cleansing" the garden for a power-hungry and maniacal monarch, or torturing that same butterfly to save one of his own, there were just some jobs that needed doing. Once someone, ruler or rapist, was convinced of the justness of their cause, there was no end to the evil they would do to defend it.

It didn't matter that, effectively, the two conniving liars were his parents—and *that* was some nightmare to wake up to—Jump's job . . . was to do the job. That was what he was good at, the best at.

Protection just called it "Taking Testament." And though most of their language was meant to distort and deny the truth, the process of beating and raping a confession out of someone. . . The name was about as literal as they ever got. They *took* testament from someone . . . along with a whole lot of other stuff. In fact, when an interrogator was finished, there wasn't a whole lot left to take.

Jump fluttered his wings and landed in front of the portal. He still couldn't understand why Fury wanted to leave Hell. She was twice as angry as him and probably just as damaged and depraved. Hell was home . . . for them both. But one truth he was able to lift out of the lies in Rain's book: whoever a Protector was going to resurrect, they had to want to go back. "Free" will—he was starting to get a handle on Life's understanding of the concept.

Push a person into a tight enough box, and they will beg you to let them out. In the version in Life's head. . . In fact, when Jump thought about it real hard, he had to laugh out loud and his voice echoed through the empty arena. *Obey and you will be blessed. Disobey and you will be cursed,* he thought. Lies aside, for an interrogator, or god gone rogue, there was no truer *Bible* verse than that.

Jump stepped toward the portal. Time for Life—God—to taste her own words. The portal twisted open and Jacob Oliver Blake, Protection interrogation agent #1, stepped through the entrance to the dungeons. And before the portal twisted shut behind him, he shouted to the entire cadre of caged creatures in the place, "Ladies, before this is over, you shall worship no god but me!"

— XXXI —

GO BACK TO move forward. Life and Lived both told Faith it was the only way. Save himself, then save Babette. And he wondered. Faith knew the exact moment he had failed her . . . and that was exactly where he would resurrect.

Father Benito listened. The voice seemed far away when it spoke to him, "Clear." And his chest heaved upward, and a blinding spike of pain shot from his chest to his eyes. Then it felt like he was choking—not breathing.

And then, all of a sudden, it just came over him and he was in it. Benito was in that light, and he came to a beautiful place, a sense of knowingness. Then everything made sense. It wasn't a dream—dreams were never clear. This . . . this was like fine crystal, and he felt himself smile. It had been years since he had lost his faith, and now—now it was coming back.

State doctors—if you could call the experimenting butchers that anymore—called it the "dying brain hypothesis" and they tested it as often as they had protectants to experiment on. It was the idea that when the brain was under stress, it released a flood of neurochemicals that created flashes of light, peace and calm.

The father knew that these weren't brain impulses, and he saw his body floating below him and he saw a bright light again, and then the voice said it again, "Clear." It sounded farther away this time. He felt a smaller fist hit his chest.

He wasn't afraid, after all he had been through this same feeling before. At least four times that he could remember.

During the thirty-three minutes he was "gone," Benito remembered spectacular music and aromas he had never smelled before. Beautiful scents like a cross between jasmine and lavender. But others . . . others were vile, and they violated his nostrils with putrescence and he faltered.

Could it. . .? Surely he wouldn't go there if it were? He had been faithful and he had served, and more importantly, he had yet to fulfill his destiny. Yet no one had spoken to his heart. Then he saw Babette —his dove—lying on a silver table, torn to shreds, bleeding and alone.

Then he was jerked back to the bright lights and there was a magnificent gate made of pearls. And they all—he had no idea who the others were—stood in front of it as it pulsated brightness. But when he looked closer, there were people—his people—and he recognized them. There was Babette, and a woman he had performed marriage rights for, and Babette's daughter and others he recognized but couldn't remember. Those seemed like decades-old acquaintances, now familiar friends again.

But the calmness and lack of pain—the serenity was everywhere at once.

Then he was jerked away from it and he remembered something about being beaten and bleeding . . . and bullet casings falling silently by his face . . . and the flashes of fire, and his ears were hurting. And he was above it watching an agent fire his rifle in slow motion and then the little brass casings fell like shiny tan snowflakes, slowly to the floor, right by his own head.

Then it just felt like sleep and he couldn't tell if he was awake or resting. And he wondered if he would wake up. If he did, he would tell them, all of them, Heaven was a real place.

That had been Benito's job for more than half of his life, but he had lost the fire of faith in that belief. He had needed only to look around him at the vileness and sorrow of Man to extinguish that flame and believe in the mission his own father entrusted to him. Then he preached from his pulpit with such an obvious lack of conviction that his own clergy leaders began to question his commitment.

The church investigated him and spied on him constantly. He was even sent back for re-seminary in order to rekindle his resolve. But he recoiled and turned inward, praying to God as his mother taught him. And when no comfort came from his faith or from the Lord, Benito had turned to the comforts of Man.

At first, it was just a sip of State swill now and then. Then it was more—liquor. But then in one euphoric night—too much swill and a late-night confession from one of his parishioners—he fell through the cold cracks in his faith, down and into the warm and wonderful wings of a dove. And it was good.

But no matter what Benito did to convince himself he would not burn for it, he couldn't silence the little voice in the back of his mind, telling him that somehow, someday he would be punished for his sins. The liquor helped douse the flames of his guilt, but it could hardly extinguish a fire that was started and stoked daily by people who blindly accepted the truths they were told.

Benito knew if the church ever found out. . . They could never find out! Excommunication was for offenses that the church could cover up, but a priest of the largest church in Seattle, breaking a covenant? Fornicating and falling in love? Such events were heresy of the highest order and would simply wind him up at the *Fifty* downtown, quietly condemned as an inconvenient truth of the church. Then that would lead them to the *other* thing.

Condemned would be better than anything at the *Fifty* after that. The father knew that. Dead and in Hell for his sins, or strapped to a chair at the *Fifty*, slowly going insane? The father figured there was precious little difference.

"Clear!" and the voice was louder again. Almost too loud, and the father winced at the pain in his chest and he tried to grab at it, but his arms wouldn't move. Then his eyes were blasted with bright white light again and then . . . nothing—darkness.

Then Benito heard it, "Waaake uuup!" This was a different voice, it felt far away and it sounded like . . . a bird screeching at him?

The darkness turned brighter and then a light descended down at him from above. Benito was back on the table in the middle of the room, staring up at a doctor and the two nurses from the hall. And behind them the two agents with their guns pointed at him. But he ignored them and looked straight up to the bright light. *Beautiful,* Benito thought as the light slowly grew bigger. *Simply magnificent!*

"Benitohhh, you have to get . . . up. . ." and that was squeaking and cooing—the voice *was* a bird. But it . . . spoke to him.

And the bright light grew steadily closer, and it got larger and then there were wings around it.

An angel, was the thought in Benito's head. *More real than I dreamed!* But if seeing was believing, the father's faith in his purpose was slowly fluttering back down from Heaven.

He watched the wings flap in slow motion, like a huge duck or a goose, landing on the river, lazily hovering downward to alight in the middle of he and his father's decoys.

And as the wings grew closer, Benito noticed that the feathers weren't normal. Then there was the sound of steel against steel, like pouring the metal credits from an offering basket into a drum. Even that sound was like music in his ears. "Get up, Benito," the voice said again. It was more familiar to him when it cooed this time, "You do not die today. You cannot."

As familiar as the voice was, it felt like it was more sure. . . Almost as if it knew when he *did* die, so certain that it wasn't today. Benito watched the wings get closer and closer. And then the bright light cleared up and became a shimmering bird. It was covered in feathers, the same as its wings. The only parts not covered with metal plumage were. . . *Talons?* Benito thought. But its palms weren't feathered . . . neither was its face.

Benito smiled up at . . . himself . . . as an angel. He frowned—he was hallucinating again—just like then—this wasn't an angel at all. *Another dream*, he thought. *Your mind still plays tricks on you.* Then he remembered. *You are dead . . . again.*

It was the only explanation. The last earthly thing he remembered was the orderly being shot to death and the blood. Then he had failed to give the man his last R's. So if this was really an angel, he wasn't going to Heaven. It hardly mattered—he knew how the *Fifty* worked.

Sooner or later, they would wake his mind back up and he'd wish he was dead.

"You are stronger than this, Benito," the flapping bird said, hovering barely above his chest now. "And I told you, you cannot die today."

But Benito was too tired, much too tired. "Let me go to Heaven," he said. Then he softly whispered to himself more than the hallucination he was having, "I must. . . God help. . ." It was more exhaustion than anything else, but habit from his mother as well. "I can't take any more suffering, Mother."

Then the bird spoke again, "For whosoever shall call upon the name of the Lord shall be saved," and then Benito saw the angel's talons come out. *On its feet, too,* he thought.

"So, my little fallen friend, to prevent further suffering and injury"—Benito smiled at the bird's words. He knew their literal translation—"you shall appoint as a penalty life for life, eye for eye, tooth for tooth, hand for hand, foot for foot, burn for burn, wound for wound, bruise for bruise." Then the bird sank all twenty of its razor-sharp talons deep into his chest. "Awake, little sleeper, and arise from the dead!"

— XXXII —

I WAKE UP to a *serious* bunch of bitching down the hall. At least, I think it's—sounds like it's down a hallway. Someone is screaming and screeching, like a dying. . . I have no clue, but it's kinda like . . . like birds killing each other or some crazy shit.

And I can't move, and holy—I'm face down! *Oh my God, I can't move!* And I'm . . . I feel. . .

I turn my head a little and the pain spikes into my spine so hard! "Aaaah!" the screaming doesn't help my back or anything else, because I can feel it—I—I know.

I scream through the thought, and I finally get my head turned. Brie is gone and so is the gurney that Tessa was on. And I'm in this— *Where am I now?* I try to turn the other way, but every move is killing me and I'm in here all by myself. Nothing looks the same.

I need my father to show up—he needs to get his ass in here, because like, I'm seriously—*Tessa is dead! How did this. . .?*

But when I try to move this time—*Which time is this?* I'm hallucinating or—*Please let me be hallucinating*, I think. Or . . . I don't know what. And then pain shoots though my chest and it's—it's just kicking my ass just like . . . just like. . .

They beat the shit out of me in the lobby, and they killed them both, back there. I try to scream again, but it comes out too quiet, and the pain burns into my breasts. "Jesus!" I manage a scream this time. Then bright spikes of light and pain hammer my head. And like, everything is fuzzy but bright in this—*Mexican Protection cell?* That's where I was—am—I don't know anymore.

The pain finally goes down enough, and I try to—I can only turn my head a little and I can feel the searing in them—I have breasts now? But the pain shoots again and shoves that shit out of my head and I—I'm . . . I just don't know shit! "Help meeee!" I scream it as loud as I can, and *mother . . . fucking . . . shit* the pain!

I start crying—sobbing down onto this steel table. And I'm cold . . . so cold. I wish I was back.

I barely remember the words—so zoned out when she dragged me there. But I can remember my mother chanting them by her bed at night, crying herself to sleep after my dad did that. I can hear her words in my head, *God . . . save me from my . . . my . . . my weak self. Save me from greed . . . and power. Save me from pleasure. Save me from betraying you, God. Amen.*

— XXXIII —

WHAT DID YOU little purgatories think was going to happen? I told all of you that! No! No one is coming. I'm dying right in that room. Don't you get it? Whenever he gets back, he's just gonna kill me. You think I would be *praying* if everything is just going to be. . .? You need to figure this out. I'm not supposed to help you. You have to do it for yourself. What the hell do all of you think redemption is, anyways? You have to *do* something—sacrifice something . . . for somebody else.

Goddamn squawking little purgatory hatchlings. Stop *whining!* Damn, if I ever do get back, you are answering to Rain about all this blasphemy, because *seriously*—not my fault. What? . . . What if you don't sacrifice? Then you just get trapped in your own little hell, that's what!

LIFE AND LIVED rested on their perches on opposite sides of their cell. "At last," Life said, observing the last stages of Fury's fall. "That should be sufficient."

Lived was not as certain. "She utterly butchered—you believe that was. . .?" he said. "She failed to recite even *half* of it."

"It is a small concern," Life replied. "The interpretation is the same —the important verses were included. And she spoke my name far more than the requirement."

"You and your 'small concerns.' That is two then," Lived said. "One final feather remains . . . to pluck from under his hell."

They both heard the portal door open and shut.

Life stood up, and then she walked slowly to the iron bars of their cage and grasped them, turning her hands—gripping the bars would assist with the sting of the whip. She peered down the dark tunnel. Then she spoke softly, beneath one of her last calm breaths, "The worst one."

Lived pushed his face between the bars and peered down the tunnel. "Ah," he muttered, "fashionably late."

Then the words wafted back down the tunnel, like the smell of Man-monkeys and misery. "Ladies, before this is over, you shall worship no god but me!" their son said.

— XXXV —

JUMP'S PLAN WAS simple—they always were. They typically resembled something like using a sledgehammer to pound in a spike. Finesse was not his strongest sin. "Break down the door, go down in their nasty little love nest, shine the light on the two of them, stuff 'em in a sack," was how he had so eloquently put it to Rain and Salvation. Then he went down to the lake to get something.

Whatever Jump retrieved was safely concealed beneath his feathers when he got back. Then he gave Rain and Salvation one last reassurance. "Nothing to it," he said. He leaned over and kissed Salvation on the forehead. Then he left.

But something had gone wrong. And when Jump didn't return on time, Salvation and Rain both got nervous. Since her husband had been pretty specific that they were not to go looking for him under any circumstances, Salvation knew even Rain was concerned when she said they should go check on his progress.

Rain had felt or understood, or some other sense that a Protector couldn't explain to a mere archangel, but whatever it was, Salvation could see fear written all over her daughter's face.

When the portal to the dungeons twisted open in front of Rain and Salvation, the foul stench of souls, burning in agony, blasted them both.

Salvation bent over and almost retched. "Son of a—what *is* that?"

Not that every time she had ever been to the dungeons they didn't stink worse than Hell itself—before Jump cleaned it up, anyway—but this . . . this was something else.

Rain held her mouth. She motioned for the two guardians standing watch to enter. Then she and her mother waited while they flew in to scout ahead. That was their purpose—protect the Protector, deal with danger, so a deity didn't have to do it.

A few moments passed, and with the portal door wide open, the tide of terrible smells was starting to recede. However, the guardians had not returned.

Salvation and Rain were just about to go in when the two golden angels flapped back out onto the arena field. They fluttered wildly and then crashed to their knees, and coughed and spit and shook their feathers. Ash and blood fell from their plumage and blanketed the arena floor, forming little circles of red on the ground around them.

When the guardians finally stopped, they both stood and the first one informed Rain that, though it was decidedly not dangerous inside, she should consider staying out.

"Mother," Rain said to Salvation, "I'm not certain you will want to see any of this."

Salvation felt older somehow and she didn't like the taste of it. But after cleansing the garden, what could her husband possibly do to an angel that she hadn't seen done to a Man-monkey . . . ten billion times before. She looked at Rain. Her daughter smelled older now. Some scent she recognized between the wafts of angel urine, shit and . . . blood? "I've seen more than you know, little girl," she said.

"I'll be fine." When she finally recognized the scent, she looked at Rain with her face full of motherly glow. She was concerned, but curiously and to herself, secretly happy. "You . . . you're—"

Rain frowned. "I am fully aware, Mother," she said. "However, now is certainly *not* the time." Then she turned her feathers to their full brightness and fluttered in front of Salvation toward the portal. It was never a question—they were going in to find Jump.

And Salvation flew, following behind her daughter, smiling and shining.

"*Mother*," Rain said without looking back, "don't."

Once Salvation and Rain got through the portal door, they quickly realized they would have to walk. The rock on the ceiling of the tunnel was burned black and when they flapped their wings, burnt, ashen blood fell on their heads. So they fluttered to the floor and walked down the tunnel toward the two liars' cell.

There was charred blood everywhere, caked and crusted to the rock walls and iron bars, like a tale of torment etched on old parchment.

As they passed each cage, every creature in it was in varying stages of melding back together, having obviously been blown apart and burnt. The ones that were further along in the process had long thin wounds oozing blood and puss from their flesh. And the moaning. . . Asylums were quieter.

Salvation and Rain kept walking, covering their mouths and noses with their hands. Slowly stepping over the blackest sections of the floor. They walked past Rain's self-denial of what she had sent Jump to do, stepped right over the burning corpse of Salvation's disbelief that her husband was capable of such things. And as they got closer to

223

the truth—approached the one cell they had come to see—the faint odor of burnt vanilla and the smoking smell of charred souls tore away any delusions Rain had had about the difficulty of ensuring, much less enforcing "To the Benefit of All."

Standing in front of Lived and Life's cell, neither Salvation nor Rain could believe—it just wasn't possible. The man they knew could never. . . They stood in silence, not even wanting to look at each other for fear that they would have to admit the truth.

Lived had a broken wing and singed feathers and when he limped his way over to help Life to her feet, Salvation could see what looked like . . . whip marks on his back?

Life took Lived's hand and winced and chirped as she struggled her way to her feet. Once she stood up, she favored one leg and held one of her arms with the other, like a sling. Then she pushed her wings forward, covering the front of herself as best she could. Her gaze was down and the look on her face was none that Rain or Salvation had ever seen. It was the look of a person who had been thoroughly beaten —had the will torn out of them.

And lying in the corner, limp and completely still, was one of Lived's snakes. Lived hesitated before he looked at them. "I am very reticent to inform you, Your Eminence. . ." Then he looked Rain in the eyes. It wasn't a look of defiance or his gaze of condescending curtness. To Rain, it looked . . . meek. "It seems our son. . . The apple . . . did not fall far from the proverbial tree." Lived glanced at his severed snake, and then he said, "Though it was very decent of him to leave me with one, don't you think?"

* * *

Guilt. That was the lynchpin of her plan. Life slowly raised her head, making sure to avoid eye contact with Rain. She had no idea how powerful the little whelp was yet. "I . . . I am sorry," she said softly. "I just find it. . ." She paused and looked down the hallway at the mayhem her second son had wrought. Holding back the smile was the hardest part. "I cannot reconcile. . . How is *this* to the benefit of all?"

— XXXVI —

WHILE RAIN AND Salvation attempted to get information that her son had already brutalized out of them, Life had felt the churning in her stomach growing. She was worried that she might actually retch right in front of them or "precarry" from the beating she endured.

Somehow, Life managed to keep both of them at bay. All four, when she thought about it, because neither she nor Lived had divulged any further information.

The wailing from down the dungeon tunnels subsided, and Life turned her head toward it and smiled. "They prepare."

Lived followed her gaze and took a deep breath, enjoying the sweet smell of burnt flesh and blood . . . and the aroma of impending birth. "Ah, the dawn of gods," he said. "Soon . . . very soon."

Life touched her belly and grinned. "Yes, she is almost ready." The aroma from Lived's bitch down the hall was masking her own scent. Hole was useful in more ways than Lived knew.

Life bent over and hunched her back and then she vomited a long stream of blood and bile onto their cell floor. When she was finished, she fell to her knees, and then slumped back against the wall. She slowly slid her knees up to her chest and crossed her arms around them. Her head hung down. "He *is* your son, isn't he?"

"Are you. . .?" Lived asked. Then he paused. Life never was one to accept assistance or pity. He considered asking anyway, but thought better of it and limped to the corner. His snake lie motionless. He bent over and picked it up. He shoved it inside the feathers on his waist, and then sat against the opposite wall. He stared across their cell for several seconds before he spoke, "And yet, he has somehow acquired your . . . charm, don't you think? Though, the irony of his words as he worked was more to my taste."

The entire time Jump interrogated them, while the other watched, tied to an adjacent cell, powerless to help, their son had quoted scripture. Neither of them could break free from the heavily-prayered Rosary beads that bound them, legs and arms spread like eagles caught in a web of iron bars on the cells.

When Jump began, they had both growled and roared in defiance and anger. But they quickly succumbed to exhaustion and the misery of trying to escape his whip, and their defiance turned to moaning and wailing for mercy.

It would take longer than it usually did to repair themselves. That much torn flesh and loss of blood was not easy to restore. So they passed the time doing the one thing that that kept them sane during their half-eternity incarceration, they traded quips and quills to amuse themselves at the other's expense.

"Your snake," Life said, "beaten by its own fruit." She let out a small caw and then she laughed. "I pray you find the irony in that."

Lived's face tightened as he pondered her words, frowning as he remembered Eve in the garden. Still healing himself, he found none of his clever responses. "Yes," he said. Then his face loosened a bit and he smiled. "As I said to them, your apple is an . . . acquired taste."

Life leaned back against the bars. The feelings in her womb were getting more powerful now. There were several times during Jump's "questioning" that she feared he might beat it out of her. However, she could feel the seed growing again. The girl—though male or female hardly mattered—the life inside her would be a god . . . and it would rule.

"That," Lived groaned and scrunched his face. "Ah. . . I was worried for a moment." He started to laugh, but the pain in his ribs made him stop.

Life looked up. "It was difficult to—I think I . . . I nearly giggled. How odd?"

"Did you see her expression?"

Life tucked her wings behind her. "Whose?"

"The whelp, of course," Lived said. "I was never worried about her bitch mother."

"Ah, yes," Life said, "she hasn't any idea."

"Neither of them do."

Life smiled at him and stretched out her damaged wing. The metal bones in it cracked and snapped as she popped them back into place. "I've told you this many times," Life said, wincing, "Guilt—it carries twice the potency of fear."

— XXXVII —

JACOB OLIVER BLAKE—Protection Agent Blake—badge number 333, freshly promoted from the interrogation division to PAIC, stretched his tight, black leather gloves over his hands. He stared straight into the interrogation cell as he reached in his pocket and felt for the syringe full of Judgment.

He was inches from the bastard—the man who destroyed his life, took his daughter, Amy.

It had been two years since he lost his little girl. He and his wife, Kelly, had never been the same since. Before Amy was gone, everything made sense and the three of them were happy. It was a good life. The PAIC lived well, and the way things were . . . well, that's how they were supposed to be, how they had always been.

In the beginning, Jake was worse than a rook—an agent in training at the Rookery academy, where Protection "Forged the Force" that would protect the citizens.

Jake figured he already knew everything there was to know about Protection, more than the instructors, for sure. After all, his father had prepared him for the rigors of training, and that man had been one of the most highly decorated agents in the history of the "Rook."

But stories weren't experience, so until he "got his feathers wet," his dad liked to joke, he would never fully understand what it meant to be an agent of Protection. "Get a little blood on your shield," he had told the eager young Jacob, "you can squawk after that. Be careful, though, because it doesn't wash off."

Despite his father's warnings, at Protection's "invitation"-only academy, Jake was an up-and-coming rook, soaring his way through his flock, faster than any other hatchling who graduated before him . . . except for his father, of course. But that was a different breed of old buzzard—a different time where mighty eagles bared talons and puffed out their chests for all to flee from and fear—an eternity ago.

Finally, Jacob was kicked out of the nest—he graduated. He was a freshly "cracked" hatchling agent, shining wings and shield insignia on his back. And he wore the badge like he'd earned it—bloody, hard and proud. Jacob Blake was a mighty agent of Protection . . . but not.

Until a graduate earned their wings and became a full-fledged agent —and there was only one way to do that—they were a hatchling, envied by rooks at the Rook, desperate to graduate and end their misery, and condescended to by every other full-fledged agent on the force.

Caught in the middle between being entrusted with heavenly duties as an agent and the hell of training at the Rook. And unless another agent took a hatchling under their wing, it was going to be a long flight through "purgatory."

Some agents feared they would never be called anything but a bunch of "humping hatchlings" or "pissing purgatories." Derogatory names almost as bad as being labeled a "citizen."

PAIC Blake wrapped his hand around the syringe in his pocket.

* * *

But something happened to "Jake," most people called him. No agent had seen fit to tuck the arrogant hatchling of the infamous Agent Blake—Jake's father—under their wing. "I don't want *junior* under my protection," they joked.

It seemed like every other purgatory from his class had found a place to perch. They had effortlessly flown from sentry to agent to citizen compliance. Some of them even went to Prime Officer protection—they became POPs guarding rich businessmen and powerful clergy. Others, with hardly a flap of their wings to glide them, landed at the peak of Protection's great mountain of misery itself—intelligence interrogator.

Meanwhile, Jake learned to do things that "other" way, the hard way. Every young agent, pissing purgatory or humping hatchling, knew what that meant—twice the patrols, twice the traffic-ticks, and twice the time taking testament from panic-pissing people on the street.

Disgruntled citizens marked Jake's career as he screeched and screamed his way through pedestrian compliance, traffic compliance, and he even did a stint of the shit duty on a clean crew—the ghosts.

It was hard to come out of a Protection clean crew and not have a little dirt on you, and he knew it. So many secrets, and he had to burn them all to ash—papers, prints . . . people, and not necessarily in that order. Jake burned every last trace of so many citizens, even he didn't remember their names.

But clean crews were where they sent burned-out agents to serve out the remainder of their sentences, feather-dusting furniture and firing the fingerprints off of every last ounce of a citizen's life. It was meticulous, meaningless and mind-numbing duty. But Jake dug in and did the job like he did anything. "Suck it up and do it to the best of your ability and better," was all his father ever asked of him.

But he finally made it to compliance, a full two years after every other fledgling from his flock at the Rook. Then he put on the coveted black mask and boots of a "snag and bag" agent . . . and he went to do "real" work.

PAIC Blake placed his thumb on the plunger of the syringe. It was the same shit this bastard had pumped into Amy. He smiled a little downturned grin and then wiped it away. Frank King, was about to get a taste of his own medicine . . . literally.

After the clean crew duty, Jake had settled into citizen compliance, and things sped up. He had a sort of "sixth sense" for the one duty that every citizen-stomping, beak-breaking, testament-taking agent loved—gutting the gogos—grabbing the guns from the God-fearing gun owners.

Agent Blake could sniff out a weapons cache like a "hump-hound sniffs for whores in heat," the old buzzard vets would laugh about it in the smoke-break room. After a successful raid, they would all smack him on the back and say, "AK, AR, or A-hole—shit, he smells better than a drone. If it fires something more dangerous than a fart, Blake's the first one to bust through the door and bash brains with his billy."

And he earned such a reputation by being so efficient at disarming dangerous dissenters that his department turned to no one else to lead the assault teams.

It got to the point that if the Scent-seeker module on a Vengeance drone caught a whiff of gunpowder or explosive, the whole briefing room groaned the next morning when the PAIC read the daily raid roster. There was no question who would be Agent #1 on the three-man team for that. And that only left two scrap spots for the rest of the flock to squawk and fight over.

Because by the time Agent #1 silently held up his fingers, counting to three outside a protectant's bedroom. . . After first fire, what was the point? The unlucky weapons-harboring citizen was as good as gone—checked into the *Fifty*. Agents #2 and #3—what fun was that?

Life was good for Agent Blake from then on, and through hard work and guts, not to mention a few thousand guns and the countless tens of thousands of rounds of ammunition that went with them, he was poised to arrive at the pinnacle of his "chosen" profession—PAIC. Then he did what no mere mortal should: He started thinking . . . for himself.

Just a quick stick, PAIC Blake thought, running through the plan in his head. He always ran the plan in his head. *Then hit the stairwell, down to the garbage alley and disappear.* That plan was already in place.

Thinking. . . Normally deadly for a citizen, whose best chance at survival was compliance and submission, but for a god-like PAIC of Protection? Jake figured he could keep it in his head.

Sure, he and his wife, Kelly, and their daughter, little Amy, were happy . . . happier than most. And why shouldn't they be? Agent Blake was at the top of the roost now, finally responsible for "Ensuring Peace and Prosperity. . ." It was a job that he'd excelled at for years. And the job rewarded him for doing it well. He saved citizens from themselves. The Rook taught him that, too.

Because a disarmed and compliant citizen was a peaceful citizen, and peace brought prosperity to all. "Ipso-facto," the instructors at the academy liked to joke. Though when rookie Jake Blake looked it up, he figured they messed up the true meaning.

"All citizens must endure to keep the peace at all costs," they said. Sometimes that cost was high. Agent Blake knew that—he had brought about that cost on more than one occasion.

Ensuring peace and prosperity . . . "for all." It was that last part, the one that was never spoken, that stuck in his craw like grain he couldn't swallow. A little nuance left to interpretation. That was how language worked. Nuance and translation—make sure that whatever was said could be interpreted any way the people in charge saw fit. But they didn't teach that at the Rook.

Over twenty years after he was cracked, Jake still learned everything that "other" way.

The easy way—compliance—was Protection's preferred citizen response. Yet PAIC Blake could not understand why so many citizens chose the hard way to their own certain death.

Compliance brought peace and commerce, and commerce ensured peace and prosperity. There could be no simpler logic than that. He never saw the irony of forcing compliance to—why would he even wonder? The things Agent Blake did, he did because he was Protection, and Protection kept the peace and the peace brought prosperity . . . for all. That's what he was taught. He never understood why citizens resisted it. And he might never have . . . if it hadn't been for Amy.

For all. . . PAIC Blake thought. He gripped tighter. The tiny syringe full of Judgment might not be enough "wet on his wings" to quench his thirst for revenge. Today, it would have to do.

When he finally slowed down and thought about it, Jacob Blake . . . because at that point he had already made his decision. . . But as Agent Blake stood in the rain outside the State Med-mart, his tears mixing with the drizzle and the futility of life, before it all ran down his face, he finally understood the price of compliance.

"For all," actually meant that occasionally, but really more often than that, an individual citizen's peace and prosperity would *not*— could not—be ensured. For doing so would jeopardize prosperity . . . for all.

PAIC Blake could hardly contain himself now. *You killed her, you evil bastard! And now—*

Set aside the fact that no one really knew where the framing tenet of the new world came from, it didn't really matter. What did matter was what the highest levels of State and Protection interpreted it to mean.

An individual citizen's prosperity could not be assured when weighed against the prosperity needs of so many others. Only afterward did Jake realize it was just a convenient way to cover up the truth.

Regardless, the result was the same: suspend all dissent, force compliance on each citizen individually. Then a select few would be able to control an increasingly common and overly-available work-force of billions.

As Agent Blake, none of what was behind it had mattered. Until one day, just another ordinary citizen compliance day, a name popped up at the Utah datacenter—"Amy Ann Blake."

A common enough name, to be sure, but one that would change the fate of humanity and the Earth itself . . . eventually. It was a tiny mistake—a "citizen slip"—but that's how catastrophes happened. A spec of fly in the ointment and the trajectory of one's life changed forever.

And as the Protection paper-pusher in Utah typed the name on the printout into his computer, the auto-complete-tech on the application filled in the name and then the man pressed "ENTER" before he finished typing. Then up popped, "Amy Anne Blake." Anne . . . with an "e." One tiny little letter—small enough to go completely unnoticed, yet one that would have mountain-shaking consequences.

Agent Blake would have never even considered that his child might be randomly selected for inclusion in one of Protection's contractor trials. And it was unthinkable that she would be given that contractor, K&T Enterprise's, experimental interrogation drug without his consent. Unfathomable that his little angel would be stuck in the arm with a needle by a monkey-minion follower of the very man next to him . . . *twice* before Agent Blake ever found out.

His daughter had fallen victim to an unfortunate clerical error. She was sentenced without trial or consent to a living hell of blinding headaches and screaming nightmares . . . before she was finally condemned at the State Med-mart downtown. Wars in Heaven were started for less.

And why would Agent Blake have considered any of it? Every

Protection agent's entire family—right along with anyone who had the credits to exempt them—was flagged as "NP," non-participatory, excluding them from many things that an individual citizen had to "endure" for peace and prosperity to be "ensured."

Two years ago, Agent Blake stood outside the State Med-mart downtown, directly adjacent to the very building he was in now. It was in that very moment—his tears mixing with Seattle's mind-melting drizzle—that Protection Agent Jacob Oliver Blake, Interrogator, badge number 333, finally met the demons of frustration, helplessness and rage that ordinary citizens made friends with every day. And it was also when he decided that no matter the cost, he would bring judgment and justice to the one responsible for it.

It took another year for him to claw his way to the coveted PAIC position he now held. And another to make his way to being in charge of all Prime Officer Protection agents. An eternity, it seemed to him. Interrogating, intimidating and violating all manner of man—mother to monster—in a cell just like the one they watched from the observation room.

Those demons flew around in his head most days and screamed and screeched at him like angry eagles in his dreams each night. But like a good compliant citizen . . . he endured.

PAIC. There wasn't a hatchling or rookie at the Rook who didn't dream of it. But the only thing that PAIC Blake dreamt of was dragging this murdering monster out in the street and sending his citizen-raping soul to Hell.

— XXXVIII —

FATHER BENITO'S CHEST heaved violently, up and off the steel gurney, and his whole body tensed up and he screamed out, "Aaaah!" And his eyes got wide and he screamed at the pain again, "Aaaah!" The straps held him down.

Then the nurses started picking and poking at him, but he could hardly hear them.

And he barely heard the wave behind them, "Bravo eight-six, this is Kilo, over," the voice squawked over one of the agents' mini-wave. "I need a drone up here. We got heavy contact—repeat, heavy contact from an—it's a—"

And then a response cut the wave off, "Negative, Kilo. Primary tasking, priority—"

"Aaaah!" and that was the first voice squawking again. And then the wave terminated.

Something exploded and the entire building shook.

"Son of a bitch," one of the Protection agents against the wall said. "What now?"

Benito turned his head toward the agents. He recognized the one who shot the orderly in the hall.

That agent looked at Benito's face briefly, before he looked at the doctor. "You got this?" he asked the doctor. "I want him judged and preparing for testament when we get back."

The doctor looked at the nurses and said something to them.

Benito didn't hear what it was, or didn't understand it—he was focused on the waistband of the first Protection agent from the hall. He stared at his little King 9mm, tucked in the agent's pants.

I need that, he thought. Then he felt his restraints being loosened and then something—someone placed something in his hand. *Cold*.

The little veteran nurse from the hall was fed up and done with the *Fifty*. The constant fear of rape at the hands of the orderlies, and the condescending and often brutal treatment from the butchers that called themselves doctors. Seeing all manner of poor citizen come through the front doors, only to watch them leave through the alley in a body-bin. And now they wanted her to help them condemn a priest to Judgment?

While everyone in the room reacted to the explosion outside, and then the squawking on the radio, she loosened the father's straps. She knew she had little hope of helping him now, but she also knew that sometimes a little hope . . . went a long, long way.

She slipped the tiny scalpel from the instrument tray and gently placed it into the father's right hand. Then she wrapped his fingers around it and gently squeezed his hand three times. That was it—all she could do. She knew she had even *less* hope of resisting Protection agents. At least this way, she wouldn't end up face down on a gurney being "interrogated."

She had almost let go of the priest's hand when she felt him respond—his fist tightened two times. He understood!

Father Benito felt the three squeezes. "I love you," it almost felt like she spoke the words to his mind.

You too, he thought as he squeezed back.

Then he felt it all over him—the angel who came to him while he was dead on the gurney. And he also felt something he hadn't in a long time—faith. In fact, for some reason he knew that was the angel's name—Faith. Then he felt something else from that angel, something—a feeling he hadn't had in a long time. *Power*, he thought.

As strong as that feeling was, he hesitated, frozen in fear. But then Benito gritted his teeth and did the one thing he knew might help him overcome it. *When I am afraid . . . I put my trust in you!*

Before Benito realized it, he sprang off of the gurney and the doctor's throat was cut and the man clutched at his neck and blood sprayed between his fingers, turning his white coat red. And then Benito was on his feet and the second nurse screamed and then the room went into a slow motion cinewave.

And Benito saw the fear in the young nurse's eyes, but he wouldn't harm her. Then the other nurse was running at the one screaming, plowing her way toward her colleague through the sticky slowness of Benito's perception of time. He read her citizen-badge. *Thank you, Agatha*, he thought. The two nurses were headed for the door, and their screams were muffled and he barely heard them.

Then things sped up for an instant, and the scalpel stabbed into the doctor's belly and the man fell to the floor.

Then the molasses feeling again. Benito could actually smell it. And he was stuck, watching the barrel of the first agent's submachine gun slowly raising up at his chest.

And the room sped up again—this time lightning fast—and the

father rammed his forearm up at the agent's rifle, caught the bottom of it and it pointed above his head and—*Brrrrt!*—bullets ripped into the ceiling and rock rained down.

Then the scalpel rammed up and into the agent's armpit. And a muffled yell, and then it sliced through his black face mask and along his neck and blood sprayed, and the agent hunched over and then three stabs to the back of his neck, a crunch into a vertebrae, and the agent's body dropped like a sack of rocks.

Slow motion again . . . blood pumped from the first agent's neck . . . and then the muffled voice of the second agent came like a faraway loudspeaker, "Benito . . . Octavio . . . Benedetti . . . you . . . are . . . hereby . . . remanded . . . to . . . protect—"

Then the father's world went into fast-forward and his mind raced—*gun-coming-up, keep-the-barrel-away-from-you, push-it-away-with-your-other-hand. Go-Benito, faster*, the thought raced through his head. *Grab-his-arm-stab-him-in-the-elbow, neck-neck-neck, pull-his-goggles-off, eye-for-an-eye!* And two stabs, deep into the agent's eye sockets, and it was over!

Benito stood in the middle of the room. He stared down at two dead and bleeding Protection agents and one sack of blood doctor at his feet. And the door was just swinging closed and he caught a glimpse of the back of the little veteran nurse, whisking her panic-stricken trainee down the hall again.

Benito's father had trained him his whole life for this moment, but the fear was deafening. He knelt down next to the first agent. The artery in his neck was just finishing pumping the last ounces of his protective fluid out. Benito pulled his pistol from the man's waistband

and then he paused for a second and looked at the little gun in his hand. Then he looked at the agent's submachine gun.

Benito stared at the gun for a few seconds, and then he looked at the agent's black boots and uniform and he smiled.

Then the building's alarms sounded.

— XXXIX —

SALVATION WAS LOST, and more than a little bit panicked. She stood in the middle of Rain's throne chamber and stared at nothing.

The scenes from the dungeon assaulted her mind, tearing apart the image of the person she knew as her husband. Sure, she had seen Jump commit every type of violence during the great cleansing of the garden, but that wasn't completely his fault—he had no choice. But did he . . . have a choice?

From the look of the dungeon—a person, or angel, had to like doing that. The scene down in the tunnels was gruesome, but the thought that her husband was responsible for all of it was worse. It was unbearable to think that he had done that over and over in life, but that's what that devil bastard told her. Jump—her husband Jake Blake . . . had been a monster.

But Lived was a liar, wasn't he? That devil would say anything to get what he wanted. "I just can't believe. . ." she muttered, "He did all of that. And that wasn't the first ti—"

"Mother," Rain said. She searched for the words. She felt that the two liars in the dungeon were manipulating everyone toward an end that only they understood. Yet Jump was gone, Fury was still missing, and from what little Life and Lived divulged, Faith was with them. Which was to say nothing of the flock of little hatchling purgatories that Fury was "training." Yet, the immediate issue seemed more pressing to her. She had never seen her mother's love and trust in her father falter. "You cannot believe anything they said. You know this."

"You saw it," Salvation looked at Rain and said. "You saw what he did. You sent him—wait, you *sent* him down there. Did you know he. . .?" She really didn't want the answer.

"He chose to go," Rain said. "He knew what needed to be done, and he did it."

"But you," Salvation said. "What kind of. . .? That was monstrous. He's an—"

"He is the Great Dragon of Judgment!" Rain shouted. "You say I am naive. Do not delude yourself. Judgment . . . justice, these things have cost."

"But what about mercy?" Salvation asked her. "And compassion? What happened to you? Isn't there any of that left?" She shook her head and put her face in her hands. "What about love? How will. . .? How can he . . . after that?"

Rain fluttered over, and gently pulled her mother's hands down from her face. "Those are the most beautiful of things, yes," she said. "However, they also come with the highest sacrifice. And though I may disagree with her on most things, Life is correct about some. To the benefit of all. He can find peace, for those who are well, have no need of a physician, but those who are sick. . ."

"He is lost," Salvation sobbed. "I don't know if I can ever. . ."

Rain's tone was sadder this time. "Do not be hasty with judgment," she replied. "It is a sharp and dangerous sword, as likely to kill with its hilt . . . as it is to condemn with its tip."

Salvation looked up slowly. Tears trickled down her cheeks as she looked into her grown-up daughter's eyes. "How did you get. . .?" she said. But there was something behind Rain's words. When she looked closer, there was the tiny start of a tear, welling up in her daughter's eye. She hadn't seen that since. . . And no mother's own suffering could take priority over that. "What's wrong?" she asked. "You don't cry, not since . . . the Med."

It wasn't the time, but then again when was it going to be? Rain had hidden herself as long as she could bear, sheltering in front of her parents' blindness and denial that she had long since grown up. The fabricated acts of a little girl, peaking from behind the hidden truths that she was becoming a young lady.

It had helped keep her father's "talk" thankfully delayed. She knew if they ever had it, he would smell it on her right away. Rain knew her father was not the monster her mother feared him to be, but whatever he was, he was certainly not naive. He would know.

Salvation had been easier to fool. Rain knew her mother's mind still lived with her little angel back in Life's life. The Amy that Rain had been was etched into her mother's right heart. Her mother most likely harbored images of stroking Amy's hair and humming softly to lull her to sleep. What mother would want to leave that memory behind?

Rain pondered her response, but she could feel the time running out. Life and Lived had a plan, she smelled that in the dungeon. She could also smell something else—something foreign and unfamiliar to her and that could not be good. But try as they had, she and Salvation had simply been talked in circles by the two lying devils. Whatever it was would have to wait.

Even with half an eternity at her back, the relativity of how long time could be had been hard for Rain to understand. Until she had something that she desperately wanted . . . immediately. The liars' plot would soon be rooted out—her father was single-minded once he pointed his anger at something. Rain had finally witnessed the truth of that in the dungeon. But her new urgency needed to be dealt with.

"Mother, she has to. . ." Rain said. Then she stared into the fall.

"She has to what?" Salvation asked.

"She has to . . . find herself."

Salvation's face went blank and her eyebrows raised up. "Rain," she raised her voice, "you . . . you're in love."

Rain stopped and fluttered to the floor. She stood motionless, staring at her mother, and then she slowly folded her wings behind her back. There was no going back now. To lie would be to go against her own word. "We must get her out," she said. "She has to find forgiveness in her hearts . . . or she will never be redeemed to Heaven. And we can never be—"

"Oh my *God*," Salvation said, blasphemy or not.

— XL —

WHEN FATHER BENITO peeked out of the medical room, the long hallway was lit up with flashing red lights. The lights above the big steel doors to each cell alternated the darkness from a crimson, hazy bright to total black.

He gripped onto the first agent's submachine gun and felt the pockets of the man's black combat vest for the extra clips. He didn't know why, but he knew who the voice in his head was, spurring him forward and giving him advice. The first command was, "Get all his gear . . . and the weapon."

But he wondered what the voice meant by, "You won't fail her this time, Benito. I won't let you."

This time? he thought.

The sound from the alarms was louder in the hallway. He eased to the center of it. *Where am I?*

"Interrogation wing," the voice in his head answered almost immediately. "They were preparing you."

Benito knew what that meant—he would have been put on trial, given Judgment, and then raped and beaten in that room until he was condemned. *I have to get to her!*

"We—you will," the voice said.

Then all of the speakers above the cell doors blared a horn-like blast and then a voice crackled a little too loudly, "Benito Octavio Benedetti, you are hereby remanded to Protection. State your compliance."

Benito found the remote wave-eye peering at him from the ceiling. Then he slowly raised the agent's MP7 and sent a short burst of 9mm rounds into it—*Brrt!*—getting the feel for the gun. And the wave-eye's lens burst, and metal and plastic and glass showered the floor beneath it.

"Time to go!" the voice shouted to him. "She's down the hall, number five. Go!"

Benito looked above the door to the room he'd just killed three people in. He shook his head as he read the number. *Three*. . . She was only two doors away. He turned and ran.

Another explosion outside rocked the building again and Benito stumbled and fell to the ground. *You will never make it*, he thought to himself.

"Get up," the voice said to him. "Have a little faith."

Faith. Benito didn't have much left, if he had any. How could he? If there was a Hell, he couldn't imagine it would be any worse than the building he was trapped in. He pushed himself to his feet.

The clanging alarms were deafening now, and the alternating red and darkness made the place feel like Hell, too. What he imagined it to look like. And he wondered where the—

Brrrrt-brrrrt-brrrrt! Bullets zinged past Benito's head so close that it made the alarms sound quiet, and he instinctively grabbed at his ear and then he ran. He searched for the number on the door through the dark red alternating light.

The darkness was helping him, as a Protection agent would have surely been able to hit him from the other end of the hall. But the black was also making it hard to find the number above the door. *It's only two doors, Benito*, he thought to himself, *Mother of Mercy.*

And then there it was, and he rammed into it with his shoulder as he pushed on the big bar handle. And he grunted. *Locked!*

"Shoot it! Shoot it!" The voice in his head was more urgent now.

And Benito backed up two steps and a bullet grazed the back of his thigh—"Aaaah!"—and he raised the gun and sent a huge burst into the lock—*Brrrrrrrt!*

Sparks flew, metal blew back from the door, and brass casings showered the floor, clinking on the concrete, barely audible between the alarm clangs.

"Ram it down!" the voice shouted.

Benito rushed at the door with his shoulder and burst into the cell. When he saw what was inside, the last two ounces of faith he was holding onto were ripped out of his soul.

The two men had their interrogating, raping black pants halfway up. And Benito went wild.

Brrrt-brrrrrt-brrrrrrrrrrrrrrt! He sent the remaining rounds in the gun into the first one, the one behind her. The bastard flew backward, body jerking and jolting wildly until he slammed into the side of the room, and then fell sideways to the floor, leaving a huge stripe of blood on the gray rock wall. And then—*click-click-click*—the submachine gun was empty.

Number two had his pants up, and he rushed at Benito.

"Hit him in the face with the gun!" the voice in his head shouted.

And Benito punched with both arms, just as the second one got to him, catching the man just under the nose, and he heard a crunch and the bastard flipped backward.

"Knife," the voice in his head yelled. "Use the knife!"

Before Benito realized it, he was on top of the second bastard, stabbing the combat knife he'd taken off the agent. He yelled and screamed, and then he grabbed the handle with his other hand and he stabbed down at the man's chest with both hands. High over his head and back down again he plunged the blade, until he heard the voice again.

"God help me. . ." it said, but this voice wasn't inside his head this time, and it was softer. It was in the room and it sounded beaten. "Benito . . . please . . . please help me!"

— XLI —

I KNOW HE'S a priest! Like, what did you little purgies think? Look, I don't care if you resurrect as a man, a monkey or a moron with a robe on, you think Life gives a shit about that? She'll crack you like a rookie, just as soon as look at your dumb asses. So get it straight! This isn't redemption in there, this is pure revenge, plain and simple. You either do it—

What? . . . No, I just told you, this is resurrection, not redemption, and resurrection's a bitch. First time or the fifth, doesn't matter. Not to him, not to her, not to—Who? . . . Ha, ha, ha, very funny. Yes, smartass, it matters to them. But like, those agents died a *long* time ago. They're soulless. . . . Redemption for them? Like that's happening. Jesus Christ, that job is all about suffering! Can't you see that?

Could they? . . . I guess they—shit, I don't know. That's like, up to Rain or some shit—I don't have the power to—stop asking me stupid questions that aren't about this. You little bitches, you are never going to leave the nest, are you? Why they stuck me with a flock of pee-pissing purgies. . .? That's what you are, you know—humping hatch-lings.

You try to do this job . . . this dumb . . . Man-monkeys will eat you alive! Get hard, whining little purgies, else Life's gonna spike you to a cross and burn ya. Why am I even. . .? Start figuring it out or I'll cut your wings off myself.

What? . . . Me? They already caught me. You know that. That's how this mess started, remember? Bet your tail feathers that the clock's ticking on that shit. I figure I got like, one day left before they find me in here. Once they do . . . they're finding you too.

Oh my G—stop squawking, stop squawking! Listen, fold your wings around you and hang onto your talons, little purgies, because Hell's about to get hot.

— XLII —

FROM INSIDE THE nothingness, Jump watched Fury's fall.

One day, he thought. That's what those two liars told him. *Parents . . . prisoners . . . punishers*, the thoughts drifted through his mind.

By now, Jump knew that Rain and Salvation had probably figured out that he wasn't coming back. And that meant they would go looking for him. They wouldn't like what they found.

To someone—citizens, gods . . . angels, it didn't matter—anyone who hadn't had to do it. . . Until they were held accountable for the truth in the words of a testament, no one had a clue how to interrogate someone like that. Misinterpret the words of a protectant? Your fate would be worse than theirs. That was a certainty. God or government—failure was for the fallen and that was not what anyone at Protection "signed up" for.

Language was like that—words started wars. That was another universal constant. Mess up the translation . . . burn in Hell.

Been there, done that, Jump thought. *Not goin' back.*

Jump *was* going back to Hell, though. His own, not Life's life. He knew she was planning on trapping him back in the garden. The rest of them, too. And it wouldn't be one eternity this time. She wasn't satisfied with two thousand years as God on the first. . . Come to think of it, he had no idea how long she had been the Protector. But there was no reason for him to believe she'd settle for only one more shot at it. Life was a lifer—she would never retire.

No, he got that information, although they probably thought he couldn't smell it on them. Life and Lived each planned to take back the garden and rule over it forever. Little tyrants didn't like their toys taken away.

That meant Rain's prayer book was right. If a fallen went back and took revenge instead of seeking redemption. . . Hell, salvation, forgiveness, or vengeance—it didn't matter which one they prayed for. If they wanted it bad enough, they would have to ask "God"—the one from *that* eternity, not Rain's. And that meant Life would have to exist . . . as a god, not some ravaged and raped prisoner in a dungeon between Heaven and Hell. Life would have to be the ruler—the Protector—to answer a fallen's prayer. And Jump knew there could only be one of those.

It was the same as the garden. One day in eternity—longer than he realized back at the great cleansing. Life couldn't build the whole thing in seven days, any easier than Jump could burn it down in one. But burn it he and Salvation and Fury had, and that day lasted . . . forever, it seemed.

But one day to an archangel or a god wasn't the same as it was for a Man-monkey, or the little Woman-monkey he had to go and "save."

Relativity of time, he thought, *what a bitch.*

Not only did it feel like some events took forever, while some raced by like Fury flapping her wings, but the eternities overlapped on themselves, too. One Man-monkey's events might happen at a totally different time than an archangel's perception of them. The two liars tried to explain it to him. And in between dodging his fire-feathers and Jump pounding Life with the literal interpretation of her "Word," they had almost twisted his mind in a knot.

He knew that's what they were trying to do. So after he paused to take a rest, when he started back up, he said, "Then this is going to feel like two eternities for you."

Next week, next month, or the next ten seconds watching himself as a PAIC in life, Jump knew what Fury wanted more than anything. He didn't blame her—that incestuous, raping bastard's soul ended too quickly . . . both times. Pitched out a window for serving Judgment to Jump's daughter, Amy, or cut to pieces at the Battle of the Books under Fury's wings and talons, Frank King hadn't suffered nearly enough either time . . . in Jump's not so humble opinion.

That's what Fury went back for—revenge on her father. It was the only reason she would seek out the assistance of the two liars, because if Jump had it figured right, the girl would never ask Rain.

Faith. . . That one had been harder for Jump to understand. The man was hiding something when he was a priest and it seemed he still had secrets as an archangel. But once he whipped and beat the disgusting creature that Lived kept for a whore in the dungeon, the whole thing made sense. That part of it anyway.

The brief period Jump knew the father back in life, the man had been searching for something more than faith. You couldn't talk to faith, smile at faith, laugh with it or any other thing that would give a man comfort.

Blind, boozing old cocksucker, Jump smiled at himself. Faith was blind as a bat . . . back in life, anyway. He could barely find anything without his glasses. But what the father was really searching for was love, and when he didn't get it from God . . . well, that wasn't really the type of love that a Man-monkey went looking for in the first place.

Jump almost laughed out loud. *You can't fuck faith*, he thought. Though after his interrogation of the creature-bitch, Babette, apparently that wasn't true.

And when sucking on his little tin tit full of State swill didn't give the father enough comfort, Babette had offered him something else to —Jump scrunched up his face at the thought.

His last recollection of the hideous creature was from the dungeon, but back in Life's life, he had caught a glimpse of her at Frank's loft.

She hadn't looked all that good after he sent a couple of feathers through her chest, though. He guessed she looked good enough to a priest who had long since seen the backside of middle-age, especially one who had probably *never* seen the backside of a woman in his entire life. Anyway, blondes weren't his type.

The father ending up in Purgatory and then Hell for abandoning Babette at the *Fifty?* . . . Only one place the archangel, Faith, was going to go back to for *his* redemption.

Redemption or revenge, Jump knew those were the stakes. For an angry archangel there could be no greater reason to tempt the Devil or his concubine bitch, Life, for that matter.

So once Jump beat the truth out of them, he cut his own deal with the two liars. That was in the book, too. He had to willingly "ask" for Life's help. Never mind that by that time, she was pretty compliant. And he said to her, "Wages of sin—stings like a bitch, doesn't it?" He remembered her trying to go back on the deal she cut with his father, the Devil. Only this time, it would be Jump who reneged on their deal.

Jump watched Fury's fall. He stared at himself as a vengeful PAIC, all dressed up in his black attack-suit. His rook-rags at the Rook never looked so tightly pressed. And he watched himself reach his black glove into his jacket pocket. That's where the syringe was. Jump knew that from before. He would never forget that day.

The next ten seconds would send Jump's mortal life on the trajectory that brought him to where he was now, reunited with his girls, Kelly and Amy—Salvation and Rain. Failure to bring ultimate success. *Wife in Hell and my little angel in Heaven*, though, when he thought about it that way, the wife part didn't sound so great.

If Salvation had gone down in the dungeon—and there was no way she would let Rain go down there by herself again—then his wife was probably wondering if ruling in Hell with her husband was worth it. He'd deal with that when he got back. *One ass-beating at a time*, he thought.

Revenge—kill Frank King, the bastard that experimented on his daughter, rob Mercedes of her own revenge—or redemption—forgive and forget and let things stay the way they worked out in the first place.

He *had* gotten revenge on Frank eventually, and so had Mercedes at the Battle of the Books, so what was the point of doing it a different way . . . again?

But the toughest part about revenge, Jump had found out that other way, was that it was like pouring blood into a big dark cave full of vampires. No matter how many wastes of blood he threw into it, the hole would just never fill up.

Jump stared into Fury's fall, at his own hand coming out of his pocket.

It was a failure the first time. A rarity in Agent Blake's career. And he would have gladly taken the whipping for it if he was back at the Rook. But a whipping wasn't what he would have gotten, so he had run, escaped, disappeared. And he never had any clue how Frank knew what he was going to do to him.

— XLIII —

INSIDE THE INTERROGATION observation room, the PAIC continued his little pre-bribe negotiation speech and Frank King listened, as they both stared into the dark half of the cell. Little Mercedes' body was still limp in the chair on the bright side of the cell. Once Frank was done negotiating credits with this agent, he would have an orderly go in and strap her face-down on the gurney—get her ready.

The observation room was tight—it would only fit a few—but it didn't take much room to house an orderly, a doctor, and a flunky from research and development. In the past, they'd had a nurse from the *Fifty* present, just in case there was some nasty cleanup, but none of them could handle it once the interrogators showed up. Many of them just ended up running from the room crying, so Protection stopped requiring their presence during the interrogations. They could clean up when it was over.

The observation rooms *did* have some safeguards that made the tight space even more cramped than it should've been. A ballistic film on the one-way glass was a pretty standard precaution, but after a protectant smuggled a bomb into one of the interrogation rooms and blew out that glass, killing the observers behind it, the rooms were retrofitted with ballistic barriers. No one at Protection was taking chance on that mess again.

They stared into the dark half of the cell.

Frank leaned into the glass. "Who *is* that?" he said under his breath.

Had Jump been focused on anything but watching Fury's fall and himself as a PAIC, pulling the syringe out of his pocket, his piercing angel-eyes might have noticed the other figure in the interrogation cell, bathed in darkness on the left . . . and covered in blood.

"Oh, son of a bitch," he said when he saw her. "Little playin'-possum pain in my ass. Clever girl."

"Had we known she was a twin," the PAIC said to Frank, "it might've been easier to stop them from—"

"What twin?" asked Frank. "Stop who?"

"Her," the agent said. Then he pointed into the darkness. "They martial-lawed her up pretty badly in the lobby."

Frank strained his eyes, trying to see into the left side of the cell. The basement of the *Fifty* was no better equipped than its upper floors. Quaint old-world techno still permeated its walls like ancient arteries, barely bringing enough electro to run the dark dungeon. Frank reached for the switch to the spotlights over the left side of the cell.

"Don't . . . do that," the PAIC said. He moved his hand back into his pocket. "I'm keeping her in the dark until I get someone in there. The serum will have her sensitive to it. I don't want her injuring herself before they can take her testament."

"Whose testament?"

The PAIC turned toward him. "Her sister," he said. "Wait, you're saying she *doesn't* have a twin?"

Frank chuckled. "Not that I know of," he said. "Unless my wife was

—" He thought about it for a minute. He had the wave of the birth. He'd watched it a few times in his office just to see Babs screaming again. He would know if there was another—*Ridiculous*, he thought. "No . . . no twin." But he was curious now, and he reached for the light switch again.

— XLIV —

JUMP SAW FRANK reaching for the light switch. In his heightened perception of events and time, the bastard's finger was moving ultra-slowly. But it didn't have to move fast to get to the switch and flip it, and if he did. . . Jump could see that the whole thing was about to turn into a "feather-fuck," his instructors back at the Rook used to call a screaming and screeching shit-storm of mayhem.

If Fury did it now, they might all get stuck back in life. *Shit*, Jump thought, *I didn't even have time to explain it to her.* He'd been searching for Fury for hours, so he could tell her the way out of this, but there she was. *Right in front of my face. Dammit!*

He knew it was the best place to hide for an ambush, training or not. And just when he thought he had the whole thing under control.

"It's just a training scenario," Jump's instructors at the Rook had drilled that into every rook, "no more real than a dream. If you think of every situation that way, you'll survive. Freak out, fly or freeze, and we'll be scraping your shield off the wall for breakfast."

So Jump ran it in his head as fast as he could—*Syringe in my pocket. Gotta stick it and miss, then run. Frank's gotta live—cocksucker, anyway. Kill that fucker later. That's Mercedes on the left—shit day for her. Stop Fury from—*

And he saw Fury's head lift up a little and then she opened her eyes and whispered something to Mercedes.

Shit, Jump thought. Because that's where every plan went once the shooting started.

Then the lights came on.

— XLV —

I THINK I blink—some light hits my eyes and I squint. And that sends a shard of pain right behind my eye like a migraine, or a bad hang-day with Brie and Tessa, and then I see like, blinding light and my head.

Head's on fire, I think. The pain is—it's killing me. Everything hurts.

Where am I? I try to move. *Still strapped to this . . . chair? Not where I. . .? The gurney—I was on my stomach.* I try not to think about it, but it's in there, burned into my mind.

Then there's like, a voice . . . in my head. "Don't move," it says. And I'm just about to talk, when—"Don't talk either."

And I can't help it. "What?"

"Stop!" the voice shouts into my mind. "Just like, *think* what you wanna say, okay? But don't say shit."

"Who are—?"

"Shut . . . up!" the voice is so loud that I wince and the pain spikes into my face. Then the voice is quieter, but not much, "Jesus, you're such a stupid. . . You need to start listening. Another one of you I gotta tow. Listen, I say shut up, then like, *you* . . . shut up! As in, don't talk out loud. They're gonna hear you. And if they think you're awake. . . I know it doesn't make sense, just do it. Think *at* me."

Who are you? Right now, that's the only thing I wanna know. I'll get to this chick bitching on me in a second.

"You won't believe me," the voice says, "so I'm not even telling you. But you're in deep shit. And I'm not—it's not happening, so I need you to stay quiet while I figure this out."

Where's Brie and Tessa? I think, and then I try to adjust in my seat, but the pain hits me hard and I groan a little.

"I said *don't* move," the voice says. "Anyways, they're. . . It doesn't matter."

It so matters! I think at her. Maybe I'm cracked, but the voice in my head is a she. And I know Brie and Tess are dead, but I ask anyways, *Are they. . .?*

And there's a pause and I hope that maybe my inner cracked-voice has skipped out on me, because—"Yes," she says.

I know. . . I think. And I pause, trying to remember which time that was. *We were in Cancun—the Tuaca and the Mexican Protection cell . . . and they got—I got—*

"We're fixing that," my little voice says, "right now."

How? I ask. *My brain's obviously cracking wide open like an egg, and you are like, some stupid voice in my head.* And I guess I just wanna know. So I ask myself, *Why do I hurt so bad?*

"You jacked the mike and stole those Betty boots with Brie and Tess," my voice says. "You don't remember that? . . . Those PAs martialed you so bad—messed you up. That sick fucker! How can he . . . after that?"

What? I ask. My conscience is speaking in riddles now—Tess does that same shit. Totally pisses me off. Anyways, that's what this voice is. I didn't even think I had a conscience. *I'm high*, I think.

"You're not high, idiot," my conscience says. "And I'm *not* your conscience."

I finally wince through it and get one eye all the way open and the other one a little bit, and I can see in front of me—"Oh . . . my God?" I mutter it softly, and then I try not to talk again. *That's me! I am so cracked. They shot me up with J and I'm sitting across from myself, and—*

"Don't lose it!" her voice booms in my head, but her lips aren't moving and like, her eyes aren't even open.

And we're in a cell and I can see she's taped to a chair like I was, and her head is down.

"I can smell them over there watching us," she says it in a tone that scares me. And I mean, she's not moving her mouth! "Pervs," she clucks—like, that sounded like a bird.

I know I'm cracked, I think. *Voice in my head and I can see myself?* I check to see if it's a mirror—no mirror.

"You're not cracked, idiot," my voice says. "You're. . . Don't try to figure it out," she says, "just listen. In a couple minutes, two guys are coming through that door, and if you don't do exactly like I say, you're gonna get . . . you're gonna get fucked up again. But I'm not letting that happen, redemption or not. I decided that shit."

Raped. I know that's what she's talking about. *I already. . .* And when I tense up, like, every bone in my body feels like it cuts into my skin. And I grunt and wince and try to stop the pain. But I don't scream this time. Whatever this is—Tuaca Blonde Bimbos, hallucination, bad Judgment trip—I don't know, but everything before this felt real. So I'm listening, but this is another bad one. *Why can't I have the smooth trips?* I think to myself.

Her voice says, "You're not getting ra—"

Spare me, I think at her. *I been in this dream—I know.*

"No," my voice replies, "because like. . ." Then she pauses for too long, like when I'm trying to make up some bullshit story about where I was before my dad had to credit-spring me from minimum. ". . .because you're OD'ing right now, that's why. *God*. . . Oh, now dammit, look what you made me—*listen*, you aren't gonna remember most of this, but I gotta make sure you remember something."

Who are. . .? I think, because I don't like taking orders from—I don't care if it is me, that's just not happening!

"You already know," my voice says. "Now, I want you to remember this. No matter what happens from here, you are *not* cracked. Don't let that psych doctor tell you that shit. He's fucking his secretary, anyways. I saw her touch his—"

Eww, I think. *I don't wanna hear that stuff. What's that got to do with. . .?*

"Sorry," my voice says. "Anyways, don't listen to him. Now, this is important, so you *have* to remember it. You're gonna meet this girl, and you're like, protecting her for me, okay. No bullshit . . . you're doing it. Say it."

What?

"Bitch, you're gonna do it!"

My voice is pissed off now, because that's how I get—I hate repeating myself for dumbshits who don't listen.

"Because once I kill him," she says, "I can't go back . . . but you can . . . and you will."

She is—now my inner voice is talking cracked. *Kill who?* I ask. *Wait, go back to where?*

"Look, it's not that bad," she says. "The dude's an asshole, but he's cool when it counts—he'll take care of you. He's kinda like . . . Mr.

Nick."

Nicholas? I think. *That poly-psych guy?*

But she isn't listening to me. "You're gonna go there—the fall's the worst part," she says, "but I couldn't let him off for that either. Anyways, like I said, it's better than this."

Where . . . am I going?

There's another one of those pauses. "Heaven," she says, but I know that's bullshit—that's my lying voice, "and when you get there—"

Stop lying, I think at her. *You want me to take care of . . . who do you want me to watch—oh . . . my-God . . . I'm dying?*

"You're such a bitch," my voice chuckles at me, "I'll tell you one thing, don't say 'God' . . . like, ever!"

Why not? I ask, but I don't think it long. *So I am dying? Oh, that sucks.*

"No, not now—you die later. You just have to—"

Look, you suck at this guardian angel shit, ya know. Because that's who this bitch is.

"I'm not—"

Don't even, I think to my little inner-*angel* voice. If I took a double dose of Judgment, I'm like, already dead. And an angel? I'm dead. *Don't bullshit me. What's happening to me . . . right now?* And I know this is just a Judgment trip, but my mother dragged me there, so I got that church shit in my head. *Seriously, we're going to Heaven?* Then I hear the door handle.

My little inner-angel opens up her eyes, rolls them up without raising her head, and she looks at me. Then she smiles a little, but I never smiled like that before, and she—my face looks freaky. Then the smile goes away and that look is worse. And then she says, "Time's up."

The light flickers and then the floods hit me in the face—blinds me and I squint at them and the pain slices into me and I yell, "Aaaah!"

And then two men burst through the door . . . and the alarms start clanging.

— XLVI —

ARE YOU LITTLE hatchlings ready? Because this just went from a round-trip to Cancun to a one-way to Vegas. You little purgies are about to get your wings wet, and there's no Salvation here to help you.

Quiet! Do *exactly* what I tell you, and every last one of you pissing little shits will get back to the lake. Jack around whining like you been doing. . . Like I said, there's only one way back now, and we better hurry, because—*shit*, they're coming in the door!

Get in the shadows, get in the—put your wings behind you—shields, now!

— XLVII —

JUMP HADN'T NOTICED them before, but when the lights came on, they were pretty hard to miss. Hell, everyone could see them.

And the two men stopped cold in their tracks. They were so confused by it that they forgot to fire their weapons. Jump knew Fury would not.

"Aaah!" he watched her yell and spring up and out of her chair, tearing through the tape like it was paper. Then her wings ripped out of the center of her back and she screamed again. They spread wide and shivered and shook, and blood and chunks of flesh fell to the floor, destined to mix with the stains of countless other guests' blood as it all headed to the stainless steel drain.

Jump watched Fury shiver her wings again like a dog shakes off water, and the remaining blood sprayed like mist and floated to the ground. Then all of her armored feathers pushed out and she let out a loud caw above her head.

The men who came through the door were highly trained and deadly, but Jump could see they had focused their initial attention and then confusion on the six little purgatories hovering along the left wall.

The hatchlings had probably been hidden since Fury resurrected— it wasn't easy to hide hatchlings with no camouflage training—but with the rest of the spotlights in the room on, now they were too obvious *not* to stare at. How could someone ignore a bunch of black-feathered, soon to be archangels in the first place? Jump almost laughed. *Right in front of my face*, he thought.

The interrogators stopped and stared like they were seeing . . . well, like they were seeing angels for the first time. Jump imagined they might even be thinking about all the souls they had tortured, raped and murdered in this very cell. And if these little angels in front of them were real, then what else was? Though . . . probably not.

Jump's perception of the entire event, probably Fury's too, was that of watching a slow-motion playback. To the interrogators, about to become meat, not to mention himself—the PAIC and Frank, the entire event would take less than a couple of seconds. Seconds that would ripple into the future of all their eternities, like the altered trajectory of a bullet—who knew what it would rip into now.

So when Jump saw Fury fold her wings and then spin and release a hail of orange-streaking fire-feathers at them, he wasn't as surprised as the interrogators were.

Relatively speaking, the whole thing was over in an instant, but to the interrogators, watching a fully-fledged and feathered, avenging archangel from Hell shove out her plumage—come out of her Man-monkey camouflage right in front of them—the last few seconds of their lives felt like an eternity.

For about one instant, they might have thought that they could shoot the fairytale creature, but once it spun and fired flight feathers from its wings at them, they would soon find out just how a soul got those wings.

Orange quills cut through their arms and legs, severing at least two limbs that Jump could see. Then he knew what Fury was doing. She was a mean bitch when she got mad. He watched her casually walk over to both of the writhing and screaming interrogators, now on the floor of the cell, bleeding and pumping out their raping blood onto the floor.

Fury kicked their weapons away from them and then she knelt down. She picked up one of her glowing orange feathers from the floor, held it by the cool end, eyeing the glowing tip for what must have seemed like eternity to the screaming interrogators. Then she blew hard on the pointed end for a few seconds, heating the tip back up.

In the meantime, the six little purgatories she'd had in tow since leaving the hell of the dungeons, gathered around behind her. They squawked and chirped and hopped around like . . . well, like little humping hatchlings on their first training mission to the garden. *With an archangel from Hell*, Jump thought. He almost smiled. *Trial by fire-feather—only way to train.*

Whatever trouble they were all in now—and the clock was ticking on that—it was satisfying to take a break and watch Fury work. Jump could see that she had learned a little more since the great cleansing. The only angel he figured a Man-monkey might want to have pay him a visit *less*, would be the devil, Jump, himself.

Fury turned and whispered something to her flock of fledglings, and then each one of them blew on her burning feather. It alternated glowing brighter and then cooling down slightly between each of their turns stoking it.

When Fury looked like she was finally satisfied that they understood how a fire-feather worked, she spun back toward the first screaming interrogator and rammed the hot steel feather into the bloody stump where his leg used to be.

And the screaming got insane for a couple of seconds, and smoke wafted into the air, flesh sizzled, and blood vessels and arteries seared shut, stopping his loss of blood. Then the first one passed out. Jump knew that would happen.

A Man-monkey's body had a delicate threshold for handling excruciating pain. Jump taught interrogators to take a protectant right up to the edge of it, but not over. Too much and it would take forever waking them back up. And a good dose of Judgment only lasted about a day—there was no use wasting the effects of it on unconsciousness. Because once someone recovered from the first one, if they had to judge someone up again? Second trip was always worse than the first.

Protection interrogators had proven time and time again, the best case after a second full dose of "J" would be blinding headaches and insomnia that drove a protectant nearly insane. Worst case, it would produce a hallucinating, rage-filled, whack-job whose only mission in life would be to kill whomever they believed had wronged them. And at the *Fifty* there were plenty of people walking around that fit that bill. The only use for a monkey like that would be to scare inmates into submission at a Protection prison.

At first, it looked like Fury didn't understand that, but when she shoved the blazing-hot quill into the second man's severed arm socket as hard as she could, Jump knew what she was doing. His screaming was pretty brief—she wanted them out cold.

Once the interrogators were both unconscious, Fury turned and ran right at the observation room's one-way window. Then she spread her wings as wide as they would go—probably shielding her little flock of trainees from the blast, Jump figured—and she let out a huge screech.

Then any delusion that the PAIC and Frank King had about their safety behind the bulletproof glass shattered in at them, showering the floor of the room and them with flying chards of razor-sharp guilt.

The two fell backward onto the floor. When they recovered, they both looked up at Fury—the PAIC with his hand still halfway into one of his pockets, and Frank with a look on his face that screamed fear and panic. Neither made a sound.

"Keep your filthy Man-monkey mouths shut," Fury screeched at them, "and you might get to enjoy a few more minutes alive. Say *one* word, and I'll send you to a place you can't even imagine."

Jump almost sprang from the nothingness to stop her, but at the final instant, Fury jerked her head behind her.

Jump sensed them a split second later.

And the door burst open and six black-armored Protection sentries with MP7's stormed into the interrogation room.

Fury cawed at the little purgatory cherubs behind her, still busy hovering over the two passed-out stumps on the floor. As soon as the little angels heard her scream at them, every one of them flapped and wrapped their wings in a cone around themselves. They looked like a nest full of huge dinosaur eggs.

It was actually one of the first things newly-hatched angels were taught after being condemned. "Shield then wing-wrap," Fury had told them. "Learn to protect yourselves . . . *then* you'll learn to fight back."

Fury leapt at Mercedes, still taped to the chair, and she slammed her wings around her, wing-wrapping them both. Then she screamed at the two Man-monkeys in the observation room, "Get your stupid monkey asses down!"

Jump figured she was wasting her breath, because as soon as the sentries burst into the room he—the Jake PAIC version of himself—jumped on top of Frank and shoved him down onto the floor of the observation room, behind the ballistic barrier.

The hot lead flew like stingers from a hornet's nest, pelting anything and everything in the room. And glass flew and bullets ricocheted off of the purgatories—now screeching from inside their "eggs." Fury and Mercedes' egg got sprayed too, and then bullets pelted the ballistic barrier in front of the observation seating until the six sentries were all out of ammunition.

Then the clicking and clacking of clips being changed, joined the echoes of gunshots and the plinking sound of brass hitting the concrete floor. Then the whole thing started over—*Brrrrrrrrt! Brrrrrrrrt! Brrrrrrrrt!*—long bursts of suppressed gunfire and smoke swept back and forth through the whole room, filling the air with the sweet smoking smell of burning gunpowder.

Clean crew, Jump thought. He knew a clean crew's job was to kill everyone in a room and then mop up like nothing ever happened. When they finally ended their second hail of hate, the room felt to Jump like a thick foggy morning on a Puget Sound ferry, furiously plowing ahead at full speed, bow slicing its way to a destination that only radar or bats could see.

An archangel's senses might as well have been both, because the clicking and clacking sounds of reloading barely started before Fury screeched at the purgatories. And then all six of them burst out of their wing-wrapped shells, and they each hopped onto a dark figure in the smoke. And then they clawed and cawed, and ripped and rammed, using talons and teeth and wings and feathers to tear at the black-clad men until there wasn't much left but black uniforms and blood.

Ferocious fear would do that. Flying around and hiding from danger in the Man-monkey world was stressful, not to mention having your trainer yell and berate you every time you were confused or asked a question. So for a pissing-scared purgatory, still in the process of earning their wings, it was hard to control all that pent-up fear. And Jump figured that from the looks of it, these purgies had been scared angel-shitless since they got there.

Fury unwrapped her wings from around Mercedes' quivering body, checked her over a little, and then she walked back to the observation room.

The little hatchlings tore guts and plucked eyeballs behind her. They clucked and squawked and cawed like eager little eagles fighting over a fresh fish their mother just brought.

"Now," Fury said when she got to the edge of the blown-out observation window, "what should we do about you two? Because those cocksuckers just like. . . They cheated me out of pounding those two pussies on the floor." Fury looked behind her at the two interrogators' limb-severed bodies, freshly bleeding and riddled with bullets from their buddies. "I guess that only leaves you two pussies to pound."

Jump clucked a little when Fury said that—it was something he might have said. With the absence of Rain. . . To attempt to replace his little Amy with a daughter figure he could mentor in his Hell, Jump had found Fury—a raging archangel after his own vengeful heart. They had enjoyed an evening chat or two beside the lake a few times, and he would tease her and joke that she was too "serious-angry" and she should enjoy her work a little more by sprinkling in some colorful commentary every once in a while—get more "sarcastic-angry." Otherwise the job of ripping apart souls—games at the arena or gutting souls in the garden—would get boring.

It appeared that Fury had taken his words to heart, because taunting someone before gutting them wasn't her style. All the same, Jump could smell that was what she was about to do next.

The consequences of allowing Fury to get her revenge were bigger than her. Not to mention that Jump didn't really want the memory of her gutting him as the PAIC in the past indelibly burned into his memory, regardless of what repercussions that might have in altering all of their futures.

He looked into the nothingness, back at everyone watching her fall. The sands of that day-long dream were quickly running down. Revenge or redemption—she didn't have long left to choose.

But Fury had chosen. Jump could see that. A poor decision in his opinion, given the consequences. However, probably one which she hadn't thought out. He couldn't blame her, he rarely got past his pissed-off stage in making decisions in a battle. But on this one, he had taken more time to ponder.

If Fury took revenge on her raping father—probably killing the PAIC in the process—it would be a lose-lose . . . lose-lose scenario. In fact, the only ones who *would* get what they wanted out of that were the lying bastard and his benevolent sex-slave in the dungeon. *Life back in charge of the garden?* Jump thought. *Not today.*

Jump sprang from the nothingness, just as Fury was readying her combat spin. And he spread his wings wide between her and the observation room, just as she spun and unleashed as many glowing fire-feathers as she could.

And glowing-hot, steel feathers ripped into Jump's wings and chest and legs—he barely got his steel plumage out, as the bulk of them hit him and ricocheted away. It wasn't quick enough. Some of them pierced him before his armor could stop them.

When Fury spun down, she looked down at Jump, lying on the floor of the interrogation cell. Her feathers were burning out to cold steel, sticking out of his breast and body. And her friend from Hell—Jump—was dead.

— XLVIII —

SALVATION AND RAIN had finally succumbed to the fact that they would have to watch the falls just like everyone else. Rain convinced her mother that they should worry about their "discussion" later. Three missing angels and the debacle in the dungeon. . . Her father's delayed "angels and demons" conversation could wait.

Rain wasn't powerless to help a fallen, but the cost of her intervention had been high enough already—three falling archangels, Salvation convinced her, would have to be enough. The consequences of the third lay bloody and beaten, bathed back in glowing darkness, slowly repairing themselves, in the depths of the dungeon.

Even if Salvation hadn't been adamant about staying out of it, Rain knew that the "benefit of all" would have to start being respected. Otherwise, what type of Protector would she become? Breaking and trampling her very own words and those of her predecessors? She would be no better than Life.

And yet despite all of that, Rain had an overwhelming urge to reach into the fall and pluck Fury back from the depths of her resurrection and redemption. Because if her friend didn't hurry—if the dark night of resurrection turned into a day full of failed redemption—the dawn of revenge would burn her soul to ashes.

They sat on the steps up to Rain's throne and stared past the nothingness at Fury's fall. Rain worried that Fury had descended too far, and Salvation wondered if her husband had fallen far enough. That is, until she saw Fury kill him.

"Oh my God! Oh my God!" Salvation yelled on impulse. But she was beyond blasphemy charges by now. "She killed him!" And Salvation stood up, looking like she was about to go to war. "He's—he's like a father to her! . . . I'll kill that little shit!" And she leaned in, preparing to jump into the nothingness.

Rain stood up quickly and grabbed her mother by the arm. "She didn't do it on purpose," she said. Hasty decisions at this point would not help anyone. She stared back into the fall at her father and her . . . her . . . she had no idea what her feelings for Fury meant. But watching the girl who had helped save her from Life's clutches. . . A young lady who had endured so much and harbored such hatred, yet somehow found a place in her right heart to help Rain understand "the real world you lived in," as Fury liked to put it. And how to protect herself and others from harm in the one she now ruled. To Rain, Fury was more than a friend when she needed one the most. She did love her as her mother suggested, but what did that mean?

One of the best lessons Fury taught Rain—a lesson that was too difficult to grasp from her father—"Things are not always as they seem," she said to Salvation. "You do not believe that the Great Dragon of Judgment is so frail, do you? This angel of man is your husband, remember?"

— XLIX —

THE BRIGHT LIGHTS pounded Jump's eyes. He blinked and squinted and tried to open them twice. Then he moaned at the sharp pains in his chest and the fire in his legs. He tried to reach for them, but something held his arms and legs down.

"Aaaah!" he yelled out in agony and his eyes opened wide, just as Fury ripped the last burning feather from his thigh. "Goddammit, that is—I'm gonna *kill* you!" He tried to move, but was still pinned down.

When he finally opened his eyes all the way, Jump looked up at Fury.

She smiled back at him. "Welcome to my little nightmare," she said. "Now, what the *fuck* are you doing in here?" she asked. "I almost killed your old ass."

Jump tried to move his arms again—he might not kill her, but at least he could give her a good smack in the jaw. "That's the second time today that one of my friends has *shot* me," he said.

Then he turned and looked at the six little purgatories, wide-eyed and shitting themselves, concentrating hard on holding down his arms and legs, like he was sure that Fury had told them to.

"Oh, you better get these little shits off my wings or Salvation help me, I'll gut every one of them!"

And the purgies screeched and all of them let go at once, and they ran behind Fury to try and escape.

Jump stretched his arms and wings rubbed his chest, then worked his legs up and down to his belly, groaning and moaning a little as he did it. Fire-feathers were nothing to scoff at. Salvation pulling one of the feathers out of his back hurt pretty badly, but almost a dozen, plucked out and then the wounds cauterized by one of his own faithless fairies—that stung worse. He sat up and leaned to the side to look at all of Fury's "trainees."

Fury was busy handling it. "What did I tell you?" she said. "You don't *ever* let go of someone once you got them down on the ground. Jesus Christ on a cross, I should let him rip out your tail feathers!"

All the little hatchlings shivered in fear, as she turned back to Jump.

"What am I gonna do with these whiny little bitches?" Fury said. "Like, every class, whinier than the last one. Where do you dig these purgies up, Jump? And like, why is it always me who has to train them?"

Jump looked at Fury and smiled. He spoke without his filter, "You're the best one I got, little girl," he said. "You think I can just hand them over to Salvation? She's way too easy on 'em. They'd be blathering basket-babies by the end of it. All them being so humping hot. . . I figure gotta match 'em with a cold-hearted bitch."

"You're such an asshole," Fury frowned and said. "Like it matters." She looked back at her flock of purgatories, busy clucking and bobbing their heads. "What, like, you think this is over? Hah, we aren't even to the redemption part yet."

Some of the smiles left their faces and the clucking laughter died down.

"Yeah," Fury said, "you better shut your beaks. You keep acting like that, you won't make it. Guarantee that. Right now, I wouldn't even jack an old lady at the Mike with you flock of flying. . . Look, we got about—I don't even know. How much. . .?" She glanced at the observation room—at the two heads peaking back over the barrier, and the one little pistol barrel pointing right at her. "You think I forgot about you two monkeys? Whatever, pitch that gun down or I'll stick it up *your* ass and pull the trigger. See how you like the view from the other side of that window." She frowned at them as they ducked back down. "Old cocksucking assholes," she muttered. "And you better lube up, *Daddy*, because I'm making this last. Bet that."

Jump turned to look behind him and caught the last glimpse of the two heads, ducking back below the barrier. Then he turned back to Fury and opened his mouth to speak.

But Fury was pumped up on the rage and the piss-smell of fear that lingered in the air from everywhere. "There, how's that for like, trash-talking while I work?" she asked. "You are such a drama queen. Can't you just like, kill someone and be done with it?" She reached her hand down.

Jump hung his head and he clucked and chuckled a little. Then he reached his hand up and grabbed onto Fury at her wrist.

As Fury pretended to help Jump to his feet, she said, "I'm talking to Salvation. Between all your chirp-chirp and the fashion with the sunshields"—she put her nose to the air and sniffed in a couple of times—"I think I'm like, smelling . . . yep, there it is! You got a little bitch in you. I can smell some tinkerbell." Then she laughed out loud.

Jump stood up, rubbed his chest, and then looked at all the half-smiling little hatchlings behind Fury. "Don't any of you get any bright ideas about talking right now," he said to them. "She's earned the right to that." And four billion reaped souls in the garden later, Jump was telling them the truth. He towered over little Fury, and he turned back and looked down at her—into her eyes. "And you, young lady," he said, "you're in deep dolphin-shit here. And you got about six clicks to fix it."

— L —

GETTING BABETTE UNSTRAPPED from the gurney had been painful. For her more than Father Benito, but his heart hurt almost as much as her wounds hurt her.

Babette had screamed and cried for Benito to leave her and go get her daughter, but he wasn't abandoning her again.

After Benito got her unstrapped, he tried to help her stand up. Babette fell to the floor and started crying. He had no idea where the strength came from—Benito wasn't a muscular man—but he hoisted her off the floor and slung her across his back, one arm between her legs and wrapped over to hold the butt of his stolen submachine gun, and the other wrapped around her arm, holding her to his back.

Little Benito looked just like the Protection agent he stole the uniform from, carrying a fallen friend out of a firefight.

Everything was foggy to him and the world seemed slower than paint drying. But Benito's reactions were lightning fast in comparison. And then he knew his guardian angel was helping him.

Father Benito shot two agents in the hall as soon as he carried Babette out of her cell. And he shot two more as he headed toward the elevator to the lobby.

On the way, he barely heard Babette whisper, "No. . ." And when he hustled up to the elevator and pushed the button to bring it, she said, "We have to go back."

Go back? Benito thought. "For what?" he asked her softly. He scanned the hallway for more agents. All he wanted to do was get out —get his love out of that hell. And the clanging and red lights blinking made it hard for him to think. He was on impulse and adrenaline now. The truth was, he wasn't thinking.

"We can't leave her with him," Babette said.

Benito could barely carry Babette any farther. He rolled her off of his back and sat her next to the doors to the elevator. Then he knelt in front of her and caught his breath.

The fear and the hopelessness crept back into his soul. He wondered if he would ever be redeemed for his sins. "Leave who?" he asked. He couldn't go back for someone else. He didn't even know if he could get Babette up on his back again. "We can't go back."

"You have to," Babette barely said. She raised her frail-looking face. "He's going to—we have to . . . get her away from him. Leave me here, Benito . . . and go."

"I'm not leaving you again," Benito said to her. "God help me, I can't lose you twice."

Babette's voice was weak. "You don't have much time—he's going to. . . You can't let him do that. She's . . . just a girl," she said, trying to raise her hand to Benito's face, but she was too weak and her arm fell back to her lap. She let out a big sigh as she said, "She's yours. . ." And then Babette closed her eyes and slumped sideways to the floor.

And the elevator dinged . . . and its doors opened up.

REDEMPTION

LIVED AND LIFE observed the fall from the miserable confines of their cell. They had nearly recovered from the torture at the whipping hands of their only son.

Despite her condition, Life grinned an evil smile. Her plans were progressing perfectly. The little bitch, Fury, had simply to flick out a feather and end her father, Frank's, life. Then predictably, she would beg for "God's" forgiveness. From there, Life would smite her raping oppressor cellmate, and all would be as it was before—she would rule over her children and he would be her slave. "Perfect," she said softly.

Lived knew Life had planned some sort of treachery—that was her way. Yet when it came to deceit, Father Benito—Faith—had written the book. And Lived would be Life's devil forever. It was written in the *Book of Blood*. He almost winced as he watched Fury shoot their son with . . . nine feathers that he could count. "No," he said, "ten of them. Your bastard appears slightly burned, Your Majesty. And he has interrupted your plan."

"Once again," Life said, "I believe you underestimate the female of my children. Sadly, it seems that is your blind spot. For you forget—" Then Life leapt to her feet and bared talon and teeth and shined her light as bright as she could, blinding Lived. And she pushed out all of her armored white feathers, just before she jumped and sunk the talons on her hands into Lived's chest. "The debt of your vile vengeance against me is mine," she screamed and clawed at him. "And I shall repay it ten times into eternity!"

— LII —

WHEN THE DOOR to the body-filled and gunsmoking interrogation room swung open, no one inside was prepared for what would happen next. And there wasn't an angel in the room who could comprehend or react any faster than waiting for molasses to pour in winter.

And the black figure stood motionless in the doorway.

The hatchlings, flock-shocked as they were, actually saw the figure though the smoke first. And they all fled in slow motion, to the edge of the room and slowly slammed their wings behind them. And a loud faraway echo of clanking steel feathers reverberated in the room as they put up their shields.

And Fury tried to spin, but her turn started so slowly that it felt like her wings and legs were in a tar pit at the edge of the lake of fire. Her perception of time pulled on her legs, as she tried to flap her wings through a time full of sticky black grease that was determined to hold them in place.

Jump tried to flap one wing at her and shove her aside, but he winced and cawed out at the pain still in his chest and arms. Then he swooped a long powerful beat of his wings as pain crawled up his limbs and face like snake venom, slowly working its way through his bloodstream. He felt every muscle, every feather and every breeze all at once. Even the smell was so slow that he couldn't get a whiff of the intentions of the figure coming through the doorway.

And then the figure was in the cell and yelling something, waving arms like wings at them.

Jump and Fury both saw the gun.

Jump had been shot enough for one day, but he could see that Fury was about to unleash, so he turned toward Mercedes. It made him angrier than he already was, that even his voice felt slower. "Motherrrr . . ." was all he could get out, before two more black figures appeared in the doorway, both of them shouting and yelling at the first one.

Jump's feet moved like he was running in sludge, and it felt like it took forever to take one step.

By the time Fury spun halfway toward the first black figure, two more had appeared though the smoke. She aimed at them as they raised their guns up toward the first figure.

Fury and Jump watched the action and bolt on the second black figure's MP7 slowly open and close in between the faraway muffled sounds of suppressed 9mm fire. Every last detail etched into their eyes like a stonemason chiseling granite statues as they watched.

They saw and felt the agent squeeze on his trigger and they heard the tendons in his index finger popping as they tightened. And the hammer released and slowly shoved the firing pin forward, and then the pin pressed into the tiny primer on the bottom of the bullet's casing—*Pssshhht! . . . Pop!*

And they heard the powder charge catch fire, expanding and crackling as it burned. They felt the pressure of the gases as they expanded beyond what the little brass bullet casing could contain, forcing the crimped-in lead projectile on its tip to break free and start slowly moving down the barrel of the gun, twisting along the rifled grooves in the barrel, headed toward the tip—its only pathway to escape the rapidly expanding gases from the explosion behind it.

They saw the tip of the bullet poke out the end of the rifle's barrel and small puffs of white smoke escape to the side all around it, finally free to find another pathway of least resistance. And the lead projectile inched forward like a snail, heading for some faraway piece of fruit to slowly chew into and eat.

And then the faraway-sounding report of the submachine gun—
Ber . . . er . . . er . . . er . . . er . . . tah. . .

The first black figure's uniform depressed slowly until it ripped, and the bullet slowly ate into his arm . . . and then his legs and then his chest and then the world spun back up like a shooting star through the black of the night!

Fury spun and released—she had no idea how many—and glowing orange fire-feathers cut into the second set of black figures, cutting them to pieces faster than their minds had time to realize that they had walked into a hornet's nest of avenging archangels. And then they were dead—black chunks of protection and pain.

And Jump hurled himself toward Mercedes, still strapped to her chair. He surrounded her with his wings as stray rounds ricocheted and pelted him, then fell to the floor, bouncing and coming to rest as lifeless as their masters.

And it was over—nothing but smoke and echoes left!

— LIII —

SALVATION AND RAIN'S perception of the falls were different. Inside a fall, an angel was at the mercy of their perception of time; an observer saw everything as it occurred and all at once.

"What the hell does he mean, I'm way too easy on them?" Salvation asked no one. "I'm not too—I mean, I'm tough enough. You don't have to beat on them *all* the time."

Though Salvation was most likely speaking to herself, Rain had embraced and accepted her new role as the mediator between her father's true nature and her mother's understanding of who he really was. "You are quite forgiving, Mother."

"What?"

"It is not what they need," Rain said. "If they are to survive out there, they will require a more firm hand. Fury has this capability."

Salvation jerked her head toward her daughter. "Oh, now it's Fury has this capability, huh? Little—I am still your mother! And though you might not know it, I'm a little more *worldly* than you might believe."

"Forgive me," Rain said. She continued to watch Fury fall. "I only wish to—I am worried she will not choose correctly. With revenge only a few feet from her, how can she?"

"Rain," Salvation said, trying to calm herself, "you can't will it. You have to let it show up . . . on its own. You said it yourself at the beginning of this very day. Let her figure it out. The harder you tug at her, the worse it will get. Trust me on that." She looked back at her own love and Fury deep in their fall. "If she is supposed to"—she shook her head—"I *still* can't believe it. I guess maybe I am a little too naïve. I had absolutely no idea."

Rain smiled. She liked that it had confused her mother. "Do you think I would have bared myself in front of him if. . .?" she asked. "Ich, disgusting! I have no idea how you and—I may have to take Fury's advice and ban you from this."

"Don't push it," Salvation said. "First things first. Are you sure that we can't go down there and pull their sorry butts out of this? It looks like they're making a complete mess of it. And your father doesn't look like he's helping at all. He just got himself shot . . . again." By now she knew that a few flaming feathers weren't going to be enough to murder the mean out of her husband.

"You know," Rain said, "he told me once that getting shot in his chosen profession was simply an unfortunate—"

And Salvation completed her husband's only explanation for coming home bruised, beaten or bloody, "Occupational occurrence," they both said together.

— LIV —

FAITH STARED FROM the nothingness into his fall, looking at himself as Father Benito, kneeling in front of Babette. It couldn't be. How could it have happened? She had never said a word to him about the girl—nothing in over sixteen years of their affair.

Faith had gone half-mad back in life, writing a book as protest in secret and turning to alcohol over the guilt. But God had spoken to him—sent him word after all. Given him an answer in a voice so loud and clear that there had been only one way he could have missed it. His answer: Benito's daughter was hidden right in front of his face.

Faith remembered seeing the girl—Mercedes—over and over again, throughout his and Babette's secret affair. All the while he was distracted with his own guilt, trying to conceal his sin from anyone who might catch him. He hid and cowered whenever Mercedes was around, sure as the devil that she would somehow know why he came calling so much.

Babette had assured him that the girl had no idea about the true nature of their relationship. To her daughter, Babette was simply another crazy mother, attending services and sermons regularly, occasionally dragging Mercedes to church, kicking and screaming if she had to.

When Mercedes was small, Babette even went so far as to have her little girl baptized. Afterward, the father's own guilt could simply bear no more. He finally pleaded with Babette to stop attending church and only meet him in private and away from the reminder of his fallen faith.

And what of Faith's book? Over twenty years of writing it. Another reminder that he hadn't really been a man of faith at all. He hadn't been for a long time . . . for more reasons than Babette knew.

But he *had* been sent a message. One of love and beauty and innocence. Yet he had ignored it, or not recognized it, or worse. He had openly neglected his responsibility to protect the girl.

He watched Mercedes fall into mischief and then sin. He even had conversations with Babette, trying to—now that he thought about it, she always referred to Mercedes as "our daughter."

When Faith was Father Benito, he had thought Babette simply meant her and her husband, Frank. Now that he tried to remember the events more clearly, Faith realized that she had been trying to tell him all along. She must have harbored such guilt, such condemnation of herself. She was trapped in a mansion built on the foundation of her own lies . . . and his.

The love and beauty that Faith had longed for in life was delivered to him in the form of a beautiful little girl . . . and he had squandered the gift, seeking the "right" response from Heaven. One that he had been taught and trained to look for and understand.

Once Faith thought about it, Life was cruel enough to deliver her messages in exactly that way. Love and faith and joy, wrapped in a package—exactly what someone asked for—right beneath their blind, begging-for-forgiveness noses. So obvious that no one would see that was what they were—faith and meaning in a baby-bin, bouncing bundle of resurrection and redemption, fresh from the Med-mart.

But now, Life had manipulated Faith into allowing himself to be resurrected, not for redemption, but to punish him with knowledge like she had punished Man and the snake in the garden. She was a twisted woman whom Faith finally understood created her own ant farm, so she could burn the ants and watch them scurry around, trying to escape the searing misery . . . for her own pleasure and entertainment.

And as he stared at himself by the elevator, holding his own face and crying into his hands, he could feel that she was using him to help her get that power back.

When the elevator chimed, he dropped his hands and watched the doors open up.

Father Benito cried into his own hands, barely noticing the elevator doors as they opened.

The first perception he had of them was a bright blinding light and then pain that shot through his face. He fell backward and clutched at his head, and blood ran into his hands. Then there was yelling and wave-units squawking and he knew he had failed again.

His love sat dying by the elevator, violated and abandoned by her faith in him. How could she hold faith in him after that? If she wasn't dead already. . . Benito didn't want to think about it. He just wanted to join her—die next to her.

It had all gone horribly wrong. Every plan he had made, every dream he had dreamt, every call in the night he had answered from Babette, knowing that she would seduce his soul from his faith and into her flesh. It had all brought him here—a beaten blasphemer with a bastard child. But Mercedes was not at fault for his failures. Should she suffer simply for the sin of being born to weak and wanting parents?

Benito had made so many mistakes, and he had barely escaped judgment for most of them. It seemed that justice had caught up to him and he was at failure's doorstep again. Would he ever fulfill his purpose? He wondered.

And the boots kicked into him and his blood flowed onto the black uniform he'd stolen. "Help me," he muttered, more hysterically than directed at anyone who might provide assistance.

Faith watched himself as Benito, being beaten. This was not what he had returned for. This was not redemption—this was Life's own revenge for him having written the *Book of Blood*. She had somehow found a way to punish him. And he had given her the power of his own free will to do it.

Surely Faith had some power left, didn't he? He could save himself. This was not how his life had ended anyway. Then he realized—his own daughter had had to kill him—Life was more cruel than he imagined. He had seen enough of the cruelty of her creations to know that the only thing her kind of power respected was equal response in return.

Faith sprang from the nothingness like a great eagle from a cloud. And he bared talons and loosed feathers in such a ferocious flight of fury that it even surprised himself. But it was nothing compared to the barely remaining chunks of the Protection Man-monkeys after he tore and plucked them apart in rage.

When Faith was done, he tilted his head back and screeched above his head. And all of the blinking red lights above the cell doors shattered and the loudspeakers blew up, and all of the remote-wave feed cameras exploded.

Then there was nothing left in the tunnel with Faith but Benito and Babette, both nearer to the darkness than the bathed-in-black tunnel —closer to death than to Life's horrid version of living.

Bright light always made him squint, and Benito instinctively reached for his glasses. *Nothing there*, he thought, touching the empty pocket. *Where are—where am I?* He felt the smooth, slippery wetness on his fingers. *Sticky.*

Benito tried to lift his head and look at his hand, but fire shot though his chest and arms and pain pierced into his mind from everywhere. But he didn't cry out. And the light was so bright.

Benito tried to look directly at it—that's where his guardian angel had come from before—but it was blinding. Then he felt like he was floating, and he remembered. *Mercedes*, he thought. *Have to get to her —have to save. . .* "Mercedes," he mumbled.

Then, almost as soon as he said it, there was her face, right over his, blocking out the blinding light. He smiled up at her. "You are. . ." he could hardly speak. He licked his lips. "You're . . . beautiful."

— LV —

FURY RUSHED TO the first black Protection agent that had come through the door. The bastard needed to be finished off. But when she got there and saw his wounds, there was nothing more she needed to do. The agent was just about dead.

She looked at his black goggles and his helmet and then to the bullet holes in his uniform. She poked her finger into one of the holes and the man winced in pain. "Hurts, doesn't it, bitch," she said. "That'll teach you, won't it?"

Fury looked back at Jump, still wrapped around Mercedes. "Is she okay?" she asked. Then she looked at her little purgatories, cowering in the corner behind their shields. "Get your whining asses out here, purgatory little—come and look at him."

They all stood up and fluttered over to the Man-monkey's body, but they were afraid to get too close.

Fury frowned at them. "Put your faces down here—get a good whiff."

They all leaned in as instructed and sniffed a little, then recoiled back from the smell and moved their heads to what they thought was a safe distance.

"Jesus Christ," Fury said, "like he's gonna bite you or some shit. That's what they smell like before soul security comes and gets them. Once they do, they'll mark them, and then they are their responsibility to carry back. Like, they *can't* go back without them. You got it?

Because that's—shit, you ever get out of this and you'll end up ferrying these monkeys back and forth out of here as one of your first jobs. Rain help us, Jump, can you imagine that?"

Jump clucked and chuckled from the other side of the room, and then he pulled his wings from around Mercedes. The girl was seriously messed up, but she would live. At least until the next time he had to visit her. "She'll live long enough to take her first flight."

"Oh, very funny," Fury said, remembering her first fall. Then she looked back to the first Protection agent through the door, busy moaning and mumbling and leaking his lying life out onto the interrogation floor in the corner. "Think I should finish that one off."

Jump looked down at him. "Let him suffer."

She watched the man trying to move his lips and she walked over and knelt down next to him. She leaned over closer, putting her shadow on his face. "Mercedes. . ." the dying agent whispered.

"Yeah, yeah," Fury said. "Like you're getting to her. I don't think so. You failed. No more sticking your cock where it doesn't belong for y—"

Then the agent spoke again, "You are. . ." Fury watched him lick his lips—there was something . . . something familiar about it. ". . .You're . . . beautiful."

"What he saying?" Jump asked behind her.

Fury reached down and took the goggles off of the agent's face. "Holy shit. . ." It was all she could say.

"What?" Jump asked. He wasn't really paying attention to Fury. He was watching and wondering what to do about the two cowering loose ends in the observation room. He didn't understand why the PAIC hadn't come out shooting yet. That's what he would've done . . . back then—now. "Don't mess around with him too much, he might surprise you. We taught them how to take you with them when they kicked."

"Jump," Fury's tone said it all.

Jump walked over, shoved a couple of the little cowering purgatories out of the way, and then he knelt down next to Fury. "Son of a bitch," he said. "Goddammit, what's he. . .?" And he looked around at the carnage.

Two dead Protection interrogators, two cut-to-pieces sentries at the door, chopped up by Fury's feathers, glass and rubble everywhere, and this one lone—Protection agents never went anywhere alone unless it was to take a piss. This was the boozing little priest—it was Father Benito.

Then Benito spoke directly at Fury, "I can't—I never saw you before now. Too scared. . . I'm so sorry—she never told me about you."

Fury raised her head and looked at the ceiling and the light of the truth of the room, blasted into her eyes and she squinted. "God-*dammit*," she said. She had killed—well, she didn't actually shoot him, but she hadn't smelled him in time to save him either. "I gotta sit here and watch him die again?"

Jump knew what she meant. Fury had felt so guilty after the last time. But back then, the father had known it was coming. Still, Fury always had some unexplainable love-hate thing going with Father Benito—Faith—in Heaven.

Whenever she visited Rain, she would drop by to see him and chat or something. She never really talked about it, but Jump knew something was weird. He figured it might have been the guilt over cutting his head off, but in Jump's own messed-up mind, he entertained the possibility that they might have had some kinda weird "older-man" thing going on. He teased Fury about it once—fishing for the truth—but she had almost beaten him senseless with her wings.

"Dammit," Jump said, looking down at the father, "told you about what?" he asked.

Benito didn't take his gaze off of Fury—he was almost spent. "I never. . . I would never have allowed him to. . ."

"Shit-shit-shit!" Fury shouted. She looked up at the ceiling again. "Is that all there is down here, lying and death?" She knew Life had to be watching. "You're an evil bitch!" she yelled. Then she looked back at the father. "It's gonna be okay, they'll be down to get you. I'm gonna—I . . . I'll check on you when I get back." It was a lie, but it would make him feel better. "Try not to give any speeches until I get there, okay?"

"I. . . Father. . ." the father said to her, barely able to make sound now.

Fury looked at her little purgatories. A tear was forming in her eye, but she wouldn't let them see that. "Take a good look," she shouted at them, "because it doesn't get any better than this. So you need to like . . . like, show some respect! Because I told you, that bitch will—"

"I'm so proud of you," the father whispered. "You had such a hard. . . I wish I—I wish I had known. . ."

Fury couldn't hold it back this time, and she leaned down to look at him as he left. A tear dripped on his face and she wiped it off. "Knew what?" she asked softly.

"I didn't know I"—his eyes started to flutter—"the father," he muttered. And then his head went limp and his eyes stared at the ceiling above her.

Fury stared down at Father Ben's corpse. "Old cocksucker. . ." she mumbled. Then she looked at all the wide-eyed little purgatories, staring at her. "What are *you* looking at?" She looked back down at the father's open eyes. "You see that? See what she did to us? It's like . . . can you make this any worse. Delirious at the end of—no peace at all. Babbling his own name. It's just. . ."

Jump leaned back and stood up. There was still work to do, and so far his little "loose ends" had been content to hide behind their wall. It was a good thing for now, because if they did pop their heads out after the "father" thing, he might not be able to hold Fury back this time. Jump stared through the blown-out window to the observation room. "That's not what he said."

Fury looked up. "What?"

"He wasn't saying his name," Jump said. Once he got up close, he could smell it on him. Too much love for an old man's lust. Only love smell stronger was—"He said 'father.' "

"Yeah," Fury said, "that's his name—father."

Jump eyed the observation room, looking at K&T's huge logo on the back wall. He still couldn't figure it out. *Wings and snakes and a spike*, he thought. *Devils. . .*

Rain was right. Some things people needed to figure out for themselves. It was actually why Jump had delayed his talk with her for so long, pretending to let his daughter weasel her way out of it time and time again. He wasn't one to let anyone weasel out of anything. He was surprised that Rain hadn't caught on. But that's what love did—blinded everyone who looked at it.

The truth of it was that Jump wasn't sure Salvation was ready to hear it. She definitely didn't know. But ever since that night in the father's church, Rain and Fury had become more than good friends. And though he knew neither of them had figured out what to do about it yet, sooner or later that shit had a way of "figuring" itself out. "Look," he said to Fury, "I'm gonna go ahead and let you get to this one on your own. Because when you see him again, you need to tell him the truth."

"Truth?" Fury said. "What truth?"

"About how you feel," Jump said. "They deserve that."

— LVI —

FAITH STARED DOWN at Babette. She was still limp next to the elevator, but now surrounded by the blood and brains of the half a dozen Protection agents that he had just torn apart.

In life, the elevator was his moment. One of them, anyway. He'd had many of them, really. Chances at redemption—opportunities to do the good thing. Turn left and hide or turn right and live.

Looking back, they all seemed so simple. Lean a little this way or that, look the other way at the immorality and depravity that surrounded him. Stay silent in fear and not roar like the lion his father told him to be. In the end, there had been consequences on both sides of each decision he made.

Playing it safe hadn't offered any more safety than throwing himself into the arena with the lions. Those he could have helped, should have helped, languished under the weight of his inaction—his fear and lack of conviction.

What would have become of them if he had thrown himself in front of the flames that now burned around everyone he loved? Would he have suffered any more than he already had by doing nothing? Would they have suffered less?

The most good he had done in his life was at the threat of death from an ex-Protection agent who had seen the error of his lying and brutalizing ways. Certainly if Jump could find redemption, Faith could find his own truth? Was his book his only destiny? He hadn't believed it, but he had lived the lie for so long that each time he imagined the consequences of facing it, his fear chased him back to the comfort and warmth of his own deceptions.

Faith hardly noticed the tiny red specs at the other end of the pitch-black tunnel. With the lights freshly blown out and the long hallway bathed in the black of deep, dark lies . . . he should have. When the red specs finally got close enough for him to notice, it was almost too late.

He spun away from them and slammed his wings behind his back, just as the first of the red fire-feathers sliced into him and burned into his shield. And he yelled out and whipped his wings wide open, breaking the ends of five feathers, burning their way into his steel.

"I can smell that you've finally figured it out," the voice laughed from far down the hall. "Naughty, naughty, Ben. Always poking your stick where it doesn't belong. Now look at her. And her daughter? Shameful, it's just shameful!"

Faith knew the voice. But lost in self-loathing it was hard to protect himself. "Did you do this to her?" he asked. "You filthy dog!"

"Wages of sin," Dogg's voice came back. "You should know that better than anyone."

"She's not dead," Faith said. "Which is lucky for you," he muttered. He could just make out the outline of the archangel, Dogg, at the far end of the darkness. And he spun and fired as many fire-feathers as he could, releasing the telltale golden streaks of the followers of Rain. Then he watched as they grew smaller and smaller and then hit their mark. And he heard the echo come back—flaming metal piercing steel shield. And a few seconds later they all fell to the floor and their lights flickered and burned down.

And a growl and a howl wafted back from the darkness. "Owooooah," Dogg's voice echoed down the hall, "nice to see you're not impotent. Man of your age—need to be careful firing all those feathers at once. Never know when they'll turn up limp. Looks like you got a little sting left in you, though. Then again, so do I. She wakes up, you can ask her about it."

Faith paced back and forth at his end of the tunnel. He glanced down briefly at Babette on the floor.

It was another test—another crossroads to face. Run like his instincts begged him to, or stand and fight as he wished he had in the past. "I feel for you," Faith said. He pushed out all of his armored feathers and tightened them against each other and they scraped metal on metal. And a loud squeal reverberated as sparks flashed and fell, burning down to the floor.

"Aw," Dogg yelled back, "don't you worry about me. She felt enough for me and you both."

Faith stopped and faced him. He had made his decision. "Then I shall put to death the sinful, earthly things lurking within you," he said.

"Damn," Dogg's voice wafted back, "you are one helluva hypocrite, Ben. Spouting that *Bible* shit at me like that. Right after she told you that she—you're a priest, for God's sake! How did you think that that was okay? I mean, what did you tell yourself . . . when you were about to stick it in her? What, you just hold your hands over your eyes and plan on asking for forgiveness later? How do you even get it—how did you think you were getting back after that?"

"I may not go back," Faith said. "I may never return to my faith, but I'm sending you back, so you may beg for forgiveness from your master."

"Don't worry about her either," Dogg's voice shouted back, "there's begging all right, just not for forgiveness. So what do you say we stop —?"

Around a hundred tiny pinfeathers pelted Dogg all over his body and wings and arms, stinging him like little wasps. And a couple even streaked through his cheeks and he yelped like a hound getting whipped with a stick. "Dammit!" he yelled, and then he ran and took off flying toward Faith. "Sneaking son of a bitch," he said, flying faster and wiping blood from his face.

Dogg could see Faith, flying at him from the other end of the tunnel. Closer and closer the angel streaked at him, and faster and faster Dogg flew.

Then Dogg twisted in mid-air and loosed pinfeathers at Faith—he could play that same little trick.

And the pinfeathers streaked into Faith's plumage and ripped and tore at metal. Then he twisted himself and loosed as many glowing-gold fire-feathers as he could. Golden-yellow streaks burned down the dark tunnel.

And Dogg fired his red fire-feather tracers—the color of Lived and Life's armies in the dungeons.

And burning gold feathers passed raging red ones, in a fireworks display that would have looked beautifully magical had it not been for where they were headed . . . and what they were meant to do.

And flaming feathers pierced both of their armored feathers and they both broke wing quills and crashed, sliding along the slick floor of the tunnel until they slammed into each other.

Dogg rolled and pounced on top of Faith, and he grabbed around the angel's neck with both hands, sinking his talons in, and Faith coughed and choked.

Faith beat at Dogg with his wings and cut and sliced Dogg's feathers. Sparks flew and Dogg growled and Faith flailed at his attacker. Neither could fire feathers this close together.

Faith sunk his talons into Dogg's side and legs, and the animal let out a horrible yell and then started yipping.

Then Dogg let go of Faith's throat and sunk all of his talons into Faith's chest and stomach, and Faith screeched and screamed back.

Feathers broke and talons dug through metal and found flesh, and red and black blood flowed—from right hearts and wrong ones—and they both screamed and growled and screeched in anger and agony.

Faith rolled with Dogg and he got on top of him, and then he flapped and slapped his wings at Dogg's face, cutting and slicing into his cheeks. But Dogg rolled back on top of him and choked Faith again.

Faith coughed and struggled for air and turned blue, while Dogg growled and laughed out loud. "You wanna spout the Word?" Dogg said. He gripped tighter as he spoke, "Any slave who knows his master's will . . . and doesn't prepare himself for it"—Dogg beat his wings at Faith's head—"will be severely beaten!"

After a few seconds, Dogg could feel Faith's strength starting to leave him and he let up just enough so the fallen archangel could breathe—come back to life. There was no sense killing the little bird quickly. He wanted to toy with it before he ate it.

Dogg shoved himself off of Faith's chest and then stood up and spit. He looked at his wing—feathers missing and broken at the tip. Then he frowned down at Faith. "You want to hear the Word from her *Bible?*" he said. He swung his other wing down at Faith and clipped off the tip of Faith's wing. "There's a little wing for a wing for ya."

And Faith's wingtip sprayed blood across the floor and he screeched and folded it over his chest, grabbing onto it with one of his arms. He rolled to the side and spoke softly to himself, "I have done all that I can to live in peace with everyone." And he tightened his wing and he held it firmly back with his arm, tensing every feather in his body. And God or Life or Rain or no one at all, Faith spoke softly to himself at the end of his fall, "I am a servant for good. But if you do wrong to me or those I love, be afraid, for I shall not bear my sword in vain"— he even rolled the dice on defying the blasphemy covenant, because he figured he wasn't going back anyway—"for I am a servant of gods, an avenger who carries out their wrath on wrongdoers."

"What are you muttering down there?" Dogg asked. Then he leaned down and turned to the side a little, so that he could hear. And he opened his wings just in case he had to pin the old angel down again.

Faith tensed up even harder, pulling on his wing until he thought he might break it, then he released it from his arm's grip and let it spring loose like a rat trap. His wing sliced through the few feet that separated him from Dogg's back and his steel feathers and bone cut clean through the base of Dogg's outstretched wings, and both of them flapped one last time before they spun to the side of the tunnel —cut off.

Dogg howled, yipped and yelped, and his back sprayed blood, and he cried out and whimpered, "Aaaaaah!" He rolled on his back trying to make the pain go away. But when he did, the stumps of his wings shot pain and agony into his spine and he cried out again and flung himself at the wall, trying to make the pain stop, and everything he did just made it worse.

Faith rolled over and watched as Dogg bounced, hopped and howled himself down the hall. Until he finally stopped and whimpered against a wall.

"Look what you've. . ." he growled. "You whore-fucking bastard! Now what am I going to. . .?"

Faith stood up slowly and stretched his wings wide. They were hurting and damaged, but still attached, unlike Dogg's. He was alive, and also unlike Dogg, Faith was still an archangel of one of the two Heavens. Which one would have to be decided when he got back, but for now the fact that he was an angel was enough.

Faith knew that was more than Dogg had, because every angel in the two Heavens understood what would happen if their wings got cut off. He walked over to the whining, whimpering mutt, Dogg. "And now you can feel what it's like to be mortal again," he said. Then he swung his wing as hard as he could, lopping off Dogg's whimpering head.

As Dogg's head rolled across the floor and blood pumped from the stump on his body, Faith limped back toward Babette, dragging a badly injured leg as he went.

And now he knew what he had to do to get back.

— LVII —

I'M STILL STRAPPED down to this chair. This dream's getting old, but I. . . My eye's still swollen, so I guess—maybe it is real, I don't know. I'm beat to shit, I know that. Like . . . "Aah," I let out a little groan. She said not to do that, but—she was. . .?

"She's waking up," I hear her voice clear enough. That's me—my voice.

I struggle to get my eyes open this time. It's like, a bad hang day, or some stupid shit. Groggy. . . Whole body is. . . It's a slow ache now, kinda like . . . like too many liqs and—who are all these. . .?

I'm hallucinating again. There's a big, burly-looking—yep, I'm jacked up on J, because that's like . . . an angel or some stupid fairy shit. But I—there was like, a copy of me or something. She was all *bitching* at me. I was—there she is. Still here, I think.

Then I see them. How many? Six little. . . What the hell are those things? Like little winged midgets or something. Baby angels. I am *so* tripping on J!

"You're not tripping," my bitchy-self's voice again. "Well, technically, like, I guess you are fucked up, but you're not drunk."

I look closer at the little ones. It's like, they're confused, or—shit, I'm confused. "What are those things?"

Sounds like I—she chirps at them, like a bird or something. And they all go running behind me. I can hear them back there, cheeping and chirping like little baby chicks. This is some bad J. I'm gonna kick

Brie's ass. She never gets the good stuff. Total gullible bitch. Have to get her credits back. I guess it's better than those other hallucinations —that was harsh. I hope he didn't—

They're whispering to each other—the big one and—I think I recognize him. No idea, but he's leaned over and she's—I'm—"Hey," I say to her, because I don't think I'm yelling at him, "that's just . . . rude. I'm right here. Anyways, it's my dream, so untie me, guardian angel fucks."

They walk over to me and stare down. I know who that fucker is! I seen him on my dad's Protection—"I know who you are," I say to him. "Untie me. My dad's gonna—"

He looks over at . . . me—angel-me. That's still spinning my brain. "She doesn't know," he says to angel-me. They're like, ignoring me— totally rude.

"Hello, right here, asshole," I say to him this time. "Rude."

He laughs a little, still ignoring me and looking at her. "Your charming vocabulary hasn't changed much," he says to her.

And angel-me frowns at him. Then she looks—I look down at me. This is a serious trip. "Do we like, untie her?" she asks. "What if she runs away?"

He's like, a foot taller than her. "Where's she gonna go," he laughs, "Cancun?"

"So not funny," she says to him. At least my angel-me doesn't take any shit off assholes, because I'm starting to feel like . . . like I shouldn't like this guy.

I close my eyes and my head slumps down—I'm . . . I feel exhaust-ed. I guess I should be—spinning through all this shit. Where did all that come from? Like flashes of my—oh, shit. . .

I open my eyes back up, kinda slow, because I'm not sure if I want to know. But angels and little angels and being in—"What . . . in the fuck . . . is that?" I say when I see all of it.

I was too busy looking up at them before. The floor's got like—there's dead people everywhere!

"I told you little purgies," angel-me says to the little ones, "she's gonna freak. Now drag them out of here like I told you."

But I'm still like . . . dead bodies! "They're dead?" I ask.

Angel-me looks behind her at the little ones wrestling with the bodies, and . . . and chunks of bodies—shit!

The little ones—they look all black and they have little . . . like wings? They're dragging everything out the door.

They still aren't untying me. What the. . .?

Then angel-me looks at me. "How's she going to—how can I do that shit?" she asks the big one. And she is pissed—I know my voice.

Then the big angel looks me in the eyes. "Not a question of how," he says, "she . . . you *have* to do it. Otherwise, no one's going back. And we still gotta find Faith, because he's fucked too. Right now, no time for this. Tell her and be done with it. I still gotta wipe my own ass over there and deal with your daddy." Then the big one walks off muttering to himself, "Can't believe—it's your lucky day, Frank. Nothing's easy."

I'm a bitch, but I'm not stupid. "Am I . . . dead?" I ask angel-me.

"You wish," she says.

I frown at her, because that's like, my own sarcastic voice she's using . . . on me. "Tell me what?" I ask her.

By the time angel-me is done whispering my fate to me . . . I guess . . . I guess I do wish I was already dead. "Well, what if like, when you untie me, I just jump right out a window or some shit? Or maybe run away? How 'bout that, bitch?"

She smiles at me and I know it's shitty, because that's like, what I do when I tell someone something they don't wanna hear. "Trust me," she says, "you do not wanna do that. Falling is totally scary . . . then and probably scarier now. Anyways, you're not hard enough to handle. . ." She looks behind her at the big angel, staring into the room with the blown-out glass. "Better to let him do it," she says.

"He's throwing me out a window?" I say. Then I look over at him and scrunch my eyebrows. "Fuck him."

Angel-me turns and looks at him, too. "You sure she's not remembering this, because like—"

The big angel doesn't look back. He just keeps staring into that room. I try to lean to see what he's looking at, but he must hear me or something, because he spreads his wings way out—they're huge—and I can't see around them. "She won't remember," he says. "Do you remember?"

"This shit?" angel-me says. "None of it."

"Ipso facto. . ." I think the big angel mutters.

What the. . .? I think.

And then angel-me reads my mind? "Yeah," she says, "don't think about it too much—it'll judge up your head. Have a couple of Blonde Bimbos, hit a little J, you'll cruise right through it. It's only a year—like that's . . . barely a second."

For some reason, I don't think she's talking about the dead bodies. I don't know how I will forget any of this, though.

Then the little midget-angels start filing and fluttering back into the room . . . and they've got another one with them. *How many. . .?* But when I look closer, I definitely know who that one is.

— LVIII —

WHEN FURY SAW the look of recognition on Mercedes' face, she spun around and almost fired feathers at him . . . again.

"Heaven help—whoa-whoa," Faith shouted. "Easy . . . easy." Then he limped into the room. His wings sagged and his body slumped—he'd been in some kind of fight.

Fury turned back to Jump. His wings were still wide, shielding the other two. "We cleansing the garden again?" she said. "Like, every angel with wings, flying around down here." Then she turned back to Faith. "What are *you* doing here . . . old cocksucker?"

Faith frowned a little. Daughter or not, her vulgarity was—she was a singular force to be reckoned with. "Good to see you, too," he said. Then he looked around the room. "You've been . . . busy."

The tearful reunions would have to wait, as would Faith accounting for shooting a fire-feather into Jump's back. When they started bickering about it, Fury told them both, "Stuff a cock in it because we don't have time for you bitching at each other! Faith, watch the hall while we clean this shit up."

Once Jump grumbled past his need for retribution and Faith explained his own return to the garden, Fury sent Faith into the hall to stand guard and they got to work cleaning up her "feather-fuck." Because that's what the whole thing was turning into, Jump told her.

* * *

When they were done, Fury summoned Faith back into the cell and he looked around. He had missed a few things in their haste to put him back in the hallway. Now he could see why.

Remnants of body parts that the little purgatories had obviously missed were strewn across the floor. Fury and Jump stood angrily on opposite sides of the cell, and Frank—the real one—and a Protection agent that looked like—*that's Jake—Jump?* Faith thought.

The PAIC—Jake—and Frank were duct-taped to chairs and their mouths were taped shut, too. Mercedes was taped up behind them. Faith limped toward her, dragging his leg a little quicker now. "Untie her!" he shouted. "Why are you—?"

Fury stepped in front of him. "Can't do it," she said. "It'll all get fucked up."

Faith almost threw his good wing at her to get her out of his way, but technically Fury was his daughter, too. He looked past her, at Mercedes again. The girl was badly beaten and her eyes were swollen, and he could see that some of her hair was ripped out and on the floor at her feet. "God help me," Faith said. "Who did this?"

Jump frowned. "You're gonna wanna stop talking like that," he said to Faith. "Shit's getting a *little* too real."

"Stop saying what?" Faith asked.

"The G-word," Jump replied. "The mercy shit, too."

Faith frowned. Jump was a disbelieving blasphemer in life, but after what they had all seen in death? And all this? "Why?" he asked.

"Yeah, why?" Fury asked. She was curious, too. "Rain's not down here."

"Not that it would matter," Jump said. Then he looked up at the nothingness. "But she's not the one I'm worried about. Something I read. . ."

— LIX —

THE PAIC AND Frank both flitted their eyes around the room. Taped down to chairs, in the middle of an obvious Judgment overdose, neither of them could speak or move. But who had shot them. . .?

Images of angels and cherubs and winged warriors, coming to take souls to Heaven, filled their minds. The hallucination was so real that they could even smell smoke and gunpowder and feel the pain and panic in the room.

And when the PAIC looked closely, he could see that the girl angel was this bastard Frank's other daughter—the twin had turned pissed-off angel from Hell. *Gotta make it through the Judgment,* he thought. *You're remanded, Jake, wait it out. Did I stick that bastard in the neck?*

But that girl angel wasn't the only pissed-off fairy in the cell with them—the big angel wore a familiar scowl that Jacob Oliver Blake, PAIC, saw every morning when he shaved in the mirror. That big angel . . . was him.

And when that angel turned his attention back to the two of them in the chairs, Jake got a little nervous. It had been a while since anything had scared him, but a big angel that looked just like him? That did the job.

Jake's personal guardian angel caught him trying to work on the tape with his fingernails. Then the angel walked over, spread his wings wide, and squatted down in front of him.

The wings were impressively huge, and Jake figured the fairy had to spread them out in order to squat down. That's what a PAIC was trained to do—catalogue details.

The angel looked at Jake's hand. "You can stop that shit," he said. "I'm not killing you." Then he looked at Frank in the chair next to Jake. "But I can't let you kill him, either."

Then Jake struggled against his tape even harder. He had to kill the bastard—he'd come too far to let a hallucination stop him.

"Don't worry," the big angel said, "you'll get to him later." Then the angel held up the syringe from Jake's pocket. He smiled. "Right now, he's just gonna take a nice little trip. You missed his artery anyway." The angel reached over to Frank's collar and pulled the man's shirt down a little, revealing his mesh-armored under-suit. "Little paranoid, don't ya think?"

Jake struggled some more, but he was taped tight.

The big angel looked right into Frank's eyes. "That's the thing about assfucking people, Frank—pretty soon, all you're doing is looking over your shoulder, clenching up all the time, trying to make sure it doesn't happen to you."

"Wait," Fury said. She walked over behind Jump. His wings blocked her from getting at her father . . . and the other "loose end" they still had to clean up. She could see now that the guy was Jump. "You're not even like, letting *me* do it?"

Jump paused. Then he turned his head behind him and looked into Fury's eyes. She was still wild with pent-up rage. "You're gonna cut his head off," he said. "It's all over your face. You know I can't let you do that."

Then Frank started bouncing up and down in his chair and muffled screams came out from behind the tape over his mouth.

Jump turned back and clucked a little chuckle at him. "Shut . . . up," he said slowly. "I *should* let her. Be doing you a favor." He shook his head. "You have no idea. Eh, but since I kinda like my life the way it is now . . . well, I guess Miss Mercedes and I will just have to crack your little eggs in your nest." And then Jump raised up the syringe.

"No, no, no," Fury raised her voice behind him. "I didn't like, fly all the way down here, dragging these little purgie bitches, so you could deliver him judgment. That's bullshit! That's not what you said."

Jump paused the needle in front of Frank's face, letting him get a good look at his company's "wonder" drug, dripping out of the tip—that was his agreement with Fury. He looked at her while he hovered the needle behind him. "Hmm. . ." he said, "maybe . . . but you have to *promise* not to cut his head off. That shit in the church—I could barely handle all that blood, spraying and spewing out of his neck like that. You are one sick—you might be meaner than me."

Fury looked into Frank's eyes. They were wide as her wings. Then she looked at Jump. He could hardly stop from cracking a smile. "What if like. . .? Ooh, I know," she said, "I'll cut off his cock. That—that's fair." She would like to do that very thing, but after she and Jump's little chat, the stakes were now beyond her need for revenge against her father.

Jump frowned at her. Fury was enjoying torturing the man. But that was their deal, so he shrugged a little and moved the needle closer to Frank's neck. "I don't know," he said, "how's he gonna piss? And he'll get all infected. Messy, too. You ever cut a cock off? They bleed like a stuck pig—messy . . . very messy."

And sweat rolled down Frank's forehead and nose and he started hyperventilating, sucking in the salty liquid through his nostrils, and then he choked and tried to cough behind the tape.

Fury frowned and pouted her face a little. "Balls?" she said. "At least let me take his balls. That's like, *totally* fair."

Faith could see that Jump and Fury were simply torturing the two of them, wasting valuable time. He could feel the sands of eternity galloping at them—somehow he knew there wasn't much time left.

The torture didn't bother him as much as he thought it should. Frank was a filthy dog, in life and after. And Faith wondered.

What was Dogg doing—where was his soul? Faith hadn't heard a soul-security gathering angel since he let Life resurrect him. And from the looks of the bodies piling up in the hall, not to mention the ones he and the father had left in the other interrogation wing, there was a huge backup of waiting souls to take back to Purgatory.

But Faith had sent Father Benito looking for Mercedes. When he stopped to think about it, he was nowhere to be found.

Distracted by Jump and Fury's little game, Faith hadn't checked the edges of the cell. "Excuse me," Faith said to them both, "but when you two are done with him, can you tell me what the *hell* is going on? And where am—where is Father Benito?"

— LX —

RESURRECTION, RAIN THOUGHT. She knew the tide of re-demption could go out as quickly as it came in. If Fury wasn't careful, it would sweep her out to sea with it—a little bird, lost in an ocean of her own self-denial. If Rain's friend harmed a hair on her own father's body, she could never be redeemed. She would simply repeat her trial, and her judgment in Heaven would be the same.

Salvation continued to watch the fall with Rain. Seeing Jump and Fury toy with Fury's father, she felt a darkness in him that she hadn't known before. He enjoyed watching the man squirm in fear. Yet, the man was an evil animal. Salvation had overheard Fury and Jump speak about it. And then there was Vegas.

Fury had alluded to it the whole time she and Salvation cleansed Sin City. Watching older men parade through casinos with young hookers barely out of high school, Salvation hadn't really understood Fury's contempt and joy as she killed them. Now, watching Fury delight in torturing her father, it seemed more obvious.

Rain looked into the fall. "Mother?" she said.

"Oh my—Rain, don't listen," Salvation said. She stopped watching and looked at her daughter. "That's just—does she always talk like that?"

Rain giggled a little. "Not always," she said, "sometimes it's worse. But . . . it's kinda cute too, don't you think? She just shouts about nothing, and it is—she likes to hear herself talk. I think it keeps the memories out of her mind—calms her down. I just . . . I just want her to get back here."

Salvation rolled her eyes. "Just like your father," she said. "Heaven and Hell have mercy. I have to deal with two of them now? I can't handle one." She looked into Rain's eyes. "Are you sure about how long this takes?"

Rain was worried. Fury was wild and many times unpredictable, and the moon and the sun would only pause for a few more hours—her friend had to repent in order to be redeemed before that. She read from her book, following along with her finger, "The sun stood still, and the moon stopped, till the nation avenged itself on its enemies. And time stopped and delayed the passing of one full day."

She looked back at the fall, at Fury torturing her father. "She has but a few hours left. She has this time. How she chooses will free her soul or trap her forever in Life's eternity. And that is why she has to hurry."

"I'm starting to hate the books," said Salvation. "Where do they. . .?" She looked at Rain. "How do you think all this up? It's—nothing makes sense."

— LXI —

FURY LISTENED TO Jump's theory about Rain's Prayer of the Protectors. He *was* a conspiracy-ranting old cocksucker, always cursing and muttering about dictators and shit. Even in Hell, even after Rain cast Life and Lived into the dungeons, he brooded about authority. He used to say that Life was just like the overpopulating monkeys she made in her garden—she always found a way to fill the world with more shit.

But *this* shit. He wasn't a believer, so how could he. . .? "That's why she helped me come back?" Fury said. "She needed fresh believers? Jesus Christ. Hah, like that's gonna work. I'm not begging forgiveness for anything." Fury *was* here to be redeemed, but Life had never said anything about—"Oh, that bitch," she said, "she lied to me."

"Ya think," Jump said to her. Then he frowned. "For a smartass, you can be pretty dumb. So, now you got me chasing you around down here—cleaning up after you again—because you wanted to. . . What exactly are you doing down here, anyway? And don't say training purgies, either." He glanced at the six of them, looking a little more other-worldly, black feathers covered in red blood after dragging chunks and corpses to the hall.

The little purgatories hopped and clucked in place, obviously enjoying their first duties in the garden.

"Look at them," Jump continued, "they're a mess. There's better places to teach them this shit. And revenge? You could do that up there on any Judgment night. Shit, walk right down in the dungeon and kick the dog any time you want."

"Lord almighty, Jesus!" Faith shouted. Fury and Jump jerked their heads toward him. They hadn't noticed, but Faith had finally found Father Ben's body, in the corner where Fury told the purgies to put him. "I told him to—oh, no-no-no. You killed him! Why did you kill him? He was your—"

"Hold it together," Jump raised his voice. "And I told you to stop with the begging for Jesus shit. She didn't kill him. Those Protection agents in the hall shot him before—nothing she could do about it. We both tried. Not that we shouldn't have shot his ass—running in here all waving his gun, dressed up like an agent." Jump raised his eyebrows and scrunched up his face at Faith. "And she needs to figure that *other* shit out herself. So, keep your mouth shut and let her. And by the way, we still have to get back to you shooting me in the back!"

"What other. . .?" Fury said.

Faith gave Jump a fatherly look. "Yes . . . well," he said. "That was . . . an unfortunate. . ." Then he nodded a couple of times at Jump. "I am sorry for that, but—"

Jump frowned back at him. "I liked you better when you were sucking on your tin tit," he mumbled. "Goddamn booze—aw, shit!"

Fury jerked her head toward him. "I thought we weren't supposed to say—"

"Why again aren't we supposed to say 'God?' " Faith asked. "Or Jesus?"

"Stop!" Jump shouted. It was getting messy and there were bound to be more Protection agents showing up any minute, suspension of time or not. He looked at Fury and said, "We don't have time for—

here it is: Life's only reason for you to be down here is to torture you somehow. And she's using her pretend puppet-master to help her. Only way she can do that—put you through some suffering." He paused and pointed to the father's dead body.

Faith stared down at himself as Father Benito. He shook his head. "I just can't believe. . ."

Jump continued, "That's the only way he—the only way both of them got people following them in the first place. Guilt-ridden, suffering citizens—they make good sheep, don't they, Faith?"

Faith was silent, but he did look up and over at Jump briefly before he stared back down at his own dead body—Father Benito.

"Yeah. . ." Jump said. Then he looked back at Fury. "Anyway, I'm guessing you've suffered"—he pointed to Mercedes, sleeping in her chair, smiling as the Judgment slithered its way through her blood-stream, probably causing her to dream about pixie-fairies and warm beaches in Cancun—"she's suffered plenty for both of you. So the only thing you have to decide—because the rest of us are just along for the ride on this little Judgment trip of yours—are you gonna condemn him or are you not? Because I've made my decision—I'm gonna let this bastard wake up to his little nightmare the same way I did last time. So, what's it gonna be?" And Jump held up the syringe, offering it to Fury. She was a big girl. It was time he let her act like it. "Get him cracked or let's get back, because time is gonna start ticking again *real* soon, and I got a feeling that that bitch is getting exactly what she wants."

"Stand him up!" Fury shouted.

As soon as Jump cut Frank free and jerked him to his feet, Fury raced at him and grabbed him with all of her talons—wrapped them around his arms and legs, and then she knocked him to the floor. He went down with a thud and she landed on top of his chest.

Fury spread her wings wide and pushed off the floor, holding herself and Frank up a couple of feet above it. Then she reached behind her back and held her hand open at Jump. As soon as she felt the syringe in her palm, she said, "Franklin James King, you are hereby remanded to my *fucking* Protection," She said. The vial was three-quarters full—the PAIC had planned on double-dosing Frank.

Jump had gently injected a quarter of the syringe into Mercedes' neck and she was out cold, dreaming the sweet angel dream.

Fury held the syringe tightly. Half of a full vial would send her raping father into a euphoric fantasy dream about flying with fairies and banging his secretaries, no doubt. When he woke up, no one would believe a word he said. But he would know to keep his mouth shut anyway—crazy talk got you killed. If Fury gave him the rest of the vial—three quarters—he would end up a psychotic, religious nutjob.

Fury hovered the needle inches from Frank's neck. It was all she could do to stop from eating the man's eyes out. She leaned in close enough for him to get a good look at his future. And she let a little bit of her saliva drip onto his lips—taste the rage in her. Then she gritted her teeth and spoke slowly, "State your compliance, bitch. And you *better* submit to judgment too, or I'll tear your guts out and eat them while you watch."

"Please," Frank said. "I—"

"Wrong answer," said Fury and she jammed the needle into her father's neck.

"Aaaah—wait-wait-wait!" Frank shouted. Then he stared into his daughter's demon-angel eyes. There was nothing there to bargain with. "I submit to . . . to—to your judgment." And then he closed his eyes.

Fury grabbed the two twisting snakes on the side of the syringe and she pushed down hard on the wing-shaped plunger at the top, injecting him with about a quarter of the liquid.

Frank's eyes rolled back, and the whites turned black and he started to shake in Fury's grip. Then she slowly pushed in another quarter of the sleep serum, debating in her head. She held herself and Frank there for a couple of seconds, still pressing the needle into his neck, drinking in the pleasure of feeling him shake.

"No!" Rain shouted at the fall. And she lunged toward the nothingness, preparing to stop Fury from killing her father.

Salvation stepped in front of Rain and let her slam into her, then she grabbed the tops of Rain's wings at their base and held her back. "You can't!" she shouted. Whatever came next, intervention wasn't the answer. "She's not—she can still save herself. You don't know what—"

"Don't touch—she can't!" Rain shouted back. She struggled in Salvation's grip, but her mother held her firmly. Then Rain closed her eyes and looked away from the fall. She stopped struggling and went a little limp. "I cannot—please, I don't want to see it."

Salvation turned Rain away from the fall and held her slumping daughter in her arms. "It'll be okay," she said. "Have a little faith."

Fury looked up and screeched out a long, loud scream above her head. When she was done, she ripped the needle out of Frank's neck and threw the quarter-full syringe across the cell. Then she dropped her father's body to the floor and watched him spasm and shake.

She stood up and looked at Mercedes, sleeping in her chair. That's what a quarter vial of J would do to someone. Fury knew that. Now, so did Mercedes. "Don't fuck it up," she said to her sleeping "sister."

Then Fury sucked in a deep breath of air, trying to calm herself down. She looked across the cell at Faith.

Faith stared back at her. The fear was just leaving his face.

"Stop pissing yourself," Fury said to him. "What's *your* problem? Afraid I was gonna kill my own father?"

Faith stared back . . . at his daughter sleeping in the chair and then at his vengeful child staring back at him as an angry archangel. "I . . . I—"

"Yeah," Fury said. "Ya-ya—you. Why *are* you back down here, anyways?"

Faith stood and stared at her. He still couldn't bring himself to admit it.

Fury looked over at the father's corpse. "Couldn't save her, huh? Sucks again," she said to Faith. "So your trip's like, a total waste." She stared at Faith, waiting for him to respond, but he said nothing. "Why do you keep trying with her? She's totally gone to the darkness. Growling around down in that dungeon. She reaped that for you, ya know. Yeah . . . and you got to live all *righteous* in Heaven." She glanced over at Jump. His eyes were a little wider, too. "Uh-huh, I figured that out. Calling me a dumbass. Whatever."

"How did—how did you. . .?" Faith stumbled on his words.

Fury looked back at him. She folded her wings a little tighter behind her back. "Couple of old cocksucking idiots, you two are," she said. "Duh, my loft is like—I had to sleep right above you two humping. . . You guys—sick! I don't even wanna *think* about it. No wonder you're—"

Faith still couldn't believe she knew. "I am sorry. I never—that does not mean—" he said. "You . . . you have red hair like . . . and—"

"Jesus," Fury said to Faith. She slowly shook her head. "And—and what? I looked that up on the feed, ya know. Hello, two parents with light eyes. You don't get brown eyes from that. And you . . . your eyes are scared as shit brown. You flew down here for redemption? Good luck on that, because the denial's not helping you get it."

— LXII —

AFTER FURY FINISHED ripping the denial off of Faith's wide eyes, the three of them stared down at the father's body. The little purgatories crowded around behind them, peaking through legs and jostling each other to get a better view.

Fury swept her wing back and sent a couple of little hatchlings sliding across the cell's concrete floor.

They rolled and jumped up and scurried back to their positions.

They're learning, Fury thought. She looked back down at the father's body—her father. "Miserable old—why isn't it coming out?" she asked, herself more than anyone else.

It had been almost a full day back in the garden and the only return ticket to Heaven or Hell that any of them could think of wasn't showing itself. There wasn't a wriggling, squirming maggoty-soul coming out of a single one of the dead bodies that were piling up in the bottom of the *Fifty*. Surely Rain would be sending down some soul-security angels to start gathering them up.

It was a dirty job—ferrying spent souls from the garden to the pearly gates of the arena for recycling—but they had all done it. Fly down through the portal, grab the little maggot with your talons, fly the screaming, screeching thing back to Purgatory. It was disgusting duty, but pretty simple, too. That was why it was one of the first real tasks a freshly cracked hatchling was given.

"Why isn't she sending some purgatories down to clean up the corpses?" Fury asked again. This time she *was* looking for an answer.

There was jostling around her legs again as the little hatchlings shoved at each other and bumped into her legs.

"Knock it off!" she shouted down at them. "You fidgeting little—I can't hear myself bitch. If you pissing little purgies don't knock it off, I'm—"

Jump laughed out loud. Then he got control of himself and put his hand over his mouth. He looked down at Fury's feet. The little hatchlings were all over her legs—in and out and between like cats.

"I know," said Fury, "they're annoying little shits, aren't they?"

"Purgatories. . ." Jump said, hoping she would get a direct hint. The moon and the sun were setting on this day, and that meant they had to hurry up. But just like the garden, souls were the only way in and out of Purgatory. And carrying one or burying one, they were shitty business, best left to newly cracked hatchlings. "Eh, what are you gonna do with them?"

Fury adjusted her wings and cocked her head sideways. He was her father, and he had been her friend, kinda, but the feelings just weren't there. Why would they be? She didn't have a bond with anyone.

Rain, she thought. Those feelings were weird, but right now her benevolent Protector was starting to piss her off. She looked at Jump, still holding his mouth. "Why doesn't she send me a pack of purgies to clean this—?"

Jump and Faith cawed a little, laughing at her.

Fury closed her eyes and frowned and shook her head. "Aw, shit," she said. "Go suck your own dicks, you bastards. I can't believe I—son of a bitch!" Then she turned to her pack of little purgatories.

The little purgatories hopped and clucked and cheeped with excitement.

"Listen up," Fury said to them, "you annoying, little maggot-movers. All you gotta do is reach in, grab onto it like, real tight, and then drag its ass straight up. Once you get up above the city, you'll see the way. Then turn your asses around and come down and get another one. Unless she decides to help us, and then maybe you won't have to get them all." Then she pushed the first little fidgeting fledgling over next to the father's body and nudged him toward it. "Go ahead, sink your talons right into him . . . just above the belly button."

The three archangels and the rest of the little purgatories watched the little hatchling reach tentatively toward the father's midsection.

"Stop pigeon-pecking around," Jump said. And then he reached down, rammed his talons into the father's corpse, rummaged around for a couple of seconds and then he ripped out the father's writhing soul.

The maggot wiggled around in Jump's hand and moaned and wailed like it was in pain. Then Jump handed it to the little purgatory, making sure he had a good grip before he let go completely, and then he looked at Fury. He motioned with his hands for her to send the little hatchling on his way.

Fury looked at him like she always did. "What the—"

"No time for that shit," Jump said. "Next. Get him out of here and let's get back to it."

Fury sent the little purgatory on his way and ordered the rest of them to start cleaning up the hallway. Once they left the cell, she said, "Well, there's how *those* little bitches are getting back, but like, how are we?"

Then an alarm blasted like a great horn. One long harbor-clearing . . . heart-stopping . . . haunting moan. And the building shook and rumbled on its foundation.

"Holy shit!" Fury said. "What the *hell* was that?"

Jump knew exactly what the blast was. He recited it to Fury and Faith exactly as he had read the passage in Rain's book, "And upon the great moan of the trumpet, the sun and the moon ground the gears of eternity again, and the darkness of night crept forward toward the burning truth of dawn"—he gave Fury his trademark half grin-half frown—"and judgment and damnation followed."

— LXIII —

JUMP PAUSED FOR a second, cataloguing the carnage around him. He had done it countless times while in charge of Protection clean crews when he was a Man-monkey. "Loose ends, loose ends," he muttered. "Gotta clean this shit up. Come on, Jake, work it."

"We fucked up," Fury said. "Shoulda left the father's soul—"

"He was dead," Faith stated the obvious to her.

"Well," Fury said, "*you* were supposed to make sure that didn't happen! So now—"

They could all hear the boots coming down the hallway. Fighting off Man-monkeys, running for your life—the garden hadn't changed much since the cleansing. *Maybe a little reversed*, Fury thought.

"Time to improvise," Jump said to Faith. "Bring his body."

Fury looked down at the empty husk that used to be the vessel for Father Benito's soul. "What good is that gonna—"

"Bring him!" Jump shouted. *Still got the Judgment syringe—quarter full. Gotta swap out the father. Only one way for Fury and Faith to go back. That leaves me*, he rocketed through the list of things to clean up in his head.

The PAIC had finally "fingernailed" his way through the tape on one of his wrists. When his arm popped free, he ripped the tape off his mouth, and then he said, "Where's Amy?"

Jump stopped and looked at him. Thinking he was in a hallucination Judgment trip or not, that's what he would have asked. Technically—he smiled at the thought because it was just too insane—he *had* just asked it. "Sh—she's fine," he said, "but *you* gotta get outta here."

"Bullshit," the PAIC said, "I don't stutter. Just tell me if she's okay?"

Just then, one of the little purgatories—the one that took the father's soul—came flying back into the room. And gunfire echoed down the hallway behind him. The little guy looked completely flustered.

They all glanced at him briefly, and then Jump looked at Fury and said, "We're taking too long. You gotta scrape him."

Fury ran at the PAIC.

"Wait-wait!" he said. "I just want to see her—"

Fury touched both of her hands to the agent's face and his eyes rolled back, and his head and then his whole body went limp. She let go of him and his head tilted forward and bounced off his chest once before it was still.

The little purgatory stopped cold. He just stared at Fury.

Fury clucked a laugh at him and said, "Didn't know we could do that, did ya? So much to learn, so little time to like, burn it into your stupid little feathers. Now, get out of my face—fly and get me another maggot to Hell." She watched the little angel leave. "And don't get shot, either . . . idiot." Then she looked back at Jump. He was taking the tape off the PAIC—himself—from the chair. "What the *fuck* are you doing?" she asked him.

Jump kept cutting. "Loose end," he said. He didn't even look up. "He's coming too."

"Where are we going?" Faith asked.

For an angel, trying to outrun the Word, the fastest way they knew was to fly. No better place to do that, in Jump's opinion, but before he could get the words out—

"The roof?" Fury shouted.

— LXIV —

IT WAS A furious fight to get to the stairwell. Once Fury, Faith and Jump heard the first long alarm blast, there were Protection agents everywhere.

Feathers had flown and blood had spilled and limbs had severed. Carrying bodies while they fought had Faith and Jump at about half their normal worth in a fire-fight. And they certainly couldn't use their shields with one wing around a limp Man-monkey. Fury did most of the blood-spilling.

And spill she had, but as fast as she cut Protection agents to pieces, more showed up. They were like rats, scurrying and racing at them as they fired. Finally she just couldn't keep up, and all three of them took a few rounds through their armored feathers. When they finally made it to the stairwell. . . The purgatories had their first work as soul-security gathering angels cut out for them. Or cut up, if they listened to Jump's sarcasm while they fought.

Jump was leaking black blood, Faith was limping worse, and the tip of one of Fury's wings was broken. Then another long moaning trumpet blast shook the entire building.

"Dammit," Jump said, "that's two." He struggled to shut the door to the stairwell behind them. "Clock's ticking too fast. Burn it shut!" he yelled at Fury

Fury popped one of her fire-feathers out and started welding the steel doorjamb with it. Sparks and molten metal fell to the floor around her. "What clock?" she asked. "Two? Like, how many do we get?"

Barely one flight of stairs up—none of them knew how far down they were—Fury yelled behind her at Jump, talking between breaths, "How many . . . do we get?"

"Seven," it was all Jump had to say. The truth was, carrying himself as a Man-monkey PAIC and climbing stairs, it was all he had breath for.

"Mother of mercy," Faith said behind Jump.

"What?" Fury gasped back at Faith. Then she caught her breath again. "What are you bitching about?"

"You don't. . ." Faith yelled up the stairs at her. He coughed a little, choking on his words. "You don't . . . want to know."

— LXV —

SALVATION AND RAIN both looked away from the fall at the first blast of the horn.

"What the hell was that?" Salvation said.

"I . . . I'm not—I don't know," Rain said, but she had an idea where she might find out.

"What?" Salvation said. "I thought all of you Protectors knew everything. Not so smart *now*, are you? Damn. . ." she muttered. "Well, I might know what it is. Not good, not good at all."

Salvation leaned in next to her, while Rain read from Life's book—the *Bible*, "And the citizens shouted and the walls came down. And a second son was brought to life."

Rain stopped reading, and they both turned back and watched the fall. Fury was busy welding the edges of the door—melting the metal with her feather—locking their three archangels into the stairwell.

"Oh my God," Salvation raised her voice, "she's sending another Jesus!"

"Mother!"

"I'm sorry-I'm sorry," Salvation said. "It's just—she can't—how can she do that? She's in the dungeon."

"It is written," said Rain.

"It is—honestly?" Salvation said. "I wish all this stuff wasn't so much interpretation." She reached for the book. Rain gave it up only slightly grudgingly. Then Salvation looked at the last line. "Such a tiny little thing," she muttered. "One little letter . . . capital—her name's not capitalized."

Rain knew it hardly mattered. "Blind faith, Mother," she said. "The words only have meaning as one believes in them."

And then the second huge horn blasted and they both looked at the fall.

Rain turned back to Life's book and read out loud, "And a second trumpet plunged a great burning mountain into the sea and—"

"I forget," Salvation said, "what happened on the first one?"

Rain ran her finger back up the page to the description of the first trumpet. "Upon the first," she continued, "hail and fire, mixed with blood, was hurled to the garden, burning up trees and all the green grasses. And the oceans became blood."

"We already did this," Salvation said, "cleansing the garden—Armageddon. That's over."

Rain looked up from the book. "That was then," she said. As a Protector, she understood many things, some more than others. But now she knew what Life was doing. "This is now. And now is punishment and suffering. She wants her children to fear and—"

"And what?"

Rain looked into her mother's eyes. "Pray for her to deliver them."

— LXVI —

FURY AND JUMP and Faith ran a few more floors up the stairwell, and then bullets started raining down on them from a few flights up.

And Jump dropped the PAIC and spread his wings wide to protect him. Bullets pelted him and ripped wing feathers and a few made it past him and hit Faith.

One bullet grazed Father Benito's empty husk. And Faith yelled up at Jump to tell him.

Jump looked back at him and frowned. Not that it would harm the dead and soulless corpse, but he had an idea.

And a long blaring sound . . . wailed . . . and moaned its way through the stairwell.

"Wormwood. . ." Faith shook his head and muttered.

Then the stairwell shook again.

As Fury stumbled, she fired hot feathers up the center of the stairwell, in a hail of bright tracer streaks that lit up the whole shaft of stairs like a shining star.

Screaming echoed back down at them—men crying and raging at their misery and pain. They all called for God to save them.

"What's Wormwood?" Fury yelled above the screams.

"It's a star," said Jump. Then he stood up, scooped up the PAIC with a wing, and started climbing stairs again.

Fury yelled after him, "How do *you* know that shit?"

Jump shouted back at her between gasping for air as he climbed.

"Try . . . popping the wave tablet . . . off your ear . . . once in a while," he gasped. "Read . . . a book. Could"—he sucked in some air—"save your life one day."

Fury flapped and hopped up a couple more steps. "Fuck you," she muttered up at him. Then she gasped for air. "Hello . . . the books are . . . *kicking* our asses."

Jump knew she was right . . . about *those* books, anyway. "Wormwood," he muttered. Then he sucked in hard again to catch his breath. "She's a bitter bitch."

— LXVII —

FURY OVERTOOK JUMP and passed him as she stepped over dead Protection agents in the middle of the stairs. Then the fourth long horn blasted and sent them all crashing up against the wall along the outside of the stairwell.

Fury sat up, breathing hard, and she said, "Can we like . . . just skip to the end"—she panted a little—"on this horn shit? It's *pissing* me off!"

Jump got back to his feet, grabbed the PAIC's limp body, and pointed his wing in front of Fury, up the stairs. "Keep moving," he said. "You don't redeem yourself . . . by the time the seventh one goes off . . . we're stuck down here with the locusts. You think those purgies are a pain in the ass. . .?"

The fifth huge alarm moan sounded like a voice. It was so loud, it felt like the whole planet should have been able to hear it. "Woe, woe, woe, to those who dwell on the earth, the remaining warnings of the three angels who are about to sound!"

"What . . . was that?" asked Fury. "That sounded like . . . Life?"

Faith followed behind them. "Don't worry," he said, "she won't hurt you."

Fury rolled her eyes and kept pumping her legs. "So relieved."

Faith kept running and he yelled ahead at them, "The locusts just"—and he gasped for air—"torment you."

"I don't give a. . ." Fury yelled back, "about any locusts!"

Jump switched the PAIC's body to his other wing. He shouted back at Faith, "I thought these . . . were supposed to. . . Aren't they months apart?"

"The 'day' is . . . speeding up," Faith yelled and then coughed.

"*Perfect*," Jump said.

Then the sixth horn blast reverberated through the stairwell and they all stumbled and fell to the floor.

"Four angels," Faith said. It was barely loud enough for Jump and Fury to hear now. "Plague . . . fire . . . smoke . . . brimstone. Get up," he tried to yell, but it came out quieter, "we have to get to the roof!"

— LXVIII —

ON THE FIFTH horn, Rain looked away from the fall. She could not bear to watch. If this was Fury's end, she wanted to remember her a different way. "They won't. . . She does not have time."

Salvation put her arm around her daughter. She stared into the fall, watching and listening as the sixth trumpet blasted. And then she got mad. Maybe they did need to intervene. That bitch in the dungeon wasn't playing by the rules, anyway. "Come on," she said, "we're stopping this bitch."

They raced from Rain's throne room, down the steps and out onto the Great Mountain of the Eternities, then they both flew as fast as their wings would carry them.

Rain grew brighter as they soared—she could feel Salvation's determination raging beside her.

As the roof to the Hallowed Hall of the Words rotated open, they both twisted in mid-air and then dove at the floor of the Arena of Reckoning. And they opened their wings wide and vapor trails swirled as they decelerated, then they landed at the portal entrance to the Dungeons of the Damned.

When they folded their wings back, Salvation said, "I'm still not sure how she did it, but that evil woman restarted her eternity. Time for it to finally end, because I'm getting tired of cleaning up after her."

Rain flapped toward the portal. Salvation flapped beside her.

The aftermath of Jump's torture had been an intolerable horror to witness. Rain pushed out all of her brilliant bright plumage and steeled herself to wade through the stench again.

By now, most of the evil angels in the dungeons had more than enough time to meld their disintegrated bodies back together and were most likely . . . angrier than ever.

Rain pushed out her ballistic wing feathers and crouched down, ready to fire if necessary.

Salvation did the same.

The portal twisted open.

— LXIX —

FURY, FAITH AND Jump fought their way through two more squads of Protection agents before they finally clawed their way up the last flight of stairs.

The big steel door to the roof was a cold, Seattle gray. The three of them stared at it. The door would swing to the inside when they opened it—the back cover of an old book, daring them to open it and sneak a peek at the ending.

None of them had any idea what they were going to do once they got out on the roof. Some plans were like that—it was tough to imagine anything past the part where they should already be dead.

Jump had a theory, though, and so did Fury. But when she flung open the door to the roof, and the three of them ran out into the darkness . . . neither of those theories survived the first five seconds.

— LXX —

WHEN THE PORTAL to the dungeons twisted open, Salvation and Rain lunged forward, but then stopped cold.

There was no waft of misery, and no sounds of wailing demons and damned angels' souls rushed out. Neither was there the flickering flame from the fiery lake below. There was simply . . . darkness.

Rain almost fell forward, stopping herself.

And Salvation's mouth sagged open a little as she stopped.

They stepped slowly through the entrance and it twisted shut behind them.

"It's. . ." Salvation wanted to speak—say something to wake them both up. But unlike snapping out of their delusions after the last horrible dream they witnessed in the cells, waking up from this new nightmare would prove to be worse. "They are all . . . gone," she said softly. "How . . . how is that possible?" She looked closer at the iron gates to the cells. "Your seals. . ."

Rain looked at one of her seals on the floor. She reached down and touched it, moving her finger over the cracked image of her star. "She found. . ." She stood back up and looked at Salvation, remembering what her father always warned her. "Life always finds a way."

— LXXI —

THERE WAS A light layer of fog above Seattle and the mist floated down onto the rooftop of the *Fifty*, like meandering snowflakes on the mountain. The moon hung low in the sky, bathing everything in a dark, blackish-blue light. But the moonlight was poised to disappear beneath the horizon and let the sun pull back its blanket of black. Then the truth would shine down through the unwilling lie of the haze and the three of them would turn to ash.

That was the last thing Jump told Faith and Fury before he let her open the door to the roof.

They stood motionless, barely outside the door to the stairwell. The city was silent. The only sound in the night. . . The only hint of life. . . The great wings on the steeds of a force of. . . It wasn't easy for Fury to count that many mounted dark and evil angels, hovering in the sky in front of them, backlit by the moon. It seemed to her, though—a wild guess at best—like . . . a hundred million, at least.

They were mounted on horses . . . well, at first glance they looked like horses to her, but when she zoomed closer. . . Their heads looked like lions and their tails were like snakes, hissing and flicking their tongues at the night. And smoke billowed from the horses' nostrils as their fiery hot breath mixed with the cold, damp air.

The riders rippled armored feathers that flashed the color of singing fire and sulfur. The feathers glinted and clanked, as riders adjusted and held their mounts at bay. And the angels' wings and the fangs on the horses dripped red with the blood of a third of mankind. Faith provided that little piece of information, right after the sixth long horn blasted.

And five months' worth of plague and torment hovered and snorted and clanked, like they had all the time in eternity to wait.

"Fuck me. . ." Fury muttered. She and Jump had faced a plague like this before. But those were Man-monkeys, soft and weak at their core. Soulless liars, put to death at the command of a vengeful deity when they had become too unruly to rule.

This plague—this horde of whores and hounds—were nothing less than the demon and archangel army of the Devil himself. Though when Fury thought about it, she knew there was very little difference. Life or Lived—maybe both of them, it hardly mattered—had found a way.

Jump dropped the PAIC. Then he dropped the syringe, still a quarter filled with Judgment next to him. No need to send himself into a dream after this—he wouldn't even believe it himself . . . if he lived to believe anything again.

Faith dropped the father's body, and then he fell to his knees right next to him. His head hung down, and his wings sagged and his wounds bled down his arms and chest. He was spent. He panted and prepared.

Fury slowly turned her head, eyeing the horde as she did. Then she looked at Jump's face.

Jump's chest heaved as he sucked for air. He shrugged his shoulders and shifted his stance. Then he tightened all of his feathers and a few sparks popped and fell to the roof. "It's your nightmare, little girl," he said. "Blaze of glory or redemption in the rain. Either way, I'm tired a running."

Fury turned back toward the hovering horde. One lone rider spurred his snorting steed down toward the roof, and they both landed at the edge with a few scrapes and some snorting.

The rider dismounted and walked slowly toward them, angling his way toward Fury. He sang a little song as he walked:

Rain's reign go away
Boil my blood another day.
If the night turns into day. . .
Burned to ashes you shall stay.

When he finished, he stopped in the middle of the roof. "Matilda Mercy King—Fury of The Fallen," the man shouted loud enough that the two Heavens could hear.

"Matilda-what?" Jump whispered to Faith.

"Mercy," Faith said. "That's what her mother—"

"You have just got to be *shitting* me," Jump said. Then he turned to Fury. "Your name's not Mercedes?"

"It's a nickname," Fury said. "Go fuck yourself."

Faith whispered to Jump, "That's one of the spellings . . . of the blessed saint, Mercy. Babette—her mother told me that she hated being called Matilda."

"Hey, Matilda," said Jump. *Let's see how bad she wants it,* he thought. "We battling, or you gonna go all maiden on me?"

* * *

Fury ignored Jump's taunt.

The singing was familiar—Fury even felt like she had heard the words before—but there was no mistaking the voice. Life had sent her cellmate to murder, rape and ravage the garden. And now he looked to be Fury's judge, jury and executioner.

She glanced to his waist, just above where he kept his violating snakes. *Shit*, she thought. *Angel axe.*

The double-bladed hatchet, tucked into the feathers at Lived's waist, shined and glistened in the moon. A long spike for a handle, half-moons for blades—one shining silver, the other onyx black —"Angel's End," this particular one was named . . . because that was exactly what it was for.

Lived looked at Fury's stare. He smiled and continued her Judgment, "You stand accused of adultery, blasphemy, and idolatry . . . in offense to the one and only God of this eternity."

Across the roof, Fury whispered out of the side of her mouth at Faith, "What the fuck's idolatry?" she asked him. She knew what the others meant—guilty on both charges.

"That means you worshipped Rain above God—above Life."

Jump raised up his eyebrows and tilted his head a little. *Not even the half of it*, he thought.

And the Devil, Lived, shouted across the roof at her, "State your intention to submit to this judgment!"

Fury whispered back to Faith again, "Like, what's the punishment for *that* shit?"

"Doesn't really matter," Faith said. "In Life's version of the Word"—he shook his head—"death . . . they're all death."

* * *

It was the only way. Jump and Faith were both certain of that. Sacrifice was a cold and heartless mistress and she didn't give a shit about Fury. That was what Jump told her. Though Jump had probably said, "Bitch." Fury couldn't remember.

Faith was a little less "colorful" in his explanation, but the end result was the same. Fury knew they were right—Life and Lived had told her the same thing. Fury had to give something up . . . something big. Other than her wings, her immortal angel-life was as big as it got.

Fury walked slowly to the center of the roof. When she got to Lived, she could see the satisfaction all over his face. "You're a miserable liar!" Fury screeched at him. "It was *nothing* like she said."

Lived smiled at her. "Coming from you," he said, "I shall consider that a compliment." He looked toward Jump and Faith. "Careful, however, you are far from fulfilling your part of the agreement."

Fury looked behind her. It was the last time she would see them. She turned back to Lived. "I'm ready," she said.

Lived spun quickly, turning toward the horde of riders. "Fury of The Fallen," he shouted, slowly turning as he spoke, "you have submitted to your crimes and received your judgment. The punishment for these offenses is death . . . at your own hand."

"What did he say?" Jump asked Faith. "At her own what?"

Faith hung his head and closed his eyes. "Her own hand," he said. He shook his head slowly. "She has to—"

"She can't do that!" said Jump. Then he tensed up.

Faith opened his eyes and raised his head back up. "Easy," he said. Not that it was easy for him to hold back either, but by now, Faith knew Jump's tendency toward violence . . . a little better, at the very least. "Have a little faith in the girl. She has suffered so much. She's gotten this far. I can assure you, if she wanted to cut his head off. . . She can defend herself." He smiled next to him at Jump. "Maybe you should pray. Try that."

Jump chuckled a little at Faith's memory of his own Judgment. "Fat chance on that," he said. But then he thought about it. He had a little itch in the back of his mind. *She recognized me. Not that I was an angel* —he looked down at the PAIC—*but . . . me.*

THE DUNGEONS WERE completely empty. Not a sound or a smell, nor a drop of blood remained. So Rain and Salvation left as quickly as they went in. They flew to the center of the arena and then watched the fall again.

Salvation listened to Faith's words. "Maybe *we* should be the ones praying," she said.

Rain knew Life's book. Probably better than the vindictive, lying woman herself. There wasn't much time before the seventh trumpet. She put her hands together and prayed for Fury, "Judge not according to her appearance, Eden," she said, "but rather judge righteous intent. Let her therefore go boldly to her judgment, that she may obtain mercy, and find grace in her time of despair."

Salvation looked up, a little bit surprised that her daughter would use Life's own book. "That was . . . beautiful," she said. Then she turned back to the fall. "I think you changed it just enough."

— LXXIII —

FURY DEBATED—CUT the lying head off this devil right now, or earn her place in Rain's eternity.

The decision with Frank. . . There was still a twinge of regret, welling up in the back of her mind. Why hadn't she killed him? She should have. She had plunged the needle into his neck and his greedy, raping soul was inches from her final judgment against him. Something held her thumb back—willed it to deliver mercy instead of murder. Listening to Lived tell her that she had to take her own life, her thoughts filled with regret.

As if the bastard could read her mind, when Lived turned back around, he was . . . he—he was Frank!

"You should have judged me up when you had the chance . . . Matilda," he said. "Now, I'm down there with her and I'm just going to wake back up and—all alone in that room. I wonder what I could do to her in there?

"After all this. . . You've run up a pretty big tab. More than your mother's ass can pay back, that's for sure. . . . Eh, that hole was getting too big to fill anyway." Then Frank—it was him, wasn't it? He looked across the roof and shouted, "You got a decent size cock there, Ben . . . for a priest. Nice to see you didn't waste it on chastity." Then he tilted his head back and laughed and howled.

"You motherfucker!" Fury yelled, and then she raced at him. Devil or Frank—she didn't care.

And Frank lowered his head, revealing his neck. "Yes. . ." the devil inside him said softly. In a split second, Fury would be his slave. And Lived changed himself back from Frank.

"No!" Rain yelled at the fall. "Please, no-no-no!" Then she turned her head. She would be lost . . . and so would Fury.

Fury had come too far. She ran by Frank, screaming and screeching as she passed him. And she slipped the Angel's End from Lived's feathers and then she fell to her knees, sliding across the roof.

When she stopped, she held the axe above her head, and then she leaned her head back and screamed into the heavens, "Rain, forgive me!" A long and loud cry over lost vengeance and the bittersweet love that she would never find.

She stretched her wings as wide as she could—angled them above her, pointing them at the two Heavens. "I tried!" she yelled. Then she hung her head down and cried. She muttered softly now, "You know I tried. . ." And then she let out a huge screeching scream that shook the roof.

The concussion pushed the riders and their horses back a few feet.

And then Fury swung the bright blades of the axe down toward the roof and then in a fast circle up and over her head, and then down behind her neck, slicing through the bases of her wings, shearing them off in one loud, steel-against-steel clang!

Red blood sprayed from Fury's right wing and black liquid spewed from her left, and she screamed in a long, mourning howl and then slumped forward, down onto the roof. And she shook as she wept.

* * *

Thunder boomed through the heavens and lightning lit up the sky, cracking bright, white spikes of light through the moonlit black.

"There's no time!" Faith yelled to Jump. "She has to do it now!"

Then the thunder boomed and lightning flashed again and the building shook, and small pellets of hail began to fall.

Fury pushed herself up. Hail pelted her bloody wing-stumps and she winced and groaned as she stood. She dropped the angel axe and it clanked on the rooftop. "I won't!" she shouted up into the sky. "I don't wanna do this anymore!" she raged at Life. She was mortal now . . . and her death was her own. She wouldn't give them the satisfaction.

— LXXIV —

SO NOW YOU know. "Matilda." You believe that shit? What was my mother thinking? Like I'm walking around with *that* on my back? My back kills me enough as it is. Meds. . . Don't do *shit*. Crazy-ass dreams and—

Oh, come the fu—I'm on the *balcony* again? . . . Hail? You gotta be shitting me. "It's Seattle!" I yell up at the night. "Like, hello, it doesn't hail here." The little drops of ice hit my back and it stings. And my head is killing me. "I won't . . . I don't wanna—don't make me do this anymore."

I peek over the edge a little and the hail kinda like, falls in slow motion, down to the street. *Weird*.

And I get a good look at myself. "Oh, goddammit," I mutter. *Soaked*. I look up. No idea why—I already know there's like, no one up there. "These are my favorite underwear."

I slip a little. "Whoa!" *Shit, I could sleepwalk right off of this— damn, that's a long way.*

Gotta keep that door shut, I think, trying to remind myself. That would be so. . . I mean, did you see how far *down* that was?

— LXXV —

FURY RAN TOWARD the edge of the roof. Hail pelted her face as her feet pushed hard against the rooftop. She was naked now, having sacrificed her immortal life—her wings and feathers—to Life's plan for her. Well, except for her favorite underwear and tank top—like she was giving those up to that bitch.

It wasn't much of a plan. The whole thing seemed pointless, like Life was just making everyone miserable for the fun of it. *Just like jacking the Mike*, Fury thought as she neared the edge. This dream. . . It was *her* life—she'd end it her way.

"She kept her underwear?" Jump said to Faith.

"Seriously?" Faith said. "That is what you. . .? Mother of Mercy."

"What?" Jump said. "Oh, shit. I get that now." He shook his head and smiled. "You're a blaspheming bastard, father." He had no idea why he even cared. "Why didn't she just use the axe?"

Faith frowned at Jump and knelt down. He had so thoroughly failed. Babette lie near death in the basement, Mercedes had to stay and endure her hell, and Fury had to forfeit her immortality for redemption.

In Life's eternity, he hadn't done much for whom he now knew to be his one, only and last daughter from Heaven. Even during the half eternity since Rain's rule started, he had barely known the archangel, Fury. It might be too late for him to find peace and forgiveness, but he could help Mercedes and Fury find theirs. He prayed, "My angel from

Heaven, forgive me my sins and my failures. For I am your guardian, my love brought you here, and from forever this day, I shall remain at your side, to light and guard and guide you from evil."

Fury leapt off the edge of the building . . . like an angel taking flight from the top of the great mountain.

And Jump and Faith watched as she drifted out a few feet—arms wide and blazing red hair flying everywhere. Then she arced down . . . and disappeared over the edge.

The riders above the roof watched in silence, broken only by occasional snorts from their mounts and the clanking of steel-feathered armor.

Faith walked to the middle of the roof and slowly picked up the Angel's End axe. This was his fate now—his newfound faith against Life's old one. He would not help her any longer, unwittingly or otherwise. He lifted his head toward the dark night sky. A tiny sliver of light pushed its way up from beneath the horizon—there wasn't much time left.

"Rain almighty," he said, "I am heartfully sorry for having offended thee, and I detest all my sins and prepare to meet thy just punishment, but most of all because I have offended thee, who is all good and deserving of my love. I firmly resolve, with the help of thy grace, to sin no more as I have, and to avoid the near occasion of sin in the future."

Lived ran at Faith, grabbed the axe from his hands, pulled his wings back, and cut them both off—one quick swing and a loud clang for each.

Faith fell to his knees and hunched forward, moaning and spraying blood from his back. And he cried out and fell over.

"You insolent hypocrite," Lived yelled down at him. Then he flipped the axe up in front of him, grabbed it by the top and plunged the spike through Faith's back, into his right heart. "Go then"—he jerked the spike back out and sunk it into Faith's left heart—"to your new god!"

Jump walked to the middle of the roof and stood next to Lived. They stared down at Faith.

"Miserable. . ." Jump muttered. "She sure wants her pound of flesh, doesn't she?"

Lived kept staring down. "If one is not vigilant," he said. He adjusted his shoulders, feeling into the fresh wounds that Life gave him in their cell, "she will take two."

"One day," Jump said to him, "there'll be a reckoning for all this shit. You know that, right?"

Lived was silent. He put the axe back in the feathers at his waist. Then he stared blankly into Jump's eyes.

"Yeah," Jump said, "you know. It's gonna be a helluva thing, too." He walked toward the edge of the roof. He wanted to see Fury one last time. He didn't look back as he spoke. "I just hope you're still alive to see it."

Lived walk toward his mount. When he got there, he stepped in his stirrup and swung his leg over his steed. Then he folded his wings behind him, forming the twisting snakes and wings of *his* Hell's warmark on his shield. "Until that day," he said, "I bid you the same."

— LXXVI —

THE ARCHANGEL FAITH stretched his shining new wings and then closed them behind his back, forming the bright shining star—the emblem of his Protector—the great god, Rain. He stared into the empty cell in the dungeon where she had been.

Every dark archangel condemned to the dungeons was gone . . . and so was Babette. But what had she done? Rain's forgiveness and his own redemption aside, Faith's failure sent her there and he would never forgive himself for that.

He stared at the star on the seal on the gate. Rain had all the cells in the dungeon resealed. "In another eternity," Faith said softly. "I will find you there."

But she would never be redeemed for what she had done after the fall ended. She could not be. Some decisions were final.

Babette lie on her side and pushed into her misery. She could never go back. She *would* never go back. Hope and love weren't even memories any longer.

Her love had abandoned her again—Benito had left her to her vile fate. Her death had barely slipped from the sharp claws of one filthy dog, only to be chained in the yard at the beck and bone of another dirty devil.

If this was what Life had delivered to her, she would finally embrace her devil, Lived . . . as she would embrace the evil growing inside her.

Misery. . . In the only way she knew how, the Babette that she knew had searched for nothing but love . . . and she had only been delivered a choking throat filled with the insidious seed of evil and misery.

She gritted her teeth and growled at her master as she pushed.

"Now, now, Babette," Lived said. He smiled and ran his long fingers through the snake-hissing hair of his newest pet. "It is not such a terrible fate, you realize. I can imagine far worse things to put inside you."

Babette whimpered and her whole body tensed up at the pain. Then she relaxed and lie limp when it subsided.

Babette. . . she thought. She would never be that hopeful woman again . . . to anyone. She felt that deep in the sliver that was left of her sacrificed and forgotten soul. And if she could never know love again —never feel the warmth and glow of her right heart—then so be it. Neither would anyone who had ever used her up and thrown her aside.

If she would not find love, she would make sure that anyone who tried to taste its fruit would draw back a mouthful of ashen anguish instead. From now on, anyone who had wronged her would harbor only love's envy in their hearts. "Hole," she said to Lived, "my name is Hole."

Lived smiled a little wider. She was his now. "And what do you ask of your master, Hole?" he said.

"Now," Hole said, "I ask only for you to bring us revenge." And then she screamed and pushed as hard as she could. And the vile spawn of her new master ripped and clawed its way out of her womb and into its new world with a screeching and screaming noise that made her ears burn.

"And so I shall, darling," Lived said. He pointed to the loosed souls that had languished in the dungeons "So we all shall."

— LXXVII —

SALVATION STARED UP at the portal to the dungeons above. The emptiness above the lake was unsettling, but that wasn't what was making her nervous. She thought past the empty dungeons, through the silent arena, and out the roof . . . to the top of the great mountain —Rain's chamber. *I hope she is. . .* her thoughts drifted.

"What the hell do you mean, how did I get off the roof?" Jump said behind her. He was deep into his *Flight of Fury* story. It was required redemption training for every new hatchling in Hell.

Salvation turned around and smiled.

Six curious and seriously annoying little purgatories sat by the edge of the fiery lake, listening intently to Jump's story.

It was one of the newest flock of hatchlings' favorite tales—a story of the pain involved in a fall to resurrect lost redemption. It wasn't clear whether the little purgatories liked hearing it more than her husband liked telling it—they all looked intense.

Salvation rolled her eyes and rocked her head back and forth as she whispered under her breath, "I'm an angel—I flew." Then she smiled to herself.

"I'm an angel!" Jump raised his voice at the purgatories, "I flew, that's how. Now, stop interrupting me. Jesus, I don't know how the hell she did this job. You little shits are so—dammit, let me finish the story."

There was chirping and cawing as the purgatories jostled and shoved each other for the best spot, right in front.

When they finally settled down, Jump continued. "Get in close," he leaned in at them and said, "because this is so scary, I don't want Salvation to hear it. Gives her . . . bad dreams."

Salvation listened for a couple of seconds, then turned her attention back to worrying about Rain.

"Salvation," Jump said, then he raised his voice behind her, "Salvation, come on over here." Then he realized what his wife was doing. "Let them alone. They're—she's fine. You need to leave it. The more you imagine it, worse it's gonna get."

Salvation turned around and gave him her "look."

"Come on," Jump said, "I forgot to do the prayer. I'm sick of—why don't you lead them this time?"

The purgatories loved Salvation's prayers. They were long, but wild to listen to. The excitement ramped up and they flapped their wings, and cawed and cackled, hopping up and down on their perches.

Salvation grudgingly walked back beside the lake. They still had duties—responsibilities and rules to follow. "All right, all right," she said. "Let's see . . . which one? . . . Which one?" She glanced back up.

Jump knew that Salvation was still steaming over Life trying to take back the garden . . . and what it would have meant for Rain. So he wasn't surprised at the long-winded prayer she chose. It wasn't one of her standards.

"Oh, Rain our Protector. . ." she started slowly, so the newest ones could follow along.

Jump knew that one—chapter and verse—and he leaned back to

enjoy *listening* to a rant for a change. Salvation had a different style than his—old-world ambiguity and long-winded waling, but if he listened closely, she buried the point underneath pretending to be nice. And that was one of his favorite things about her.

"Rain," Salvation continued, "from whom vengeance we only borrow, and for all innocence that's holy, show thyself. Lift up thy judgment under your power—find us redeemed yesterday from the eternity of our sins. O Rain, how long shall evil triumph over the wicked? How long shall they utter and speak hard things in Life's name?

"Break in pieces Life's evil angels, Rain, and afflict the heritage of Life—let insidious, vile evil die. Drown the deliverer of God's gluttony in his own bile. For they slay the mother and the sister, and murder the fatherless. Yet they say, Rain shall not see. Understand these most brutish among Life's fallen and faithful.

"Yet, be merciful, Rain, on those fallen hearts who harbor only love's envy. And be wise—know the thoughts of Life, that they are vanity. Teach us your laws that they may give us rest from these days of adversity, until the pit be dug deeper for the evil . . . than it was for the wicked. Will you, Rain, resurrect for the wicked, rise against great evil? Will you stand up for us against the workers of iniquity, while our souls dwell in wicked silence?

"For they gather themselves together to stand against your wicked in Hell, and they condemn your innocent followers to blood in Heaven. O Rain, rock of my refuge, bring upon them their own iniquity, and cut them off in their own evil. And, Rain almighty—Protector . . . we beg of you, cut off their heads and spike their evil hearts."

* * *

Wide-eyed and silent, the little purgatories stared up at Salvation.

And Jump stared with them. It had been a while since he had seen his wife deliver a good fire and brimstone tongue-lashing. He had only heard about the one at the *Battle of the Books*. The way Fury had explained it.

Jump stopped and thought about her. He missed having another raging, angry angel around to bounce hate back and forth with. And he wondered how she was doing in her new role as the protector of the Protector. "Now, ya see that, you little shits," he said to the silent little purgatories, "*that's* how you deliver a declaration to kick someone's ass. I'm not prone to all that pretty prose myself. Gutting, that's what I like.

"Nothing like seeing the look on an evil bastard's face when you show him his guts. But . . . that's just me, *you* . . . you get out there on your first flight, you don't have to go gutting and grinding right off the bat. Find your own style—put a little fear in someone's hearts before you tear them out. Trust me, it helps calm you down."

— LXXVIII —

THE GOLDEN GUARDIAN archangel, Fury, flexed her new, gilded wings, tightened her golden feathers, and tip-toed up the steps inside the throne room of her Protector. The dust on the steps down to the library, scraped softly under her feet as she descended the secret entrance. Once she was beneath it, she crept forward.

A light flickered far down the long, arcing corridor, and she eased her way down the passageway, slowly walking toward the source as silent as she was able.

Fury glanced at all of the books along the walls as she crept—so much knowledge and so much understanding. *Look at all the misery you've caused*, she thought. She shook her head and frowned as she approached the source of the light.

Rain sat at her desk, reading the book. She felt the hand gently squeeze her shoulder. The grip did not surprise her—few things did after the Flight of the Fallens. Regardless, she knew Fury was coming. She had smelled her newest guardian since the redeemed archangel crept into her chamber upstairs.

Rain lifted one of her hands off her book and put it over Fury's.

Fury leaned in close and rested her head on Rain's shoulder. "Did you find the bitch yet?" she asked.

Rain squeezed Fury's hand tighter.

"I can't help it," Fury said, "the fu—she's out there like, plotting on you and shit. You *know* that. I just can't let that go—I'm killing her. Don't even *think* you're stopping me from that. You watched that—you know what she did. I'm gutting her—end of this story."

Rain let go of Fury's hand and ran her fingers gently into her friend's crown, massaging the feathers on her scalp. "Calm yourself," she said, "that is how she fooled you in the first place." She smiled down at her book and put both hands back on it. Then she frowned at the pages as she continued reading.

Misdirection—diversion and escape—Rain had been tricked by the same ruse that Life used on everyone else. So busy flying and finding and saving, that no one had noticed her slip out of the dungeons . . . with two hundred million warriors of her Word and her devil, Lived, back under her power.

Not that there weren't billions of faithful and fallen left in Rain's two Heavens, but that many dark and desperate angels was a concern, at the very least. Dynasties had toppled from the fire-feathers of far worse outnumbered armies, smashed upon the shields of blind believers, willing to die for a book. Rain was learning about that.

"Fooled?" Fury said. "I was—she made me—"

Rain giggled. It was easy to get Fury worked up. She was learning that too. "I am simply like . . . shitting on you," she chirped.

Fury tried to frown, but could only manage a smile. She stood up. "Oh, that's just," she said, "so not right. You are getting *meaner*"—she smiled and bobbed her head slightly—"and I *like* that about you."

Rain stood up and faced her friend. She shined brighter. "What else do you like . . . about me?"

Fury squinted behind her sunshields. "Mean *and* bad," she said. "Look at you, hiding down here, pretending to be all blinding and benevolent and shit. Fooled. . . You're not fooling anyone."

Rain moved closer to Fury. "And yet. . ."

Fury's feathers ruffled, clicking and scraping as she tightened them. "And yet, *nothing*," she said. "That—"

Rain tilted her head slightly to the side. "Shh," she said softly. "Boiling and boiling, always spoiling for a fight, my furious little guardian. Have you learned nothing?"

Fury relaxed a little, but she was still worked up. "I've learned that if we don't go find her she'll come back and—"

"There is time for her," Rain said, smiling. "Does your blood not boil for . . . *anything* else?" Then she pulled back her plumage and moved closer.

Fury cocked her head toward the lake and listened hard. The voice was faint—she could barely hear it. "Is that. . .?" she said. Then she listened. "Salvation is like, delivering a sermon again . . . and it sounds. . . She's not too happy with you."

"I am aware," Rain said. She put her arms around Fury's neck. "She is not very patient after your fall. She wants me to take some action against . . . her."

"Maybe you should," said Fury. "Teach the bitch a lesson."

"Maybe," Rain said. "However . . . to the benefit of all. It is not some childish rhyme. I must protect the misguided as well as the murderous monsters."

"Why the. . .? Saving monsters," said Fury, "I'll never understand it. Why would you. . .?"

"I've told you, balance," Rain said. "If the scales tip too far one way or the other, good becomes evil, and evil becomes good. So much so, that you might never tell the difference between them again. Now . . .

shall we continue this conversation, or shall we. . .?"

Fury smiled, but looked back toward the fiery lake.

"Do you miss it?" Rain asked. "The lake? My parents? . . . My father?"

Fury turned and looked back at Rain. "I . . . I'm where I should be." And then she pushed back her plumage.

— LXXIX —

Life watched from the nothingness. Cast out of her own Heaven—an unacceptable fate. The garden belonged to her, not some whelp and her furious friend. Yet she had no need or desire to take it back herself. Such continuing wars were beneath the efforts of a queen. She would not reclaim the garden herself. And soon . . . she would not have to.

Life turned away, and then she pushed into her womb, bearing down as she screamed at her pet. "You are a dirty, filthy dog!" she yelled at him. "And when I am finished, I shall—" And she let out another loud screech and then a scream like an eagle. Then she let up and breathed quickly, and winced and squeezed her eyes shut.

"Stings, huh," Dogg said, turning his head to the side a little to get a better look at his master's opening. "I think he was right."

Life looked up at Dogg and snarled. "Regarding *what?*" she asked.

"Maybe you shouldn't have made this so painful," Dogg said. "Looks like that's coming back to bite you. But don't you worry, everything's gonna be fine . . . juuuust fine. . ."

Life scrunched up her face and bore down hard again. Then she screamed so loudly that Dogg had to howl along with her.

"Ow, ow, owooooah. . ." he howled, "Daaaaawwwwg!"

To think that her second child would be born of her insidious lust with this animal. . . When Life finished pushing this time, she spat at him and growled. "You are a disgusting canine," she said. "I should never have created you."

Dogg smiled back in his most evil grin. "Aw, that might hurt my little puppy feelings," he said. "Anyway, I'm *Man's* best friend," he said. "If you wanted cute and cuddly, you should have made me a cat."

Life smiled up at him. However vile he was, Dogg was a devious and delectable treat. He reminded her of. . . Even the thought of Steg made her long for him—not who he'd become, but the way he was—again. She would guard those feelings as she had once guarded the great dungeons. "If I were so *inclined*," she shouted at Dogg, through the pain of another tight push, "I should have you *gelded!*"

Dogg laughed out loud. "You know us dogs," he said. "Faithful to the commands of our masters. I'm just spreading your word, Your Majesty. Multiplying the fruit, so to speak."

Life smiled a little. "Indeed. . ."

END OF TESTAMENT

Congratulations! You just finished *FURY*, the second installment in Steve Windsor's *THE FALLEN* series.

Turn the page to find out about upcoming book releases for loyal fans of *THE FALLEN* series. >>>>>

FAITH

THE FALLEN: TESTAMENT 3

A FUTURISTIC RELIGIOUS FICTION THRILLER BOOK

STEVE WINDSOR

Prepping for the afterlife is loads of fun!

If the streets of Seattle really were paved with emeralds. . . you wouldn't enjoy *FAITH* nearly as much. This third installment of Steve Windsor's *THE FALLEN* has you wishing they were if only to make the protagonist happy. It doesn't matter how many mistakes he's made, you'll root for our favorite long-suffering, swill-nipping priest even if it kills you. Why not? It's killed him several heart-stopping times.

For someone who describes his faith as a "glass house," Father Benito Benedetti is awfully hard on himself. And so he remains throughout Windsor's brilliantly formidable character study. You get one of the clearest, most intimate rides through the life and afterlife of Benito, renamed Faith in a most ironic eternity, before and during his time as a priest. Like an honest cleric of any era, Benito simply cannot bear to blame anyone other than himself for his loss of that ecstasy of certainty his religion has slammed into him all his life.

"Like all glass houses, mine would be brought down by stones thrown from inside it . . . by my own weak-willed hand." Faith just can't give himself proper credit for questioning platitudes. And he looks sadly and sardonically at the bleakness his world has become. We're taken through several stops back to that dark, rainy, Protection agent-littered Seattle that has seen more democratic days.

Windsor has once again bestowed upon his readers a study so thorough and profound in its simplicity that you can't help but come out of it thoroughly knowing Benito and why this seemingly kind, upstanding priest preaches through life as lost as his enslaved parishioners. A cleric who lost his own faith, alas, before he ever approached a pulpit.

The story begins at a defining moment of Benito's life as he witnesses the literal fall of a prominent character from the heavens whom we've seen before, then takes you back to a farm upbringing where religious indoctrination and truisms of wisdom bestowed by "the Colonel" should be enough, you'd think, for smooth sailing to a clerical role where questioning gets you nowhere.

This is also a time shortly before the main power-that-be becomes the Protection agent, to a time before the Constitution is relegated to a quaint relic, to Faith's memories of a waning "old world." Readers of "The Fallen" haven't seen this before – a glimpse of society as we still know it. You can't help to understand why the good father takes a nip now and again because it "helps me stomach the lunacy we let happen."

But never fear. Hearty reminiscing and a trip to the "Mike" — totalitarian black market—for some celestial emergency supplies isn't the only treat you get here. Windsor just can't resist a return visit to the hilarity of the Dungeon of the Damned, that afterlife prison that houses anyone who fails to please the supreme being of the current eternity. Yep, here's more "cawing and clawing and biting and baying" of the most motley and exotically named ensemble we've met yet. Lucifer—remember Dal, the Dark Angel of Light?—and his crazed crew of demons are busy plotting the downfall of the supreme leader, Life—no prize herself with plots galore up her own godly sleeve.

And Faith's bucolic childhood Colonel? Of course he's had a taste of that Great Mountain of the Eternities we've all heard about. His reference to "the Arena of Reckoning on Judgment Night" wasn't a dream, was it? And we get enough hints that some other characters

Faith meets on his earthly errand are also visitors from that realm. I'd stick around for more if I were you. There's plenty in this series so far to hook you for Life!

Ana - (Vixen ink Ambassador)

GET BOOK 3

THE FALLEN series continues in *FAITH : Testament 3*.
Get your copy of *FAITH* before anyone else.

vixenink.com/faith-fallen/

THE FALLEN Series of Religious Thrillers:
JUMP, FURY, FAITH, DOGG, HOLE, BURN, LIVED, LIFE, RAIN, SALVATION

Oh, and one more thing>>>

"Look . . . Mercedes. . ." angel-me starts up on me again.

I'm getting sick of her shit. Taking care of her BFF in Heaven, my ass.

". . .before I forget," she says, "I would love it if you could do me a favor."

Now she's just being too nice. It's gross—total turn-off. *What the hell else does she want from me? I'm letting that asshole throw me off the balcony!* "What?" I ask her out loud. Because I'm done with that mind-thinking crap.

"Don't get bitchy," angel-me says, because she knows the voice. "It would just help me out a lot if you could give me some . . . feedback."

"Feedback?" I say to her. "I'll give you some feedback. This is a seriously fucked up—you got issues, sister. These dreams you're putting in my head are just not right. I can't tell if all this is real or—"

"I don't have time for this shit," angel-me says. "Can you take five minutes and review the book or not?"

I fuck with her a little. "You mean Faith's book?" I ask.

"No, dammit," she says, "I want you to review this one—my book. Faith's book comes next."

Now I'm confused again. "I thought he already wrote—"

"Christ," angel-me says. "I told you, time isn't like that. It goes in circles. And that book is the *Book of Blood*. *This* one is *FURY: The Fallen* . . . on Amazon. This is the one I would like you to review . . . please."

Now I know she's cracked—she never says please. I look at her, letting her think I might not do it. "Oh, *fine*," I say to her, "but you . . . owe me."

"As if I didn't know that," angel-me mutters. "Thanks."

About the Author:

Steve Windsor is the author of the *THE FALLEN* series of religious suspense thrillers. *JUMP, FURY, FAITH, DOGG, HOLE, BURN, LIVED, LIFE, RAIN,* and *SALVATION*.

He lives with his wife and two daughters in the real world . . . and many, many other cool people in the imaginary world in his mind.

Connect with the author:
EMAIL: steve@stevewindsor.com
FACEBOOK: vixenink.com/facebook-page

Thank you so much for reading *FURY*.

"I write fiction novels, because the truth . . . is just way too scary."
—Steve Windsor